SUPER SALES

ON

SUPER HEROES

5

By William D. Arand

Dedicated:

To my wife, Kristin, who encouraged me in all things.

To my son, Harrison, who is always an optimist.

To my daughter, Amelia, who only has one joke to tell and it's simply "joke".

To my family, who always told me I could write a book if I sat down and tried.

Special Thanks to:

Niusha Gutierrez

Nyx Wylder

Bill Brush

Sarinia Phelps

Travis Ledlow

Thank you to my Patrons-

Tier 5(A-Z): Alex Lindsay, Andrew Bazhaw, Anthony Catt, Bob , Bootleg Sid, Brian andrew valek, Brian Hansen, Brian McDonald, Caleb Cassiday , Caleb Jamison, calob Rose, Capitalskr , cesar cazares, Chace Corso, Christopher B., Christopher Hall, Christopher R Yanas, clinton cuzzort, Colt McIntosh, Corin Forst, Darkserra, David Borelli, David Fletcher, David Hoerner, Dekciw , Derek Fincher, Direwolf1618 , Doomed_One , Drew Risch, Drfman, Edward P Warmouth, Eliseo Rios, Eric Beauregard, Garrett, Gavin , General Raith, Jack Coldborne, Jacob, Jake Minor, Jakob Scafer, Jameric, James Breaux, James Domec, James E. Coleman, Jeff Ford, Jeffrey C Reed, Jeremy Schultz, Jetfire , Jose Caudillo, kaldigo, Ken Maloney, Kenneth Darlin, Kevin Duran, KiwiOtaku , Kori Prins, Kyle, LagCat, Logan Carl, Loukemia , Matthew Caro, Matthew Kelly, Michael Liebenow, Mitchell L. Redinger, Nathaniel Wilkey, NerdrageSr, Nilas Hjalte Lundt Simonsen, Peter, Quill526, Rafnar Caldon, Riley Dunn, Robert , Roland Jackson, Ryan Cormier, Sam Ellis, Samuel Chesser, scott hank, SilverCrow, Stephen Chernishoff, Stephen Howe, Streak123 , Tanner Lovelace, Tavian , Tetsu-nii, Thomas Lindsay, Thomas Todd, Trav3lingman , Travis cox, Vlarto , William Brown, william hayes, yo dude, Zac Ski.

Tier 4(A-Z): Alin Simionoiu, Allen Goerl, B liz, Baelets , Bruce Johnson, Chris Doyle, Chris Eckert, Dan A., Daniel Smith , Darwin Baide, Dragon35 , Fenrisulfr, Harry, Jacob , James Hughey, james turner, Jenn Pedersen-Kahler, Jeremy Patrick, Joe Carr, jongre1512 , Josh Tumlinson, Justin Cox, Kri Grey, Kyle, Kyle Ryan`, matt12349, Matthew Parikka, Maxx Gonzalez, Nukin Futs, Omoz Osadebaima, Otis Coley, Patrick Ketcher, Paul Mikkelsen , Raul Rodriguez, Rika, Robert Muir, rodger norred, Silver Winter Night, Sonicblackfox , Tenpoundtarantula, The Agent Colson, Zachariah Beasley.

* * *

Tier 3(A-Z): Aaron Barlow, Aaron Holden, Aaron Winklebleck Winklebleck, Adam H. Bostic, Alex , Andrew, Andrew Kerr, Andrew Notohamiprodjo, Andrew Walseth, Andy, Antonio Hernandez, Archthrene, Athy192 , Atom Smashes , Aubron , Austin, Austin verm, Avoid Shisnos, Bdonovanjones , Ben Foard, Benjamin Hawkins, Benjamin J Russell, Bill Liao, Blake, BlissfulDarkness , Blucatpie, Brad Moulding, Brandon , Brandon Dixon, Braxton Rheaume, Bread Ranger, Brian, Brian Sherpe, Brian Small, Bruce Cassidy, Bruce Ewing, Burninace91, Byron Gobert, Caleb Rankin, Calvin Mekari, Ce-Ja Burke, Chace Brown, Chad Arrington, Charles Henggeler, Chase Olsen, Chase Pinkerton, Cheyene Adams, CHoobler, Chris Edwards, Christopher Tolo, chronicler49 , Chuck Powers, Clyde Spero, Connor MacDonald, Corwin Amber, Cryostorm, Curtis Brabon, Damien Osborne, Daniel Sifrit, Danielle Orban, David Cramer, David Harr, David Harris, deadeyemax , Deme A., DingBangAw, Dmc1234, Dominic Harney, Douglas Frazer, Dragonkain, Eli Page, Elias Hawthorne, Eloren Koori, Eric , Eric Hontz, Erick Malvaez, Ernie 3, Erraticcyprus , Feron Araneia, Frederick Crow, G K, George Mistkawi, GladiatorGiacomo, Glenn Broadworth, Goldenrupee , Green, Greg, Grimm-zen , Grognot , GuardianHero, HamboneTX, Heath, Heath Silvis, hiker77, Hostile El Gato, Ian Coates, IntheRaccon , Jack williams , Jake Thygesen, James, James Hastings, James Lynch, James Strozier, James Thomas, James Weed, jared snoey, Jason Davis, Jason Knope, Jason Little, Jason Phillips, Jayson Dyke, JD Kotchevar, Jens nordin, Jeremiah De Guzman, Jeremy , Jeremy Dove, Jesse S Uppal, Jim Payne, jocelyn gonzalez, Joe Kuster, Joel Magnuson, John DeBlanc, Jon Stirling, Jonathan Adcock, Jordan Gabriel Holt Smith, Jose Ibarra, Joseph Brown, Joseph Shafer, Josh Briggs, Josh rush, joshua hampton, Joshua Robertson, JT Watkins, Justin , Justin Kleven, Justin Stapleton, Kaleb, Kandamir,

Kenneth Lee King, Kenneth Palacios, Kermit Sudoku, Kevin Bagnall, Kevin McGuire, Kevin McKinney, Korbin Wilson, kyle stitt, Larry , Librado Pargas, LoquaciousT , Lord Shackleford, lucas rodger, Lui adecer, LunarLilith , Lyaruil , M, Maelstrom148, Mark Donham, mark hamilton, Mark McCaslin, Marquis Purvis, Matt, Matt french, Matt Ogletree, Matthew , Matthew Crouch, Matthew Murphy, Matthew Paulin, Matthew pfrimmer, Matthew Shealy, Michael Carr, Michael Erwin, Michael Flores, Michael Gilbert, Michael Haagen, Michael Hoover, Michael Moneymaker, Michael Rogers, Michael S Pellman, Mikael, Milksteak , Mitchel Geer, Monik , Mr. Pepper, Mtruste , Nathan Turnage , Nathanial Fritz, Nicholas Earles, Nick Cartwright, Niko , nilcaeks, No0neSpecial , noah freeman, Null_is_Void, OKMO , Ori Shifrin, Oscar Membreno, Outwardwander, Patrick Tebay, Paul Shelton, Paul Sneddon, Peefrimgar212 , Peter , PF, PhoenixCorp , R. Alexander Spoerer, Rafael, Raised And Confused, Randy Soviet, Rey T Nufable, Ricardo Sirven, Richard Stahl, Rob "Wrecki" Price, Robert Hammack, Robert Jensen, Robert Nolan, Robert Shofner, Robertlee C Fisher, Rogallaig , Rory O'Reilly, Ryan Blow, Ryan Cook, Ryn, Scott Baxter, Scott Mem, Sean O'Regan, Sean Peacock, sebastian pereira, SerHayser , Seth, Seth, Seth Grimsley, Sid Simpkins, Silent Ghost, Sir Cullen Kawano, Spellmonger, Spencer Jefferson, Ste4mpunk, Stephen Juba, stephen plecker, Stephen Roberts, Steve , Stormrall, T'Ericka , Thomas Frank, Thorland , Tilen Bogdan, Tim E., Timothy, Tionong, Tisch , TJ Severyn, Todd Kibler, Todd Zickefoose, Top Cat 269, Trent Collins, Trevor Kirke, Trey Evreux, Troy Daniels, tyller james, Voodoo , Wade Helton, Wesley Sterner, Will , Will Gossage, William Chapman, William Underwood, Yann Kuratomi, Yissnakk , Yitzhak Brill, Yitzhak Silverman , Zac James, Zachariah Miller, Zachariah Ridgeway, Zachary Nahrstadt.

Tier 2(A-Z): Aaron Gray, Alexander,

AlexanderTheMediocre , Anthony Olson, Aureliano Ochoa, Azerah, Bobby Garman, Brandon Lloyd, Brap, Brendon Quinn, Brian Brown, Brian W Steffensen, Bruce Williams, Byroz , C.G. William, Calamity , Calvin Gray, Chris Cannon, Ciellandros , Clint, Cody Browne, Colin T., Connor , Corey Billington, Corodel , Cory Fox, Cthulhu, Dan Drooger, Dan Vooght, Daniel Erik, Davey Rivera, David Dunagin, David Guilliams, David Wilhelm, Davonne Smith, Dillon Fyfe, Doug W, Douglas Winters, Dwaine Roberts, Elliot THIRY TCHEN, Ethan King, Fabien Larco, Gadfium , Georg Kranz, Greg Fedderson, H_Dingo , Jadon Aegerter, James Roberts, James Smith, Jason Jorde, JeffyThanadros, Jeremiah Harriott, Jeremy Bowman, Jerome johnson, Jlaristotle , John Dwyer, John Rooney, Johnathon Jay, Joseph Beer, Joseph Stoffer, Josh Huddleston, Joshua Nelson, JuanG., Justin Brown, KIngdome487 , kir44n , Kitsone , Kolin Fischer-Giegling, Konrad Reynolds, Lannie Leon Tompkins, Marc Ackerman, Marco Herrera, Marcus Martin, Matt Scott, Matthew Comer, Matthew Street, Matthias Jahn, Max , MechaBlerd, Mezmer, Michael Holden, Michael Jackson, michelae, Mike Longenecker, Mike Mortlock, Mike V, Mr. Flopsy Fudge, MrWilliamBlair , Nate , Nemain, Nicholas , Nicholas Connerly, Nicholas Mueller, Nick Brakhage, Orims , Oscar Leon Robbins, PaigeFault, Pancake Dressing, patrick green, paul allaire, Paul Boros, Paul Matson, Pavel Å mejkal, Raul G Harrington Jr, Raymond Jeffries, Remus WB, Robert Jackson, Robert jacobs, Robert Thornton, rory schramm, Sam , Scottie Garr, ShadowWolf , Shane Gordon, Skylar Mitchell, SolisC9, Steven Don Porto Carero, Stuart Williams, Suneral , tecto , Ted Nakata, Thomas Pruitt, Timothy Chiang, Tolovechitoge , Tyler Moylan, w0lphhh, wander , Xavier Turner, Zeuce313.

Tier 1(A-Z): Adam , Adam Beattie, Adam Hesla, Addison Baker Ford, alex kregel, Andrew, Andrew Smith, Antony Patchett, Anubis, Arthur Cuelho, assignUser, Beau

Bryant, Ben-david Singleton, Brandon Moore - Price, Brian Mason, Brownell Combs, Caleb O'Leary, Carson Caudill, Casey G. May, Chase , chester france, Chris , Chris , Chris , Chris Heilman, CJ , Clifton R Pachak, Coconaut , Cody Gorham, Corey Sacken, Curtis Sutton, Damian Paradis, Damz, DANIEL GOSSELIN, Daniel Kurniawan, David Morrissey, David Northcott, David Taylor-Fuller, Dayne Mayes, DefinitelyMaybeNotHuman, Dennis Palsson, Dentos , Derrington , DiabolicalGenius , Dion Crump, Donald, Donny Davis, Doug Northcote, Dude McGuy, eddie baker, eldenor , Esteban De Avila, FatManJiuJitsu, Felipe Quiney, Fireseal Lee, Flipsided , Fred Rankin, Freedcats , Gabriel510 , Garrett Gibson, Gary , George, Grande , Greg Harbican, groovypony , Hatcher Matheny, Havoc, Heter, Hondo Jinx, Howellman , imp , Jackofnotrade, James, Mostly Harmless, Jaws2015 , Jayare, Jeff Bourg, Jeremy Johnston, Jeremy Powell aka Valen614, jerome carsten, Jesse Garry, Jesse Peirce, Jim Possidento, Jimmy Maddox, Jog256, John Callander, John S, John Smith, Jonathan Shepherd, jordan moore, Jose Alacan Rios, Joseph Ferguson, Joseph Zimmer, Josh P, Josh W, Joshua Harrison, Juan Magallon, Justin Wright, k0dyn, Kalvelis, Kat , Kawaru, Keith Huntington, Kenn A Welch, Kevin Gomez, KingInTheNorth23$, Kyle, Kyle Kowalchuk, kyle ryan, Kylepie , L Lee McClintock, L_S87, Laigos , Lathen Carlson, Leon Redway, Light's End, Luke , M. E., Magnanix , Marauder , Marcus Bergqvist, Marcus Karlsson, Marek Rivero, mark campos, Mark de Guzman, Mark Reverman, Mark The Loot Goblin, matt huston, MattBlack, Matthew Malkin, Meia , Merwouande , Michael, Michael Cramer, Michael Nohaile, Michael Wolfe, Michel Lepage, Mr.red033, Mrdelta , Mythravael, Nabil Alanbar, Nadav, Navarre Carl Hasten, NeoPagan33 , Nicholas Fuerres, Nicole Belisle, OMEGAnaTE, P.J. Shapiro, Pope2142 , Poplast , Poppy V, Quinton , R Berkley, Randy Smith, RayRay , RedBuffalo, Richard Garrett, Richard Pearse, Robert Jackson, Robert Wrobel, Rusty , Ryan ,

ryan Luttinger, Ryan Valadez, Ryne Lindberg, Sandnoodles, Scott Braunius, Sean Jeffries, sean murphy, Skif , Sorin Jinga, Spencer Dugan, Stefan Rich, Stephen lewis, Steve Corley, Steven Gallant, Steven Sotok, Sylag , Tadrith Rashkae, Taha Markanti, Tech Priest Toaster , Terry J Bean, The Disco Option, Theo , Tido , Tim Bartlett, TitanWolf96, Tobias Peters, Tony Bates, Tristan Howard, Troy S. Cash, Unknown entity, VAN, Victor Seward, WÃ¯Ã§kÃ©Ã° KÃ°rÃ°Ã±Ã¯, waffleanator , Waldo GonzÃ¡lez Islas, Worlok, Zell.

SOVEREIGN VERSE NOVELS(In Suggested Reading Order):

The Selfless Hero Trilogy(Arand):
Otherlife Dreams
Otherlife Nightmares
Otherlife Awakenings
Omnibus Edition(All Three)

Dungeon Deposed Trilogy(Arand):
Dungeon Deposed
Dungeon Deposed 2
Dungeon Deposed 3
Omnibus Edition(All Three)

Fostering Faust Trilogy(Darren):
Fostering Faust
Fostering Faust 2
Fostering Faust 3
Omnibus Edition(All Three)

Super Sales on Super Heroes Trilogy(Arand):
Super Sales on Super Heroes 1
Super Sales on Super Heroes 2
Super Sales on Super Heroes 3
Omnibus Edition(All Three)

Wild Wastes Trilogy(Darren):
Wild Wastes
Wild Wastes: Eastern Expansion
Wild Wastes: Southern Storm

Omnibus Edition(All Three)

Remnant Trilogy(Darren):

Remnant
Remnant 2
Remnant 3
Omnibus Edition(All Three)

Monster's Mercy Trilogy(Arand):

Monster's Mercy 1
Monster's Mercy 2
Monster's Mercy 3
Omnibus Edition(All Three)

Incubus Inc. Trilogy(Darren):

Incubus Inc
Incubus Inc 2
Incubus Inc 3
Omnibus Edition(All Three)

Swing Shift Trilogy(Arand):

Swing Shift
Swing Shift 2
Swing Shift 3
Omnibus Edition(All Three)

Right of Retribution Trilogy(Arand):

Right of Retribution
Right of Retribution 2
Right of Retribution 3
Omnibus Edition(All Three)

Super Sales on Super Heroes second Trilogy(Arand):

Super Sales on Super Heroes 4

Wild Wastes second Trilogy(Darren):
Wild Wastes 4

Veil Verse Novels:
Cultivating Chaos(Arand):
Cultivating Chaos
Cultivating Chaos 2
Cultivating Chaos 3

Chapter 1 - Time Goes By -

Watching the beat-up pickup-truck roll toward the dump point, Felix sniffed and then scratched at his jaw.

After arriving in this world, he'd realized he could get points from eliminating trash.

Everything after that, had been a run up to this very moment.

From battling drug dealers, suppliers, then taking their jobs, then kicking off the first Super Hero fight at the gold bullion repository. Then selling all the footage he had to the news industry.

All of it had been for this inglorious moment.

Just so he could revel in the peculiar feeling of being far too excited for people to throw out trash into his dump.

"I'm going to go with… appliances," murmured Felix.

"Trash! Bags and bags and bags of traaaaash," Andrea countered.

"I think I'll agree with my G-Grove-husband. Appliances," argued Alma. "Old ones. Rusty ones. I'll bet on it."

"Nope! Not for me. I already owe Goldie and Faith too many Felix nights. No more betting till I'm not in debt," grumbled Andrea.

Glancing to the side, Felix looked from the Beastkin to the Dryad.

Andrea was as she always was.

Her excited mismatched blue and green eyes

were staring out at the truck, eager to see what it would unload into the landfill.

Their betting on what was being dumped had become somewhat of a serious game now. To the point that Andrea even had an Other at a whiteboard near the side that took down accurate guesses in a tally.

Andrea's short dirty-blonde hair hung around her face in the normal style she wore, though one of her non-human ears swiveled toward him, displacing her hair.

She didn't look away though.

Alma was on his other side, though when he looked her way, her head practically jerked to the side to meet his gaze.

Being a Dryad, she was of course gifted with looks and a body-type that was attractive to a fault.

Her eyes were deep, with a dark brown hue that, depending on the light, looked to be dark red instead. Medium length light brown hair was pulled back in a loose style that suited her quite well.

Long gone was the slightly sick look to her. Now she shone with vitality and life. Her and Carlotta both did.

Looking back to the truck, Felix watched as it turned to one side, put its tailgate to the pit, then began backing up.

"Appliances," he said with a chuckle. "Rusty ones. Are you perhaps cheating in our game Mistress of the Grove?"

"N-no!" Alma said with absolute sincerity.

Which to Felix meant she was lying.

Alma could say many things straight faced, though they were more often than not, absolute lies. Rather, it was when she was being honest that she tended to look guilty. As if being truthful was harder for her somehow.

"Uh huh," Felix said with a chuckle and then moved away from the window. Pulling his phone from his pocket, he glanced at the screen to check the time.

They were only about five minutes out from the official "ground break" moment. When Legion could officially open up its first headquarters and move to the next phase of the plan.

Nodding his head, he slipped the phone back into his pocket. Walking out the back door, he found Faith and Carlotta engaged in hand-to-hand combat. The former was relentless in drilling the two new Dryads.

Focusing and honing their bodies and abilities day in and day out. Often with Andrea and Miu assisting her.

This didn't look like the normal training though.

Especially since Alma wasn't being forced to participate.

This looked more like just a spar to see who could bash the other more.

The Dryads would often go until one of them was incapacitated, then the victor was responsible for healing the defeated. He was fine with letting them practice that way, so long as it was never anything that even approached lethal exchanges.

Carlotta's normally hazel-colored eyes were blazing a bright and eerie red at the moment. She was so into their battle that she'd slipped into utilizing her body to its full potential.

Being a beautiful and eye-catching knockout didn't detract from the terrifying force she was putting into the attacks. Her long brown hair in its single braid was whipping about her with the speed of the blows.

Faith's eyes in contrast were only glowing a faint green. She was tapping into her ability, but not as deeply. She'd been training for many more years than Carlotta, and had a great wealth of experience in combat.

The overly-sexually-developed Dryad was taking every blow from her red-eyed and equally over-developed counterpart.

Carlotta would come in with an elbow, which Faith calmly stopped with her own elbow, before bringing up a wicked kick into the other Dryad's thigh.

Faith's blond hair was pulled back in a ponytail quite similar to Carlotta's, though her hairstyle wasn't slashing about. It instead hung down her back, remaining mostly still.

Her movements were brief, lacking the same vigor of the other Dryad's, and were just enough to stop Carlotta cold.

Hm. Seems like Faith is doing her own training.
Training to… minimize combat and her own
power? I suppose it wouldn't be that useful for her to go all
out. Wouldn't give her much.

"Come to join us in a three way?" asked
Faith with a laugh, her eyes starting to glow more
brightly when she saw him. "Won't be as fun as last
night's, but we can try."

Unable to help himself, Felix snorted at that
and came over to where the two Dryads kept
fighting. He briefly considered going in and trying
to get in close to Faith. He wasn't as good as they all
were, but he knew he would cause enough mayhem
that Carlotta would get a chance.

"Ah… actually, don't," Faith said quickly as
he came nearer. "We can play for reals later,
Carlotta is in a bit of a—"

Pausing, Faith snapped out a jab that
slammed into Carlotta's chin and knocked her head
back. She put out a slower one at the red eyed
Dryad that caused her to move back and become
more defensive.

Ah… yeah… she's training her. She hadn't gotten
offensive until Carlotta lost her focus.

"Have fun. I'm going to go get ready for the
ground-breaking. I imagine Aunt Gaia and her
people are eager for this," Felix remarked with a
wave of his hand.

"We'll catch up," Faith grunted as she
dodged to one side.

Realistically, Felix didn't need anyone with

him. This wasn't some formal event that needed everyone on board.

He could easily handle it by himself, since it was primarily his power and his alone that'd be required.

To be frank, this was a non-event.

Everyone moving in, in fifteen to thirty minutes, that was the real event.

Felix walked a short ways away from the house to a large and slightly disheveled looking barn. You could see right through the top of it to the other side. The first floor was better, though it did look almost as bad.

Going to the front, he pulled it open and looked to the interior.

A number of Andreas were sitting at desks. Looking into monitors while typing away at keyboards or moving mice around.

Several were at the back with rifles held in their hands.

They were all smiles.

"Third, Fourth, Fifth, Eleventh, Thirteenth, Fourteenth, Nineteenth, Twentieth. A pleasure to see you all," Felix said, addressing each and every one of them. Then he grinned and pointed at one of the Andrea's in the middle of the room. "Don't even try hiding, Second. I know you're in there with Twentieth. Good try though. Or are you still embarrassed and trying to hide it."

"I'm not hiding!" declared Second as she popped out of Twentieth. "I'm… I'm just… testing you. Yeah! Testing you."

"Testing," said every Andrea in the room.

"Oh? Mm. I guess if you're all saying that, then I can't really argue the point, now, can I?" Felix confessed with a grin.

Ever since he'd poked at them for having individual memories, things that they kept to themselves to be unique, they'd unified again. In all of them being their own Andrea, they'd ended up remembering that they were, of course, all Andrea.

The bickering had ended the same day he'd pointed it out.

"I'm lying, I'm sorry," admitted Second, her head hanging low and her tail drooping. "They're all covering for me. I'm a little embarrassed. I admit it."

Felix only laughed as all the Andreas' heads dipped down. All of them pausing in their work.

"It's fine, it's fine. Alright. Open up the hatch. It's time, so be ready to let all of Gaia's children through. We'll need to get them moving quickly," Felix murmured. "It's only been three months since they got here, but I'm sure they're tired of living in the forest after being used to hiding amongst society. They'd adapted to living amongst humans and likely weren't expecting to 'rough it' anymore.

"And speaking of, it's probably about time we made that video and sent it out. We did say we wanted to time it so it'd be several months after the attack on the gold depository."

"Nn, nn! I'll have the space ready as soon as

you're done making it," announced Third.

"Yes!" agreed several other Andreas.

"We already have all the video equipment. It'll be a bit weird, might have a bit of a… uh… hehe… recorded-in-a-cave kind of feel, but it'll be alright," Third said while laughing. She turned and looked at Twelfth. "Remember when we blew up all those caves? They paid us so much money to clear out the tunnels!"

"Nn nn! With all the fwooosh we could put into it, and then the screeching. It was kinda weird though, how it then went bang," said Twelfth with a chuckle.

Felix realized they were talking about carrying out PMC operations in the middle east. Likely clearing out insurgent caves with flame-throwers and explosives.

"I mean, when you use open flame, almost anything can become explosive," Felix said, walking over to the trap door in the middle of the barn. This was going to serve as a temporary entrance until everyone got in. Then he'd close it permanently once the awakening happened. He'd learned his lesson with being obvious, and with a location that could be accessed.

"Flour is especially kaboomy," agreed one of the Andreas. He couldn't see who'd said it, but he nodded his head. He'd heard about that before.

Opening the trap door, he saw the ladder there. Grabbing it he began to climb down quickly. If he had gloves on, he'd probably slide down it as Andrea had showed him to do before.

Reaching the bottom, Felix didn't call up his point bank. He didn't want to see the number there, because he wouldn't have it for much longer.

Still kind of annoyed I have to spend so much but... this is what we need to do. We need a way to stay completely off the grid. This is how we do it. Get down under ground and then start taking care of our own needs.

Just like we did with Legion city, just better.

Holding his hands up, Felix called for his desire. His want.

To build out the plans he'd developed for the new Legion headquarters. The secured underground location that they'd work out of and where they'd house everyone Gaia had sent his way.

The same people he was using as a basis for offered manpower to offset the cost, along with all of the Andreas.

The excavated dirt would be piled up in a spot they'd cleared out for it. Not far from all the excavation equipment he'd rented out specifically for this.

Trying to do it without the proper tools or manpower would make the cost jump into the billions. Points so high in cost there just wasn't a possibility of it happening any time soon.

Then there was all of the electrical equipment and finishing materials they already owned. All of it piled up in containers not far away, waiting to be used for this specific purpose.

Lots of the stolen cash they'd taken had been

spread out to hardware stores across half the country. Most of it purchased by Goldie and flown back in a container.

A window popped up in front of him.

Type: Construction	Condition: New (Work/Tools provided)
Owner: Felix Campbell (Legion)	Construction: 482,947 points

Wincing at the cost, Felix closed his eyes and accepted the pop-up.

There was a grinding, groaning noise from the ground beneath and ahead of him.

Where there'd been hard set rock a second ago, now there was a wall with a heavy and massive security door in front of it.

This would be the front door, at least until he could give someone the ability to open portals or create a device that could open portals. Once that happened, he'd be able to eliminate the entrance.

With that being said, it needed to be able to take in any type of item down below from here.

"All set?" called an Andrea.

"All set," confirmed Felix. "Call everyone down. I'm going to head down to my office. I want to get a feel for it and see if everything is set out."

"Okay! We'll change out the trap door and get the big lifter put down. Then we'll invite everyone so they can start moving in," answered an Andrea.

The security door was already open, and Felix went through it. Entering an equally large elevator that could easily fit a tank or two.

The doors shut and the panel lit up. Felix tapped the office floor button and it began moving down.

Quite quickly, too. It felt almost like he was falling. It was very much a Legion security elevator. He had no idea how Miu, Faith, and Goldie had managed to get all these plans and things put together, but he was glad for it.

I miss Mr. White and Felicia. I'll need some new tech people.

But that's why we're doing this. Why all of this is happening.

To regrow Legion and bring it to the fore. This time as a neutral agency that stands between heroes and villains, while controlling both sides. Never to become a target while letting everyone else take the hits for us.

I have the location, I'll have some people, next is to bring in the ones I want.

There was a beep from his phone at his side.

Pulling it out of his pocket, he glanced to the screen. He'd gotten a message on the Legionnaire's Call phone app.

Opening it he flicked it to the messenger tab.

It was from Miu.

Zachary and David are dead. They were murdered. Looks a lot like it was done as an execution. No one has moved in to try and take over their positions, and no one from the inside is trying either.

    Word is that it was done by Stephen.

    What do you want me to do?

    Also… I love you.

    I love you, I love you, I love you, I love you, I love you —

Felix stopped reading the endless line of "I love you"'s that probably went on for another sixty or seventy times. It was a fairly standard close of a message for Miu honestly.

He took the phone into both hands and tapped out a quick reply.

The fact that Zach and David were dead was unfortunate. They'd been quite useful to him. However, their demise did also help him.

They unfortunately knew of his existence as the Legate, and that he was their supplier. They were connections from Legion to the underworld that he didn't want.

He needed a layer between himself and the dealers. The money was needed, but the exposure was very much not.

Miu, I need a favor. Take whatever resources you need and kill Stephen. Then kill Stephen's boss, and that man's boss. Make sure no one ever comes looking for us again.

Either before that, or after that, I formally am giving you permission to go find the you of this world. We've put it off long enough and this feels like a suitable

reward for you doing this.
    Any concerns?

    Staring at his phone he waited. He knew that
Miu had been watching the screen. Waiting for a
response from him.

    More than likely, she wouldn't have stopped
until he did respond.

    At the bottom of the screen, he could see that
confirmed.

    "Miu Campbell is typing," he murmured
and shook his head with a smile.

    The elevators dinged and opened out into a
security room.

    It was empty of people since he was the first
person inside.

    Moving through it, he found he was now in a
near duplicate of the original Legion Headquarters
office floor. Everything was laid out in a near
similar way.

    Holding onto his phone, he walked through
the area. Looking around, he felt an odd echo.

    It was familiar, but also, not.

    The windows were all monitors. They would
end up projecting a computer-generated view in the
future. The program was currently being worked on
by Jay's team of programmers, but was planned to
be handed over to Felix in the very near future.

    He'd modify it after that, and it'd be added to
the library of Legion programs. This one would be
for generating images, videos, and scenes that were

realistic, through using existing footage of other things.

Can't wait to use it to make a dead person send video messages. That'll be interesting to say the least. I bet I can rile up a whole bunch of people.

Wait till a few influential people die, say they're in hiding, then start posting videos. Let it really just rip through everyone and see what they come up with.

Felix made it to his own office and entered it.

Everything was exactly where it should be.

Even the desk that Felicia had worked out of so often to keep everything on track for him. Without her, he'd never have been able to get the last "twenty percent" out of himself and Legion.

It was always easier to get eighty percent and leave it there, moving on to the next project. Trying to get percentages past that started to invariably cost more than they were worth.

Sitting down at his desk, Felix looked to the laptop and the dock it sat on.

Tapping the power button, he leaned back in his desk and looked to the monitor. It began to flash through its bootup sequence.

"Alright… first things first," he said to absolutely no one. "We record a message to the governments of the world. Offering to help them evaluate people for Super Powers. That if they endorse us, we'll be able to be the licensing and registration point for them.

"In return for that endorsement, we'll provide them with every single person's power type and a general psychiatric work-up. We'll act as a third party, hire up the Supers we want, flag them for either the League of Villains or the Guild of Heroes, then push it all along."

Felix nodded his head at his own words.

"We play everyone against each other, hold the center, and roll along. All the while controlling it all from the background. We'll just set up everything from the very beginning. That way no one can really come at us," Felix concluded. "First things first then... the video that's going to be sent.

"A video from Legate to the nations of the world. That now that he feels more comfortable with his role, he's offering for his Legion to take up the mantle as the neutral party. A force that can stand between Supers and Normals. Offering to measure, analyze, and determine powers," he continued.

Looking to his phone, he saw it'd received a new message and he'd missed it.

Tapping it open, he found it was from Miu.

I will take care of this!
I love you! I love you! I love you!

Felix once again skipped over the endless long list of I love you's.

He really didn't want to send Miu out on this job if he was being honest. She was one of his best resources and closest allies. In her, he could tell her anything and she'd only smile at him and offer to eliminate everyone and anything in their way.

That or that she loved him.

Stephen needed to be eliminated as quickly and efficiently as possible. That meant using an ace in the hole, even if he couldn't afford it.

He wasn't done making moves yet though.

Moving to Goldie's contact, he brought hers up.

My dear Golden One.

We lost our dealers, as I'm sure you're already aware. I need you to go set up the business with whoever's in charge since they're dead. Get it back on track and running smoothly.

Don't mention Legion, the Legate, or anything else.

While I regret their deaths, this is an opportunity for us to break free of the association they had with us.

Putting his phone away, since Goldie wasn't likely to respond quickly, Felix let out a breath.

His next task was obvious.

The video for the world.

Looking to a closet in the wall, he stood up and then walked over to it.

Opening it, he found his Legate armor on a stand inside.

He pulled it off the stand and began getting into it.

"Oh! Oh! Video time? Video time!" cheered a

mob of Andreas as they stormed in through the door. "We're making a video!"

"Yay!" called a second, while two others started into some type of dance.

"We'll make a dance video when we're done!" stated yet another Andrea. "With masks on! Then upload it. We'll be the Beastkin Girls!"

"Let's make a different kind of video. One just for Felix… with Felix," said a different Andrea. Her tone and volume had been just enough to break through the cacophony of what was going on.

The effect was immediate.

Every pair of Beastkin eyes had snapped toward Felix and were now gazing at him.

Don't look. Don't look. Don't… don't look.

We can just do the video to the world, send it out, and then wait.

We have lots to do while they consider our offer. It'd probably be a month before they can even really give us an answer.

Focus on the work and —

"Oh my yes," said Faith. "A video just for us. I really do like the sound of that."

Felix heard the door slam and then lock.

"How fun," murmured Carlotta. "I'll get the camera."

"I w-w-want to go first!" demanded Alma.

I fucked up. I should've waited for Goldie to get here. She would've stopped them if I promised her a reward.

Damnit.

Chapter 2 - Build Out -

Standing in the middle of the open field, Felix felt quite strange.

On either side of him was Alma and Carlotta, standing behind him was Faith. He'd hyper charged them to a point that they were brimming over with power and energy.

If they weren't wearing Legionnaire armor that included helmets, their eyes would be akin to LEDs behind a magnifying glass. They were here to make sure nothing funny happened on the part of the government of the United States.

He'd been surprised that in the end, they'd been the first to reach out to him, and it'd only taken several days. They weren't sure of the details of his offer and had wanted to work through it all with him.

Miu had responded through the messenger system that she felt it was a trap and wanted to be there. She had yet to complete her task though, so Felix ordered her to continue with that instead.

He wanted her with him, but he needed Stephen dead, more.

Goldie had felt the same, but was also still engaged with the dealers. She also couldn't attend.

He'd decided to go with his Dryads to this meeting as they were all quite well versed in combat. On top of that, they could easily put out enough magic to shield them, and then push them into a veil of invisibility.

"Probably a trap," growled Carlotta, her voice transmitting through their helmets only. Their external speakers had been turned off.

"Even if it is. W-we'll handle it," answered Alma. "It'll be fine. It always is, with Grove-husband there. He fixes everything."

"Campbells are the best thing to ever happen to Dryads," Faith responded earnestly. "In my homeland, Dryads were treated poorly more often than not. Felix's younger brother has changed that for the better. A great deal better."

Felix could only nod his head at that.

He wanted to do better by everyone in this world. Not just Dryads, though they'd certainly be included.

The problem was, there weren't many of them in the whole world. Many were ailing and sick on top of that.

Of those that had come, Faith had kept to her original numbers. The number of added Dryads to his personal grove hadn't grown beyond the other seven she'd mentioned.

They'd planted their seeds in his chest and quietly went to rest. They'd been resting ever since, regrowing their strength.

Faith had been adamant about not charging them up as he'd done to Alma and Carlotta. It would be better for the others to grow naturally back into their health.

Rather than having it slammed into place.

Faith had warned him that, in about a year,

he'd actually have to perform the seeding ritual. It was much slower for them because Gaia had granted them a great deal of power just to make it here.

"They're not late," Alma muttered. "Y-yet. In another minute they will be."

"We leave the moment the clock hits eleven-oh-one," ordered Felix. "We won't be waiting around like a stood-up date. They can come back to us when they're ready to be serious. Until then, there's no point in dealing with them."

Even as he got confirmations from all three Dryads, his armor picked something up. It was beyond normal human hearing, but it was enough that the suit could catch it.

In seconds, he got a small notification in his heads-up-display that it was a helicopter. Several helicopters, in fact.

"Seems like they decided to show up," muttered Felix, his head turning to look in the direction the noise was identified from.

There, on the horizon, he could indeed see a great many helicopters coming toward him. Quite a few of them were very large.

Likely filled to the brim with the materials he stated he'd need to build the "Superhuman Association" building. Where Legion would "technically" work out of, as far as anyone was concerned.

The government had demanded it be in a location of their choosing, and with the ability for themselves to monitor everything that was going on. To screen, speak with, and look through, everything that happened there.

Felix agreed to all their demands, except when it came to data and information. They would have no rights or access to anything that went into a computer.

He'd been very strict, to the point of nearly giving up on it all if they didn't accede to this one. There would be gathering of electronic information from the government in this building that he was in control of.

Legally obtained data.

He imagined they'd try to do so illegally, but that was fine.

He already knew that his programs were unbeatable. The vast majority of points he'd spent to make the bare-bones programs work, were used to achieve exactly that unbeatable state.

Even if someone got into the system by stealing an open laptop, PDA, or just sat down at an unlocked computer, it wouldn't take long for it to lock them out. The information they'd have available in such a situation would be limited as well.

It'd been rather simple in the end.

Even if physical security was breached and someone did indeed get ahold of hardware, the software was more than capable of doing its job.

The only person will full access to the data was Felix. Even Jay had never seen the code, system, or how anything worked after Felix had modified it.

Not to mention, he could see at a glance everyone that was logged into the system through his own power. One that was filterable by "those who don't belong".

That wasn't even taking into account a few other security features.

Like the Tribune.

This'll be easy.

While lost in his thoughts, Felix had missed it when the helicopters began to land.

Disgorging their contents rapidly.

A great number of people were all heading towards Felix. Most of them were unarmed and wearing political "office wear". Suits, dresses, blouses, and anything you'd see a politician wearing on camera.

There were a few with weapons, but not many, nor did they seem bothered by Felix and his Dryads. Giving them a quick once over, he figured it was the president of the country with his cabinet. Likely a number of advisers, and probably a few generals.

The rather large group of people came to a stop in front of Felix.

He didn't really care much for any of them, what they looked like, or even what their names were. They really didn't matter to him.

After this first meeting, it was very likely most things would be conducted by email or phone call. He'd have individuals he had to work with that he could learn and begin dealing with personally.

What he was looking at right now was more of a cluster-fuck committee that probably wouldn't get anything done.

"I take it you agree to the contract?" Felix asked as the group came to a stop.

"Well... we certainly don't want to be behind any other country. Especially since you're already clearly a citizen here," said an older white man. He had white hair, dark brown eyes, and looked like he was probably the president.

"Great. Contract?" Felix asked, holding his hand out.

"First, we want a demonstration of your power. Both the construction and that you can identify powers," said an anxious-looking blond haired man. His blue eyes looked watery and he had a complexion that didn't look healthy.

"Uh huh," muttered Felix with a shake of his head. "Fine. I'm sure you have some sort of test arranged for both. Let's get this over with. You're wasting my time.

"I have a meeting in two hours I still need to prepare for and travel to."

"Is it a foreign nation? Who are you meeting with? I—"

Felix sighed loudly and looked to the president. Ignoring the man asking questions entirely.

"Well?" Felix asked, not bothering to listen

to the other person anymore. Felix also decided to lie without lying. "Let's get the tests over with. Out of respect to my home nation, I put all my other meetings after yours. You're the first to speak with me, so you'll get to announce it to the news stations first."

It was the truth of course, because no one else had set up a meeting with him yet. The one in two hours was just to check in with Goldie, and he wanted to be home to chat with her.

Nodding his head, the president made a beckoning gesture to the people behind him. Felix had been right in guessing that they had the tests already prepared for him.

"I guess I'm not surprised," complained Carlotta through their private helmet line. "I'd probably be suspicious as well. Supers didn't exist for them only half a year ago."

"Y-yes. I don't really like the man next to him. I want to kill him now," Alma growled.

Felix was once again reminded that the quiet Alma was actually very aggressive when it came down to action. Carlotta was bold and very direct up front, but slowed down a bit when the time came.

"Hush, girls. It'll be fine," chided Faith. She let out a soft laugh and turned her head, looking toward one side. She cleared her throat. "Please advise your people that encircling us is a bad idea. It wouldn't help anyone if we decided to leave, and we had to do it going through your soldiers back there."

Felix turned so that his helmet would be facing the president directly. He also squared himself up and tightened up his posture slightly.

"I promise you, that isn't something I ordered," the president said quickly, holding his hands up. "I'm sure they're just sweeping the area."

"I'd believe that if they weren't already in position, laying down with weapons trained on our backs," Carlotta added, her own voice carrying beyond her helmet.

Felix had the impression she was now inhabiting the large army of plant-based golems that were spread throughout the field. They were more like clumps of grass, bushes, or weeds when laying down.

"It seems that maybe this is over before it begins," lamented Felix.

"No! No, I didn't order any of that, and I guarantee this is a mistake," growled the president, turning to look at the closest person in a military uniform. "Fix this, now. Get everyone to back the hell off!"

The general looked rather upset, but had already turned away and was talking into a handheld radio.

"Units Six through Eight, stand down, back out. Unit One remain in position and —" Alma said aloud, clearly being spoon fed information. The man had frozen as he was speaking, clearly hearing Alma relaying back his orders. "Even now they attempt to betray us. Unit One is to remain in position despite being ordered by the president. It would appear the government can't even listen to itself?"

"It's certainly impossible for us to become a neutral agency for them if this is how they behave," remarked Faith. "It's a pity. Maybe the Canadian government can be more trustworthy."

"Someone, lock that man up for treason!" demanded the president pointing at the general. "Get him in cuffs, shipped to a federal prison, and whoever is in charge after him, get those soldiers to follow my damn orders!"

There was a pause as all the soldiers considered the order they'd just been given.

Oh? Oh.

Well.

That's actually... alright.

Fast thinking, willing to act immediately, prioritizes the salient points. We can work with him. We'll have to make sure we keep the carrot firmly in view though.

The stick is less likely to work since... well... he's a politician.

They've already been through the ringer more often than they'd like to admit.

The general was wrestled to the ground and quickly subdued. Then he was gagged since he was yelling, then dragged off without another word.

Someone else had already been calling in orders for everyone to fall back immediately. That if there was anyone out there in two minutes, they could just stay out there. That disobeying this order would be tantamount to treason, and would be treated with extreme prejudice.

At the same time, someone had brought over a large cardboard box and a man.

One that was in chains, their arms wrangled behind their back, and a bag over their head. The fact that his chest was bare was why Felix knew it was a man.

"What is it you expect me to do?" asked Felix, turning his head and looking away from the man. He suspected they believed he had a power and wanted him to confirm or deny it.

Then tell them what that power was.

In the cardboard box was an unassembled doll house. There were no instructions, and on closer inspection, "unassembled" was a charitable way to say that it was trashed. Someone had busted it apart with a hammer.

"This is junk, right? No one owns this? If I screw it up, no one will care?" asked Felix, pointing at the box.

"I… no one owns it, no. No one will care," agreed the president. He didn't seem to think the question was completely valid, but it was obvious he wasn't quite sure how to answer it either.

Felix pushed out to the doll house and wanted to reconstruct it. Put it back to its original state, before it was smashed to bits.

A window popped up and the point cost was quite low. Only several hundred.

Felix accepted that and looked to the man.

He wanted to know exactly who this man was and what his stats were. His character sheet, as it were.

Name: Rodney Fell		Race: Human	
Alias: Rod (Over 10 items. Click to expand.)		Power: Fire Manipulation: Partial (Touch)	
Physical Status: Drugged, Wounded, Exhausted.		Mental Status: Depressed, Drugged.	
Positive Statuses: None		Negative Statuses: None	
Might:	17		Add +1? (170)
Finesse:	13		Add +1? (130)
Endurance:	10		Add +1? (100)
Competency:	07		Add +1? (70)
Intellect:	09		Add +1? (90)
Perception:	16		Add +1? (160)
Luck:	03		Add +1? (30)

Faking this interaction was part of a setup they'd worked out. They needed this to be something that could be performed by others, not just Felix. Or at least, perceived to be performable by others.

Pulling out a small nonsense device that he'd prepared for this moment, Felix held it up in front of the man. He moved it across Rodney's brow and then tucked it away again.

"Fire manipulation. Uses his hands to do it," Felix answered and looked up to the president. He was staring at the now newly rebuilt dollhouse that was sitting to the side.

It was exactly as it had been before whoever smashed it, smashed it. Even down to the fact that it'd clearly already been broken. The porch on the front of it looked like someone had fallen and put their hand through it.

"Oh, looks like whoever broke it, hadn't broken it first. I can restore it to like-new, but this serves as a better example anyways," muttered Felix and then flicked a hand at the doll house. "Does that answer your tests? Answer your questions? Provide you with a resolution that'll help move this process forward?

"Because I'd really like to build the association building and get moving. Let's be honest, you've put this near a nice and busy city, that has a good airport, but there's no real direct road here. Someone is going to have to spend some time putting that in.

"And unless you want to pay me, give me the land it's going on, and provide me with materials, you'll need to hire contractors to get this done pretty quick."

"Contractors. It'll be done as fast as we can. Round the clock work crews," the president said in a half-whisper, slowly shaking his head back and forth.

"Great. Anything else? Or can I get that contract with your signature on it so I can sign it myself," Felix prompted.

"Yeah, no, that's... fine," answered the president. He seemed to wake from his thoughts and turned to one of his aides. They held out a clipboard with a paper and pen attached to it. The president signed it, flipped over a second copy of the contract, then signed that as well. Then handed it over to Felix.

Glancing at it, he confirmed that it was the same contract he'd given them. The listing of the items matched what he'd given them. This was the original he'd provided as well.

The second was a duplicate of the first and was listed as "duplicate".

Felix signed both, took the duplicate, and handed them back the original. He didn't mind letting them have the original.

"Great, now, all those materials… I need them a bit closer. So go ahead and unload them completely and bring them over here. I'll have the association building up, lickety split," Felix said with a nod of his head. "I hope you brought everything I asked for as well. If there's anything missing, or wrong, I'll know.

"Then it'll be a matter of finding what's wrong and correcting it. This'll be a fine balancing act for my power set, but I can definitely make it work. Then we —"

"Hold," Faith said, interrupting him. Her head was tilted to one side, and she was looking off into the distance. "Caught a spy. Surveillance equipment. Bringing him over."

Everyone slowly turned to look the same way that Faith had been. Looking to the distant horizon and wondering just what they were about to see.

Slowly, several plant golems came marching into view. Between them, they had a man tied up in vines and held aloft. Another golem was carrying a backpack that looked rather full.

"A spy. Huh, that's a surprise," Felix admitted. "Let's question him right here and we can get his real name as well. See who he's working for."

The golems kept coming on as the man struggled and writhed in their grasp. There was no escaping them though, as the only leverage he had was his body weight.

Felix knew firsthand those golems were much stronger than you'd expect.

Reaching Felix, they dropped the man down on the ground and left him there. Though they didn't untie or unbind him.

"Right, so... let's just do this the easy way," Felix said and then called up a status screen for the man. He also belatedly pulled out the nonsense device, that was literally nothing more than a nose-hair trimmer he'd modified to look strange and stuck a few LEDs into, and held it over the man.

Name: Xhuehua Shan	Race: Human
Alias: Michael Shan(Over 5 items. Click to expand.)	Power: None
Physical Status: None	Mental Status: None
Positive Statuses: None	Negative Statuses: None
Might:	11	Add +1? (110)

Finesse:	17	Add +1? (170)
Endurance:	18	Add +1? (180)
Competency:	21	Add +1? (210)
Intellect:	24	Add +1? (240)
Perception:	19	Add +1? (190)
Luck:	13	Add +1? (130)

Felix felt like the name was certainly different. It didn't tell him enough though.

Next, he wanted to know who he would need to speak with, to own this man's contract. Such a man likely had a contract and could possibly have that contract purchased outright, or at least, make it so he could hire the man indirectly.

There was a pause, followed by a window popping up.

Government of Zhongguo.

Clearing his throat Felix put the nonsense device away again.

"His name is Xhuehua Shan. He works for the Government of Zhongguo. Other than that, you'll need to take him apart to figure out anything more. That should be more than enough to start digging though," Felix offered and looked to the president. "Now... materials? If I'm going to put up the Association, I need to get cracking."

Chapter 3 - In Summary -

"Hm. Everything really went exactly as planned," Felix murmured, walking in to his office. Moving to the armor stand, he began taking it all off and putting it up. He wasn't going to need it for a while.

Legate appearing in person needed to be somewhat out of the ordinary. An expectation that he would make an appearance was the wrong thing here. He needed to be as neutral, in the shadows, and not discussed as possible.

"Felix, Edmund is here to see you," chirped the intercom on his desk. One of the Andreas had taken up his personal assistant duties.

The A-Net had been reborn, and Andrea wasn't going to give up her position this time. She'd spoken of it previously and he was now seeing it in truth.

She thought she'd have more time with him in relinquishing her positions to others. When in fact, it'd lessened her time with him.

He was always working, after all. What better way to be close to a man that always works, than working with him.

"Great, send him in," Felix muttered as he continued to get his armor put away. The side-arm, he kept in his desk though. Pulling that free, he walked over and sat down.

Pushing the pistol into the holster that was secured underneath the desk, he felt it sit right. He ran a finger over the five magazines for it and found them all there.

After being surprised in the past, Felix really didn't like going around without a weapon close by anymore.

Thankfully Edmund was someone he trusted.

The young man reminded Felix a lot of himself in mentality, if not his life or situation. Edmund had already gone through a lot worse than Felix could have ever imagined for himself.

Looking to his monitor, he tapped it and waited for it to power on. He still wasn't quite used to having to wait for his computer to start up, even though it only took seconds.

Not to mention a physical keyboard. So very strange.

Pressing physical keys with an actual tactile response to them.

Hard to get used to.

Felix reached up and stuck his thumb to the Legion hardware add-on that came with all computers. A thumbprint scanner.

Leaving his thumb there for a second, he looked to the door as it opened.

Edmund walked in, looked around a bit, and found Felix.

After being fed regularly meals, getting clothes that fit with some quality to them, and having a place to actually sleep in, Edmund looked much more like a young adult.

Rather than the scarecrow in rags Felix had seen him as at first.

His pale-green eyes locked to Felix, and he grinned at him. Stepping into the room, Felix was glad to see the man was wearing office-casual clothes.

Just because Felix preferred to dress in suits when he worked, didn't mean he expected everyone else to. He wanted them to be as comfortable as he was.

Felix noticed that Edmund had once again changed his hairstyle. Today his dark-blond hair was trimmed and swept back with a part in the middle.

He'll find himself eventually. Just gotta give him more time. It's not like it will hurt him either to really explore.

"Hey boss. You had a meeting set up?" Edmund asked, closing the door behind himself.

"Oh. Yeah. Sorry. I forgot about it, honestly. Just finished dealing with the government. They signed the contract I gave them and we built the facility," Felix explained.

He really had forgotten, despite receiving the reminder for it this morning.

"Ah! Yeah, yeah. I saw that on the calendar. I wanted to be there but I don't have my armor yet so... couldn't attend," Edmund said and took the seat directly in front of Felix across the desk.

"Sorry, was trying to save as many points as we could just for the Association building," Felix apologized with a grin. "We'll get your armor squared away soon enough."

"Err… before we really get started… can you explain the contract and everything? I'm a little fuzzy on it all," asked Edmund. "Sorry, I really did try to follow along, and Faith even explained it to me. I just… didn't catch it all."

Felix nodded his head as his computer finally got to the desktop screen.

A meeting reminder popped up in the corner, stating that he had a meeting with Edmund to discuss his position in the Association.

Smirking, Felix let out a soft sigh and leaned back in his chair.

"Okay, which parts do you understand?" he asked. He didn't want to cover it all if he didn't have to.

"Right, okay, so, yeah… okay. We made a deal with the government. Legion is going to be the Association and handle determining who is a superhero, what their power is, and register them accordingly," Edmund said.

"More or less, yes," Felix agreed. That was all accurate.

"But that's all conditional based on a three-month temporary contract. That's the one you just signed," Edmund continued. "If that contract goes uh… successfully… then the next one, the ten year one, goes into effect."

"Yes. The three-month temporary contract is what we just signed today. It's a test period to iron out any concerns or problems they have," confirmed Felix. "We're trying to make this as painless and neutral as we can for them, while retaining all property, intellectual rights, and ownership over everything we do and use.

"That really got stuck in a few of their craws, but there was no way I was going to back up on that. It's a must on our part, not a 'nice to have'."

"Got it. That's why you've been fiddling with all those things lately," Edmund pushed.

"Yes. That's right. I'm developing technology through my power-set so that others can use them to identify supers, the power level, and what it is," Felix said with a chuckle. "I didn't finish any of them because I wouldn't have owned them. Now that I'll own anything I finish, and the intellectual rights for it, I'll get them finalized and moved to the Association."

"Yeah, okay, yeah. Right. Got it. Won't... they steal our stuff though? They're not idiots."

"They'll most certainly try. I can easily lock-out anyone from our systems that I don't want snooping around. So it isn't really an issue of making sure they can't get in if I don't want them to," murmured Felix with a shake of his head. "But we don't want them paranoid of us.

"We're going to run a watered down database in conjunction with our actual one. One that'll be encrypted, hidden, and made to be secure. If they really wanted to push and dig around, that's what they'd find. It'll even have some data in it. Though most of it they'd already have had access to.

We'll add some other things to make it look like they managed to get in.

"They'll never find the Encampment database, though. I've… modified that program to the point that it might as well be from centuries in the future. It honestly runs on a type of code that isn't known to anyone. Not even me. I don't understand it at all."

It was the truth too.

The Encampment OS had been upgraded to the point that it had a Virtual Intelligence that ran alongside and within the original program. It actively monitored all users on the system and data going in and out.

A Virtual Intelligence that served the Legate and had been dubbed Tribune.

Felix had plans to make more Tribunes for all the various tasks he needed a virtual pair of hands for. This world would live and die by programming and its ever-increasing hold over the world.

"They're welcome to poke around as much as they want. Even to steal a laptop or other hardware. Won't matter," Felix continued with a nod of his head. "All the hardware and machines we use for Legion are owned by Legion as well.

"Any and all of them can be disabled instantly. Even without knowing where it is, who took it, or why. Though… if they did manage to steal a laptop, I'd rather let them load it up and start looking around. It'd tell us a lot about what they know and what they don't know."

Edmund nodded his head slowly at that.

"Did you know you have a Super Power?" Felix asked, deciding this was a good time to shift gears. It sounded like Edmund already had a good idea of what was going on, he'd just wanted to confirm it.

Freezing, Edmund didn't move. Then slowly, he looked up at Felix. He looked disbelieving and suspicious. Like Felix was trying to sell him a bridge.

"You do, really. I've looked at it several times," Felix affirmed. "I can even tell you the name of it but... honestly... I have no idea what it means. I can usually guess at a power by its name, but yours is rather vague."

"What... is it?" asked Edmund quietly.

"Polymorphic," answered Felix. "I have no idea what that means. I've done a number of searches and read through a number of dictionaries, but it doesn't really help. Sometimes it relates to a computer virus, sometimes biology. Then there's the possibility that whatever the hell it is, isn't described accurately by my power."

"Polymorphic," repeated Edmund, looking even more confused now. "Not a word I've ever heard before."

"Mm. I'm sure it'll make more sense when your power activates. By the way, before you ask, no, I can't activate it early. I've already tried," Felix said with a chuckle, not telling Edmund the whole story.

The point cost to push Edmund's power into an active state early was incredible. Astronomical in fact.

It was so high that it was expressed in scientific notation. Right up there with turning the planet into cheese if he happened to own it.

Though, those kind of thoughts were why Felix was now investing into the ability to get into space. He wanted to start collecting space debris.

He was already putting together a contract to clear all the space debris from orbit. So long as he was granted ownership over it all, that was.

Except in your case, Edmund, this isn't an issue of converting something of great worth or value. It's a power.

Which means someone has a great worth or value assigned to your power.

There's only one person I can think of that would put me on a path that was likely to run into you, who would value your power that highly.

Grinning, Felix felt quite pleased with himself. He was almost certain he'd already found the reason he was sent here specifically.

"Now, with that out of the way, I wanted to talk to you about your future in Legion. Where you see yourself, what you want for yourself, and honestly, when you want to see that."

"I… what?" asked Edmund, his face still a sheer mask of surprise.

Damn. The super power was the wrong way to open this up. He's too flustered to get his mind working.

"Your future. I want to talk about it. There's a lot to discuss about it. With Legion just starting out, it makes it almost more imperative as well, since I'll be opening so many different departments soon," Felix tried again. "What would you see yourself doing? What do you want to do?"

"Uh," Edmund provided elegantly and with clear thought. "I don't know. I've never thought about it. I just… I just wanted a chance to escape. Get away. To… to kinda… live, ya know?

"I have no idea what to do with myself, or even what I could do. Does… does that make sense?"

Taking in another breath, Felix let it out shortly. It was more or less what he expected.

With someone like Edmund, his entire life had been aimed at just getting the foot in the door. To get that opportunity to do something.

Felix had swooped in and simply stuck him on that path without any warning. Everything after that point was a massive question mark to Edmund.

This was something Felix had actually planned for.

"How about we just… pick randomly to start, and work from there," offered Felix, pushing ahead. "I'll assign you to a department, you try it out, see how it goes. After that, we'll move you around to another.

"Obviously I'll be your boss regardless of the department since… well… there are no departments yet. Kind of why I wanted to talk to you, in fact. We'll be going through interviews for the Association.

"We'll hire them on there, then move them to Legion if we find that they're capable and we like them. Most everyone there will be working for the Legion without ever knowing it. Our list of personnel to work directly for us will be somewhat... short."

Felix grabbed the cup of pens he'd deliberately put on his desk a day ago when he came up with this plan. Emptying its contents onto the desk he then opened a drawer next to himself.

Pulling out the piece of paper he'd put there this morning, he set it down in front of himself. It was a list of departments, as well as a bunch of fake scribbled notes he'd written down.

He wanted this whole thing to feel more random than it was, because he'd be pushing at something he likely shouldn't. Disturbing someone he really was better off not bothering.

Ripping off the department names, he dropped them all into the cup and then shook it around. Looking to Edmund, he grinned.

"Any department you'd rather not be in?" he asked with some amusement.

"I don't think I'm evil enough to be in management," Edmund muttered.

"Good thing management isn't a department. Though that's not where the evil goes typically, you know. That's HR and Finance. That's where evil goes," he said with a laugh.

Shaking the cup, he then pushed on his power.

He wanted to know how many points it would cost for him to pull out the exact department he needed to, for Edmund to be perfectly suited to Ryker's long-term plan.

For Edmund to be ready for the day of awakening.

Everything slowed down suddenly.

There was an almost imperceptible whining noise that Felix could but couldn't hear. A sound that felt a lot like someone breathing out next to his ear.

There was a flicker, and the world became black and white.

"You know, I'm getting real sick of you, Felix," said a voice from nowhere. One he recognized immediately.

"Uncle, good to hear from you," Felix replied happily. He was quite glad to know he'd been right with his assumptions. He had to be careful going forward though.

"I hate you. I'm going to make sure Andrea and Goldie go into heat for several years," hissed Ryker.

Now that he knew he was right, he had to be more conservative. Others could be watching and paying attention.

"Sorry, I just really wanted to know which direction to take Legion in. You know, to make sure things work," Felix murmured.

Come on Ryker, you're a smart man. We both know you're not angry at me. You're terrified I'm going to say something stupid.

Don't worry about that, just help me out to pick the right department to put this kid in.

Because I'm aware of what he is, it makes it almost impossible to guess at what I should be doing.

So we're fucking pushing this whole fiasco at you, since it's your damn problem.

Though… heat for years… there's good and bad in that.

There was an audible sigh from Ryker. Whether out of relief or frustration, Felix wasn't sure. Time began to quietly tick by before he heard Ryker clear his voice.

"Project management should probably be your focus for a bit. You're going to have way too many things to work on all at the same time. That'll be the department that requires the most focus from you," grumbled Ryker.

A moment later, the world returned to color, and he got a popup screen.

Type: Department Creation	**Condition**: Input from Consultant
Owner: Felix Campbell (Legion)	**Construction**: 1 point

Smirking to himself, Felix accepted the cost, stuck his hand into the cup, and pulled out the slip of paper he touched first. He had no doubt in his mind it would be exactly what he needed it to be.

"Well, would you look at that. Project Management Office, business division," Felix said, looking to the paper he held in his hand.

"Huh. Alright. I guess… that's where I'll start then," Edmund mumbled. "What… do we do first?"

"Candidate resumes and scheduling interviews. These will mostly be by phone, since a lot of them won't all be in the area," Felix answered. "I'll have the appropriate files sent over to you. Read them over and start sorting them out.

"You can use your friends we hired. Consider them your first quasi-reports. They're just spinning their wheels as far as I know since we moved away from getting more involved in the underworld."

"Reports?" asked Edmund.

"Those who report to you. Now… thank you Edmund, but I need to make a quick call. Let me know as soon as you're done with that. Consider it a priority task, since we only have a few months to get the Association really up and running.

"While I can do most of it myself, I'd prefer to have people the government can look into and see how normal it all is. To really peek into those we've hired and see they're all quite normal citizens."

"Course, not a problem boss," Edmund said and hopped out of his seat. He made a hand wave at Felix and exited quickly.

Felix waited until the door shut before he pulled out his phone.

Opening it, he switched it to Legionnaire's Call, then tapped it over to the message tab. He selected Goldie's icon and name.

There wasn't a new message from her, but he needed to get in touch with her. If he didn't have to rely on the somewhat emotional-based readings from Carlotta and Alma, he wouldn't.

Goldie was a much more accurate gauge on other people.

"My Golden One, will you be returning to me soon? I could use your help. That and I do miss you and that rather fetching smile of yours. Dragon or not."

Frowning, Felix then flipped over to Miu's message window. There hadn't been anything from her in a week. The last message was from him to her.

It'd been read, but she'd never actually responded.

Deciding to throw some caution to the wind, Felix hit the call button.

It wasn't as secure as text, since someone could record the audio if they were close enough, but he needed to try getting a hold of her again. The Dryads were good, but he wanted Miu around as much as he did Goldie.

That, and he genuinely missed both of them.

Ringing quietly through the phone, Felix

waited, hoping she'd pick up.

On the third such ring, it clicked.

"Yes?" asked Miu on the other end. She sounded stern to the point of being angry. It reminded him a great deal of when he'd first met her.

"Hey Miu. I'm sorry I just... well... I missed you. Ugh. This was a mistake, I shouldn't be bothering you," Felix groaned and leaned his head back, looking at the ceiling. "I know you're working on what I asked you to, and I should just leave it at that. It's just hard. I was thinking of you today dur — and it led to this. Well... I'm sorry."

There was a shuffling noise on the other end, followed by Miu clearing her throat.

"It's... it's alright. I understand. I miss you, too," she said in a much warmer voice. It sounded strained, but far more like her normal self. He imagined she was having a tough time of it.

"If you can't make it work, just go find yourself and come back to me. And if your... self... doesn't want anything to do with it, just make sure she's alright and then head on home. Make sure you leave a way for her to contact us, too. She might not be you, but she's still you in a way. I'd want to take care of her," Felix ordered with a shallow nod of his head. "I'm starting to really feel like it isn't worth sending you out on stuff like this. We'll need to find others for it. I really don't like you being away from me."

"I'm... I... yeah," mumbled Miu, finally completely reverting to how she normally was when he talked to her like this. Embarrassed and sounding very flustered. "Okay. I'll do that. It isn't a problem."

"Alright. Then… I'll let you go," Felix said, feeling rather stupid for calling her like this.

"Tell me?" she asked in a quiet voice.

He knew exactly what she wanted. She'd never asked for it so directly, however.

"I love you, Miu. Come home when you can. As quick as you can," stated Felix with a chuckle.

"Yes. I'm coming home. Soon," she answered quickly, then hung up.

Felix stuck his phone in his pocket and considered what to do next.

Alright. Interviews are coming soon. Departments to open and a lot of people to hire. We'll need to really push everything out and start the process.

Thankfully… part of that temporary contract was that Legion and the Legate wouldn't pay income tax. Just sales and services.

That means I don't have to worry about disguising where all the cash came from. We can just deposit that into the bank and declare it outright.

Time to push that commercial with Alma and Carlotta out into the world, and start showing it everywhere. Especially on the internet. And sponsor some podcasts and programs.

Hm. Not too terrible, all in all.

Now we just have to dodge the government while they likely try to spy on me, without it looking like we're dodging them.

Okay!

Chapter 4 - Open Doors -

Felix couldn't deny that he was actually impressed.

The president had followed through with his promise.

There was a large four-lane road that ran right up to the association building. It was a straight and well laid out street. Heading off into the distance and likely to the nearby interstate freeway.

"Still feels weird they picked Kansas," Carlotta said over the radio. She was currently running a patrol through the nearby areas with an army of plant golems.

"I already t-told you. Easy to roadblock, surround, and surveil," Alma replied while providing front door security to the building.

"She's right. It's more like having a super max prison in the middle of your country, in the middle of a desert," agreed Felix, turning his head to look at the mass of people in front of the building. They'd all been brought here at his own expense.

These were all the people who'd passed a resume over-view and a generic phone screening. He'd paid to have them all brought out one way or the other. The nearby local hotels were completely filled with them.

Actually that's not a bad idea. I should have a hotel put in. Then buy up all the other hotels, motels, and possible rest spots nearby.

I could put in surveillance to everything.

"Edmund, you there?" Felix asked.

"What's up, boss? I'm in the lobby. Almost done here, and then we can start ripping through interviews," replied the young man. His Legion armor had been finished up and he was now assisting directly.

"I want to buy all the hotels near here and have a really big one built," murmured Felix, marching toward the front of the building.

It was a large and modern-looking thing. With glass doors, glass entry way, and several very large monitors above the front.

Information would be displayed there as needed. He'd read a number of opinions on the idea of data presentation in the workplace, and most employees found it helpful.

So long as it didn't show how bad they were failing, that was.

More cars pulled past him and moved into the large parking lot that was looking almost full already.

He imagined that there would still be a stream of cars showing up to the building as more and more people arrived.

Likely, quite a few were those who wanted to get here under their own power, rather than relying on him. There would also be those who wanted to just see the building, government spies, or spies from other governments.

Please do come in. All of you. I can't wait to gather

all the delicious information on you all. Just a quick note here and there about who you are and what you're about and then, done.

In fact... we should probably make sure Tribune is ready.

"Tribune, status?" asked Felix.

"Ready, Legate," the VI immediately responded. It was a feminine voice that sounded quite human. Human to the point that it actually bothered Felix.

He'd been very careful with the program, but he still felt like he'd possibly crossed a line or two.

He wanted it to assist him and provide him with more tools, but he desperately didn't want a Sci-fi story to start up because of him.

The very last thing he needed was an VI to go rogue on him.

"Legion systems ready inside the association?" he asked.

"Yes, Legate," answered Tribune.

The chatter and talk of people began to die away as he made his way to the front. Reaching the doors, he paused in front of them.

"Good morning," Felix called out.

He knew without looking that the monitor above his head would be spitting out everything he was saying.

"Good morning," came the response from the crowd.

"Welcome to the Association. I'm sure at some point, someone clever will joke about 'Ass' in some way or another," Felix said wryly and got a smattering of chuckles from people. He could feel the mood starting to ease up a bit. This was where he wanted them. "First, some of you are here for an interview to work for the Association. It's a facility and group that owns, runs, and maintains this building, Legion tech, and Legion information. They're neither a part of the government nor of Legion, but rather, they're a third party I own that will be operating as the in-between point of contact for Legion and the government.

"You'll enter and proceed to the left. Please follow this Legionnaire if that's why you're here."

Felix held up his hand and positioned it over Alma's helmeted head. He knew Tribune would be posting an arrow on a monitor behind him, along with a brief bit of information.

"If you're here to be evaluated for a superpower, you'll be coming with me to the right," Felix continued, letting his hand drop back down. He gestured to the other side now. "You'll be coming with me and going that way. I'll be performing your evaluation and interview personally.

"Now, you should have received an invitation to be here along with a number. You will be allowed to enter the lobby, but moving further than that will require your invitation, and waiting for your number to be called.

"Refreshments will be provided throughout the day. The wi-fi is 'Ass' the password is 'withclass'. The bathrooms are, of course, open to everyone. There are no remotes for the TV, but you can tune in to the audio for the movie through the wi-fi. It'll push you to a webpage that'll link you to the audio. Just let it run in the background.

"Providing you're willing to do all that on your own phone."

Turning, Felix moved into the building. Alma was on his left now as they entered the lobby.

Edmund was standing behind a podium in his armor in front of them. Likely inside the podium was a Legionnaire's rifle. One of the few Felix had spent the points to have made, just in case something happened.

Really need more people. Once we start hiring people into Legion, we can have everyone move about more freely. Just another Legionnaire in the Legion.

Even I could start moving around a bit more.

Partition glass began to slide up from the floor and then sank into the ceiling. Separating the back of the association, and Edmund, off from the lobby. A lot like how a bank had barriers designed to pop up.

These could go much faster, but for this situation, going slow was closer to the desired goal. To show people that approaching the front desk in the future wasn't going to be easy if someone wanted to assault the place.

Felix turned off to the right as Alma moved to the left. She'd be in charge of hiring people onto Legion with Faith as the leader interviewer.

Together the two of them would be able to

find the right personnel for the association, as well as pick out potential Legion candidates.

Felix would be working by himself until Carlotta joined him. He hoped she wouldn't take too long.

She was a bit stronger with determining how others felt than Alma, so she'd be a useful asset to him.

Not for the first time, he lamented he'd given Goldie a task he needed her to finish. If they didn't have the drug money coming in, they'd have much greater problems.

Though, overdose deaths have significantly decreased in the area. The violence over turf also more or less ended.

If it wasn't for Stephen, there'd have been no violence at all really.

Entering the room he'd be conducting the interviews in, Felix sat down at the desk and tapped the computer's identity login with the back of his left wrist.

The Legion armor provided whatever coded signal was required and unlocked the terminal. It was just another change he'd made with his powers and points to help secure everything.

Someone could log in normally to the computer, but it'd be with the false-front end OS rather than Encampment.

"Tribune, send the first one in for me," Felix commanded and then sighed.

It was going to be somewhat of a long day he

imagined.

***

Felix felt rather strange. He knew he was projecting the mannerisms of a middle-manager at the moment, but he was also wearing the full Legate armor. On top of that, Tribune was keeping him updated with how things were going elsewhere, while also taking information down for him.

Carlotta had joined him quickly and was at his side, providing what information and assessment she could on the candidates. It helped, but it didn't make it as easy as it would be with Goldie around.

Or Kit. But… Kit's not really an option.

Though that does raise the question. We haven't come across a telepath yet. Once we do, we need to make sure we get them hired in quickly.

"Done," Carlotta said and then shifted to one side. She lifted up her right arm and shook out her hand. She'd taken off her gauntlet so she could take notes freely.

Felix had actually done the same and removed both gauntlets so he could type on the computer. He was mildly concerned about the idea of leaving fingerprints behind, so he'd been incredibly diligent about touching nothing except the keyboard and mouse.

"Transcribed," reported Tribune. "Dryad Carlotta, it is advised that you simply speak your notes aloud."

"Yeah, I heard you. Thanks. I wanna write'em out, alright? Alright. Great. Thanks," growled Carlotta. She didn't much like Tribune from what Felix could tell.

"You're welcome, Dryad Carlotta," answered Tribune, the sarcasm lost on the VI.

"Next, please, Tribune," Felix asked.

"Right away, Legate. Reminder, it is now approximately lunch time," responded Tribune. "You should have lunch, check in on Dragon Goldie, and then reply to Assassin Miu."

Felix sighed and nodded his head.

"Thank you. Just prod at me again after this interview with those reminders," grumbled Felix.

"You have already requested this twice before. I've been instructed by Dryad Faith to intervene if you attempt to do this more than four times," reported Tribune. "Your orders do not supersede your own health. I will be forced to comply with Dryad Faith's directive, as she is the acting medical officer of the Legion when it comes to you."

Groaning, Felix looked up to the ceiling.

"Fine, okay. Fine. Send the next candidate in," he said and then looked back to the door.

"Already done. Their name is Georgia Marin," announced Tribune. "Fifty-five years old. No living family recorded.

"Suspected of possessing a super power that gives them uncanny identification, per the candidates own admission."

Felix's head snapped to the door and he stared hard at it. As if it would explode inward and slam into him, smashing him to the wall behind himself.

Instead, it opened in a timid way, and a woman entered. She closed it behind herself and smiled at Felix and Carlotta.

She looked exactly as she did in his memory. He hadn't seen her in so long that his heart ached and he felt his lungs seize up.

"Ah, hello," she said, nodding her head. She had dark brown hair that was pulled up in a small bun behind her head. Her eyes were the same grey that that he saw so often in the mirror.

"Good afternoon Miss Marin," Felix said after forcing his body to cooperate. "Thank you for coming. I believe you suspect that you own a super-power?"

"I do! Yes," Georgia said, coming over to sit down in the chair directly in front of Felix. "I've always been able to identify something. Especially if it had a connection to me.

"Things that shouldn't have been possible, really. Like knowing exactly which coat is mine at a glance, even if it's hung near others.

"Or knowing perfectly which order happens to be mine when someone gets lunch for the office. Those things come real easily and almost without trying.

"I can also figure out what an item is by

touching it and focusing on it. It doesn't always work, but it works often enough that it's... it's always been uncanny."

Felix nodded his head.

Identification did indeed sound like a super power.

"Have you tried envisioning it as a pop-up window?" he asked curiously.

"What... like... in those video games?" asked Georgia with a laugh and a shake of her head. Then she paused and looked thoughtful. "No. I'd never considered it. It was always just a voice in my head."

Felix picked up a gauntlet he'd taken off and set it down in front of her.

"Please, identify that," he asked of her while pulling up her character sheet.

Name: Georgia Marin		Race: Human	
Alias: None		Power: Identification	
Physical Status: Tired.		Mental Status: Excited, concerned, nervous.	
Positive Statuses: Curious.		Negative Statuses: None.	
Might:	06		Add +1? (60)
Finesse:	07		Add +1? (70)
Endurance:	08		Add +1? (80)
Competency:	78		Add +1? (780)
Intellect:	31		Add +1? (310)
Perception:	91		Add +1? (910)
Luck:	01		Add +1? (10)

Felix felt his eyebrows crawl up partly. There didn't seem to be a limiter or a break in her power. It was fully active from what he could tell. He had no idea what that actually meant in the grand scheme of things, but it was noteworthy.

Up to this point, he'd found a great number of people who would have super powers, but they'd all been limited.

Georgia was staring at the space between herself and the gauntlet. She was holding it in her hands but had gone completely still.

In fact, it seemed a lot like she wasn't breathing.

"Ah… it worked," she said after a few seconds. "The… window… popped up."

"Oh? Wonderful. As to your power, you most certainly do have one. You're correct as to what you think it is. Identification," Felix confirmed for her. "I'd suggest taking on a role here at the Association directly.

"We'd be happy to hire you on here. I imagine your power would easily be able to identify people as well. In fact, I could easily modify your power so you could identify people at a distance without touching them. That'd be, if you signed the appropriate contracts with the Association though."

Because right now… super powers aren't owned by anyone. There is no case law or precedent for it. I'll have to do my damnedest to make sure none ever occurs either.

So long as that never happens, I can own other people's powers so long as they sign it over to me. That means I can modify a power, but not a person.

"I— alright. I think... that would be best. I wouldn't mind having a job come out of this. I've spent most of my life just... working in an office. Data entry, to be specific.

"Pretty boring and, honestly, I could use a change in my life."

Georgia had set the gauntlet down, then placed her hands to the desk. Likely she was identifying that as well.

"Not a problem. I'll have the paperwork drawn up tonight and presented to you tomorrow morning," Felix said with a small nod of his head.

He was having a bit of a difficult time dealing with what was essentially his mother. Just a different universe version of his mother, one who never had any kids.

"That'll be fine," murmured Georgia, finally looking back to Felix. "You... do realize that you told me how to figure out who owns a thing.

"The way you described it presented me with a lot more information than I originally would have."

Huh. I guess that means she knows my real name.

"No, I hadn't considered it. It makes sense though," Felix admitted.

He could feel the tension coming from Carlotta next to him. Even if she hadn't moved, he could feel it bleeding off her.

Though that was likely due to the fact that her tree was planted inside of him.

"There's more to it. That's of course... not... the end really. My power is a bit different than just that," Georgia said with a slow nod of her head. "I can also properly identify what's related to me more clearly. That made it a lot easier to figure out what people were to me.

"Like... never finding the right man to marry. Never finding that person that would complement me perfectly. That I never found him no matter how hard I tried.

"I'd sit in nearby busy areas and just watch people flow by me. If they were related to me, I could feel it, even if I couldn't quite identify them. I found a cousin that way once. One I didn't even know I had.

"Apparently my grandfather had an affair and didn't tell anyone. It was an interesting experience to find them. Never found the right man though."

Felix had an ugly feeling right now that he'd misjudged the situation.

If she could figure out who the owner was of an item, yet also discover if someone was related to her personally, there was the distinct possibility she had an inkling of what he was to her. Perhaps only a nebulous feeling of connection but not one of being a direct link.

"You feel like my cousin did. A relation

but... not directly to me. Someone related to me but also not. Could you explain that to me?" she asked.

"You probably wouldn't believe me if I told you," Felix said with a chuckle, his voice catching slightly. This wasn't how he expected this interview to go at all. Not in any way shape or form.

"Oh, that's hogwash. There's a lot I'd believe right now. The very world around us is changing. Super Heroes! Powers! Abilities!

"A Dragon was even on tv! A Dragon! I'm sure I can allow for a little bit of belief to creep into my world view for whatever it is you could tell me."

Felix snorted at that and shook his head. He looked away from the woman who was this universe's version of his mother.

Then she clicked her tongue, let out a soft huff, and sighed.

"Don't be that way. Communication is how everything gets solved," said Georgia.

"Because all relationships fail when communication dies," Felix said at the exact same time as Georgia did.

It'd been a common phrase of hers. One that'd followed her after she'd died and been told to him even from others.

So much so that his response had been automatic.

"We'll talk about that tomorrow with the paperwork," Felix said and then stood up. "Please... forgive me, but I need to have lunch. I'm

75

afraid that if I put it off any longer one of my Legionnaires will likely try to brain me and drag me off to feed me."

"Not a problem," Georgia said and stood up with a hand wave. She adjusted her purse and then chuckled. "I look forward to hearing your answer."

"Before you go, how much were you expecting to make? What would it take for you to accept the first offer made to you?" asked Felix as Georgia began to exit.

"I don't need much, really. Just above my current rate of pay would be fine. I only make about ninety thousand right now," she answered. "That's mostly because they can't really get rid of me. Their back end would fall out if I left."

Opening the door, Georgia exited.

"Apprentice Edmund has reported that he needs you to assist him. He believes he's witnessed suspicious actions and needs you to review video footage," Tribune declared.

I... okay. That's better than thinking on my not-mom.

"Additionally, Dragon Goldie left instructions that you needed to be taken off site if two names showed up in the admissions and testing lists," Tribune continued. "Both names have showed up. Lillian Lux and Kit Carrington are in the next batch to arrive, next week.

"Miss Carrington has applied to be a psychologist in the Association, while Miss Lux has applied to join the legal team."

Wincing, Felix looked down to the ground in front of himself.

Of course. Because they're both driven individuals, why wouldn't they apply?

I mean, that's seems perfectly logical, Felix. You're clearly trying to make more work for yourself.

Oh! Hubris! How kind of you to join me. Seems like you're right. Really outdoing myself, lately.

I know, I know. It's getting to be pretty amazing. You really were just so confident that you could handle it all and didn't even consider it.

Yeah, I'm just awesome like that. Anyways, gotta go, Hubris. I'll see you later.

Chapter 5 - Sideways -

Sitting down at the table, Felix felt drained.

Pulling the Legate's helmet off, he set it down in front of himself.

He immediately felt cool air rushing over his face and hair. He suddenly very much wanted to somehow put in something that might cool the interior of the helmet down.

He did have a momentary thought about the fact that he was fairly certain it already was climate controlled.

Then he deliberately pushed that thought away.

Staring into the void, Felix just let his mind wander. Seeing nothing, hearing nothing, and letting his mind unwind from the knot it was in.

"I've prepared all the contract work that will be needed for tomorrow, Legate," Tribune offered from the polycom in the center of the table.

"Oh," Felix muttered then blinked several times. He shook his head and looked to the phone. "Thanks, Tribune. Anything I need to be aware of?"

"No, Legate. Everything fell within parameters," reported the VI.

Felix made a short nod to that and began to look through the table as if it wasn't there to the nothing beyond it.

He was so focused on nothing that he didn't realize Faith was there until she was next to him, bent over, and looking into his face.

Her helmet was on the desk next to his own.

Already knowing what was about to happen, Felix turned to face her directly. She'd just move him to where she could access him better anyways.

In doing so, he realized Alma and Carlotta were there as well. All three Dryads were looking at him critically. Each still wearing the Legionnaire armor, sans their helmets.

Peering into his upturned face, Faith's focus was absolute as she inspected him. Her hands came up and she gently cupped his face in them.

Her fingers were slightly cool and dry. Like earth just beneath the surface, but not deep enough to retain moisture.

Gently, carefully, she moved his head to one side, then to the other. Looking at his eyes from different angles.

Her fingers began to gently push and prod at his neck and just beneath his jaw. Massaging lightly at his skin and just beneath.

"He feels worn. Maybe the back-and-forth driving has gotten to him," Faith murmured quietly. "We've spent a lot of time on the road lately, going from Kansas to Alassippi and back again."

"Very possible," Alma allowed. "We divide up driving duties, but we all have spent more time behind the wheel than we're used to.

"That and… well… he's human. An amazing human that's unlike any I've ever met before but… still a human."

"A fair point," Felix agreed. While he could do a lot, could change many things, he was still, ultimately, a human.

"Maybe," Carlotta murmured as Faith gently peeled down his eyelids.

"Look up, dear?" asked Faith.

Felix looked up and found himself watching Alma.

She smiled at him and tilted her head to one side.

Faith leaned in and kissed him next, her tongue moving into his mouth for a moment, brushing over his own. Then she drew back.

Alma and Carlotta moved in and kissed him as well.

"Imbalance in his diet," Faith concluded. "A bit too much sugar right now."

"Yes. More protein, less carbohydrates are needed," suggested Alma, looking to Carlotta. "You tasted him last night. Was he off?"

"A little, not this bad though," offered Carlotta. "Must be whatever he had this morning. It's fine. Easy to fix."

All three Dryads nodded.

"Alma, go get what you can from the fridges in the break room. I put all the leftovers in there," ordered Faith. "Carlotta, can you go grab several water bottles. We'll increase his fluid intake and that'll help him flush everything."

The two Dryads left quickly, leaving Felix alone with Faith.

"How'd we do today?" Felix asked her.

"Very well," Faith answered with a smile. "We were able to identify everyone who would be an issue in one way or another. Given our recent… empowerment from Aunt Gaia, we Dryads have been able to pick up on a bit more than we used to.

"I sorted them out further by 'personality issue', 'foreign spy', and 'domestic spy'. They sent quite a few people from the government. Several from an agency called the CIA, and others from the FBI.

"They were perfect for the positions they applied for, of course. Their resumes were also perfect. Everything about them was perfect. They even sent a young woman from each, who was more than attractive enough to catch a man's eye.

"They both applied for the secretary position. I, of course, started the process to hire all the domestic spies. I also did so for a few of the foreign ones, of course, only for the ones you said you wanted here.

"None of the personality issues will get though of course. Spies we can work with. They'll do their best even. Nobody wants a bad attitude though."

Felix laughed at that and felt better for asking her. This was precisely what he'd wanted to hear.

"Knew I could trust it to you, Faith Campbell. Grove-mistress," Felix observed, looking at the Dryad's pretty face.

She smiled at him and wrinkled her nose a

bit. There was a very faint glow starting in her eyes.

"Did you?" she asked.

"I did. I realized as much as I wanted you with me, it would be better having you handle the other group. There was just too much to do for just myself," he admitted, then he sighed. "I'll also need to talk to my dear therapist at some point. Met this world's version of my mom. Kit and Lily from this world will be arriving with the next group as well."

"I know. I already booked some time in your calendar to talk about it tonight, and then again in two days," Faith laid out. At the same time, she's started to lightly run her fingers through his hair. Her fingertips grazing along his scalp. "We'll be fine, dear. Just a matter of helping you to get the words and emotions out. Nothing wrong with it, and you'll be better for it."

"Thanks. Tribune, how many listening devices got slipped into the interview rooms and lobby?" asked Felix.

"Twenty-six in the lobby, nineteen in the interviewing room that Dryad Faith was in, eight in the room you were in, Sir," reported Tribune. "They were all disabled upon deployment.

"At some point they should be retrieved to determine the ownership of them. That would help understand who is actively interested in us at the moment."

"Great, we'll just need to make sure we don't get rid of all of them, actually. We'll break all of the ones we don't want listening in, keep only a few of those we want to allow to have some idea, and leave the real impressively hidden ones," Felix summed up. "The more they can see and hear, the less paranoia they'll feel about the whole thing.

"We have to let them see some of it, so that they at least feel assured they can keep an eye on it in a way."

"I do find this direction to be strange, Felix," Faith confessed.

"If we're going to take over everything so our rules dictate what happens, doing it from a neutral position that's behind the scenes will be a lot harder, won't it?

"I'm not really that great with human politics, let alone human politics in such an advanced world."

"It'll certainly be harder to dictate which way the world goes without being directly in control, sure. But It'll be safer for us all as well," answered Felix. "We just need to make sure we've got our hands on the steering wheel at all times. Guiding us along the track we want.

"When we reach the destination we want, it won't even matter anymore. Even if they wanted to change the course, it'd be far too late for them to do anything effectively."

Faith clicked her tongue, sighed, and then shrugged her shoulders.

"Alright, Felix. Alright," she said, clearly not quite believing him or his words.

"Sir, you've just received a message from Dragon Goldie on Legionnaire's call," Tribune interrupted. "Your phone is currently inside your armor, and you won't be able to access it easily. Shall I relay the message to you, Legate?"

"I… yes, please, Tribune," asked Felix.

"I'm sorry to ask for help like this, but I need you," said Goldie from the polycom. It felt a touch robotic, but Felix was surprised Tribune could copy her so well. It sounded almost exactly like her. "I'm afraid the situation with the dealers and suppliers is getting out of hand.

"I've been forced to step in to the situation more than I wished, because there's a turf-war of sorts that's starting to get out of hand. I think a super is involved, but I can't confirm that.

"What I can confirm, is that I do need help. I can't do this on my own and would really appreciate your guidance."

There was a pop after that followed by nothing.

"How would you like to respond, Legate?" asked Tribune.

Thinking on the situation, Felix didn't have an immediate answer.

If there really was a war starting up, it meant there was a major player moving in, or a power vacuum across the board. In either situation, he'd likely have to change his plans accordingly.

"Tell her to come pick me up," Felix said after a minute of consideration. "Effective immediately, Faith is the acting Legate in my place while I take care of this issue."

"Yes, Sir," said Tribune.

Faith blinked several times while staring at him. It was obvious she really didn't know what to say to the sudden change in her rank.

"It'll be fine. Just keep following the plan we laid out," Felix said, patting her on the stomach. "Realistically, you shouldn't need to change anything. This was a massive build-up phase anyways. If you need anything, just reach out and let me know."

"Dragon Goldie has responded. She has stated that she is 'on her way', Sir," Tribune informed him.

"Great. There we go then. Any questions or concerns?" Felix asked, watching Faith.

"I don't want you to go," she mumbled, her face turning into a pout.

Every now and then Faith slipped into a spoiled princess' role. It was typically when she was disappointed or upset and needed him to fix it.

"Well, how about I help you get back to a good mood before I go?" offered Felix.

Faith rapidly nodded her head to that, though she was still pouting.

***

Goldie landed in the dead of night on top of the association building.

The giant Golden, sparkling, and gold-chain wearing Dragon was an impressive sight to behold.

Her bridal gold clattering and clinking as she settled down carefully on the roof.

Her golden eyes swung toward him and Felix simply hopped up on top of her. He'd leave his Legate armor in the Association for now. He didn't want to be spotted getting onto Goldie, or on Goldie, while in the armor.

Right now she was registered as a Super Villain and terrorist.

"Oh my, thank you Nest-mate. I'm so glad that you think so highly of me. That I'm 'impressive' to you," purred the mind-reading Dragon.

Clambering up atop the Dragon, Felix got as comfortable as he could.

"What can I say, not everyone gets to ride a sexy and amazing Dragon," Felix said. "No reason to try and hide how I feel about that from said sexy and amazing Dragon."

Goldie laughed at that and then jumped into the air. Her wings began to beat, and they climbed up into the sky.

"What's the run down? I feel like you left a lot out. Especially if we're going to have to figure this out," Felix asked, holding as tightly to the Dragon as he could.

"I honestly didn't. There isn't much to say. I didn't want to get too deeply involved, as that isn't our place as the supplier," Goldie answered quickly. "It's a massive war between the dealers and gangs to try and sort out who's in control and how.

"There's been a lot of deaths, and it feels like it's getting even worse. Spreading further and further. I heard some things on the news while I was out and about one day."

"Really? Huh. I haven't paid as much attention to it as I probably should have. What else do I need to know?" he asked instead.

"That's really it. The remains of Zachary and David's groups merged together and they're holding their own," said Goldie. "They haven't really lost any ground, but they're having to fight a lot more than they were.

"We'll make less money, of course, simply because of that. What do you think we should do?"

Felix forced his mind away from the fact he'd missed Goldie and tried to get it working on the situation at hand.

To not think about the fact that he missed her smile, her voice, and just being around her. The way she would nuzzle and tenderly nip at him in a strange way after their bed-play.

Instead, he brought his brain around to the work they'd need to do, rather than Goldie.

He really didn't want to get involved in this whole situation if he was going for the core issue here.

He also needed to force it to bend in the way he wanted it to though, as he needed the income. There was no legitimate way to raise as much money as he'd had with drugs.

Well, maybe this is a good opportunity to get the

League of Villains started. This can become the backbone for it if I just push hard enough on it.

Force it to all become one organization, all bound beneath the League.

Then give it to someone else and let them run with it and become the lightning rod. We can step into the background and just handle supply again. That's all I really want to do.

Dealing with drug dealers is already bad enough, but at least we're changing it to a degree. Making it more commercial.

With regulation comes safety, and we can at least start wrangling it. Pulling it somewhere more manageable.

You can't stop people a lot of the time when it comes to vices, but you can at least redirect and contain it.

"Oh, those are all very good ideas. I like it," Goldie said with a laugh. "I really am quite flattered by the way, Felix. My nest-mate. My love.

"I know you said you missed me, I believed you, but I had no idea it was that bad. That you wanted to call me back to you if only to hold me. You're such a romantic in the end, despite working so hard to hide it."

Felix rolled his eyes and tried to be as good natured as he could about it.

After losing Kit and Lily, he'd promised himself he would work to not hide his feelings anymore. That he'd stop trying to bury them and pretend they didn't exist.

"Yeah, well, I love you. I missed you. My big beautiful Golden One," grumbled Felix. "Now, where are we going?"

"Home first," Goldie declared with an edge to her tone. "I'm going to capitalize on your feelings for me right now. Then we're going to go to the landfill and we'll clear it out.

"The people Edmund connected you with to operate it have been doing their job well enough, so it's time to harvest it. We'll need the points."

"Oh? What am I altering?" Felix asked.

"Got a Dragon bone," Goldie admitted, her tone becoming quite serious. "One of Gaia's people brought it to me, actually. They formally gave it to me, and I'm formally giving it to you.

"That means you can probably bring it back to life, right? You can't own Alma and Carlotta, they're people. Citizens. The Dragon never was part of a government. Its bones are a lot like finding a tin-can on the ground."

"A Dragon," Felix whispered in surprise.

That'd help clean up the gang-war. They could become the contact to the League of Villains as well. Since I'd own them, that'd be a point increase, and it'd prevent them from betraying me.

Though… I'll need to make sure they have the opportunity to decline it.

"Aunt Gaia? I'm sure you're aware of my plans," Felix called out as they flew onward.

"I am indeed Felix Otherworlder," agreed Gaia.

"The bone you gave indirectly to me, you knew what I'd do?" he pushed.

"Of course. I'm well aware of what you're going to do with it," Gaia agreed once again.

"Will the Dragon be angry about it?" Felix asked. "Do they have a say in this? I wouldn't want to drag them back from death just to have to deal with an angry and unhappy Dragon."

"She'll be quite fine and is more than willing to go ahead with this," answered Gaia. "Though you'll have to help her acclimate to the world. She isn't quite... up to speed."

"Well, I'll just plunk her down in front of a TV and tie her in to a line with Tribune. She can ask questions of the VI until she's ready to go. This'll work though," Felix remarked in an off hand way. "Will she mind being used as an enforcer?"

"I'll need someone to keep the League of Villains in line. Someone to crack heads and generally be... not so kind."

"Also not an issue, and if anything, that'll work well for her," Gaia replied. "She's a Void Dragon. A Dragon without color. They're a blend of all the colors and can be... quite... unstable until they mature."

"Ah... teenager Dragon of some sort. Great," lamented Felix. "Fine. This'll work and it's fortuitous. Yeah, fortuitous. This isn't a mistake. It's a good thing. A good thing that'll work out well for us and... and... it'll be fine. Fine."

"A Void Dragon," mused Goldie. "I've never met one. They were around briefly in my time, but they didn't last long. They didn't have a Primordial to watch over them and they were hunted to extinction.

"Mostly by Reds who didn't want another source of competition. They really are the wild ones amongst Dragons. It's almost a shame, their Maidens can be so lovely to look at, yet their personalities are so terrible."

"Not everyone can be a gorgeous golden goddess, my lovely one," Felix remarked. "By the way, I think we should start adding a gold ring to your bridal gold for every Dragon Maiden you put into your Wing. Thoughts?"

"Yes," she said without another word. It was a word that was more like a steel trap slamming shut. There would be no escaping from that expectation in the future.

Though she did begin to loudly purr as they flew on through the clouds and the dark night.

Chapter 6 - Dire Charm -

Taking a sip of his coffee, Felix leaned into the arm of the couch.

The TV was on and the morning news broadcasters were doing their thing. Rehashing any relevant updates to older stories and what happened overnight.

" — see where this 'Association' goes. So far, they're positioning themselves as a separate entity entirely. Or at least, that's what they claim.

"We were able to get some footage of the Legate welcoming everyone inside. The video stops just as they enter the lobby, though they were able to take some photos. We'll be reviewing those later," reported the anchor.

Felix smirked and shook his head.

Tribune had told him that they could disrupt recording devices, but not photography. If someone had a regular analogue camera, then they'd be able to take photos without a concern.

The screen flipped to a video still of him standing in front of the doors. Then he began to talk.

"It's been on the news quite a bit," reported Goldie, walking into the living room of the trailer. She'd brought him back here in the end, after they ditched all forms of identification at the farm.

While they were here, they were operating as their underworld personas.

"I mean, it's a big change, so it isn't a surprise," Felix replied as the Dragon sat down next to him on the couch. She snuggled up to him, then laid her head down to his shoulder.

When she didn't have her horns out, the gold chains simply rested across the top of her head, almost like a golden shawl of sorts. It blended quite well with her bright-gold hair.

She was wearing it in a very simple way that hung straight down without any braiding, ties, or bands, other than her bridal gold.

Her normally elongated ears were quite human-looking at the moment. She was in her fully disguised form and blending in with humanity.

Though even in this form her full, hourglass figure, continued to demand the attention of everyone nearby.

Regardless of her mask, Goldie would always be a woman shaped from fantasies and artistry.

"Artistry? Well, that's rather flowery. Though I do like it," Goldie murmured, rubbing her cheek against his shoulder. "I'm afraid this is just how I was born, though. I was quite blessed in my physical appearance.

"Amusingly though, there were many times throughout history and across cultures where I was not considered very attractive. Beauty is always in the eye of the beholder, after all."

"Stupid. Anyone who wouldn't think of you as beautiful is stupid," grumped Felix, laying an arm around the Dragon's shoulders.

The TV flipped to a commercial break and

began showing a soda product.

"Well… thank you. Anyways… I haven't been able to really get this all worked out because there's something going on," murmured Goldie. "Every time I got them stable, people would just start acting strange. Strange to the point that it was obvious something had changed.

"Then after a week or two, or when I started to look into them a bit more closely, they vanished. Without a trace.

"When I looked into their thoughts, I found there was a connection between all of them. There was a strange… gauzy-like… blanket over their thoughts. They were thinking quite normally, but it felt like a set of rules had been put into them."

"Rules?" asked Felix, curious and concerned in the same breath.

"That's the only way I can describe it. I've never encountered it before. No matter what I do, I can't get ahead of it either, which is why I asked for help," Goldie said, then sighed. "I really don't like asking either. I wanted to solve this on my own. It feels like a simple turf-war, but there's most definitely a super involved."

"Nothing wrong with asking for help, my Golden One. I ask for help as well you know," Felix murmured comfortingly. "Asking for help from your companions is a perfectly normal thing."

Goldie nodded her head but didn't respond.

The TV flickered from one commercial to another and suddenly Alma, Carlotta, and Faith were on screen.

"Feel like maybe you're not just Joe Schmoe?" asked Alma with a beautiful smile.

"As if there's something more in you that hasn't been brought to the surface?" asked Carlotta with a purr to the question.

"We've all applied to the Association to determine just that," Faith said with her own smile, a wrinkling of her nose, and a nod. "You should too! Just fill out a form on the website!"

Then the commercial turned off and went to another.

"I hate how single-minded it is, how stupidly simple it is, but it's worked," growled Felix. They'd hired several male models to do a female aligned version of the commercial as well.

"Humans are no different than any other race, you know. We're all animals in one way or another," Goldie mused. Then she sat up and gave him an inspecting look. Her eyes moving from his head, down to his waist, and back up. "Speaking of animals... wanna do it like they do on the discovery channel?"

Unable to help himself, Felix laughed.

"Andrea has completely corrupted you," he said, though he did put his coffee cup down and gestured to the bedroom. "Though... not as much as I plan on corrupting you, my Golden One."

Goldie's eyes flashed and they began to glow a golden color. Breaking through the illusion she was wearing.

Then her ears began to elongate out and her horns started to grow in.

The purr she was letting out was loud and obvious.

***

Sitting at a table outside the property that Zach had last been using as his headquarters, Goldie and Felix were acting more like a couple out to eat.

Considering that the property itself, a cafe that specialized in coffee and bagels, was now closed, and they had the remains of their meal in front of them, the disguise worked rather well. Or Felix thought so at least.

Goldie was rummaging around in the minds of anyone who passed by. Their goal today was simple. Find whoever had this "gauzy blanket" over their thoughts and follow them for a bit.

It wasn't a great plan, but given that Goldie hadn't been able to determine anything from their thoughts or memories, their options for figuring the situation out were limited. Doubly so since the numbers in Zach and David's gangs had been steadily decreasing since the leaders had died.

"You know, it's a bit odd," Felix remarked with a shake of his head. "Every time the police bust a dealer, they just open up the door for others to take their place. Where those people can move into the vacancy or expand their own operations.

"It's almost like... a form of consolidation. Where it becomes further and further strengthened and concentrated. Almost like the waste disposal industry.

"There's a bunch of big corporations running most of it. We lucked out that we got dropped into a city that had such a rickety contract we could take over."

"Oh? I wouldn't figure you for the type to think law and order wasn't the best course of action," murmured Goldie, taking a sip from her coffee.

Apparently it was the last sip, because when she set it back down, it sounded rather hollow. That meant that they could only stay so much longer without raising suspicion.

"I'm a big fan of law and order. Especially rules that are easy to understand and move through a society," Felix confessed, followed by a small shake of his head. "But this is stupid. This is right up there with prohibition.

"All they've done is move everything into an underground market. You might as well compare it to... eh... it doesn't matter. That's just politics and I don't care. None of it will matter once I take over.

"But yeah, it's just like prohibition. If their goal is to stop the dealers and the market, legalize it. Commercialize it. Make it no different than pot. I mean... I can't speak to this world, but in my own, heroin used to be sold over the counter. They put it in cough medicine and all sorts of things.

"If the goal is to put drug users in jail, then

mission accomplished. They just happened to create a massive organization of power and money at the same time. Outside looking in to the decision made, it seems almost silly."

Goldie laughed at that and then sighed.

"I don't care about any of this. I just want to be a housewife, putter around in my little garden, admire my gold, and occasionally knock over a casino. Or a bank if I'm feeling grumpy," the Dragon admitted. "This is all… all that stuff just isn't something I worry over. Laws, politics, government. It's, whatever."

Felix smirked and couldn't help but nod his head. He could certainly understand how she felt. Many people felt like that.

They just wanted to make their way as best as they could in the world. Everything beyond the circle of overlap to that wasn't important to them.

"Hello," said a young woman, stepping up to their table.

She looked mildly attractive, with light-brown hair, blue eyes, and a normal physique. If Felix had to guess he'd put her at about twenty-six.

"Afternoon," Felix said a bit suspiciously. There was no reason for her to approach them as she had. Not unless she was a lookout of sorts.

Well. Let's pull up her character sheet and go from there. That'll be more than enough to… I… what?

A slow and strange force was pushing on his mind as he stared into the woman's face. Gazing into her eyes, he felt like they were infinitely deep and without end.

That force circled up around his mind and began to solidify itself there. In a moment, he felt like this woman was the very center of his world. That he had to do whatever he could to make her happy.

For her to smile.

"Perfect," said the young woman. "Can I join you? Or would you two rather go elsewhere?"

"Elsewhere," Goldie said firmly. "We've been here too long and will raise suspicion if we remain."

"Elsewhere," Felix agreed. "Same reasoning."

"I see," the woman said with a slow nod of her head. Then she turned and started walking away toward a work-van. "Come on then. Let's get going."

Felix felt a pull on that command that came with a sense of completing the duty as quickly as he could. That doing anything else was the absolute worst possible choice.

There wasn't a single thought in Felix's head of resisting, either. In his mind, this was exactly as it should be.

Clambering into the van, Felix took a seat and then buckled his seatbelt. Goldie sat down next to him and did the same. Her eyes were the dull illusion color at the moment, and she seemed almost bored.

The woman got into the passenger seat and

looked the driver with a smile.

"Let's start heading back. They didn't want to stay here because they might get noticed," said the woman with a chuckle. "Betting they're cops. Wouldn't hurt to add more of them to the collection but... well, you know."

"Yeah, I know," grumbled the man. He put the transmission into reverse and began moving them out of the parking space and into the street.

Sitting there, Felix was quite happy to have completed the task she'd given him so easily. That all was right with the world and all he had to do was keep following orders.

Then there was a golden and warm poke against his mind. If anything, it felt a lot like someone testing water with a finger.

It retreated after a second, then a much larger presence oozed down around his mind. It created a shell around the suffocating slowness that'd locked Felix's thoughts into place.

Several seconds drew the feeling out before Goldie's presence snapped through the barrier in his mind. It crushed it completely and discarded the remains as one might crack an egg.

Oh... uh... huh.

Huh, well... I guess that answers that.

Super power or magically enhanced power, but still the same thing in the end. Some type of... come hither spell.

A charm I suppose.

Next to him, he caught Goldie as she gave

him a glance, then focused ahead again. From the very beginning she likely had been unaffected by the power.

Dragons are extraordinary creatures.

Should always keep you at my side, Goldie.

The corner of Goldie's mouth turned up a fraction, before it flattened out again.

Yes… we'll play the part of the charmed man and woman for now. I'd say… gang associations. People who were doing drug mule runs between Zach, David, and the 'supplier'.

That way we can propose a linkup to the supplier again.

Beyond that, I say play it straight other than our names. You can be Dee. I'll be… Bruce. Seems fitting somehow.

Bruce Campbell.

Goldie made a small nod of her head to that, yet remained motionless otherwise. Staring ahead just as he had been.

" — on the way, can we swing by the store? I need to pick up some things," said the woman.

"Michael should do it since it's all for him," complained the man. "It's not like he's got anything else that's pressing in on him."

"He's doing all he can to lead us. You should trust him more," replied the woman.

The man said nothing, but he spoke volumes just by shaking his head.

***

* * *

"Alright, both of you come with me," announced Anya. Felix had checked her character sheet and found that she was quite normal in every regard.

Other than the fact that she had a Super power, and that it was "limited" in activity, labeled as "Dire Charm".

Which meant she could probably become significantly stronger in the future and might be able to hold anyone in thrall. Though Felix was curious if there was a numerical limitation.

As in how many people she could have charmed at the same time.

The man was named Thomas Todd and was equally as normal as the woman. He had a limited activity Super power as well. His was listed as EM Field control.

Felix took that as to mean he could effectively go after any electronics within a certain distance to him. That perhaps he could even feel electronics and then take care of them.

You know... putting their powers together would make it nearly impossible to break into their organization.

Felix stepped out of the van after Goldie and began following Anya inside.

Charm anyone and everyone who comes close and find out who and what they are. If anyone has electronics on them, Thomas can just wink them out of existence I bet.

That means surveillance in person, and by electronics, would be difficult to say the least. If I had these two working for me, I could easily build up a mafia like outfit.

Or... is that the whole point? What they're already doing?

I wonder if this Michael is another Super, or just someone they trust to manage the whole thing. Could go either way.

Though it seems like Thomas isn't a fan of "Michael".

I can probably use that to my advantage later.

Anya led them into a bar of some type, though it looked like it was a restaurant as well, given the layout.

Felix didn't look away from Anya's back and was just trying to play the "charmed doll" role that he imagined everyone would expect, while also trying to keep an eye out and notice everything that he could as they went.

He'd noticed that someone had flipped a placard in the window as they entered as well. Possibly to indicate that Thomas and Anya had returned, but Felix wasn't sure. He'd have to look into that as he went.

Moving through the dining area and by the bar, they quickly got to the back. A small private dining area and open door that led into an office.

A man was sitting in one of the booths there, fiddling with a phone.

He had dark black hair, pale brown eyes, and a face that looked to have been in more than a few fights. He even had several small scars about his mouth and cheek.

Must be Michael.

Anya walked up to Michael, bent down, and kissed him wordlessly. Then she slid in next to him, all while the man in question just sat there. Receiving the kiss as if it were as simple as a wave or a handshake.

Right.

Is that it?

Anya is dating Michael, Thomas wants Anya, Michael doesn't give a shit but wants to use her. That'd be the likely scenario, right?

Hm. Also need to investigate that.

"Found these two outside Zach's base. They didn't belong and looked out of place, so I snagged'em," Anya explained, watching Michael with a smile. It was obvious she was infatuated with the man. "If they're just nobodies, we can take a small donation from them and send them off."

Michael finally looked up from his phone.

His eyes moved to Felix, then flicked away from him to Goldie. Then stayed on Goldie. In a way that was more like a buyer looking at merchandise.

As if realizing what he was doing, Michael quickly looked away from Goldie and to Anya. While he clearly didn't feel the same way about her as she did him, it was just as obvious he wasn't going to endanger his meal ticket.

Felix used the moment to open up a character screen for Michael.

Which after reading the pop-up told him exactly what he needed to know.

The man was ordinary.

With a bit more strength than the average person and lower wisdom. Otherwise, he was interchangeable with the vast majority of men on the planet.

Meal ticket indeed. Without Anya and Thomas, the man would probably be swimming in bad ideas and in debt from going off with too many half-cocked plans.

"Alright. Makes sense," Michael said gruffly. "Just make sure you get them out by nightfall. I'm still feeling weird that the gold horned lady hasn't come back. It's been almost forty-eight hours.

"She's never been gone that long, and no-one's reported seeing her. I told you we should have moved on her first."

"If we hadn't kept pulling people out that we got into their organization it've been fine," Anya countered with a pout. "Besides, if she's gone, that just makes it easier for us. She was able to identify all our people far too easily."

"What? We definitely did the right move by pulling people out. You probably just didn't do it right," Michael said with disinterest now. "You even said it yourself. That you'd probably given them bad information."

Anya's face clouded in what looked to be confusion and disagreement. She didn't fight him though.

Gas lighting, maybe?

That'll be hard to break. Gotta go about it carefully.

But... I think I can make this work.

I'll become the advisor to Anya and Thomas after removing Michael. Become their supplier, tell them everything they need to do to succeed, and let it run.

Then, in a while... turn them into the League of Villains.

Perfect.

"Who are you two" Anya began, directing her question to Felix.

"Dee and Bruce," he answered succinctly.

"Do you work for the government? In any way?" Anya asked, looking to Goldie.

"No. I was an exotic dancer until I met my husband," Goldie said almost blandly.

Dancer? Damn.

That'd be a sight to see.

Anya turned to look at Felix.

"You're her husband?" she asked.

"Yes," he answered directly.

"And what do you do?" Anya prompted.

"Waste management," Felix said with a sour tilt to his mouth.

"Ask about the dealers," growled Michael, his eyes sliding back to Goldie before jumping away.

"Did you two have anything to do with the dealers around here?" Anya asked.

"I was the connection to the supplier," Felix said as Goldie answered with a negative.

"How?" Michael demanded.

Felix didn't respond.

"How were you the connection?" Anya asked.

"Supplier only talks to anyone electronically, so I was the in-between. He wouldn't talk to anyone but me after there was an attempt on his life. He doesn't do face-to-face. Ever. For any reason," answered Felix.

"Well. There we go. We'll keep them so we can get that connection," Michael said, his eyes moving back to Goldie. Then quickly away.

"Alright. We'll… have to be careful though," Anya said, looking at Goldie and Felix. "They feel like they're still under charm but… they'll break if we try to push them too far. To do something they wouldn't want to do.

"We'll have to treat them like guest-members rather than just workers."

Michael had a disappointed look on his face, but he nodded to that.

"Let's go get some more information from you in the office and then get you settled," Anya murmured and then stood up.

Chapter 7 - Indoctrination -

Anya sighed and leaned her head back. Looking up to the ceiling above them.

"I was honestly hoping you two would have more money," she complained. "You barely have enough to get by. I'll have to move some money over to you both just so you don't end up having problems."

Anya groaned and then put her hands on her head.

"Michael will get pissy. He hates giving away money," grumbled Anya, who was shaking her head.

"His opinion doesn't matter. Only yours does," Felix interjected. He wasn't sure if the charmed would behave like this, but he didn't care at the moment. He needed to start somewhere. "Without you, he'd just be a thug. He depends on you and Thomas. He doesn't even deserve to be in your company."

Anya blinked and looked at him in shock. Felix suddenly felt the presence of her power. It settled over him and forced his thoughts back to how they'd been when he'd first met her.

On a leash.

As soon as it settled into place, Goldie popped it open again. Crushing the charm outright and scattering it.

"Tell me what you really think," Anya asked in an odd tone.

"Michael is using you. He's a detriment and likely going to be a problem. You should be leading everyone. It's by your will alone that you set all our minds in motion," offered Felix. "In fact… he's a weak link.

"If he were to be captured by a Super Hero, or brought into a federal agency's circle of attention, he wouldn't even be able to do anything. He's a weakness as glaring as having a foot wide hole in the middle of body armor."

Anya looked incredibly shocked now. Her eyes wide and staring at him as if she was seeing something and someone else entirely.

As if she'd heard this argument already before.

Thomas must be trying to steer her clear as well.

"He would never—"

"Some Super Heroes can read minds. He wouldn't even have a chance or a choice unless your protection is on him. Is it?" Felix asked.

"I… no. No he's not… no. Neither is Thomas, though," Anya argued.

"This isn't about Thomas. It's also why he's a weakness, too, however. He shouldn't be in the lead, nor should he be allowed to go out without your protection."

Anya's face was still screwed up in a picturesque view of a woman torn. Yearning for one thing while considering another. One that she really didn't want to think about.

"Leave here and go back to your normal

routine. I need you to contact the supplier. Let him know we want to do business with him in the place of the older gangs. We're taking over and… well, we're taking over," Anya instructed. "Come back here tomorrow in the morning. Preferably before noon but… stick to your schedule, too."

Felix and Goldie nodded, then turned around. They quickly left the building and stopped just outside.

Standing there, they hesitated for several seconds, looked at each other, and paused further.

"Did we want to talk about dinner soon?" Felix asked in his best "we were just chatting earlier and this is a follow up" type of conversation. "I was thinking maybe like… tacos. I could really go for tacos."

"Tacos sound fun," Goldie agreed.

Felix turned his head and looked to the front door.

In the window there was a sign that said "the doctor is in".

Ah… so yeah… that's how they determine if Anya and Thomas are in the building. Unless that sign's up, I bet they're told not to talk about anything.

To discuss nothing so there's no possibility of someone catching something said.

So… very interesting.

I can definitely use this to my advantage. The League of Villains will be able to withstand quite a bit. All without me getting involved as the master of Legion.

* * *

***

Doing as instructed, Felix and Goldie returned the next day in the morning.

They'd done just as instructed and went on a pretend schedule. One that the people who they were pretending to be would do.

No one attempted to follow them.

No one kept tabs on them.

No one was verifying their story.

It's a bit of a blind spot, but I get it. They have absolute belief in their powers.

Walking into the bar, Felix noted the sign in the window was turned out to signify Anya was here. Though in that moment Felix wondered if it was a "Anya and Thomas" was in, since when they combined their powers was when they were at their strongest.

Having only one or the other just wouldn't be as safe.

Walking through the room, Felix and Goldie went straight for the back. Where Anya had spoken to them with Michael present.

Sitting in the same exact spot as last time, was Michael. Anya wasn't present, though Thomas was here. He was in the back, fiddling with what looked to be a laptop. His black hair was hanging down in front of his blue-eyes and he seemed entirely focused on the device.

"Oh, you two," Michael growled, looking up from his phone. Then he smiled and looked to

Goldie. "Give me a lap dance. You can really work it, too."

"I could do that. But only if you wanted me to break your head open and scoop out your brains as if they were tapioca pudding," Goldie responded with a saccharine sweet smile.

"I... what?" Michael asked.

"Why would my wife give you a dance?" Felix asked, shaking his head slowly. As if they were in the middle of clearing the effects of Anya's charm.

"Never mind," Michael said quickly, looking back to his phone.

And that's that. We'll have to use this to push Anya.

"Why would my wife give you a dance?" Felix asked again, taking several steps toward Michael. Causing the man to look up again.

His face was somewhat shocked-looking and he didn't have a response.

"Answer me you piece of shit," demanded Felix, looming over the other man.

"Look, this is just a mistake. We'll just wait for Anya," whined Michael, holding his hands up.

"Why? So she can clean up after you? Are you a sniveling child? You can't own up to your own actions?" Felix continued, then he grabbed Michael by the collar. "I should pound your face into hamburger. Then we can wait for Anya."

"Whoa, whoa. Hey, let's dial it down," Thomas said, inserting himself between Michael and Felix. Apparently, he'd noticed what was going on.

"Why? He just propositioned my wife. Why would I dial it down?" Felix said, skirting the truth to a degree. It was enough to push the situation up in escalation, but not a bold-faced lie.

"You what?!" Thomas shrieked, looking at Michael.

Michael now looked like a man who very much wanted to run away. A man full of bravado on his home turf, that'd state his opinions unasked, and bully anyone he could.

Only to whine and flee when called to task.

"I didn't!" screamed Michael. "They've clearly broken their charm!"

"Anya will hear of this. She told us to come back. You shouldn't have told my wife to do that," growled Felix, letting go of Michael. He stepped away from the two men and moved back to Goldie's side.

"An... Anya told you to come back?" asked Thomas.

"She told us to contact the supplier and come back this morning," provided Goldie. "We went about our normal routine, contacted the supplier, came back."

Perfect.

Just keep making cracks between the three of them.

For Thomas, that Michael doesn't respect or value
Anya.

For Michael, that we don't listen to him and think

he's the weak link.

For Anya, we boost her confidence and her leadership.

"Slimeball," Goldie hissed. "You should treasure your woman rather than trying to demand things of others."

Thomas was wide-eyed and staring at Felix and Goldie. There was a significant amount of anger in his face as well.

"Whatever, this is stupid. I'm leaving," Michael declared and then got up. Rushing out of the backroom.

"Run coward. You're the weak link here," Felix called after him. "Everyone would be better off without you even existing! Run back to your momma. Maybe you can ask her to do what you did my wife!?"

Michael's spine stiffened but he didn't stop.

Felix and Goldie stared at his retreating back until he was gone. Then they both looked ahead and went silent. Staring into nothing as if there hadn't been an issue at all.

Waiting for Anya as any good charmed person would do.

Thomas looked at them, looked away, to his feet, then back to Felix and Goldie. Watching them carefully, he seemed extremely confused, as well as upset.

"Did he really do that?" asked Thomas.

Felix didn't say anything as it seemed like he was asking Goldie.

"He did," confirmed Goldie, not looking away from the empty space between the wall and herself.

"Great," hissed Thomas. "Just… great. I guess it was only a matter of time. And you're just… a walking wet dream so… ugh. Damnit. Damnit!"

Shaking his head, Thomas stamped off to where he'd been sitting previously. His entire body filled with tension.

Neat. That worked out rather well.

Now we just wait for Anya. Hopefully she'll get here relatively soon.

***

Anya stormed into the room some time later. Perhaps an entire hour had passed. The very second she entered, she slammed a Dire Charm onto Felix, then held it there. As if making sure this would stick and remain.

Felix briefly thought about the fact that this wasn't too terrible. He imagined Michael had already gone crying to Anya. Likely on his cell phone, and demanding she do something about him and Goldie.

This was going to be her version of an interrogation.

His only real concern was if she asked him if he was under her charm when he came in this morning.

Then his thoughts became the gooey type that Anya's power forced him to be.

Except she didn't say anything, nor did she ask him a question. She stared at him, or more accurately, through him.

There was a blank part of his mind that registered the fact that she couldn't actively hold a charm and do much else. It likely required a great deal of concentration on her part.

Eventually she finally released her hold. Followed by her panting for several beats. At the exact time Anya let go, Goldie sprung him free from the power. Leaving him in control of his mental faculties.

"Michael said you lied," Anya started.

"I did not. He made a pass on my wife and propositioned her. I almost beat him to death right there for it, the scumbag," Felix growled.

Anya winced and actually leaned away from him. As if his words were a physical assault on her.

"The only reason I didn't was Thomas stopped it. He's respectful to you and a good companion. Michael is scum," continue Felix. "If he made a pass at my wife, I'm sure he's done it to others as well."

Anya looked to the side and closed her eyes. She pressed her hands to her face and was clearly not wanting to be part of this.

"Did he proposition you?" Anya asked, opening her hands briefly to look at Goldie.

"He did," confirmed Goldie.

Shaking her head rapidly, Anya turned away from them and walked over to Thomas. They began to talk quietly and Felix couldn't hear any of it, though he imagined Goldie could.

She'd relay whatever was said back to him later if it was important at all.

Anya froze, held up a hand and looked back to Felix.

"What'd the supplier say?" she asked.

"He's willing to do the same deal with you that he had with the others. He just wants his cut and his rules followed. That's it," Felix answered. "I should mention that… he's capable of slaughtering everyone in your organization. Now that he's aware of you, it's very likely you'll receive a list of rules he wants you to follow."

Anya's mouth hung open, staring at him with shock once more.

These three seemed prone to being surprised. They didn't seem to be looking ahead to what might be coming and were just looking at their current situation only.

"He served as a counselor to Zach and Dave. He wasn't expecting a super to show up," Felix explained a bit more.

"I… but… what?" Anya asked, unable to put her thoughts into words. "He was in charge? Then… how did we take them over?"

"He wasn't in charge. He doesn't want to be. He just wants to supply you under a set of rules. They're pretty easy to adhere to. Just comes down to making it a commercial product rather than how they normally are," Felix answered.

"I… see. Okay. Well. That's not really good news," muttered Thomas. "Maybe we should just go with who we were already working with. I'm not sure we should get involved with someone like this."

"Yeah, we'll think about it. That's a bit too much for us. Especially if he won't ever meet face to face," agreed Anya.

That's fair.

Having the meeting be now wouldn't be as effective as later.

"What do we do for now?" Thomas asked, looking to Anya.

"We move ahead with our police connections. See if we can't keep expanding them," Anya decided. "These two… I don't want them here at the bar for now."

"You mean around Michael, not the bar. Since it's likely he wants to try and force Dee here into a bed," Thomas cursed. "He's a danger to us. Literally the reason we're now involved with the supplier who wants to dictate rules to us is because he really wanted to take over other crews.

"We could have just kept expanding the way we were and not causing an issue. We only did it at all because Michael wanted it and you can't tell him no."

"No! No, that's not it. That's not it at all," Anya shouted at Thomas. She was up in his face now, one hand jabbing a finger into his chest. "You just don't like Michael!"

"I never liked Michael! He's always been a drag on us. Always! Every time we start to make progress, his big frickin' mouth ruins it for us! Now he wants to rape people under control?

"What the fuck Anya! When we started this, we promised it'd be more like a club. Sure we use people, but we're going to do what we can to keep them safe! Give them a better life!

"Michael is already ruining that for us, and it's getting worse! Worse by the day! If this keeps up we'll all be done before we start!"

Anya glared at Thomas for another ten seconds before she stormed off.

"Do whatever Thomas tells you to do!" she called over her shoulder as she walked away.

Felix would say she left in a huff, if he had to describe it to someone else. A woman who clearly didn't want to believe the truth laid out in front of her.

Gaslighting and manipulation then. She's completely turned upside down around him.

It'll take a good bit to force her out of it.

Sighing, Thomas came over to stand next to Goldie and Felix. They were both watching him now. Waiting for orders like a good charmed person would do.

"Just… ugh… I'll introduce you to your boss," Thomas mumbled. "He'll provide you with tasks and your job duties. Just follow what he tells you in regards to the outfit. Otherwise just… go about your normal business. We'll get in touch with you if we need to."

Felix and Goldie just kept staring at Thomas. Waiting for him to lead them off.

"I think you were right," Felix said suddenly as Thomas stared into nothing. "I think Michael is a terrible person and he's likely to ruin it all.

"If he got flipped by the cops… that'd be it for everyone involved. They'd just use his word against everyone else and round us all up."

Thomas nodded his head and then began moving, finally. Leading Felix and Goldie off.

I wonder how organized this is. It'll be interesting to see what they've put together.

Always a pleasure to wander around a rival's place. Look at what they're doing and see if there's anything to learn.

Perform a review and see if we can make any changes.

Glancing to Goldie, he gave her a grin as they began walking along behind Thomas.

She caught his look and gave him a smile in return. There was a glimmer in her eyes that was faintly giving away her eyes weren't normal.

I wonder what that's for.

Is it because I got so angry at him for saying what he did to her?

Goldie's smile widened.

Ah. Yes. Being possessive over her.

As much as she insists she isn't a normal Dragon,

she is indeed a Dragon.
    Need to remember that, always.

Chapter 8 - Investigator -

"I don't think we'll learn anything more from them," Felix groused, staring up at the ceiling of the trailer. Goldie was dozing next to him while holding onto his arm.

"Mmm?" she asked, then began to lightly nibble and nip at his shoulder. Slowly making her way back and forth.

He'd heard about this previously, though he couldn't remember from who. This was a Dragon grooming and social thing.

"We've learned all we can from Anya's crew. There's really no reason to hang around anymore," Felix reckoned. "After a week we've seen all we need to. All in all, it's a really watered-down version of Legion. They're not even making as much profit as they could."

"Anya is kind. A limiting presence as well as their brakes.

"Without her, it'd have blown up in their faces I imagine," Goldie responded as she continued to pull at his skin with her lips. "Push for too much, too soon, and end up bringing a lot more down on their heads.

"They're not as savvy as you and your lieutenants were in Legion. They're learning as they go and are trying to figure things out."

Felix chewed at the inside of his cheek and made a ping-ponging motion with his head. Considering what she'd said and putting his own point of view out of the picture.

I can't reasonably hold someone accountable to the actions I'd take, especially if I've never spoken to them about it.

"Right. Well, this has been a useful side-trip, but it's time to end it for now," Felix declared. "I've definitely found the starting point for the League of Villains in Anya and Thomas. They could easily keep out informants and undercover agents.

"But that's something we'll have to move slowly on. To push them into the position I need them isn't so easy or quick.

"Probably time to head back and check in on the Association. It... they... ugh... this world's Kit and Lily should be coming in for their interviews in three days, if the last schedule I saw holds true."

"True," Goldie said as her head began to move more towards the middle of his chest. Then she moved up and kissed him, moving her body over the top of him. Breaking the kiss, she leaned back, displaying her naked glory to him. Her gold chains and rings tinkled lightly on her horns as she gave her head a shake. "Let's have a good morning and then get going. We can be back at the Association swiftly enough that twenty minutes just for us won't hurt anything."

***

Walking up to the front door of the Association, Felix noted that there was a

Legionnaire there. He'd let everyone know he was coming but he hadn't actually heard back from them.

He imagined they were inundated with work and simply didn't have the time.

"Legate," came Edmund's voice across the com lines. He didn't salute, but he did nod his head to Felix. Saluting was banned outright as they were a public entity, not a military. "We're going through more Association hiring reviews. No new supers since we finished up with all the previous ones.

"Miss Marin has been working closely with Faith to identify candidates for the Association. They've started up in their roles as quickly as we could so we're moving ahead faster than we expected."

I… what? Err… I guess that'd work. Wouldn't it? Using your power to identify someone who belongs in the Association.

Or someone who belongs to a different organization.

Pair that with the Dryads and their ability to gauge emotions and thoughts, and that makes it much easier than you'd think.

Though it does make me wonder. Was part of my own power given to me from my mother? It feels so similar.

"Understood. Though why are you out here?" Felix asked, coming to a stop in front of the man. Right now he was dressed in a normal Legionnaire's armor. One that could be handed off to someone else once he donned his own Legate armor.

Goldie was directly beside him, wearing her own armor. While she wouldn't be able to shift into her Dragon form with it, she could at least be "out of sight" with it on. She could blend in with the others.

All it'd cost them for the two suits was emptying the landfill, which was always getting more trash dumped in.

A few of Edmunds friends were currently making sure the dumping continued.

"People made a scene while others tried to access the terminals. Tribune shut'em down. We put them all under citizen's arrest and turned them over to the government," Edmund said with a chuckle. "Couple of them were agents for the government though so... that's awkward. Miss Marin identified them. We labeled them appropriately as well as their names.

"You just so happen to have a meeting with the government today with an unstated subject. That'll be funny I imagine."

Felix smirked and shook his head.

Entering the lobby, he heard a ping from inside his helmet as it connected to the wi-fi signal. There was a several second pause before he heard his speakers click.

"Welcome back, Legate. Should I transfer all commands to you from Dryad Faith?" Tribune asked.

"No, don't transfer them back. Leave Faith with all the powers, but also listen to mine as well. If they're in conflict, notify me," commanded Felix as he moved through the lobby.

There was a large number of people sitting in chairs, looking at phones, watching TV, or just rehearsing for their interview. Standing at the podium was a Legionnaire.

"Welcome back," Carlota said with a nod of her head. "As Edmund said, you have a meeting scheduled. We accepted it because you said you were on your way.

"It's supposed to be in thirty minutes. We've set up the Sulla conference room for it. Everything is just as Edmund said otherwise. Though… in three days, we're expecting the next batch of Supers. We'll need you there for it."

Yeah.

Can't run from that.

Felix nodded his head. He needed to go change into his Legate armor, then get into the meeting room.

It only took him twenty minutes to make the change and get to the room. He was the first to arrive though he knew he'd never been alone.

Even when Goldie had stepped out to use the restroom while he changed.

Tribune had been updating him endlessly on minutiae the whole time. Of all the work they'd done and what had been accomplished while he was out.

Sitting down in the chair, Felix let out a sigh and set down his laptop in front of his seat. He didn't want to take off his gauntlets for the sake of safe-guarding his fingerprints and DNA.

" — changed the thermostat controls accordingly. So long as I maintain this program, we'll be looking into saving money while still meeting everyone's needs on comfort," Tribune droned on.

It's just a VI, but it feels like they need recognition. So hit that, then pivot.

"Good job, Tribune. Very good job. I'm proud of you. Remind me to do something to show that gratitude for you.

"Though... I have a request for you," Felix interjected before it could answer him. "I don't want to take my gauntlets off to protect my safety. Can I rely on you for note taking and dictation?"

"I'll be recording the entirety of the conversation and will save it for later analysis," Tribune stated. "My request for your gratitude would be to accelerate your plans for the heuristics program for verbal and non-verbal communication you have the programmers developing, Legate."

Er... well... that's not a terrible request on her part, I guess.

It'd help as well to have Tribune running an analysis on everyone we bring in for an interview or otherwise.

"Push it up on their agenda as the item next in the queue for them," answered Felix. "I think they were working on the facial identification program, right?"

"Yes, Legate," confirmed Tribune.

Goldie folded her hands in front of herself after sitting next to Felix. She began to slowly twiddle her thumbs, looking for all the world like a very bored Dragon.

"I wish I had something to sew," she said suddenly, turning her helmeted head to look at Felix. "I have so much to do as a housewife and I don't like it when I waste time like this."

"Dragon Goldie, I believe your presence is vastly under-estimated by your own statement," argued Tribune. "I have noted that Felix is extremely comfortable when you're around.

"On top of which, this doesn't take into account your ability to pierce the minds of others. Your presence is required. As is Andrea's."

What?

A moment after that and Andrea came in through the door. It was obviously her, given the way she carried herself despite the fact she was wearing Legionnaire armor.

At her hip was a holstered pistol, and slung across her front was an SMG. It looked very similar to the one she preferred back in their own home world.

He imagined the armor she was wearing, was likely the very same set he'd just put away in fact.

"Feeeelix!" squeaked Andrea through the com system before rushing over to him. She slammed into him and held onto him. Hugging him tightly. "Oh it's so good to see you! So so good! I missed you!

"Also, hi hi Goldie. I missed you. I don't like it when you're away, just as I don't like it when Felix is away."

"Hello, dear," Felix said with a chuckle. Then he patted the chair next to him. "Sit down before they get here."

"Nnnn, I can't! I'm your bodyguard. Just in case things go sideways. Tribune asked me to be here," Andrea said and finally released him. "Tribune promised me she'd help me get some alone time with you if I did it!"

Andrea stepped away from him and took up position behind him. He heard a soft clatter that sounded like her picking up her firearm and holding to it.

That belief was confirmed when he clearly heard a round being cycled, and a click of a safety being turned off.

Well, at least she didn't hug me with a live weapon.

Though I'm nervous about this promise of alone time.

Tribune is an VI, right? It's always been listed as an VI.

Felix called up the ownership window for Tribune and found it was exactly as he expected. A virtual intelligence owned by him and therefore Legion.

"Oh, oh, they're coming!" Andrea said rather excitedly. He could practically hear her bouncing around behind him. "Okay. Okay. It's... it's Myriad time. Myriad. Myriad. Myriad. I'm gonna be —"

"Andrea Elex. Who was only nicknamed Myriad," interrupted Felix. "Myriad was Andrea Elex. Who all became Andrea Campbell."

There was a heavy silence followed by a long sigh.

"I'm Andrea Campbell. Once known as Myriad," Andrea said in a much firmer voice. "Thank you, Felix."

The door opened and a Legionnaire that was likely Edmund led a group of people inside. Felix didn't recognize any of them, but that wasn't much of a surprise.

People would likely be coming and going as fast as a light change in his sphere of influence. Especially for the government types.

"Thank you for meeting with us. I hope you can forgive us, but we have no time at all," said the man at the front. The five people sat down on the opposing side of the table not bothering with introductions. "We had two topics we wanted to talk with you about. The first is one you're probably expecting.

"The... agents... we sent to infiltrate the Association. The handlers in charge of them have been educated better, and those who approved it have been spoken to as well.

"There shouldn't be any other issues from

our side going forward. We'd very much like to sign the contract you presented us with as well."

Felix slowly tilted his head to one side considering what'd been said. They were trying to push through as quickly as possible and then confirm the contract.

If he had to bet, he'd bet they were afraid he'd end the contract due to their interference. Even if the operation had been completely approved, it'd now be treated as if it'd been a rogue operation.

Such is the life of covert-operations, I suppose.

"Fine. Though I expect a penalty payment for the attempts to infiltrate my organization," Felix stated firmly. He briefly considered alluding to the fact that he was aware of those they'd sent to be hired by the Association as well.

Then decided against it.

It'd be better if they at least had a partial insight to what was going on, rather than nothing at all.

Besides that, if he did it right, he could pump them for information as well.

"Of course, not a problem. We assumed you'd want to enact that part of the temporary contract and already prepared a payment in accordance with that," said the man whose name Felix still didn't know.

"They've already sent the payment, Legate," confirmed Tribune.

"Fine, we'll accept the contract. What's the second topic?" Felix agreed. It was faster than he was expecting, but not something he hadn't planned for.

Signing now or at the end of the temporary agreement wouldn't change his plans in the least.

"We need you to act as the investigative force when it comes to Supers. Just as you suggested. We made sure that it was still in the contract you gave us as well," the man said with a nod of his head. Followed by the rest of his people nodding their heads. "There are several groups we want you to go investigate.

"To confirm if they're using powers, how they're using them, and to what end. We need to know if they're committing criminal activities with them, and if so, how.

"What to look for as well, really. We don't even know where to really start such a thing. We're looking into something that's more or less a black hole."

Makes sense.

I wish Miu were here for it but… Andrea and Goldie should be fine for it. The others can all hold down the fort here.

"That's fine. Please email me the details. I'll move on it today. Any special powers or privileges during this?" asked Felix.

"We enacted special legislation specific to you and your role in this. The Association Investigative Act," the man clarified. "You'll have the right to enter, search, question, and collect any evidence in the pursuit of illegal super activities.

"You answer to the president alone and your power cannot be stripped from you, except for a full majority vote from all branches of the government."

Felix felt his eyebrows go up at that.

That was a lot of power to give him, and with almost no controls against him.

"I've read the full act. There are some loopholes they can use, but nothing that's problematic. Especially with us being on the lookout for it in advance," Tribune supplied. "I've also just received the data for the groups in question."

Felix glanced to a woman on the end. She'd been tapping at her cell phone. Likely she'd been the one to send the information.

"Right, we'll get right on that. Let's sign this contract and move along," Felix said, doing his best to fight the smile that was blossoming on his face.

The first step was done and made.

***

Several Andreas were bouncing around in their seats. The straps of the seat belt straining against them as they moved about.

Another Andrea was in the driver's seat and a third in the passenger's. The back of the large delivery truck was also filled with Andreas, Felix and Goldie.

"Andrea dear calm down," Goldie said with a chuckle.

"I can't help it! I'm Andrea Campbell! I was Myriad. I'm both at the same time. I'm... I'm just me!" every single Andrea declared at the exact same time. Followed by them all clapping their gauntleted hands together.

It'd been expensive to get all their armor sorted out, but Felix reasoned it was worth going down to only having a few hundred points. He needed them with him in case something happened, but also had to keep her out of the public eye.

The more faceless the Association was, the better. Especially for public facing things.

"I know, and I'm happy for you... I just wonder if maybe you'll burn up all your energy before we get there," Goldie said, trying a different approach.

The Andreas went still, clearly considering the Dragon's words.

"Okay, Goldie. Only because you said it," said the Andrea closest to them.

"But also because we have a funny feeling for you," said a second Andrea.

Felix was having a much harder time identifying which Andrea was which in their armor. Without being able to see them in person it felt more like a guess.

Goldie snorted and then laughed with a shake of her head. For a while now, Andrea had claimed an attraction to the Dragon.

Who said it was more a feeling of puppy love and infatuation.

"Do we need a recap?" Felix asked, deciding to clear the air. "Seems pretty simple to me."

"No need!" an Andrea announced. "Kick down the door, declare who we are, flash badges, and arrest everyone!"

Felix sighed audibly.

"Enter, announce, investigate, report," a different Andrea said. "You shouldn't have had that second energy drink, Four."

"But I waaaaaaanted it. They taste yummy."

"Yummy," came a chorus of Andreas.

"I'll be with Felix," Goldie said. "It's a shame Tribune can't really be with us. She's very helpful."

"Agreed. Her being restricted to the servers and what she can connect to is part of the reason we're safe though," Felix lamented. "Hardened network, closed to outsiders, lets us do what we do. It is a shame though."

"We're here!" an Andrea said after the truck whipped into what was likely a parking space. "I get to declare who we are!"

There was a mad dash of Andreas crawling over everyone else, bumping equipment, and then exiting the vehicle.

It'd looked uncoordinated and chaotic at first, but by the time they'd started to exit, it had more the look of a highly trained military detail.

Felix and Goldie got up after they'd all exited and followed behind. Closing the rear of the truck up before moving to rejoin the rest.

They were heading inside the front of an

impressive looking building. On the side of it was a simple and straight-forward name.

Global Co.

The government had asked them to investigate to determine what was going on, as it was a bank. A bank that had a number of regulatory problems that kept vanishing or having those in charge suffer from accidents.

Hm. I guess to them, that'd be worth sending us in for.

Any situation that can no longer be explained by happen-chance or coincidence.

Even if this is a pointless trip, it's good to establish our right to do this. It'll be handy for later.

Like when we raid Anya.

Chapter 9 - Enforcer -

"Who's next?" Felix asked, feeling worn out. After going through a bank, a franchise fast food joint, a hospital, and then a warehouse, they'd nearly exhausted the list.

Of those they'd investigated, they'd found a number of people with super powers, but no one that was actually using them or abusing them. More often than not, they were small powers that helped them in day-to-day life.

Nothing that would actually put them crosswise with the government.

The only real issue they'd come across so far had been the bank.

Someone had been actively targeting both the bank and those who investigated it, but they weren't involved with either. They were a third party that was outside of it.

Half of the Andreas Felix had started with were now running down that lead to see where it led. Hopefully it'd culminate with someone to hand over to the government.

The rest of them had left in a second truck that'd appeared at some point.

Felix really wanted to have something to show for such a wide and quite honestly illegal act the government had passed.

What they'd opened the door to was going to make a great many people very angry. Angry, upset, and calling for the blood of elected officials.

Except when it came right down to it, the government's hands were tied. There were people out there who could literally charm someone out of an investigation.

While Felix didn't quite agree with their approach and clear blurring of the lines of personal freedoms, he couldn't fault them completely for the knee-jerk reaction. It reminded him of Skipper and how she'd taken power, in fact.

Or even how he ran Legion, really.

Well. I wonder. How would I even want a country to be organized?

I'm a bit more like a monarch than a democracy, aren't I? Having people being able to subvert my will is quite an issue.

It's not like I even disagreed with what Skipper did. I just disagreed with a number of her policies regarding supers, her execution, and... well... that I wasn't in charge.

"No-one, the list is finished," Goldie answered.

Blinking, Felix wasn't sure how he'd missed that, but it was certainly possible. For most of the investigations, he'd just spend his time checking people for powers and what they were.

"The last one listed turned themselves in before we got there. Was an electronic scam apparently. They could read people's minds and then went from there. A telepath," Goldie explained, pulling the thought from his head easily. The irony of the power in question wasn't lost on him. "There's quite a bit of news going around about the Association rapidly investigating a number of businesses for criminal super behavior.

"The government got ahead of it to try and push an angle beneficial to them. The Andreas are still hunting, but they seem to think they're making progress."

"Oh," Felix said, frowning. It made sense when he considered it. He'd just been in too deep in the action and lost sight of the whole picture.

"For our first outing this was a success, though... not so much for the government," Goldie continued. "They're facing a great deal of backlash for the laws they passed. A lot of people are saying it violates their rights and the constitution directly."

Felix shrugged his shoulders.

He didn't really care.

Their problems weren't his. He was here to take over this place, not to help the government. If anything, them collapsing was more to his benefit.

In that moment, Felix promised himself that he wouldn't get involved in politics or the government more than he had to. He'd learned his lessons.

He was here to take over and build up Legion.

That was it.

"Home again, home again," he said as his mind cleared.

"Yay! Back to the Association! I like it there. I can train with the Dryads a lot!" cheered Andrea.

"That and I keep kicking every other Andrea's ass!

"I'm the Andrea champion! I get to dictate who goes in what order on Andrea-Felix sexy nights."

Now Felix knew exactly who it was driving.

"Third, are you bullying them?" Felix asked with a chuckle.

"Damn right I am! Imma pow and whap them until they whine and go 'no more Third, you're the champ'. Then I'll go get kisses from Felix and lots off mm mm mmnnnn sexy time," explained Third excitedly. "All while I know he has a secret place in his heart for me and I can't tell the Others about it because I was a Death Other."

Andrea took in a sudden gulping breath as she ran out of air, followed by a smattering of coughs.

Only for it to be replaced by laughter.

"And by being the champion, you can give me all the special attention you want! I'm the champion! I'll never lose to anyone," Andrea said in a happy voice. Followed by her voice dropping to a low tone. "I'll never lose my position as champion. Not for anything. It's how I can be given special attention, without it being viewed as wrong.

"As much special attention as you want to give your favorite, Felix."

"Don't mind Third, Nest-mate. She's just having a bit of a fall after having yet another energy drink," Goldie murmured, her voice coming in quietly over the helmet coms. "They all think they're the special one to you. Never realizing that they're all special to you. Even if you think you have a preference, you don't. You just identify more with the Death Others."

Nodding his head, Felix didn't argue that. He just wanted to get back to base and get back to work.

Anything to keep his mind off this world's version of Kit and Lily meeting up with him soon enough.

***

"You know, every now and then, when we went in the dining room, I felt a couple women glaring at me. Their thoughts were quite aggressive, too," Goldie said suddenly as they pulled into the parking lot of the Association. There wasn't anywhere to actually park a business vehicle here, now that he thought about it. "It reminded me of Dragon courting.

"Well, what little I saw of it and what my mother told me. I never actually participated. I stayed away from all of that. I slept through most everything, but I did venture out on occasion."

Blinking, Felix looked up from the newspaper he'd been reading.

Since finishing the work for the government, they'd been somewhat occupied filling out paperwork for their actions.

While legal, and backed by an act specific to

their needs, it still left a great deal of paperwork that had to be put together. Especially with so many litigious people and companies.

Thankfully, all lawsuits would be taken on by the government on Felix's and the Association's behalf.

"Uh, er, that is," sputtered Felix before his mind clicked into gear. "I mean, I guess I get it? You showing up looking the way you do would be distracting. Your Helen of Troy value is rather high."

"My what value?" asked Goldie with a laugh, looking over to him. A second passed and then she started to laugh harder. "Oh! I see! What a lovely comparison. I don't need you to launch boats or anything like that though.

"I'd really love it if you went plant shopping with me though. There's a couple things I can plant regardless of season. My little garden is turning out to be quite a bit of fun!"

Felix could only laugh, nod his head, and get out of the truck. Goldie was always a surprise.

Just as he exited the truck, he spotted something out of the ordinary. A number of people were all sitting in their cars.

Fiddling with phones, dozing, or reading something.

But sitting in their cars, rather than in the lobby.

Now, Felix wasn't going to say that every single person would be willing to wait in the lobby.

A few would want to get out, stretch their legs, or just have a minute alone.

He was looking at a group of at least twenty- or thirty though.

Not one or two.

Nor did they look like they were here for an organization or anything else. Their vehicles weren't in the best of condition.

Something… off… here. Should do a quick check.

Felix targeted the nearest person and did a contract check. Wanting to know who he'd have to work through if he wanted to hire this person directly.

Once more, a window popped up for him.

Government of Zhongguo.

Surprised and not able to completely get his mind working, Felix forced himself into action. He shut the door to the truck and began moving around to the back of it.

As he did so, he made the same contract request to all the others he could see.

Each and every one of them came back as the same government name.

Felix had no idea what Zhongguo was, or even where it was, but he had to assume they were a hostile nation at this point. That this was likely an operation for them to either assault, infiltrate, or destroy the Association.

Alright. Get inside, see if we can't get Tribune to

break into their shit, go from there.

Felix nodded at Goldie as she met him at the back and they started walking toward the front of the Association building.

Today was the day for Super interviews. They'd likely already all be in the lobby and waiting, since they were due to start in roughly ten minutes after all.

"Yes, they're here to assault the building," Goldie said over the helmet com. Felix wasn't sure if they were close enough for it to transmit to the Association building or those inside. "They want to attack during the middle of the interviews and take all the data they can. It'll start with a vehicle bomb being rammed through the front door."

"Tribune, do you read me?" Felix asked. There was no response. "Faith, Alma, Carlotta, we have foreign actors in the parking lot who plan on causing trouble. Do you read?"

Again there was no response. Felix was starting to suspect that there was some type of communications jam going on in the parking lot.

Keeping his pace steady and unfaltering, Felix did his best to look unconcerned. The last thing he wanted to do was to alert these people to the fact that their cover was blown.

As soon as he entered the lobby, he heard the tell-tale click of Tribune linking to his helmet.

"Tribune, we've got hostiles in the parking lot," Felix said, moving into the lobby and then turning left. Toward where Faith would be conducting her interviews, rather than to the right.

"Acknowledged, Legate. Spinning up all passive defensive measures and readying active," Tribune reported. "Permission to take control over all electronics within range of my network and include all Legion owned lands and facilities?"

What Tribune was asking was to infect any and every device she could reach.

Tribune was a VI, but a very dangerous one. One that could act a lot like a virus and hijack electronics that were within range of her signal.

She couldn't get too far from her actual server. It was a technology that didn't actually exist on this world yet. Pushed ahead by decades through the use of Felix's power.

"Granted, but only for those who are suspicious. Don't infiltrate anyone who appears to be a non-issue," Felix allowed. He didn't want to reveal Tribune to his friends. His enemies could make any claim they wanted and he could refute it.

It was harder to refute the claim of an ally, friend, or neutral.

"Yes, Legate. Initializing take-over," Tribune answered.

Felix had just put his hand on the doorknob when someone shouted out.

"Gun!" called a woman behind him.

Felix spun to his left, snatched at his pistol and drew it in the same motion. By the time he'd visually spotted the target, they'd already leveled a strange looking device at him.

It looked more like a TV-remote than a gun.

Then it launched a dart of some sort, to which Felix responded by pulling the trigger as fast as he could.

The boom of his pistol was loud in the small room.

Whatever projectile had been fired at him had failed to do anything at all to him. Though his response had likely just set off everyone in the parking lot.

Slumping to the ground, the woman who'd fired the device at him looked shocked. Shocked and disbelieving of the situation.

Her blood was splattered all over the wall behind her. A spray of it from Felix striking her multiple times.

"Activate defenses!" Faith called out over the com lines. "Secure the building and guests!"

All the lights turned a pale red, a number of security glass panels and steel doors blasted into place. There was a grinding and popping throughout as the building activated fully.

Felix had spent a lot of time making sure the Association building could defend itself. He didn't want to station what few people he had into defensive positions.

"Engaging known hostiles," Tribune declared a moment before the sound of heavy caliber weapons opening up could be heard from outside.

Extremely heavy caliber weapons that made

the ground vibrate and produced sound that actually penetrated through his helmet.

Ah... those must be the Avenger cannons.

I was wondering if it was overkill to put them in but... I guess we'll find out soon enough.

Walking over to the woman who'd been downed, Felix looked her over once. She was already gone. He'd hit her repeatedly in center mass. He imagined her lungs and heart were little more than fleshy chunks.

"Disengaging, weapon ineffective," reported Tribune a second after the oppressive sound of the guns ended. "Super powers have been utilized, Legate. Conventional weapons may not be effective."

"I... what?" asked Felix, feeling stupefied.

Other countries already found out about supers and started wrangling them, didn't they? Turned them into agents and weapons.

We're not ahead in this race.

We're behind!

"Alright. How did they defeat the rounds?" Felix asked, moving to the front doors and then outside. He began to scan the parking lot, but there was a great deal of dust, black smoke from a car that'd caught fire that made it a bit harder to spot anything.

"Some type of shielding, Legate," reported Tribune. "I have scoured their electronic devices of information, locked their coms, and then deactivated all their devices.

"While I cannot affect them directly, I've removed all their means of support and assistance."

Goldie stepped outside a few moments later. She'd stripped herself of her Legionnaire armor and was now standing there nude.

Her eyes were blazing and her golden horns were protruding from her head.

Damn. It'll be awkward to explain how Goldie ended up with me to the government later. Not looking forward to that one.

Maybe I can play it off as her becoming my personal prisoner, and my property. Therefore, no longer beholden to their rules?

Eh… have to think on it.

But later.

For now… I do need her as a Dragon. I'm lacking in Supers at the moment, which puts me at a disadvantage.

There was a tap to his left as someone landed and moved into his peripheral vision.

Turning his head slightly, he saw it was Miu.

The dark eyed, dark haired, athletic, and extremely lethal insane woman. An assassin that had somehow decided that Felix was her reason for existence.

"Welcome back," Felix murmured.

A second after that, another Miu appeared, standing right next to the first one. They looked identical in features, figure, and presence.

Surprisingly, somehow, one was prettier than the other, though Felix couldn't quite explain that.

Other than to assume the prettier one was his own Miu since she'd taken his order to "keep herself healthy" and applied it to everything.

"I'm back, F-Felix," said the pretty Miu, looking at him. "I brought... me, with me."

"Hello, Felix," said the second Miu. She was looking at him in a very different way though. A neutral expression that reminded him of when he'd first met his Miu.

"I see," he said, looking back to the parking lot.

He could now see a large dome that'd been erected out there. It was a shimmering blue that looked to be made of interlocking hexagons.

"We'll have to figure it out later, I guess," muttered Felix. "Is she just like you?"

"In every way," reported his Miu. "But also... not. It's interesting."

"Well. You two get out there and see if there's anyone else we can't see. If you find them, subdue them," commanded Felix. "But not at the risk of your own lives. If they're too much to handle, just kill them."

The Mius nodded and then sprinted off. One went left, the other right.

Well that's just fucking weird.

This day is weird and lame.

Goldie had transformed into her full Dragon self next to him. She was unmistakable as anything other than the Dragon that'd been seen on TV. There really was no going back from this.

A horde of Andreas all came running out from the far side of the Association building. Many of them were in Legionnaire armor, but not all of them. Quite a few had their ears and tails on full display, all armed with rifles or SMGs.

They were moving in squads and rapidly deploying through the parking lot.

Ah... hahaha... well... this is just getting worse all the time.

Let's not forget our Dryads. They'll be here shortly as well I assume. Using their Christmas themed magic and revealing it all to the world.

Tribune took that moment to open up another full barrage from her cannons. The heavy 30-mm guns shattering his thoughts with the boom and crackle of their firing.

The dome became a much brighter color as the rounds slammed into it. The concrete and cars around it being dug out, smashed, or obliterated from deflected or wide shots.

Then it cut off once more.

"That is so uncomfortably loud!" shouted a voice from behind him. A familiar voice. One he didn't actually want to hear right now.

Slowly, Felix turned his head.

Kit was standing there with her hands on her ears, peering out from behind him. Just behind her was Lily. He did his best to not register their details.

The way they looked.

That they were exact duplicates of the

women he loved, and looked to be clones of them.

Kit's brown curls were swept back from her model-like face. Her eyes flicking back and forth across the parking lot.

Lily's black eyes were doing the same. Her black hair pulled into a ponytail. She had one hand up and was slowly building magical runes out beside herself.

"I can't read any of their thoughts!" Kit called out. "Or yours, actually! Everyone is shielded here!"

Taking in a slow breath, then letting it out, Felix didn't know how to react at all to this situation.

A trio of Andreas ran past, the one closest to them waving excitedly with one hand.

"Hi Kit! Hi Lily! Love and miss you both!" called the Andrea, moving past quickly.

"Uhm, yes, hello," Kit murmured, looking very confused.

"Hi?" asked Lily at the same time.

Ah… shit. This is… this is all so wrong.

She's not wearing Legionnaire armor. Or a Legionnaire's ring.

Shit.

Hahaha… ah… fuck. She's going to scour Andrea's mind and know it all. Fuck.

Fuck!

Ha.

And I thought I could just handle all of this without much prep.

Right, Felix? It's such a surprise! I thought you wouldn't summon me up for a little while.

Oh... well... you know me, Hubris. You know me.

I just... can't live without you. Me and Arrogance are roommates at this point.

Chapter 10 - Delusions -

"I… but… I did?" Kit asked almost no-one. Her head slowly turned and looked toward him. "With you? Oh my god.

"It's a different… different… and… oh my god. Oh my god! It's all too much and… no. No!"

Fuck!

She's getting it all from every Andrea nearby all at the same time. Chances are it's just an overwhelming kaleidoscope of memories.

"Kit! You need to keep it all contained for now. I know it's hard to suppress the area effect telepathy but… do what you can. I'll fix it. Again," promised Felix with a growl. "For now, we kind of need to kill those supers over there."

Felix shook his head and looked to the dome.

Goldie had taken off at some point and was now flying low over it. She slammed her tail into it as she passed. The whole thing shuddered and sparkled with the weight of the impact.

Pulling at his power, he wanted to know who owned that power so he could buy their contract, or their power.

To know what the name of the power was, and how it worked, so he could properly evaluate the costs to purchase said power.

Once again, a simple window appeared in front of him.

Shield of Faith: Spiritual

* * *

"Lily, that's a spiritual shield. It's made of faith magic. I can reasonably bet that if you created a really strong and focused point of magic, like a needle, you could penetrate it," Felix advised. "Could you put a spell together like that, then tie in another spell to the back of it to inject an explosive like fireball through that hole?"

"I... yeah, alright," mumbled Lily, the construct at her side rapidly changing. "Err... you really do know what my power is?"

"He knows everything about us, Lilian Lux," Kit mumbled in a broken way. "He can even help your brother."

Lily's eyes went wide and her nostrils flared. Her entire body had locked up and grown still. At her side, the runes were moving faster and faster now. Building into a tightly compacted and frighteningly looking construct.

Goldie passed by the dome once more, this time laying down a massive wave of fire down across it. Bathing it completely and absolutely.

Yet once again, nothing really happened. The shield held.

"Tribune, get ready to lay them out. Use some of those non-lethal ordinance rounds we put in your systems. I'd love to question them," requested Felix.

"Yes, Legate," Tribune responded.

There was a series of loud thumps followed by a number of projectiles slamming into the shield.

Bouncing off it and then landing all around the dome.

A second or so after they landed, they began to disperse gas. A great amount of it that rapidly obscured everything.

Lily made a simple hand gesture and a roaring lance of magic shot forward from her construct. It rapidly condensed itself into an odd thermometer-looking shape.

Then it was gone, faster than Felix could follow. Vanishing into the massive cloud of gas. He heard a detonation that rumbled and shook everything.

"You… can help Lucian?" demanded Lily, pulling on his gauntleted arm.

"Contact," reported an Andrea. He could hear gunfire over the coms and also in the distance. "Multiple squads. Military gear, body armor, trained tactics.

"Taking losses, request reinforcements."

"Coming," stated Faith, who pushed past Felix. She Alma, and Carlota ran off in a triangle formation. Heading out toward the distant edge of the parking lot.

"No, I've got it," Felix grumbled and then tried to call up how much it would cost to allow Andrea to create twenty more others of herself.

Because to Felix, twenty more Andreas would be able to do more than the three Dryads. They'd likely start absorbing their dead, arming themselves from fallen enemies, or just rushing them headlong.

Name: Andrea Campbell	Condition: Determined.
If No Action Taken: None	Action >> Alter Power: Cost 74,411 points

Felix accepted the cost and then cleared his throat.

"Better, Pancake?" he asked, trying not to pay attention to this world's Lily holding onto his arm.

"Nn!" came the short happy response.

He knew for a fact that she actually enjoyed having as many Others as possible. Especially now that she was so sure of herself.

The gunfire he heard continued, though it eventually started to trickle off.

"D-1 through D-3, collect the survivors. We'll interrogate them," Felix said. "We'll... we'll let Kit poke around in their heads."

"Confirmed," Faith said and then spun away. Carlota and Alma followed her on each side.

"Lucian!" demanded Lily, jerking on his arm. "You can help my brother? How! What's wrong with him!?"

Wincing, Felix sighed and looked to Lily and Kit.

Kit was down on the ground on her hands and knees. She was currently throwing up violently onto the ground. Her entire back arching with each heave.

"Ooough... it's too much," groaned Kit, followed by a burp.

Then more vomiting.

"Lucian is just... suffering because of his power," mumbled Felix. "It's astral projection. Think of your own power but instead of mana, it's him. He launched himself out of his body.

"He's just lost and trying to find himself. That's all. I'm sure I can put something together that'd help guide him back. Not something I can do easily or quickly."

"I'll do whatever it takes!" hissed Lily, her eyes flashing dangerously.

Felix could only nod his head. That all made perfect sense of course. That was who Lily was. She'd become a soul-eating monster in her previous life because she refused to bend or bow to anyone.

She'd never break and never crumble.

To turn away from the possibility of saving her little brother would be impossible for her.

"I'm me but not me," moaned Kit, pressing her forehead to the ground. "I'm me but not me. There's other... other woouuuugghh-"

Kit once again began to throw up.

"It's... gonna be a long story," muttered Felix.

"Cloaked vehicle detected. Engaging," reported Tribune a moment before her cannons opened up. The deafening roar of her ordinance cut any further chatter off.

Not far away, a large saucer-like vehicle was starting to lift off into the sky. It was rapidly gaining altitude in a way that didn't seem normal.

Felix wasn't sure of the means of propulsion, but it was absolutely silent.

He'd bet on it being a super power, in fact.

All the rounds slammed into it. Tearing off a massive section and sending it careening sideways through the sky.

Only for Goldie to intercept it and snatch it out of the air. Holding onto it with all four of her limbs, she began to wing her way back to the Association.

"Legate, Tribune reports the situation has been resolved," declared the VI.

Yeah… no… not so much.

Lily was glaring at him, still holding onto his arm, while Kit moaned above a large puddle of puke.

Goldie landed not far away and dropped the large saucer-like ship to the ground. She hesitated for a moment and then looked to Felix.

"Leave it to the Pancakes," he said when he realized what she was contemplating. "Just wait for them to get here and then we—"

Andrea Prime, Third, and fourteen all came over. They were unarmored but armed. All smiles and looking quite lethal as well. Prime even had blood splashed across her face.

"We've got it," said Prime with a wave to Goldie. "Go get changed and help Legate."

"Alright," rumbled Goldie. Moving away from the saucer, and then shifting into her human form. Though her ears and horns were visible now. She met Felix's eyes and then sauntered over to him.

Her strut-like walk had been fully incorporated into her gait. It gave her a provocative and seductive look whenever she moved.

It often made him feel like prey.

Grinning at him, she watched him for several seconds before moving past him to Kit. Laying a hand on the woman's back, Goldie was peering at the back of the woman's head.

"There, see?" Goldie asked in an odd way.

"I... yes. I do," mumbled Kit. "Okay... o-okay. That... helps. Thank you, Goldie."

"Of course. This, too, though," the Dragon continued.

"Oh. Oh... yeah," Kit whispered, her voice trailing off.

It seemed like the conversation was continuing through telepathy now and no longer with words.

"Enemy in retreat, Pancakes in pursuit," called an Andrea. "Let none escape, we'll — oh, hi Shadow. I missed you!"

There was a thump followed by a groan.

"Andie, not so hard," moaned Miu. Somehow it managed to make it through Andrea's open microphone.

"But I missed you!" Andrea argued. "Oh!

Another Miu! Hi hi, come here. Huuugs!"

"Mmf," grunted a new voice that was likely the other Miu.

"I have two Mius, one Dragon, and one Human! I'm rich!" proclaimed Andrea.

"I missed you too, okay? Stop. Let go of the other me," Miu huffed, then sighed. "Did you take care of him?"

"Yes. I reminded him often that about everything you said to —"

Before it could go any further, someone thankfully cut the feed. He wasn't sure who did it or why, but that wasn't anything he wanted to hear.

Miu would likely have started killing as many Andreas as she could once she found out.

"Thanks," Felix got out and then turned around. Heading for the lobby, he was surprised to see all the windows were darkened and shielded.

There was no way anyone in the lobby could have seen what was happening.

"You're welcome, Legate. I closed them after I let Hero Kit and Hero Lily exit," Tribune reported. "Legionnaire Georgia identified them as Hero's Guild prospects. Encouraging heroic behavior on their part would be ideal."

Probably.

If it wasn't for the fact that Kit will likely peel my thoughts out of my head and realize what I'm doing, that is. Given her heroic nature in her other life, it's quite likely she'll be the same way here.

This is likely not… going to go very well.

"Let's wait, dear," Goldie said, lifting her head and looking to Felix. "Tribune will hold the perimeter and the road closed until Andrea's back.

"Then we'll head inside. Besides, Kit could use a few minutes. She's still processing everything."

"Tell me you'll help my brother," demanded Lily, once again.

Nodding his head, Felix felt overwhelmed. He didn't feel like there was much else he could do.

***

Felix sat down in his office. Hesitating for only a second, he then pulled his helmet off. There was no point in trying to hide anything from Kit at this point.

She'd be better off knowing all that he did, realistically. So long as he didn't think at her roughly, or push thoughts, she'd be able to work through it gradually.

Lily, Kit, Goldie, Andrea, Miu, Faith, Alma, and Carlota were all here with him. All staring at him and each other in equal measure.

All the Andreas had condensed down into their Prime, though the Mius were sticking close to one another.

Thankfully, Felix could tell who was who at a glance. He'd be concerned if he ever mixed them up visually. He wasn't sure Miu would forgive him.

"She would," whimpered Kit, her head

resting on the desk. "She'd forgive you even if you carved out her intestines and fed them to her. So long as you told her you loved her.

"And she missed me. That I accepted who she was with only a modicum of concern. But I'm not Kit. I'm not your Kit.

"All your feelings, your thoughts, your emotions, they're too much. They resonate in my head like a bomb going off with an unending echo. I can barely think."

Felix had an inkling that it was because she was Kit, but also not Kit.

That there was some type of problem with the "congruence" as Uncle had called it.

No sooner had he thought of the man, than thoughts Felix had tried to keep quiet bubbled up. Thoughts he didn't want to consider that were problematic to say the very least.

Thoughts that made Felix question the very reality of the world he was in.

That he'd somehow "soft-locked" the world.

As far as Felix knew, the only thing that could be soft-locked were computers and videogames. When he started to follow that thought further, he started to feel an incredible pressure inside his forehead.

Skittering away from that, he instead concentrated on Uncle himself. Along with the fact that he needed the man's help.

He had the feeling that whatever was wrong with Kit was only going to get worse.

Pushing out with his power, Felix simply wanted to know what it would cost to help Kit with whatever was wrong with her. As if Uncle had intervened and provided him with assistance.

There was no response.

Nothing came back to his inquiry and his power made no move.

"That's nice of you," mumbled Kit. "I'll be fine. Just fine. I just need some time to process it all. If you can fix my power like you did the other me, that'd be great."

Lily was watching the whole thing quietly, her eyes moving about the room as things progressed. She didn't say anything though, she merely watched.

"You're not wrong, Lily. They knew an alternate version of you, too. You were married to Felix," Kit got out in a whisper, one hand pointing at Felix. "He loved you desperately. Would do anything for you.

"For me. For all of us. Legion... Legion First. They're not from this world. This universe. They're from another universe. Their universe version of you and me... we... fled. Sacrificed ourselves.

"They're here to get them back. Even if it means turning the whole world upside down."

"Well, not quite," interjected Felix. "I wouldn't want to do anything that Kit, my Kit, would hate me for. Nothing that would make her despise me."

"She's a goody-goody," groaned Kit, gently

tapping her forehead against the desk. "I don't know what happened in her past, but it didn't to me. I'm all for doing the good thing, the right thing, but not at my own expense."

"Right," huffed Lily. "Let's say I believe it. There's no way you could prove it. Unless you want to help my brother. That'd make me believe it."

"I'm not here to make you believe it," Felix said with a shake of his head. "I'm not here to convince you, know you, or anything else, to you.

"I'll be honest, to me, you're strangers. You're not the people I care about, even if you look like them. Sound like them. You're not them. That's just the reality of it."

"You have a birthmark right next to your privates. On the right side," Kit whispered, still tapping her head against the desk repeatedly. "He knows you used to call it your spunk-spot.

"He knows all the details about me, too. It's almost too much. I can see all his memories of me, that aren't me. It's too much."

Sighing, Felix leaned back in his seat and looked to the ceiling above them.

"Look, you're strangers to me," he said, firming his resolve and looking to the two women. "It's nice to see you two doing so well, that there's alternate versions of my loved ones, but you're not them. So... let's just go from there.

"In fact, let's just—"

Felix leaned over and pulled Faith's Legionnaire helmet out of her arms. Leaning over, he pushed Kit's head up partially, then shoved the helmet down over her head.

"Oh," came Kit's voice, though severely muffled. "Oh that's... that's lovely."

Laying her head down on the desk, she went still. Her body started to relax.

"We'll need to make her an Augur helmet I guess," Felix guessed with a shake of his head. "As well as some type of homing beacon for your brother, Lily. That shouldn't be too bad.

"Though I do have a favor from the two of you I need you to do for me. Something I think both of you can do easily."

Lily lifted her chin up, looking down her nose at him. Her mind had clearly jumped straight toward wanting a sexual favor.

"Sure. Whatever. Just want a helmet like this," whispered Kit. "Ever since a week or two ago, I can't tune it out. None of it. It's constant. Constant and never ending. I can hear the evil of everyone.

"Their dirty thoughts. Constantly. Never ending. The cruel and criminal wishes of the many."

Err... was it her power itself that skewed her personality?

Huh. Something to consider I suppose.

"That's fine. It's a simple request," Felix continued. "I need people to lead the Guild of Heroes. Or at least, guide it if not lead it.

"People I can put in charge of it so that the guild has a good chance to do the right things. At the right times."

"Liar," whispered Kit.

Felix smirked at that and then sighed. He'd figured out how to make this work for him, but it would also be rather strange in a way.

"The second part of that favor is for you to give me control over your powers. For you, Kit, I'm going to modify it a bit so it's more controllable, but allow you to temporary modify the memories of others.

"Then I'm going to have you wipe the memory of this whole thing from your own mind, and Lily's mind. You'll receive your helmet, and your homing beacon, from the Association, rather than me.

"I'm going to make sure all my people get a telepathic blocking device so this situation doesn't repeat itself.

"That's my favor and the price I'm willing to pay."

"Yep, I'm good," mumbled Kit. "Fire away."

"Lucian will wake up?" Lily asked, her eyes softening slightly.

"He will. Though... err... did you want him to be normal? I accidentally fixed his... different... nature last time," Felix admitted. "You weren't exactly thrilled about that, but you didn't seem angry either."

Lily looked shocked, blinking rapidly. Then she shook her head slowly.

"Just... have him wake up please," she answered. "He's just fine how he was.

"If that's what the deal is then... yeah. I'll take it, too. I can do that."

"Alright. Then we can move this along," Felix said and turned to looked at Goldie.

She gave him a small nod of her head, which meant Lily had definitely agreed to it. There was no way he could make this happen without Kit being on board, but he imagined she wasn't lying when she said she'd do it.

"Uhm, uhm... nn... can I hug both of you, before you get the mind whoosh?" Andrea said suddenly. "You're not... not my friends but... you look just like them. Can you just pretend for a minute and hug me?

"Hug me like I'm your best friend and you missed me? Just... just once. Just for a bit. Please? I miss you guys. So much."

Lily's face twitched and Felix saw her soft heart become exposed. Lily could be kinder than Kit when it came down to it.

Kit saw herself as a crusader of goodness and did what she did out of duty.

Lily did everything that she did because she believed in her emotions. Good or bad.

"Okay, that's fine," Lily said with a sad smile. "Come here then. Let's give you a big hug, Andie."

Andrea made a soft huffing noise and then slammed into Lily. Nearly knocking her out of the chair.

The sorceress hugged her tightly, just as the

real Lily would do.

"Oh knock it off, Andie," growled Lily as the Beastkin began to whimper, then cry loudly. "Stop it. You'll... you'll see your own Lily soon enough I bet.

"Okay? She wouldn't want you to be like this. If she's anything like me, she'd just tell you to tough it out and push through."

"She woooooooouuld," howled Andrea loudly. "Lily come baaaaack!"

Wincing, Lily just gently patted the other woman and held her. Almost exactly as their own Lily might.

Chapter 11 - Trash Disposal -

Sighing, feeling drained, and not wanting to do anything more, Felix was wiped out.

Kit and Lily had agreed to everything, which left him about twenty-four hours to get everything finished. To fix Lucian, get Legion rings made, alter Kit's power, make her an Augur helmet, and wipe both their memories.

There'd been no time to sleep, and he'd spent more of that time rushing from location to location. Scraping up any and every point he could while running through endless hypotheticals on how to get to his goal as cheaply as possible.

"Legate, the government handlers are on their way. They're just past my furthest sensor at the entrance to the parking lot," Tribune reported.

"Right," Felix said, leaning his head forward. He'd only been sitting in his desk for a few minutes. His mind felt like it was swimming. "Tribune, I don't want to be surprised by this again.

"Put together a report of everything you'd need to be upgraded so that people couldn't be planning something from the parking lot again.

"Then a second plan beyond that so you could monitor all the approaches. You'd still need to be hard-locked here though. Away from the rest of the world. I don't think they're ready to discover a true Virtual-Intelligence."

"Yes, Legate," answered Tribune.

"I could kill them for you, m-my love,"

whispered Miu, appearing at the edge of his desk. She was crouched low over it and quite close to him. One of her hands crept over and then gently laid down on his armored knee.

"Thanks, Miu. I actually considered taking you up on that, but it's not a great solution. They'd just send more people," Felix confessed and looked from her, to the other Miu.

She was standing only a few feet away and was staring at him in a flat way.

"So... Miu," Felix murmured, reaching up to lay a gauntleted hand on the top of his Miu's head.

"Call me Mikki," said Miu, now Mikki. "I never liked my name to begin with. She can have the name since she rescued me."

"Mikki, then... what're your plans? I'd be happy to make room in my organization for you if only because you're this world's Miu," Felix said as Miu crept ever closer to him. Until she was pushed up against his side. It didn't seem to bother her at all that other than his head, he was still in his Legate armor.

"I'm not sure. Part of me wants to remain here and... learn more about you," Mikki murmured, then shook her head. "Though I don't think it would be wise. If I remained here, I could very easily end up no different than Miu.

"Then she and I would have to likely kill one another. If it were me... the idea of sharing my partner with anyone would likely make me a bit violent."

"I'm not allowed to kill his other women," Miu interjected, her head now resting against his chest plate. "I can kill Andie if she lets me. That helps a little, but not much.

"That and I don't... want... to kill her anymore. Not unless she does something that deserves punishment, at least."

Mikki grunted at that, her eyes moving from Miu back to Felix.

"Join the Guild of Heroes with Kit and Lily. I left open a back-channel in Kit's powers so that I could wipe people's memories, then wipe her own," Felix offered. "It'd give you a chance to peel out the bits you don't want and maybe move toward your own life.

"I don't think Miu here wanted you to be locked up. Beyond that, I doubt she considered it at all."

"I didn't," admitted Miu quietly. She'd crawled into his lap by this point and was plastered to him completely. "Just didn't want to leave myself where I'd been."

"Thank you, Miu. I wouldn't have been able to escape without your help," Mikki confessed. She shivered once and her eyes started to wander off to the side.

"Miu, take a breath," Felix commanded. There was a slight hesitation as Mikki's eyes locked to Felix's. Then she took in a slow breath. "Let it out. Focus. Take control and then fix it in place.

"Do an especially good job today and I'll

take all your control away and take responsibility for you."

"W-wrong, Miu, Felix," whispered Miu, who was still in his lap. She didn't sound upset, thankfully. If anything, she almost seemed excited.

Felix had completely spaced out and had forgotten that Mikki wasn't his Miu. She was this universe's Miu, even if she looked just like his.

Mikki's eyes had snapped open wide, and she was looking at him now in a way that reminded him of how Miu used to react.

"I accept," she hissed, her attention focusing on him to a hard needle-like sensation. "I will stay with Legion. I am Mikki. Miu, may I lodge with you?"

"Of course. I already offered," Miu countered. "We'll need to figure out some way for him to own you as he does me.

"That way he can make your powers like mine. Oh, and don't worry, he doesn't want to change you. What's broken with you.

"He likes what's broken. He understands it and thinks we're perfectly normal."

Mikki's mouth snapped shut and she continued to stare at Felix.

"Mikki, go get a Legionnaire's suit on. You can probably get one from an Andrea," Felix directed. "They'll fit reasonably enough till I can get you one personally.

"Act as the door guard and greet our guests. Determine if there's any issues with them, then bring them to a conference room. I'm sure Tribune or Faith has already set one up.

"Miu, go with your… sister… and help her learn how to be Legion. For now. She can re-evaluate her choice in an hour or two after she cools down. Chances are, she'll decide to join the Heroes' guild after all."

"Of course," Miu answered, then leaned up and kissed him quickly. Then she bit his lip rather roughly. Almost to the point of drawing blood, but not quite. "You're taking control for both of us for doing a good job.

"You can give me the usual, and you can let Mikki run wild in a training room. Like what you used to do for me."

"Fine," agreed Felix. He didn't let go of Miu, however. Instead, he pulled her in close to himself and kissed her. Kissed her as a woman he loved and cherished. Taking his time, he didn't let her go until he heard Mikki's boots shift around on the carpet.

Pulling away from Miu, he saw she had a glassy eyed look. Almost like she wanted to bite a chunk out of him and eat it.

"Go," he commanded her.

Miu hopped off his lap and scurried away. Grabbing Mikki by her wrist and leading the other woman out.

"Their heart-rates are both elevated and their systems are displaying rapid fluctuations," reported Tribune. "Is Legionnaire Miu going to be alright given her erratic readings?"

"It's normal for her. Did you do a medical scan on Mikki?" Felix asked.

"Not yet, Legate."

"Make sure that's taken care of," Felix asked, leaning back in his seat. "If she's planning on remaining here, we'll need to make sure she's at peak physical condition."

"Yes, Legate."

Closing his eyes, Felix just sat there and breathed slowly.

"Legate, according to the data from your armor, you're likely about to fall asleep. Please wake up," requested Tribune.

With a start, Felix sat up in his chair. Pushing himself out of it, he grabbed his helmet. Stuffing it up under his armpit, he held onto it and began walking toward the door.

"I... yeah, thanks, Tribune," rumbled Felix, feeling rather foolish. Falling asleep here and now would have been hard to explain. "Which uh... which—"

"The Aurelius conference room, Legate. It's right next to your office. I had it put nearby," Tribune answered. "I also had coffee ordered and delivered. Legionnaire Andrea is just finishing setting it up. Legionnaire Goldie is brining bakery confections.

"You will have time to drink most of a cup of coffee leisurely and half of a pastry, Legate."

Felix noted that Tribune was now addressing

everyone as Legionnaire, but didn't put any import into it. He knew that being able to select a form of address was one of the options that could be set for Tribune.

He imagined Faith had changed it, though he didn't know why as of yet.

"Thanks," he muttered instead. He didn't honestly care why Faith changed it, and it didn't really matter.

Exiting his office, he turned down the hallway, he crossed over, moved to the first door, opened it, and entered. He was struck with the smell of coffee in that instant.

Thrashing him about the nose and mouth, with an aroma that made his mouth water and his mind pluck itself up. Andrea was humming, swishing her hips from side to side, and shifting around several coffee travelers.

She was very intent on her setup.

Walking right up behind Second, he put his hands on her hips and leaned over her shoulder. Looking to what was in front of her.

"Eee! Felix! I didn't even notice you," Andrea squealed, her hands clamping down atop his own. "Oooh. I was so in my own head thinking about Kit and Lily. It was so nice to see them, but it wasn't... them. They didn't smell right, but it was so close. So close."

"I know. It's almost worse to have seen them, than to have never met their alternate versions," Felix wondered.

Andrea sniffled, shook her head, then growled. She stamped her feet and once more growled, as if she could somehow scare something off.

"I can do this. We'll be alright. Andrea is tough. Tough! Lily told us to get through it. Just like Lily would," Andrea mewled, rapidly nodding her head. "I'm tough! Tough! I can... I can—"

Her shoulders hunched inward, and she let out a soft sob.

"Hey, it's okay. Go get some rest. I need to down a cup of coffee and get ready for the government people. Thank you for setting this up, Second," Felix said and kissed her cheek. "Get going dear. Get a nap in, then share it with everyone else after you wake up."

"Nn, nn. A nap sounds great. Then... then sharing it with everyone is even better.

"Maybe later you could recharge us? We're tired. We didn't sleep last night either," Andrea said. She turned, kissed him briefly, then scurried off.

Felix picked up a cup, filled it with black coffee, and downed it as fast as his mouth could handle the burning liquid. Then did it for a second cup.

The taste was terrible and left him feeling like his mouth was full of acid, but he needed to be awake for this.

"Legionnaire Goldie was delayed. Legionnaire Miu and Human Mikki are guiding the guests up," reported Tribune. "You must put your helmet on, Legate."

"What?" croaked Felix. "Delayed how?"

"The government agents came faster than expected. Legionnaire Goldie wasn't able to get ahead of them and drop off the pastries in time. They will be placed in your office," answered Tribune.

Felix pulled his helmet down over his head with a muttered curse. He'd actually really wanted to get a hold of a pastry. He had realized in that moment that he hadn't eaten in a while.

Turning, Felix went and stood behind the chair he intended to sit in. It was neither at the head nor the foot. It was directly in the middle of one of the long sides of the rectangle.

He didn't have to wait long as the door opened relatively quickly. In walked several men along with three Legionnaires.

He assumed two of them were Miu and Mikki, the third was likely Faith or Goldie. Either of those two would be able to get the ball rolling for him as far as a telepathy standpoint went.

"As always, thank you again," said the person in the front. Felix had the impression that this group of people were in the same 'department' that'd come to talk to him last time. He was starting to suspect that they were deliberately rotating people through so he couldn't get a solid read on whoever he was speaking with.

This time it was a woman in her late twenties

with short brown hair and flat brown eyes. She was neither attractive, nor terrible to look upon.

"We received your report yesterday and reviewed it," she said, taking the seat in the middle which was directly across from himself. Felix pulled back his chair and sat down. One Legionnaire sat down on his right, while the other two flanked him at each shoulder. "Our analysis so far lines up with everything that you yourself have postulated.

"We've... we've also found that... all of our foreign assets were compromised. It's very likely there's someone who can determine who our agents are."

Felix nodded his head slowly. That'd make sense, given the situation.

Any information he might turn over to the government would likely be leaked to those bad actors as well. Which meant there were a number of people at risk if they didn't act quickly.

"I believe this would be an appropriate time to mention that you should likely begin working with the Guild of Heroes," Felix pushed. He was thankful for the mask right now, because he felt like his face was going to split into a smile if he lost control for a split second. "Or at least sanction them. Doing so would present you with a way to spin up a new faction that could assist you with your needs, but align and be part of the government.

"In fact, I even have three people I would suggest as leaders for the Guild of Heroes. One is a Telepath, another is a Sorceress, and the last would be a great asset for security and assassination."

He didn't need Tribune to tell him that Mikki was likely starting to spike with her heart rate, or something along those lines. He imagined the young woman was still riding the push he'd inadvertently given her.

Pushing her off onto Lily and Kit would actually work out better for him.

Provide her with the new version of the Legion ring and tell her to work with them. Spy for him. Report back to Miu everything she saw and believed.

"I... see," muttered the woman with a small shake of her head. "You wouldn't... want to leverage the Association or your Legion to fill that role?"

"Of course not. We're not here to stand in for the government or against the government. Legion is here as a utility to operate the Association. We're the neutral ground between it all.

"It's why I was able to broker a deal between the supers who were fighting in front of the depository. Speaking of that, there's something I need to make you aware of," Felix declared and then cleared his throat. "I captured the Gold Dragon as well as its combat partner. They're both working for Legion as prisoners under life sentences.

"I've taken ownership of them and their powers, as they refused to accept my mediation of the situation and register themselves appropriately. Their actions had put too much strain on everyone involved so it was best if I simply curtailed it outright."

The woman began to shake her head, before she started to nod it instead. Looking very much like someone who didn't want that bit of news.

"We'd had reports that the Gold Dragon had been seen yesterday battling for the sake of the Association," the woman admitted. "I was going to ask you about it to determine what the situation was, but it appears I needn't have worried.

"We'll of course leave it to your custody, so long as you can vouch for their good behavior."

"They'd be dead if I couldn't," Felix remarked flatly. "No, that isn't an invitation to turn me into a prison, though I'll happily help you design one if you ask.

"I'd also be willing to assist with building it for the right price. Though beyond that, we'd only be willing to assist with its upkeep and maintenance. As well as it's installation of equipment and proper safety features.

"Unfortunately, we won't be responsible for jailing, guarding, prisoner intake, or monitoring. Those would all be functions outside of our purview.

"Legion and the Association is meant to be here as a gateway and neutral utility. Like a power company. Not something to be wielded by a government official, party, or body."

"That'd be great, actually. I assume it'd be the same type of requirements as for the Association building, which isn't an issue," said a man to the left of the woman. He'd been quiet for the most part, but now seemed interested. "We've been having difficulties with our... super... prisoners, and having a prison built would be wonderful.

"They've been able to escape, or nearly so, from every single prison we've put them in. We're not sure how to handle this and... honestly, there seems to be more of them to deal with by the day."

Felix smirked at that with a short nod of his head.

"There's more to it," reported Faith through their helmet coms. "But he's not lying. They really are having issues with super prisoners. They'd prefer that to happen before the guild of heroes.

"Especially with all the prisoners they're loading up right now. To be fair, there are at least four supers we're handing over to them. Ones that are from a foreign country and would likely be akin to nuclear weapons if you think about it."

"If I were you," Felix said aloud the second Faith finished speaking. "I'd get the Guild going as quickly as possible, then assign them to man and watch the prison. I'll begin drawing up plans for a suitable design, blueprint, layout, and cost.

"Is there any limit to the budget on this? As well as the capacity you'd be looking for and type? As in, is it a super-max, or an after-school club?"

"Super-max, maximum occupancy, no concern for their rights," stated the third woman. Up to this point she'd been deathly quiet and still. Almost as if she weren't completely comfortable with the situation.

"Tribune, mark that speaker. Dig up

everything you can from them without alerting them to our curiosity," requested Faith. "On top of that, see if you can't weasel your way into their phones or laptops. Whatever they have on them.

"Don't do anything that they'd be able to track or notice, but if you can get in, get in. No reason to not take any information we can from them."

"Yes, Legionnaire Faith," Tribune answered.

"Of course," Felix said, doing his best to ignore Faith and Tribune both. "Though you didn't specify how many prisoners to hold."

"Modular. Make it so we can add as many as we need with a simple visit from you," the woman in the middle decided. "We'll move forward with the Guild as you suggested. If you could please provide us with a list of names you think should be in it, as well as on what positions.

"We'll take your recommendation seriously. Though of course we'll conduct our own interviews to ascertain if it's worth following through with."

"I'd truthfully be concerned if you took my recommendation at face value," Felix said with a chuckle. "It'd be best if you always had a healthy system of checks and balances that kept your own people at the top of their game."

There.

League of Villains is starting with Anya.

The Guild is starting with Kit.

My Association is getting to put itself in the middle without too much of a problem, and Legion gets to act like a vendor.

Everything… is finally moving in the right direction.

Finally.

Though… this is usually when something goes wrong.

Question becomes… what plates are going to start to wobble before I have to rush over and start spinning it again?

Chapter 12 - Follow Up -

Felix didn't leave the conference room as everyone else filed out. The government agents and employees had all collected their paperwork and filed out looking quite pleased.

Joyful, even.

In fact, if Felix had looked away from the door, he wouldn't have noticed that even the dour-looking woman had a smile on her face.

As it closed, he didn't shift his gaze away.

He stared at it.

Or more accurately, through it.

While the double serving of coffee he'd drained had prodded his mind into action, he still felt a deep and desperate need for sleep. That he wasn't at peak performance and wouldn't be without rest.

It didn't help that for the last several hours Felix had been dickering back and forth on pricing, ownership, and who was responsible for what when it came to the prison.

While the government hadn't stonewalled him, or really been much of a problem when it came to getting a good price for himself and Legion, there'd just been a lot of ground to cover.

Then he'd been forced to push the conversation for the Heroes Guild and bring it back up throughout. That they'd be the ones to handle the jail in actuality.

So much so that Felix had to bring up

repeatedly, even going so far as to make sure it was all laid out before he was willing to finish up the conversation about the prison.

Faith had undersold how much the government really wanted him to put together a prison. How much they were willing to do to make it happen was significant.

"I distinctly remember saying that I would remain with Legion," Mikki said through the helmet coms. "It seems I must restate my desire and wish as it wasn't heard as clearly as I intended it to be. I wish to remain with Legion."

"I heard you. I did hear you previously as well. And you will remain with Legion. Working almost directly for me, in fact.

"Just by being a sleeper agent inside the Heroes Guild," Felix explained. His brain restarted in that moment and he looked away from the door and to the conference table. He hadn't expected Mikki to push at the moment, but he supposed in retrospect it was obvious. It's what Miu would have done and who was she if not Miu? "Honestly... I don't think I can handle you right now, Mikki, and I get the impression that you'd end up falling into Miu's pace almost instantly if you haven't already. Just by being here it'd bleed off into you because it'd feel almost too correct for you, because you'd see yourself already doing it through Miu.

"All that means is the best opportunity for you to be your own person, find what you want to do, and how you want to do it, is probably for some time away. Away from Legion, away from me, away from Miu.

"With that said, I also want to respect your wishes, so I'll accept you into Legion. As a Legionnaire and as a part of the group. I just won't be accepting you to work directly with us at this time so you can grow into your own person.

"That and I could really use your help, Mikki. Even without me spelling it out piece-meal I'm sure you can see exactly how I need someone running the security for the guild.

"So... please... go into the Heroes' guild and act as a sleeper agent for me. It'll be fine and you can get your feet under you. Catch your breath and find some stability.

"In the meantime, I'll keep working on how I can go about modifying your powers to match Miu's at the same time. I'm sure I can figure out how to do it, it'll just take time and a lot of points."

Points I don't have right now.

Because if I have to build that prison, I'm going to have to do a bit of a tap-dance to make this happen. They're going to have to bring most materials for it to be made, but then there's the actual cost of the building.

I don't have any points at all right now.

I'm as poor as when I first came here.

Just need my landfill to be full and —

"Tribune?" asked Felix

"Yes, Legate?"

"You're already putting together a prison aren't you," Felix said. It wasn't a question, really. He assumed she was throwing it together based on what the parameters were that the government had given them.

"Yes, Legate. I'm only working to solve the basic layout, general areas, guard quarters, and oversight. I'm not working to solve the cells, holdings, or anything that involves prisoners.

"I assumed you would wish to design and modify them yourself directly, as you are likely to disagree with the parameters that were given."

Felix opened his mouth, then closed it with a chuckle.

"Good thinking. That's accurate," Felix mumbled and then stood up to his feet. "I need you to include a requirement to the building materials part of the request.

"Tell them I need access to as many landfills that they own and wouldn't mind me emptying to a degree. Phrase it as me needing to find particular elements, items, or parts. That even in a degraded state, I can still use them.

"Let them know that it's fine even if it's a radioactive site. Toxic or otherwise. Doesn't matter at all."

"Of course, Legate," Tribune answered.

"You're out of points, aren't you?" asked Faith, standing up next to him.

"Yeah. Pretty much bankrupt. Couldn't make a paperclip out of a spool of wire even if I wanted to. Spent pretty much everything."

"I don't think they'll argue about the landfill," said Faith with a tilt of her helmeted head.

"They might even respond with a few landfills they'd like you to clean out for them."

"That'd be amusing. Alright, going to go... find something to snack on. Let me know if you need anything... otherwise, get some rest. Try to sleep if you can. We'll be building a prison soon I imagine," Felix said with a heavy exhale. Moving to the door, he opened it and stepped out.

All three women followed him out, with one of them closing the door with a click.

"Alright, F-Felix," Miu said in a strained voice. "We'll... take a rain check on the control for another day. Mikki and I are going to start setting up security for the Guild of Heroes. I have a lot of experience with this so... it's best I work with her.

"Given that we'll need to also setup for a prison that'll be going up soon, we won't have a whole lot of time to prepare."

"Ah, yes. That's a good point," murmured Mikki.

"I need to get us ready for the next phase of Super interviews," Faith said with a yawn. "Alma and Carlota have been working on that in my stead for a while now.

"We need to bring everyone in to formally test for powers, provide readouts, and all that testing stuff you planned for them."

Faith hung her head forward and let out a groan. Her whole body wilting to one side.

"Why did you have to make it so complicated? We already know everything," she complained.

"Precisely for that reason," Goldie said, moving toward them down the hallway. "To obscure and hide the fact that it was that easy. That, and we do need to get the Legion technology front and center stage for this.

"That serves its own purpose in and of itself. To push Felix away from the spotlight and put it more on something or someone else."

Faith moaned loudly as if in complaint since she couldn't argue the point directly.

Miu and Mikki looked to one another, then moved off without another word. The two of them clearly having some type of wordless conversation.

Not bothering to stand upright, Faith moved away, hanging over at the waist like a dying flower left in a vase.

Moving off after the other two, she seemed resigned.

"Now, you, my dear," Goldie whispered, walking up to Felix.

She put her hands to the bottom of his helmet and then began to pull it up and off. Unfastening it deftly without any snags.

Putting it beneath her armpit, she reached up with her free hand and patted him on the cheek.

"Let's get a pastry in you, Nest-mate, because you have a meeting with Georgia," suggested Goldie. "One you can't put off any longer. It needs to happen for both of your sakes.

"Now… I may just be a silly Dragon

housewife, but I can offer some advice when it comes to this.

"Just be honest with her. Don't fret over it and tell her everything. She's already aware of far more than you think because she's been using your suggestion to push her power further. Much further."

"Oh, goodie. That's... you know... great. Great," Felix grumbled quietly.

"It is, actually. It's something that you can actively solve and maybe, just maybe, actually get to know your mom a bit better than the long distant memories you have," Goldie countered. "Because while she isn't your mother, she's very similar to the person who gave birth to you.

"As similar as someone could be without being a twin no less. Right? So why not use this as an opportunity to gain some insights into your mother, through her. I imagine there are many who would willingly take such a chance."

Felix sighed, pushed his face into Goldie's hand, and nodded his head. She was right of course.

He was just tired, sullen, and worn out.

"Good. She's in your office already. I got her some coffee and a few pastries," Goldie admitted with a chuckle. "She's a very nice woman, though I can see where you got your analytical side from. You do have a tendency to organize everything till it's a certain way."

Not waiting, Goldie patted his cheek once more, put his helmet under his arm, and then went after Faith, who was much further down the hallway now.

The Dryad had managed to stand up straight but still looked to be moving quite slowly. Goldie was also moving slower than he expected when he looked at her.

Everyone needs a rest. We're all run down to nothing.

Clearing his throat, Felix adjusted the helmet he was carrying and squared his shoulders. He shouldn't keep Georgia waiting any longer than he had to, really.

Felix forced himself and started toward his office. Which he reached sooner than he was mentally ready for.

Pushing himself, he opened the door and went inside.

Sitting at the small coffee table with seats to one side was Georgia. There were two settings down. One was clearly put there for him and had a pastry, as well as what looked to be some type of drink set there as well.

"Oh, hello," Georgia said with a smile as he entered. "I... hm. Now that I can see you, I'm honestly surprised. I thought there'd be... some familiarity, but there isn't."

"Take after dad," admitted Felix, his mouth moving to one side. "You... err... my mom would always tell me I had her father's ears though. Apparently they're a bit pointier than normal."

Moving over to the table, Felix sat down and

looked to the drink. Leaving it there, he instead picked up the pastry and took a large bite out of it.

His stomach promptly responded by growling loudly at him.

"I su-yes, you're right. They really are," Georgia remarked in a nearly shocked voice. She was leaning to one side and staring at the side of Felix's head. "My goodness they're almost exactly like his ears. Ha… that's kind of funny."

"My mom used to tell me I was a lot like him," Felix said after a hard swallow. "Swore up and down we'd be able to probably sit with one another and have a staring match where no one won."

"Oh? I'm curious then. Who won?" Georgia asked, taking a small sip from her own drink. "You or my dad."

"I… uh… he's dead?" Felix replied in an almost questioning way. Georgia's head was slowly shaking back and forth. "He died along with your sisters. It was a car crash when you were in your twenties, you said."

"I mean… they were certainly in a car crash," Georgia admitted with raised eyebrows. "Dad had a window-smasher seatbelt cutter thingie. I don't know the name for it.

"Was in his glovebox. Used it to cut everyone free and smash the window open. They got out before the car could flood. They're all alive. So's my mom."

Blinking rapidly, Felix really didn't know

how to proceed.

"Well… I should probably say it since we're just dancing around it now," mumbled Felix. He'd rather attack the one piece he knew, rather than the fact that he might be able to meet all his mother's family.

Something he'd never been able to do in the past.

"I'm not from this universe. I'm from another one," Felix deadpanned with a shrug of his shoulders. "My mother was Georgia Marin. My father was Austin Campbell.

"I was the only child they had and they… haven't been a part of my life for a long time. I miss them both."

"I see," Georgia said with an odd smile on her face. "How old are you?"

"Uh… I should be in my thirties. Time… time's been a bit weird around me. I get the impression my age isn't really… relevant anymore," Felix answered.

"That certainly wouldn't make sense. That means I would have met this Austin sometime after the accident. What… state did you grow up in?" she asked, her brows slowly pressing together.

"Wasn't a state," Felix murmured with a shake of his head. "I'm not really sure my dad exists here. In fact… I'd bet he doesn't."

Georgia opened her mouth, paused, then sighed. She nodded her head, looked down to the table in front of her, and went silent.

"I don't think he does either. Or if he did, it was a brief existence," she lamented. "I always felt like something was missing. I suppose I was right.

"Well… well that's fine! That's fine. Because you know what? I'm going to make the best of it!"

Georgia nodded her head once more, looked at Felix, and gave him a grin.

"Because you know what, Felix, you're not my son. But… you are my son," Georgia continued with a wide smile. "When I looked at your gauntlet, it said it was my son's. Not Felix Campbell's.

"So, regardless of anything else, this universe sees you as my son. So you're my son. We'll have to go visit your grandparents and aunts at some point and introduce you. I'm going to have to make up some excuse about… giving you up for adoption a long time ago though.

"That'll be rather awkward to say the least but… mm… the alternative isn't very palatable. If they're disbelieving about it we can just do one of those silly DNA tests and give it to them.

"Oh, that looks like it'd work out. Or so my power says. It's rather amusing… I'd never really considered doing what you suggested. Once you'd made the point, I'd been playing a great deal with it. I just have to run a long list of hypotheticals situations against what 'my answer' would be and I can eventually sus it out.

"Just takes a little time. That and it can be a bit of a mental work out, but it isn't so bad. It's rather nice, actually."

Felix was staring at the woman and didn't know what to say. If her power had recognized him as her son before he'd introduced himself, that meant that this world saw him as the only Felix Campbell, and her as the only Georgia Marin.

How... how close is this world to me as a person, but further away from everyone else? Is this world that much closer to my own possible life?

Or is it just how Ryker moved me over here, actually.

Is it nothing more than forcing this world to accept me?

"We'll go as soon as you have some free time," Georgia said waving a hand at him. "They all live close to one another, so we can get them all in one family gathering easily enough.

"Given who our guests were today though, I imagine there are a number of things that we'll be busy with. More than our fair share of work I'm betting.

"Though I'm finding Project Management to be far easier than I thought it would be. I just have to make sure I correctly organize, label, research, and then test each and every possibility.

"That young man, Edmund, has been quite clever as well. I swear there are times where, what would have taken me hours to do, he just manages to finish in no time at all. Almost as if he knew the answer before we even started."

Felix nodded his head a bit.

"Well, anyways," Georgia said with a laugh,

then waved her hand at him. "Look at me running my mouth. Let's talk about you, son.

"I want to know all about your life. Tell me everything. From the start, all the way to now. We have a lot to catch up on.

"Once we get yours all figured out, I can fill in everything from my side. Then we'll just go from there!"

"Alright," answered Felix after woodenly swallowing down his pastry. "Uhm… well… errr… do I really start from the beginning?"

"Yes! Please. Do. From the moment I birthed you, if possible," Georgia said with a dip of her head and her hands clapping together.

From the moment she birthed me.

I… see.

Okay. We'll just roll with it. It won't hurt me, and this woman really does seem to be exactly like my mom was. She just never met my dad.

Never found "her man" as it were.

Which she'd have discovered with her power as soon as she started dating anyone. A power that would let her know the right answer within only a handful of words.

Makes more sense now why it felt like they were perfectly matched to one another.

They had been. Without there ever being any doubt in her mind.

Which meant she'd never left any doubt in my dad's mind either, given how she was with him.

"I… you gave birth to me—" Felix started, settling in to give her their life story.

Chapter 13 - Where No Ghost Walks -

Felix was rather surprised as they flew over the landfill.

It wasn't what he could actually see that interested him.

All that was visible was what looked like a couple acres worth of trash that had been dumped, spread out, and mashed down.

No, what was fascinating to him was the rather large mountain that was below that trash.

An incredibly large mound that looked to be made of red dirt that went right to the trash-filled top. As if they'd dug a hole into the top of it and began filling it to the brim, which wasn't too far from the truth.

His interest was entirely on the inside of that mountain, as it wasn't what one expected.

The mountain was made of trash.

Everything inside of it was extremely compacted waste that'd been smashed, spread out, and then pushed down with more. Endlessly, until they were now where they were operating.

As the helicopter came around to move across the airspace above the area, Felix now noticed that there was a large number of trucks, equipment, and people all at the bottom of that massive garbage mountain.

"They've cleared out," reported the government agent in the co-pilot seat. Once more, it was someone Felix hadn't met before. They had yet to send him someone he'd met previously. It was a young man this time who looked like he was in his late twenties. "You're free to take the materials you need.

"And uh... before you get worried or anything, Legate, Sir. The dump is paying us for this. Any trash you can eliminate from the mount just gives them more room to work with. They'll be paying us on a sliding scale by what you remove."

"Oh?" asked Felix with a grin.

Maybe Legion should get into the 'unfilling landfills' business. I take a small fee to absolutely empty it of everything in there.

Even toxic ones or radioactive ones.

"It might be worth mentioning that, while I'm doing this for building materials, I could effectively do this with any landfill, dump site, or toxic hole. So long as I have permission to salvage materials to build with, I can clean it out entirely," Felix stated. "Not sure if the government has any... places... they'd really like cleaned out, but it might be worth relaying it to your boss.

"Could probably turn around and use it to build anything else. So long as I own the blueprints for it and the technology, I can construct it. There are some limitations on the power but... they're not so bad.

"That, and having building materials available makes everything else easier. Especially for spontaneous needs."

"Oh I'm definitely going to relay all of that up. I know of a few that they'll probably take you up on almost immediately. Any chance you can use that power to take out only certain things?" asked the agent. He had his phone out and was rapidly tapping something into it.

Hm.

They might ask me to refine atomic materials or something like that. We'll have to take it slow.

"Depends on what it is. I haven't experimented with many things, but it gets a lot harder if I'm not just processing it into specific parts for a blueprint," Felix relayed and then looked back down to the dump.

"Makes sense. Makes sense," muttered the agent.

Yes, and you'll move to the conclusion that I have to understand the blueprint to a degree to build it. Which means many things I don't understand, like... atomic theory... are simply not available to me.

I'm more useful than I am dangerous.

Ever the goal.

"You're clear. Go ahead," said the agent.

"They care about the dirt? Or the mountain?" Felix asked.

"Ah... no?"

"Great."

Felix reached out with his power to the mountain of trash. From the base of it to the top. He'd been granted ownership of all that junk to use as he saw fit.

He wanted to convert every bit of it to points. To leave none of it behind, except for the bare layer of dirt where the whole thing had begun.

Goldie flew by not far away. Casually moving through the sky and looking around as she did so.

Since he'd alerted the government to the fact that she was now in his custody, she no longer felt the need to hide. Wherever Legate went, the Gold Dragon came with.

Along with a number of news clips of every time she'd been spotted, came a lot of new footage. Cell phone recordings, mostly from people watching her fly through the air above.

The mountain simply ceased to exist in the next moment.

Gone, with nothing left behind.

"Alright, let's head to the site for the prison," Felix stated and looked to the agent. The man was staring down at the now-vanished landfill. "I know it's only been a week since I sent you all the Guild of Heroes information.

"Are they ready to start managing it? I feel like this is perhaps being rushed ahead because the foreign supers are becoming problems."

"I… uh… its… all gone," mumbled the agent, his head moving this way and that. As if he might see the trash mountain if he caught it from a better angle.

"Focus, agent. Prison? Heroes Guild?" prompted Felix.

"Prison? Heroes Guild?" asked the man in a robotic parrot-like way. "Oh! Yes! Sorry. Yes.

"Pilot, move to the next location. Err... the... yeah, Legate. Yeah. We're rushing it a bit, but the Heroes Guild is already established."

The agent had turned to face him now.

"They're assigned as a military force. They report directly to the president. We've already established all the precedents we'll need for them," the agent continued. "Insurances, protocol, benefits for death or injury, all of it. The legislation for it was pushed through quickly as well.

"There's... anyone who isn't part of the Guild and acting as a hero will be legally responsible for anything that happens due to their actions. Anyone who acts in the country in the capacity of a vigilante will be deemed as a terrorist."

"Wonderful. I assume anyone in the Association will of course be absent from that rule. That or you're telling me I'm going to be setting myself up for a felony here in a moment when I build that prison," pointed out Felix.

"Association members are all exempt from that rule. It exists in a separate legal structure, as was promised in the agreement with you," the agent assured him.

"Perfect. Then... excuse me, but I'll follow along behind you. Try to go quickly though, the Dragon gets bored easily," Felix requested.

Opening the door to the helicopter, he

removed the headset that he'd been wearing over his own helmet. It'd been more to communicate with the agent than anything else.

Undoing the restraints, he stepped out of the helicopter and began to immediately fall.

Goldie had apparently been monitoring the situation or reading the agent's mind. She'd already swung in low as Felix stepped out of the aircraft.

There was an unmistakable smirk on Goldie's face as she moved in below him as he began to fall. She casually snatched him out of the air with one rear claw and began flapping her wings hard. Carrying herself upward and away from the helicopter.

Gaining some height, she slowed herself until she was merely flying in place. Her wings generating enough force only to keep her relatively in the same space.

She passed Felix to a front paw, then deposited him on her neck.

"Did you get tired of them, Nest-mate?" she asked and then rolled off to one side. She moved in behind the helicopter and then slowed down once again.

"They probably wanted to talk to me about something that wouldn't do us any good," he said, expecting that the helmet would transmit the words loud enough to Goldie. "That and I'd rather just... ride you?"

Goldie laughed at that, though he did hear an edge to it. A hungry one.

* * *
***

Standing in front of the open field, Felix was reminded of how the Association location had been. There'd been some distant shrub there, some trees, even some depressions in the plains.

Where he was now though, had none of that.

It was flat.

Flat, empty, and had nothing at all in any direction but short grass.

Given the plans he'd worked out with the agents, government, and the Heroes, this was going to be a prison surrounded by a demilitarized zone. With several walls and weapons pointing inward, and outward.

Thankfully, Felix was only responsible for the prison itself.

Mentally forcing himself to do it, and to not sigh, or whine, he pulled up his point window.

	Generated	Remaining
Andrea	750	750
Alma	280	280
Carlota	290	290
Faith	450	450
Felix	2,200	2,200
Goldie	2,725	2,725
Miu	1,280	1,280
+Loyalty Bonus	1,000	1,000

+**Marital Bonus**	700	700
=**Daily Total**	**9,675**	**9,675**
Banked Total	—	**41,974,146**

Pushing out with his powers, he wanted to know how much it would cost to build the prison. What he mentally called Hero Prison v1 from the blueprints he'd put together for it.

| **Type**: Building (Hero Prison v1) | **Condition**: New |
| **Owner**: Legate and Legion | **Construction**: Cost 89,765,321,248 points |

Felix let out a soft wheeze at the price listed. He'd seen it several times when he'd been testing the plants, but it still made him wince at the sheer amount needed.

Next, he wanted to know what'd be the cost once all the materials he'd requisitioned, personnel, and equipment, arrived. To see what it would all cost once everything arrived.

| **Type**: Building (Hero Prison v1) | **Condition**: New (Materials and work provided) |
| **Owner**: Legate and Legion | **Construction**: Cost 32,321,248 points |

Nice. I mean, that's about what it was last time

but... nice. That means I'll have nine-million points left-over.

Point value must be shifting due to the ground beneath, now that we're here.

Slightly different deposits I suppose but... this is great.

It's fan-fucking-tastic.

Absolutely terrific.

This has been worth... everything.

And that even includes the new Legion base beneath the prison.

Grinning, Felix started to feel out the build. Where it'd be on the field.

"You're excited," rumbled Goldie. She was looming over him like a protective wall.

"Of course. The more bases we have like this, the better off we are. In the future we just connect the two with an underground rail and suddenly everything is even better," Felix gushed. He could see a high-speed train in his mind, rushing from one location to another, then another. "For all the land we own, we can dig down indefinitely. For where we don't... we just employ drills that'll do the work for us.

"Just load up a few carts with Andreas and the promise of rewards and we're all set. A continuous workforce that'll endlessly dig. Hell, I could convince her to do it if I promised her more Others for a set amount of distance."

"I... she... yes... yes that'd work," Goldie murmured. "You really do like burrowing into the earth."

"People can't see me there. Can't watch what I'm doing from above," Felix explained, shifting things about in his head just a bit. "Much harder for them to peek and see what's going on.

"We'll just keep adding bases like this, deep below places we're asked to build. Then put train stations at the lowest point so we can access them later. Won't be too hard.

"That and, once we get them all hooked up, Tribune will be able to function much more clearly. She's somewhat limited by having to exist where we put her.

"It's a good thing she can be in two places at the same time by copying herself, but it'd be better if she were everywhere at the same time."

"Yes, that makes sense," Goldie admitted. Then she sniffed once and turned her head to one side. "They're all coming. Though I think everything is being driven in this time."

"It's a lot more materials this time," muttered Felix. "Just have them line everything up nearby. I'm going to be focusing on this until everything's unloaded. I want this placement perfect.

"Just direct them on my behalf for now. I'm sure they'll just want to stand here and watch when it happens anyways."

Felix engrossed himself in moving the whole thing around, checking the cost, then doing it again. Making small changes here and there and checking, then rechecking.

There was a prod in the middle of his back that wasn't something he could ignore. As if a strong hand had landed in the middle of his back and bumped him a bit.

"Legate, it's time," Goldie announced.

Looking up, he found that indeed everyone was present.

Kit, Lily, Mikki, a number of supers he vaguely recognized. There was a number of agents with them and spread out as well.

Beyond all that were a lot of people with weapons and in uniforms he didn't recognize. They were all dressed in a similar fashion and had the look of either security or military as far as the design went.

"Right," he said, forcing himself to move past Kit and Lily as if they'd only just met. Since he'd used Kit's own powers to wipe her mind after Lily's, he hadn't seen them.

They'd been put back where they'd been as if nothing had changed.

The current models of Legionnaire rings were stamped with the Legion Helm and provided something different this time.

They didn't block telepathy.

In fact, if anything, it made it appear easier to the telepath.

It put out a generic stream of surface thoughts that most anyone would have, using the person wearing the ring as the source of information. All while cloaking their actual thoughts and hiding everything else.

He wanted it to work in the same way that he was attempting to move Legion into the world.

Benign, boring, expected, and overlooked.

Healing Lucian had cost him some points, but it'd been quite simple this time. He'd just created a beacon that his soul would find and be drawn back to.

For Kit, the helmet was very similar to a Legionnaire helmet, it just allowed her to focus things like a magnifying glass. Alternatively, she could also turn everything off outright.

"Any concerns?" Felix asked, looking around to the audience. He had no idea if they'd said anything, and he didn't really care. He was the builder in this scenario, so his work would be secondary to everything they'd have to do.

"Quite a few, actually," Kit observed. Her helmet was fully on, but she'd retracted the visor. He could see her eyes but that was about it. "But... none that I can fault you for, given the stipulations you've put into the contracts. I understand I have you to thank for this helmet?"

"Sure thing. There a problem with it?" he asked, curious. He'd built it after he'd wiped her mind, but he didn't think there'd be an issue.

"No. No problem. At all. Which is somewhat of a problem. It fits me in a way that feels like it could only be possible if you measured my head," Kit stated in a flat tone.

"Yes. Technology is a wonder," Felix agreed.

"Anything else at all? Otherwise it'd be best if we got moving.

"No reason to linger here and... well... my suit's great and all, but I'm not really built for combat. With Clichés tending to be founded in reality, this'd be a great time for someone to attack us."

"Can you please demonstrate one of the super cells?" asked Lily. There was a warm smile on her face that left him somewhat at a loss. "Just... for my own sake, if you don't mind... Legate."

Blinking several times, Felix didn't know how to respond to that at first. In fact, he felt like there was a problem here that he couldn't put his finger on.

Instead, clicking his tongue he nodded his head once.

"Alright. That's not a problem. I can do that," allowed Felix. "Any particular super type you want to test out? I've created an entire series of cells for any type of super I could think of.

"We'll eventually encounter a vast number of them, best we have a way to lock them away so that they can't get out any time soon."

"For me. Make a prison for me," Lily asked.

Chewing at his lip, he felt like this was a trick.

A trap.

Something that'd get him boiled alive when the day was done.

Lily had a look on her face he could have

never mistaken in the past for anything other than amusement. Amusement and wanting to play.

To toy with him and his feelings. Poke, prod, and push at him until she got what she wanted.

"Sure," Felix mumbled. He called forth a simple cell that would hold a magician without an issue. It was as simple as having magical spells engraved into the cell.

A glass cube came into existence in front of them. It was roughly nine feet by nine feet and was empty. Each wall was comprised of two panes of glass. All the interior panels of glass were inscribed with spell wardings on the side facing out of the cell. The next layer of glass was also warded with spell work, though this one had it on both sides.

It was all invisible to the eye unless they were activated. Otherwise, it just looked like a big glass cube.

"Oh," Lily said with some surprise. She walked in through the open and door-less entrance. Entering and then coming to a stop in the middle.

She lifted a hand and began to work a spell.

That collapsed on itself instantly as soon as it gained a shape. The magic bleeding away and charging the cell.

"The longer the cell is on, the stronger it gets," Felix explained and waved a hand at it. "It can only be deactivated by someone from Legion."

"Deactivate it for me?" Lily asked, tilting her head and watching him.

Shrugging his shoulders, Felix did as he was

instructed.

In the moment he did so, he saw Lucian standing near Lily. Very near her, in fact.

Beside her.

He was grinning, ear to ear, watching Lily. Clapping his hands together noiselessly as it all happened.

Then his incorporeal form was gone. In fact, Felix was sure that he wasn't even supposed to see him there.

A trick of the way the cell deactivated.

The spell Lily had been working at flickered to life briefly and then died away. It'd been made strongly enough that it lingered, even without power.

Fluttering away into nothing, even as Felix considered a problem he'd overlooked.

People like Lucian would be able to go where Felix had no ability to stop them. He needed to fix everything so that there'd be no possible trespass.

He'd overlooked a firm possibility of how someone could easily infiltrate, spy, or assist. Because believing Lucian was the only one who could probably do something such as this was a foolish hope.

Chapter 14 - Watcher -

Felix stepped into the home and paused.

It'd been a day since he'd built the prison for the Guild and the Government.

Since then, he'd been on the move with Goldie.

Flying here and there, then crossing international waters before swinging far to the north, followed by a swing east, and slowly back to the home at the Landfill.

He needed to make sure that Lucian, or whoever else might be following them, was lost. That no one would be on their tail, even if he couldn't see them.

Goldie thankfully had responded to all of this with a laugh. The idea of flying endlessly sounded quite fun to her. All it'd take is for him to recharge her stamina with a few points here and there, and they could continue indefinitely.

"Well, that was fun. I haven't been on a fly like that in a really long time. There were quite a few interesting sights to see as well," said the naked Gold Dragon moving past him. She entered the living room, looked around, and then made a clucking noise.

Walking further into the home, she began to critically look at the hardwood floor with a slow shake of her head.

"Oh, those girls! I warned them about tracking in grass and dirt," grumbled Goldie even as her eyes picked back and forth across something Felix honestly couldn't see. "Hmph. I'll make sure they clean it up themselves. Good thing I taught them how to mop a floor a little bit ago."

Nodding her head, the beautiful and naked Dragon went into the back of the home. Presumably to get some clothes, he imagined.

Felix needed to take care of something else entirely. Pulling his helmet off his head, he set it down on the entryway "key drop" table that'd been put there.

Leaving the living room, he moved into his "work room" that was in the back of the home. He needed to do some quick factoring on how to prevent people he couldn't see from getting into his facilities.

People that might as well be ghosts if they didn't even have a heat signature they could check against. Someone like Lucian who could be around him even now.

Entering his workroom, Felix paused.

He found Edmund and Ryker there. The former sitting at a desk off to one side that he'd often sat at as Felix droned on about business, and the latter working at what looked to be a circuit board with a soldering gun.

"Oh, hey boss," Edmund said with a grin and a wave of his hand as he looked up from his laptop. "I was just going through the five phases with Ryker. It... honestly feels weird going through stuff like this.

"Things I already knew, or that I had an idea about, being formed into solid concepts and stuck down. Kinda strange but… it works.

"Though I'm amused that you seem to live permanently in phase one or phase four. Everything else seems to fall to everyone else."

Felix blinked, his mind flickering backward to see if he had any memory of what the young man was talking about. He'd never gotten very deep into project management and didn't have that many memories of it.

"You start concepts or determine performance," Ryker muttered as he touched the soldering gun to the circuit board. There was a soft click as the instrument touched the wire. "Rarely do you really dig into the scope, tracking, or post mortem."

"Oh, yeah, that's about right. Not my area of expertise. If I was a part of all of those, wouldn't I be in project management?" Felix asked with a chuckle. He came over to glance at Edmund's laptop and saw he was actively going through an online course. Nodding his head, he walked over to where Ryker was working and sat down in the chair next to it. "Been a bit."

Ryker looked up from his work and gave him a smile that was more a smirk.

His dark brown eyes were brighter than normal given the light. His straight black hair was falling down to either side right now and he had beads of sweat on his brow.

Apparently he'd been head down over this

circuit board for a while.

"A bit," agreed Ryker. "Had some time. Decided to drop in. Just happened to coincide with Edmund and you being here. It's a wonder how things are coincidentally happening so perfectly like this."

"Uh huh," Felix said with a chuckle, leaning further back in his chair. He was quite tired. Spending hours upon hours on the back of Goldie without rest or sleep had drained him. "Am I starting to get on your good side yet? I fix more than I break yet?"

"Somewhat," admitted Ryker, turning his gaze back to the board. From what Felix could see, it was a commercial-grade product. Ryker had deliberately burned out a circuit and then made a wire span a gap from one section to another. There was a single chip that needed to be re-soldered to the board nearby as well. "Definitely making things a bit easier for me as of late.

"A lot less having to force things to where they should be. Then again, I removed a lot of the roadblocks you kept slamming into anyways. Works out a bit better that way."

Felix's mind wandered off back to his conversations with Ryker. They'd often left him feeling like he was missing a key piece to things. That something was incredibly wrong, and he was only a step away from figuring it out.

Except that he didn't want to know. Felix didn't want to know the secrets of the world. Didn't want anything to do with them.

William D. Arand

He had people he cared about and work to do. Those things were the entirety of his existence, and he didn't need to create an issue for himself by learning more than he could handle.

"Smart," Ryker mumbled as he picked up the chip with a pair of tweezers and pushed it into a spot that it looked like it belonged. "Better off that way, honestly. There's certainly more to the world, and you've grasped the edges of it. Some people can handle it, some can't.

"I almost ended my entire existence when I figured it out. Almost. Know a few people who went crazy when they figured it out.

"Your choice is a logical and smart one. Hold to it. As long as you do, you'll never have to worry about discovering the secret. It's somewhat of a choice in the end.

"Now... let's change the subject so you don't get a headache. Shall we? We'll turn it to this. What I'm working on."

The headache that'd been growing behind his eyes faded to nothing. Almost as if he'd imagined it.

"This is an electrical board that'll let you operate any train you purchase on your custom software. It has a few basic programs and things on it that it needed to bypass security and company lockouts," Ryker said as he adjusted the clamps to shift the board around to the other side. He then began to quickly solder the pins of the chip into place. "It'll end up attached to the master console when you end up building it. For now, you can just leave it on the desk till you need it. Should save you a great deal of points in the future.

"Cost me all of a few minutes to pick it up, and ten minutes to do this work. Not so bad and I did it willingly. So don't call it a debt or anything like that."

"Okay… then why'd you stop by? You feel like the type to maximize his efficiency where possible," Felix redirected.

"Give you some information, mostly. Vince is doing well. He's off on an adventure like you are, but still on his home planet. He already jumped my plans and did an end run on me. The bastard," Ryker said with a chuckle. He didn't sound upset at all. "Did meet his mother-in-law. She uh… we have plans to go to dinner tonight.

"Anyways. Other than that, I wouldn't worry too much about people like Lucian. There's a handful of them, but you're not likely going to run across them. Not to mention, the changes you're probably going to make in the near future will prevent them from being a problem.

"Don't focus on it, you'll solve it without solving it. Save the points. I promise. That's all I've got. Well, that and I made a few nudges here and there. Things you wouldn't notice but if you knew, you'd agree they're helpful."

Felix looked down to his boots and contemplated the situation.

Everything about this situation, about his life, felt off. Like he was listening to a symphony but had just noticed someone was quietly playing a triangle throughout.

A single shining note here and there that you'd easily overlook and miss. Drowned out by everyone and everything else, and something the vast majority of people would never even realize was there.

"How long have you been... poking around. Nudging things here and there. In my life, that is," Felix asked quietly. "Because I'm starting to think that maybe... maybe a lot of my life isn't by mistake or chance.

"That none of this was accidental. From the moment I met the Overgod I've suspected that maybe there was more to me than I'd considered. The idea of being as mundane as anyone else but managing to meet you and him seemed less likely as time went on.

"It being far more likely that I was already special to begin with, stands out as the more likely scenario. One that is a lot more likely than being a nobody who suddenly got a lot of attention."

Ryker didn't say anything.

He kept working at the circuit board. Soldering the chip into place. Upon completion, he flipped it back over and then pushed a finger against it.

The chip remained quite firmly seated.

Setting the board down on the desk, Ryker flicked a switch on the soldering iron's control base, and then turned to face Felix directly. His eyes were searching back and forth across Felix's face for several seconds.

"Hm. You've been thinking on that one for a while. Buried it deep in your thoughts and hid it away. Far, far, from the surface," remarked Ryker. "Even now, it's hard to see how far down it goes. You've suspected it for a long time.

"Though... I can't seem to find the original cause for it. There's no inciting event that this all came from."

"Wish I could tell you. As far as I can tell, there wasn't one," Felix admitted, looking up to Ryker. "Just a collecting of feelings and thoughts that slowly built up.

"My mom kinda put a magnifying glass on it in some ways. Her power is so similar to mine that it's not even funny. The fact that my father isn't here is a bit of an oddity, but it seemed almost plausible. I'd imagine my uncle Miles doesn't exist either though, and if he does, he most certainly wouldn't have a kid named Vince.

"As to hiding it... not really. Just part of the other thoughts that I try not to have. Lot of those, unfortunately. I suppose it comes with having a darker nature than most."

Ryker sucked on his teeth for a second and then clicked his tongue. He made a vague swish with his hand and the world became grayscale.

Felix and Ryker were the only things that had any color to them.

Any life.

"You're breaking things again, Felix," complained Ryker.

Felix laughed at that and held his hands up at his sides.

"I'm not doing it on purpose. At least, not this time. I'm just trying to figure things out, live my life, get what I need to go get done, and move forward. It's obvious though if you think about it," argued Felix. "Why would an Overgod need favors from me? Why would you need things from me?

"Neither one of you are lacking in power or resources. You're the creators of this world as far as I can tell. Many worlds, considering I've now seen... four? Five? I've lost track anymore. There's certainly a wide array of... things... out there for you to pick from.

"It's like going to a bar full of incredibly beautiful women, but you ignored all of them and went for the semi-cute one in the corner of the bar who was clearly trying to be alone. The action is so far outside of the expectation, that it creates its own obviousness to it."

"I get it," Ryker confessed with a sigh and a nod of his head. He slowly looked away and seemed to be considering nothing. "How much of an answer do you want? Because... well, I can tell you everything, if you want.

"We're in a place and time where things are spinning faster and faster outside of my expectations. No matter how much I rush off to fix... fix my Rube Goldberg machine, more of it starts to shiver and shake.

"Things go off early or not at all, only for the whole thing to sputter to life in a completely unrelated way. It's all on track as far as I can tell, just not in the way I'd been expecting it to.

"So... right now... at this moment... I'm a bit freer than I expected to be."

"In how many worlds do I exist?" Felix asked.

"One," Ryker confirmed with a slow exhale. "One world. Out of countless billions of worlds that I tried, only one world. Your cousin, or brother as you call him, also exists in exactly one world.

"Only in this one... strange... world... did you come into being, Felix. You are quite literally one of maybe... four people that are unique to the existence that they're in."

"Edmund is another," Felix declared, his eyes jumping across to the motionless young man at the computer.

"He is," agreed Ryker. "He exists in one world and one only. You've been around another, but never met him. His name's Rene. He ah... he has acted as a bodyguard of sorts for you at times."

"You said billions of worlds you tried," Felix murmured, changing the focus of the conversation a bit.

Looking up to Ryker's face, he waited for a second.

When the other man looked at him, Felix saw the infinite and never-ending expanse of time pass through the man's eyes. An unending sprawl of nothingness that'd been witnessed.

Endlessly.

Felix mentally shuddered away but didn't break eye contact.

"Billions. Yes. I've watched... so many worlds. Eons of human history and civilizations," whispered Ryker in a way that felt damaged. "That's assuming there was ever life to begin with. There're so many false-starts that I can't even truly explain it to you."

"In other words... you just... hit the reset button until you found me," summarized Felix.

"Not so much, but not too far off. I did all that I could without ending lives. Thankfully for each of those worlds I watched birthed, I was able to gently set them aside. Each of them living their lives and spinning away through the darkness of their cosmos.

"Living and existing until their end arrives. In whatever way that may be, but they'll all reach it."

"Then if that was just to get me started, how many times did you have to intercede just to get me to this point?"

"Me? Once, really. Runner popped in here and there. Mostly to make sure you got a proper chance when things were getting too far out of hand. We couldn't interfere too much, or you wouldn't be you."

"Why didn't you save my parents?" asked Felix in a deathly whisper.

Ryker grimaced at that and finally broke eye contact.

"Couldn't. Same reason I couldn't... keep Miles here," confessed Ryker with pain in his voice. "You wouldn't have been you without them being removed from your life. They've both been watching over you from the afterlife by the way.

"I've allowed them to keep an eye on you whenever they wished. They watch almost constantly."

The more Felix heard, the more he wanted to be angry. To rage at this man who'd watched his life more like a movie than someone he was trying to protect.

Except in those thoughts, Felix realized that 'protecting Felix' was counter to the goal. They needed Felix to be who he was at this moment.

Without the experiences of his life, both the good and the bad, he wouldn't be who he was. He was actually quite happy with who he had turned out to be.

Who he was today, was greater than the sum of all the parts of his history, good and bad. Felix Campbell was better for all of it.

"Got it. That means that you or Runner were responsible for the biggest changes in my life. There's two that I can think off right off the top of my head," Felix continued, his mind working quite quickly now. "Skipper-city is the first one. Who... set up Skipper?"

"Neither of us. She always occurred in that world no matter what we did. She used it as a recruiting world. That all ended when they ended up angering the deities of that world and they decided to blow everything up, rather than let Zeus take control of the world.

"Makes no sense to me. Armageddon makes the world kind of impossible to have worshipers on. A world controlled by Zeus still allows for worshipers.

"That's religion for you. Doesn't make a damn lick of sense to me and never has. Never understand any of it.

"Realistically, you were supposed to stay on that world for a really long time. A really long time. So long that you'd die of old age on it. You'd have come to this one only because you'd have had the luxury of time on your original one.

"I couldn't account for... couldn't account for what you encountered. She outplayed us all. Especially me."

Ryker looked like he had a mix of pride and anger at his own words.

"Right. Then... Zeus is our mutual enemy. That's who Skipper worked for, and who tried to kill me and everyone I love.

"Shirley was just a mastermind making a plan. She wasn't doing any of it with actual malice, just a need to get to a set ending. Skipper was the one who had it in for me."

"Mmhmm. Damn right on both of those, actually. Shirley goes by Bianca now, by the way."

"Err... alright. Right... then... was it you, or Runner, who was No-Name?" Felix asked with a chuckle, looking up to Ryker. "Actually, I guess that answers my question already. You told him what to do, he did it. He seems the more likely culprit rather than you."

Ryker laughed and looked like he was going to deny it.

"Just admit it. There's no way anyone would have mistaken an order of Bismuth for a person. It's so obvious that it's painful. Not to mention why Skipper would have gotten rid of those Heroes without knowing who they went to," Felix countered before Ryker could even voice a negative. "It was one of you two."

Blinking, Ryker had a no forming on his face.

"It was Runner," he said in a sudden rush. "My plan, but Runner did it. He checked in on you more than he should have. Always with the 'but he might need it' excuse. Constantly pushing things towards you thinking maybe you'd want it.

"Do you have any idea how hard I had to slap his damn hand every time he tried to put more in front of you than you needed? It's a lot like raising a child with an irresponsible parent. How was I supposed to keep you hungry and moving if everything was handed to you?

"Bad enough that we had to constantly knock Zeus' people off and prevent them from just coming to kill you. Sometimes it felt like I spent days just killing assassins that'd been dispatched for you."

I... err... I guess that makes sense.

Almost too much sense.

They were watching over me in what way they

could, all while trying to preserve whatever rules they have to work by as gods, yet doing all that they could for me.

" — thirteenth birthday, like you actually needed it. There were so many damn futures in that one with you knocking up some random girl that I couldn't let it happen," growled Ryker with heat in his voice.

"Whelp," Felix said, getting Ryker's attention back on him. "Does that make you my over-protective mom, or my discipline-strict dad? Since Runner would be my over-indulgent mom or doting dad."

Ryker blinked slowly while staring at Felix.

Chapter 15 - Reinvesting -

Felix spent another ten or twenty minutes with Ryker before the man claimed he had to go. Vanishing from view as if someone had pushed a button.

From there, he'd gone about exactly what he'd originally intended to do.

He left his work room, grabbed his helmet, stuffed his head back in it, then went to Legion headquarters. The location, of course hadn't changed, so he simply entered the barn and went through the normal security.

There were very few people who entered, since most of Gaia's people all wanted to remain below ground. Making new lives for themselves in Legion while also digging out spaces for themselves below.

Moving into the meeting room that was next door to his office, Felix pulled his helmet free once again. Setting it down on the table in front of himself he let out a breath.

"Felix! I found you!"

Looking to the door, he found two Andreas rushing toward him. One had a push cart filled with pastries and drinks, the other had utensils and plates.

"Twenty-fourth, Thirty-sixth, good to see you," Felix murmured with a warm smile. They always cheered him up regardless of his mood.

After his talk with Ryker, he'd felt a strange

heaviness settle over his thoughts. Like a heavy warm blanket.

Suffocating, but almost comfortably so.

Laughing, both Andreas did a little bounce as they came toward him.

"Second will be here soon," said the Andrea with the plates. "She'll be acting as our A-Net representative. Prime is busy working on all her projects, so she won't be able to make it."

Rapidly, a large glass of orange juice, a bagel slathered with cream cheese, a slice of lemon-loaf, and a cookie were plopped down in front of him. It was topped off with a cup of coffee that was steaming.

Both Andreas paused long enough to kiss him, then moved on. They were operating from a piece of paper that was stuck to the inside of the cart. Filling plates and laying them out according to whatever they saw there.

"Loves, what're you doing?" Felix asked. "Or... actually, I know what you're doing, but I suppose I'm asking why?"

"Board meeting!" said the Andrea who was in charge of the cart. "The A-Net is responsible for booking meeting rooms and making sure they're ready. We've actively gone ahead and gotten everyone's preferences together.

"We're now filling those accordingly. That's all. We want to make sure your meeting goes really good."

"Nn!" said the other Andrea with a nod of

her head and a swish of her hips that sent her tail moving in the opposite direction. "I heard from Five that we're probably going to get another ten or twenty Others."

"Really? Exciting!" replied the other. She picked up a scone from the box and held it out. "I bet it's something fuuuuuun. I wanna be a train driver."

"Nnnnn. It better have a really good horn. So we can go all boop-boop hoooooooooonk with a whoosh."

"I kinda wanna get hit by it once just to see what it'd do. Do you think my head would come off?."

"You're so weird."

Both Andreas laughed at that and continued to fill out placements.

Felix didn't remember actually scheduling a meeting. He'd wanted to, and had been planning on putting one together as soon as he sat down, but he hadn't yet.

Which meant someone was anticipating him.

Getting his thoughts together, Felix went to ask the Andreas who put it together, only to find they were already gone. Having finished their duty and escaped.

Sitting there, Felix didn't know what to do with himself. He supposed the only thing he could do, or at least should do, was wait.

Turning to his plate, he picked up the plastic fork and started carving into the food there. He saw no reason not to eat, considering he was rather hungry.

By the time he finished everything but the cookie and his coffee he heard someone coming. Multiple someone's, guessing by the click and pop of bootheels.

Faith, Alma, and Carlotta all entered the meeting room.

"Hello, Grove-husband," all three said in unison with a faint glow to their eyes. Each of them went and took a seat around the table. Felix found that they were actually sitting apart from one another.

With Faith directly in front of him and the other two at the far end.

"Oh, thank you Andie. I wanted something with protein," Faith whispered and then picked up what looked like a slab of meat with a hastily grabbed plastic fork. Lifting it up she took a large bite of it.

"I meant to ask, you don't seem to eat like the other Dryads I've met," Felix said, glancing over to Alma and Carlotta's plate. They also had what looked to be meat served up as well.

"Different respect of life," Faith answered after chewing and swallowing. "Especially in worlds like this. The animals were already penned and slaughtered.

"I will happily crusade for better treatment of them. Better conditions and lives, however brief they may be. That doesn't change that I will still enjoy the taste of their flesh.

"No differently than many animals would enjoy the taste of me. The Dryads you met before me were... much... kinder, you'll remember. They didn't like training with weapons unless they had to. Even then, they never quite excelled with it."

"I just like meat," Carlotta remarked. "Tastes good."

"S-same," Alma added. "We were more or less raised like Humans. I can't imagine not eating meat."

"Want to come over and give me a special dressing for this salad though?" Carlotta asked, picking up her bowl and angling toward him. "Could use some extra protein, and I rather like the taste.

"Though it makes me wonder if Succubi are real. If they are real, do they really subsist on such a thing? or is it more on the act itself?"

Felix stared at the red-eyed Dryad. Unable to help it, he'd felt his cheeks start to burn and his eyebrows shoot upward.

"Oh, yes please," Alma said and then pointed to Carlotta's salad bowl. "You can load hers up and then we'll split it between us afterward."

"Good idea," Carlotta said, nodding at Alma.

"I've never heard of them being real," answered Faith, looking contemplative and also not responding to the other Dryad's byplay. "Doesn't mean they're not, just unlikely. Neither in this world, my home world, or Felix's, at least. Though, they could be down the street for all I know."

Felix looked away from the two red-eyed Dryads. He made sure to not look at Faith either, as he had no doubt she'd ask for the same if he made eye contact with her.

Instead, he looked to his cookie.

"Possibly? Probably," he allowed, just trying to change the subject. He hadn't really even heard what they'd been discussing if he was honest. "Unsure."

"Felix? Give me some salad dressing? Please?" Carlotta asked.

"Not... right now," he said, realizing he'd have to answer her.

"Ah, good point. Someone might show up. You can fix our salad for us after the meeting," she acknowledged. "We'll set them to the side till later."

"T-true," Alma agreed. "Better idea. Others will be here shortly."

Goldie and Miu came through the door a handful of seconds later. Sparing him any further.

Miu sat down directly at Felix's right and then hard stared at him. Not looking away.

"Yes, Miu?" Felix asked with a smile for her. "You're not still frustrated about Mikki, are you?"

"I... no. I'm not. Part of me is glad, part of me is mad," Miu said, her face shifting into one of concern. "Goldie has been helping me work through the thoughts.

"She said I should talk to you about it when

I'm ready. I think that'll be soon. My l-love, can I talk to you about it?"

"Of course you can. I'll listen to anything you have to say," Felix said with a grin. Then he leaned in and kissed Miu briefly. Lingering for only a moment to nuzzle her before he got back into his seat. "Though it'll have to wait. How went the trip otherwise? I never got to ask for details."

"It was fine," Miu whispered, staring at him wide eyed. "I killed everyone again. Just like I did last time. It was more interesting this time as they were older than they were when I did it."

Felix wasn't sure how that'd make things more interesting, but he wasn't going to ask either.

"Great. You seem... better for it," tried Felix. He had definitely felt a shift in her. One that felt positive, but he wasn't sure how to broach it.

"I am better," agreed Miu with a small nod of her head. Then she gave him a beautiful smile, relaxed somewhat, and her eyes started to return to normal. Leaning back in her chair, she watched him for several more seconds before she broke eye contact on her own. Picking up one of the items she took a bite from it.

Surprisingly, she looked back to him.

"Still crazy. Still in love with you," she said around a mouth of food. Something he'd never seen her do before. Swallowing, she cleared her throat. "But better. Andie and I have been talking a lot and... and I'm glad to have comrades in arms now."

Huh. Alright.

Looking to his left, he found Goldie had seated herself there.

Andrea's second had taken up the spot next to Faith.

The table also had a number of people he didn't quite recognize, as well as one person he did.

Jay, the onetime dealer turned programmer was here. In front of him was a laptop that he was tapping away at. The sandy blonde was still in his customary Viking style. The blue eyes weren't moving away from his screen though and he seemed a bit healthier than the last time Felix had seen him.

Freezing, the man looked up and met Felix's eyes.

"Hey boss, just getting my progress chart finished so I can show you where my team's at," Jay said with a grin, then went back to his laptop.

Oh… kay.

Right.

Err… corporate life agrees with him, I guess.

"Everyone's here so we can begin, Grove-husband," purred Faith, smiling at him from across the way. There was a faint light in her eyes, but he had no idea why.

It made him leery.

"Well… it looks like it," Felix murmured glancing around. He saw a number of people from Gaia's camp, but he felt like that wasn't quite right. "Auntie Gaia, do you want to join us directly? If not, we can just leave it to your representatives but... you have every right to be here as my ally."

There was a tingling pop in his ears, followed by one of the vacant chairs across from him being filled.

Gaia had indeed joined them.

She also looked a lot like a very attractive Dryad in her middle-age. Mature, full-bodied, but starting to lose her youth and vitality. Her eyes were glowing brightly and didn't seem to have a dimmer switch to them, or if they did, she chose not to use it.

Her dark-brown hair was braided with silver and golden clasps, all designed in the shapes of leaves and flowers. What she wore looked like something taken right out of Goldie's wardrobe. A blouse and slacks outfit that fit her quite well.

"Thank you, Felix Otherworlder. Thank you so very much for asking me like that," Gaia said in a warm and rich tone. "I'm so glad for that. I'm happy to attend."

Two Andreas popped in from outside and rushed over to where Gaia had materialized. They set down a plate for her, then began to fill it with nuts, berries, fruits, and vegetables, then paused.

"Nnn... would... you like any meat?" the Andrea on the left asked.

"You're beautiful!" gushed the Andrea on the right.

Gaia stared at the pair for a second and then laughed.

"Uhm... I would, yes. Thank you. Many of

my creatures eat only meat, many eat only plants, I'm of both," murmured Gaia. "And thank you. I'm afraid I'm greatly diminished compared to my youth."

"That's okay! If you were any prettier Felix would fall in love with you," declared the left Andrea.

"Too pretty," agreed the right Andrea, holding her arms up in an X in front of herself. "Must remain as you are, even if Felix could actually fix you."

They quickly filled her plate, left her with a cup of water as well as apple juice, then scurried off.

Gaia looked unsure, though excited, and picked up some of her food. Then she realized Felix was still watching.

"Oh, you really are looking at me. With curiosity and longing no less. She wasn't wrong," she murmured aloud. Almost as if she weren't used to speaking. As if her thoughts were no different than words. "You may proceed, Felix Otherworlder."

Felix looked to Faith.

"We have a surplus of points to work with after the prison," Felix said, wanting to get straight into it. "I'd like to review where we are with everything, then to see where we can move ahead. Where we want to direct this windfall of sorts."

"Ah, that makes sense. I wasn't honestly sure when I scheduled the meeting what you'd want, but

I thought it'd be that." Faith shared. "We Dryads are fine. We've been working on getting a number of fields ready so that we can maintain our own food reserves.

"We'll be ready by next year and should be self-sufficient. We've also been making a number of below ground fields and farms. Those should be easier to maintain, but it will be the year after next before they're ready."

Faith turned and looked to Andrea on her left.

"The A-Net is building the command-center. We'll be finished just outside seven or eight months with the earthwork. After that, we'll need to purchase materials or have you put them in, Felix," Second Andrea explained, spreading her hands out in front of herself. "We'll do what we can without relying on points and what we can scrounge up, but at some point we'll need to invest.

"Money, points, or both. Whichever would work best for you. In the meantime we're trying to organize extra trash drops into the landfill. We're earmarking the loads as they come in to off-set our budget."

"Good thinking," Felix approved with a nod of his head. "I want the A-Net up and running so… that's definitely at the front of the line so far. Part of my long-term plans is to connect the HQ with the Association base, as well as the under-ground prison base.

"We'll have Tribune at all three facilities and in one form, rather than multiple versions of herself.

Having the A-Net ready for that connection would be ideal."

Andrea nodded her head quickly.

"Nn, nn, we thought that'd be it!" she said excitedly, tilting her head to one side. "We're using multiple teams to dig dig dig. Just like the old days.

"We've made a lot of progress and were advancing toward one another from both sides. It's a bit of a race to see who can get more done! I'm in team 'Felix is best on top'.

"Prime is on team 'Felix is best behind us', but I'm pretty sure she's going to lose. We've been motivating ourselves with all those home-made videos we've been recording! We got them all before Prime could, and so now, she doesn't have them."

Blinking several times, Felix only nodded his head.

Just barely.

"We'll wait to connect the Association's tunnel to the HQ before we begin the prison route," mused Andrea. "We were trying to not expand too far under the Association since we figured you'd want an underground and hidden side to it."

"I do, thank you," concurred Felix.

"Great! Nnn... I think that's everything," Andrea said with snap of her fingers. Then she looked to her left.

It was someone Felix didn't know. Likely a department head put in place by Faith so that things could keep going.

Each person shook their head, then looked left. No one had anything to add it seemed.

This continued until it reached Miu.

"Security is being settled efficiently, though we're not getting it done very quickly," stated Miu. "Force recruitment is going slow but we're being very careful with who we pick up. I've been targeting vets, ex-security forces, anyone that wouldn't need as much training or are already used to some of the work.

"It's been a mixed bag as far as results go. A number of them have views that make them inadequate candidates for our needs. Some are great and would be ideal, if it wasn't for trauma suffered."

"Mental, physical, or both?" Felix asked. He had an idea of how he could probably approach that, but it'd likely be point intensive.

"Both," Miu affirmed. "Yes, having you create a medical wing that could assist with physical injuries as well as mental hardships would help.

"It might even allow us to earn a great deal of loyalty from them for hiring on. That'd be why I brought it up. I'd like to put in a request for a medical wing as a priority.

"We'll need it for ourselves, but we could also use it as a means of recruitment. Secondary to that, we can patent that technology and see about selling some lesser-forms of it to hospitals and the like. That way we can get people to be more aware of Legion technology at the same time."

"Huh... great idea, Miu. I'll have to look into that and see what the costs are. I'm not sure where this world is technology-wise, so it might be a bit too much," thought Felix aloud. "Might get cheaper the closer we get to the day of Awakening, too. We'll just have to wait and see, but we can at least start looking into it now."

"That's all I had," Miu reported.

"I personally have nothing I haven't started," Felix offered, then looked to his left to Goldie.

"Lady Gaia has assisted me in locating a number of Dragon remains. I'll be taking some time out to go collect them and bring them back. Once I have them in my possession, I'll be working with lady Gaia to see if they're willing to live again.

"Many may just wish to remain in the afterlife. Unfortunately, that's where it ends with me as far as the bodies go. Beyond that, my little garden is growing quite well!

"I have some herbs and things that are looking splendid. I can't wait to see what flowers bloom next year. I plan on cutting some and displaying them around the house.

"I also had time to really get into the bathroom and get some of those hard water stains out. If you don't mind, please use the little handheld squeegee I left in there to get the water off the glass.

"Also... Andie... do I even need to say anything young woman? You know better."

Andrea had blanched, looked down to the

table, and was steadfastly pretending to not exist. She quickly shook her head side to side once it was obvious Goldie was going to wait for her to respond.

"Uhm… other than that, everything is great!" Goldie reported with a bright smile. "Though, I would like a vault at some point, Nest-mate. It'd be nice to have a place for our gold to remain. Not to mention, you've said before that gold is an excellent source to hold and keep points in."

That was back when I had to spend points every day, my dear Golden One. Though I'll consider it, if only because I know what you're actually asking.

That and I always want to see you smile.

Goldie grinned at him and gave her head a little shake. Making her bridal-gold jingle, looking incredibly cute and bashful at the same time.

"That's all," the Dragon said demurely, almost unable to meet his eyes.

Moving around the table, they made it quickly to Jay.

"Uh, I have everything you asked for," Jay reported, closing his laptop and looking to Felix. "It's all… well… it's buggy as fuck and jank to boot. But it's what you asked for.

"Most of my guys are just looking to get everything up and running to a minimal point so you can… do that thing you do.

"Nothing to really report or do otherwise. Did you want to look at any of it?"

"No, it'll be fine. Thanks," Felix said.

Jay nodded his head, looked confused and then slowly looked to the person next to him.

It proceeded again until it made it to Gaia.

"Ah? Is it my turn?" asked the beautiful woman with a smile. Her eyes moved to Felix and held tight to him. The bright-red glow had faded to pinpricks, thankfully.

He'd also noticed throughout the meeting that her eyes changed color. Starting from a dark-black, moving through green, to blue, then astonishingly to yellow, then back to dark-black.

"Oh… he's looking at me with longing again. I need to do something. I should leave I suppose," Gaia said with a nervous look on her face.

"Lady Gaia, you're speaking your thoughts," Faith advised, leaning over and speaking in a louder than needed voice. "Try to put your words into your head, without speaking them aloud."

"Drat," pouted Gaia who then let out a laugh. "I'm sorry everyone. It's been a very long time since I had a physical body. I'm not quite used to it. I was asleep for so long."

"It's quite alright," Felix said and held up his hands in a neutral gesture. "Please… continue."

Gaia nodded her head quickly.

"I'd really like you to invest some technology and time into healing me," Gaia said and laid a hand to her impressive bosom. "I need you to rescue me. Or at least, help me to get well. There are many harms upon me that I'd like to see addressed.

"Humanity is my child. I birthed them and coddled them. Gave them all they could want for. In their growth they've harmed me, and while they've just started to understand that and work toward rectifying it, I'd rather not wait if I don't have to."

Felix could certainly understand her reasoning. It made sense to him.

Thinking on it, Felix could imagine several ways of possibly working to help with the issue.

"What damage did you want to go for first? What part of you needs help the most?" he asked, looking at her with curiosity.

"Mm... I think... the air would be best for everyone if it were cleaner," Gaia spoke as if working very slowly through her thoughts. "There are several locations that truly need help to clean them. Especially that very dirty spot that's still on fire. It'd be great if you could handle that.

"Maybe install an ocean facility to start cleaning the trash out of it? That would also be quite lovely. Beyond that... I think the best thing for me... what'd really help me the most, is trees. Lots and lots of trees. I'd gain a significant boost to my vitality if you could do that."

"Trees... trees I can do. With gusto," promised Felix.

It was the truth, too.

Seeds were owned by anyone who collected them. He could easily modify tree-seeds to become something else entirely.

To grow rapidly and take over an entire area,

if only to devote it to Gaia.

Though… a dirty spot that's still on fire? I wonder what that is.

"On Fire? Err… do you mean Chernobyl?" Jay asked, looking at Gaia.

Chernobyl? The hell is that?

Chapter 16 – Put Out -

Felix had been surprised to find out what Chernobyl was.

Or more accurately, had been. It was now no more than a shadow of what it had been at its peak. Now it was a warning.

A shade that lurked in the corners, telling everyone to mind themselves and nuclear energy. That science was an awesome thing, but a lack of respect, or even a single mistake, was enough to possibly doom an entire continent.

"Yes, this is it," Gaia said. Looking out the window of the helicopter. Staring down at the large and impressive cylinder-like structure lodged onto the side of a building, Felix felt odd. "It's in there. Ever burning. It doesn't ache as badly as it once did, but it still hurts."

"Well… we're here to fix it," Felix murmured.

With him were Carlotta and Alma.

Goldie, Miu, and Faith were all working on things back home.

Especially the technology contracts that Felix wanted put together.

They'd decided in the end to move forward with the medical wing and the technology needed for it. In addition to that, they were moving with machines and tech to start undoing a lot of the damage done to the environment.

Those were both publicly facing and

outwardly "good" things that would benefit many people. Not just the country, Legion, or the rich.

Didn't hurt that Gaia was paying for the environmental ones with her own points.

Taking that direction in mind, they'd reached out to the government and asked if they could set up an appointment with those who owned, operated, and were in charge of the Chernobyl nuclear plant.

The offer was simple, Legion would be happy to eliminate the radiation, all the radiated materials, and do it for a nominal cost. Felix had of course stipulated that the contract would be between Legion and the government in charge of Chernobyl, not between the two countries.

"Thank you, Felix Otherworlder," Gaia said, turning around in her seat to look at him. They'd managed to fit her into Goldie's armor reasonably well. She wasn't going to need it since she'd be working on paperwork.

"I… of course, lady Gaia," Felix replied.

"Oh dear, oh dear. He's not calling me auntie anymore. He really is thinking of me as a woman," whispered Gaia.

"Lady Gaia, you're speaking your thoughts," warned Carlotta.

"I-I-I! Yes! Yes, thank you, Carlotta," squeaked Gaia. "This is so confusing. Why does being physical change so many things? I always feel so funny, too."

"L-lady Gaia… thoughts," Alma reminded

her.

"Yes!" Gaia said then went silent.

Grinning inside his helmet, Felix shook his head and looked back out the window.

"We're going to land," reported the pilot. "The hand-off ceremony will be brief, they'll hand you a small gold plaque, and then you can complete the clean-up.

"I expect they'll be monitoring the radioactivity the entire time."

None of that's a problem.

Perfectly within expectations.

"Lots of... lots of reporters," Alma murmured.

"To be fair it's kind of a massive thing. Doing what we've claimed is going to really put Legion on the map," Felix offered as an answer. "Especially if we do this as a neutral party. A non-political one that has no boundaries or borders.

"We'll likely get requests to clear land-mine fields. Maybe to empty toxic waste problems, environmental disasters, clean polluted and unusable resources. Lots of requests."

"Please. To all of those. I'd... please make me whole," pleaded Gaia as the helicopter began to descend.

"That's part of the plan. No one will be able to look at Legion without a good spot in their heart for us if all we do is go around helping out," Felix promised. "Doing it at the cost of transport, some funding for our time, and keeping the materials we pull… it'll make it so everyone wants to request us.

"I'll just have to use some of these points to give someone the power to… convert things to points on my behalf. Not that they can do it themselves, but just do it for me. Probably keep the costs down."

"Landing," reported the pilot as they started to descend rapidly. Almost touching down a bit roughly with how fast it happened.

Not waiting, Felix pushed open the door and exited. He didn't have time to waste nor the luxury of patience.

This was a risk of sorts, and he didn't want to push his luck. The longer he was in the field like this, the stronger the possibility of it turning into a type of ambush.

Realistically, a second reason for him granting someone the ability to take points on his behalf was to prevent him being at risk.

One of Edmund's friends maybe? They've become rather reliable as of late. Him and his whole group are actually rather useful.

Waiting for him was a group of people all spread out in a semi-circle. Clearly politicians, and likely the leader of the nation they were in.

Beyond that were a great many police barricades and barriers. Military and police were at it, keeping everyone back and minding the line.

There were more than a few people who had what looked like devices to record the current level of radioactive activity. Felix wasn't sure how they were read or used, but he imagined that they'd be looking to see a rapid drop.

Felix hadn't learned the name of the device, anyone involved, or even really cared. This was a means to an end, and it wouldn't do him any good to learn any of it.

The less politically charged Legion could be, the better. It'd create a lot fewer concerns down the road by and large.

A man stepped out in front of all the rest. He had a winning smile, dark brown eyes, and black hair. He wasn't that tall and seemed to be just under the average height.

Looking to be early middle aged, he still had life in himself.

Shaking Felix's gauntleted hand quickly, the man made a comment that sounded a bit like a joke. More so since everyone around laughed good naturedly.

"I'm sorry, I don't speak the language, but I'm quite pleased to be here to help," Felix returned in English.

The man laughed and then shook his head quickly.

"I said if only had suit like yours, then maybe sleep better," the man offered with a grave air. His accent was quite clearly Russian, though it wasn't too pronounced.

Felix could only nod his head at that. He knew that much of Europe was in a very tense state of affairs over the last handful of years. They'd been locked in a number of different crises that never seemed to end for them.

"More to keep my identity secret than anything else," Felix countered. He did like the man from the get-go, despite really not wanting to.

"Ah, yes. I can understand that," the man answered, then turned to someone else. He took a small item from them. It was a simple wooden plaque with a golden face to it.

On it was a globe with the helmeted icon of Legion behind it.

Ha… I like it. We'll have to use it for our global outreach program.

"And… that is that?" asked the man as Felix took the plaque.

"Is everyone outside of… there?" Felix asked, holding onto the plaque with one hand, gesturing to the large steel tomb-like structure with the other. "And have you removed everything you would want to keep from inside it or the grounds surrounding us?"

"Ah…" stalled the man looking to several others. Someone said something in the same language as earlier, to which two others responded. Then they all looked back to their leader. "Yes. All clear. Is good. Take it all."

All around at the barriers surrounding them, news crews were reporting the events while simultaneously recording the situation.

Felix nodded his head and then made a grasping movement with his hand, completely for show and those watching. For the cameras, to be more accurate.

Let's just take everything inside that structure like he said. Just focusing entirely on everything that's radioactive.

Leave everything else.

So… we'll use our power in conjunction with that.

Let's spend some points out of what we're taking to make sure we don't take anything that would cause an issue. Nothing that would weaken, damage, or destroy the structure.

We'll replace anything we take with non-irradiated materials if it would cause a problem.

In other words… a replacement while scrubbing it clean.

At the same time, let's take that massive structure around it. Get rid of all the shielding and use it as materials and points.

They won't need it after this anyways.

We'll also take all the radioactive materials from the dirt, trees, animals, air, everything inside of the "exclusion zone" as they called it.

Replace it all with clean and correct bits and pieces, since we temporarily own everything here. No sense in leaving it a ruin.

Maybe it'll help them in the long run, too.

There was a hitch Felix felt in the world.

Then, in the next moment, the massive structure was gone. The entirety of the building shifted momentarily and then rematerialized itself.

Felix wasn't sure of the differences since he'd

never seen any of this before today, but in his mind, he imagined this was how it should look if there'd never been an issue.

All around them the world had stuttered for a breath. The very earth flashing into a different color.

"All done," Felix said looking back to the leader.

He was standing next to someone with one of the devices, staring into its display. Looking up to Felix somewhat wide-eyed he then looked back to the plant.

"You fixed?" he asked in a shocked voice.

"Yes. I'm a builder. I build things. I needed somewhere to use all the materials I took away," explained Felix.

The man laughed suddenly at that, looking at the distant building. Then he slowly shook his head in disbelief. Then he turned and looked at the areas around him and froze.

Turning, Felix looked back in the same direction the man was looking.

Distantly, he could see several buildings on the horizon. They seemed quite well built to be standing as they were if they'd been abandoned this long.

"You fixed?" the man asked again, still looking at the distant building.

Felix frowned then realized what he asked.

I didn't… specifically say not to fix everything over there, did I? Huh.

Ah well.

"I'm a builder," Felix murmured. It was the best answer he could give. He didn't want to admit he'd done it on accident.

Reporters began rushing towards vehicles that'd been parked nearby. Apparently, they wanted to go film elsewhere, or needed something inside the vehicles.

Everyone began shouting in different languages as all the leaders of this country ran toward him and began congratulating him.

***

"We're here," Alma said, shaking his shoulder, waking Felix up.

Blinking, Felix felt rather strange.

He'd fallen asleep in his Legate armor, with the helmet on, wedged up against the interior wall of the Legion truck. It wasn't something he'd intended to do, but he'd gotten bored listening to the Dryads chatter with Gaia.

That and once again he hadn't slept much.

The trip to Europe, then back, had been non-stop. Filled with reporters, heads-of-state phone calls, and doing his best to respond to everything. All in a "Legion is neutral" standpoint and willing to help anyone.

Though he'd apologized many times in advance, as he'd be forced to "triage" situations. That he'd have to pick and choose who to help and when so that the most needed assistance would go first.

All that really meant was Gaia would be picking what she wanted to tackle first. She was funding the vehicles that'd be fixing the environment directly, so she got to pick where they went.

"Protesters," remarked Carlotta. "Can I punch'em?"

"No, you can't punch them," growled Felix, coming out of the sleep addled fog. Sitting up more, he stood up.

Or tried to. He ended up rebounding against the seat-belt.

Undoing it, he stood up and quickly moved to the back of the vehicle. The last thing he wanted to deal with was protesters.

They'd do nothing to help him in his goal to keep Legion neutral and would only cause him problems. Which meant he needed to nip this in the bud and make it a problem for them.

Time to push the fact that this is private property. Not government property.

The building might be the Association's, but it's owned by Legion through a lease agreement to the Association. As are the facilities, which are of course Legion's, too.

Felix was marching straight to the group of people standing in front of the association. They had picket signs, were chanting, and generally looked hostile.

Reaching the entrance, Felix found a man that was at least six and a half feet tall stepping in front of him.

"You have no right to —"

"This is private property. I own it," Felix stated, ignoring the man's words. "I'm revoking your right to be here indefinitely. Going forward, you're not welcome here without a pass from the Association.

"As far as your protest goes, I had nothing to do with what your government did to you, or the legislation they passed. That was all done by them, and I had no input in it whatsoever.

"In fact, I was as surprised as you all were when it was put into law. Now… get off my land, or I'll have you escorted off."

"You can't do that!" screamed someone in the crowd.

"How about you got ahead and make me manlet because —"

The man's words were punctuated with jabbing a finger into Felix's armored chest.

Felix snatched the man's wrist with his wright hand. Jerking it to the right, he wrenched the man's shoulder up while bending his arm down and back.

Pulling it up behind the man's back, Felix snapped a kick out at the back of the mans' knee. Sending him crashing down into a kneeling position.

Moving forward, Felix slammed the man into

the ground and then planted his knee right in the middle of the man's back.

Careful, careful now. Have to make sure we don't actually harm him.

Leaning into him, he put down more than enough force to start squeezing the breath out of the man, but Felix could still hear the man breathing.

"You will all disperse immediately, or you'll also be placed under citizen's arrest. You have five minutes to comply if you begin moving immediately. Ten seconds if you hold still," Felix commanded. "By the way, my property runs all the way to the freeway off ramp. This parking lot, the street running up to it, and all the way to the off ramp.

"All mine. You're welcome to protest anywhere that isn't my land, since it's public property at that point. Otherwise... well... you can be arrested for trespassing by me, then wait for the police to show up."

Felix listened intently to make sure the man on the ground was still breathing, which he was, and remained in his kneeling position. He had to make sure he only used the minimum amount of force necessary for a citizen's arrest.

A number of people began shouting and one even moved toward Felix.

Alma quickly intercepted the woman and brought her down to the ground in a very similar way to how Felix had done it.

By this point, more Legionnaires were

streaming out of the building. All of them in armor. Quite a few were armed with firearms and others had unholstered batons.

"Five seconds!" Felix called. "Five, four, three—"

A number of people began scurrying toward the parking lot. Likely to their vehicles. Others remained stationary.

"Two, One," Felix finished. "Arrest everyone who's still here, anyone who's on the way to their car can leave."

The Legionnaires began snatching up protesters. Dragging them to the ground and pulling zip-ties out.

Huh, hadn't thought of that. That's pretty smart. We'll need to make sure we put zip-tie cuffs as part of our standard security equipment. It isn't like they weigh a lot.

"Move over, deaaaaaaar," asked an Andrea who was now moving over the top of the man Felix had subdued.

Quite a few more people were now sprinting away from the dust-up. As soon as more people started being arrested, the rest of them got the hint that no-one was playing the game they wanted.

Felix got off the man and stood up. Andrea snatched up the man's hands and slipped the zip ties over them. Jerking them tight, she pulled his wrists together.

"Ow," whined the man. "You're hurting me. Get off me. You have no right—"

Ignoring him, Felix turned and looked to the

building, then down the road.

"Tribune, are you active?" Felix asked.

"Yes, Legate," answered the VI.

"I want plans to build a wall surrounding our property. Routers, sensors, and appropriate monitoring equipment all the way around. Put together blueprints for it based on what'd be the most cost-efficient, but which also will provide as much security as we'd actually need.

"I want it effective, not cheap. Do you have any questions or anything I need to clarify for you?"

"No, Legate. I have all the appropriate programs to make that happen," Tribune answered. "Legionnaire Jay has begun pushing my communication heuristic program. You had no other directives for him to work on and he checked into the programming wish list."

With a grunt, Felix turned and looked to Gaia. Or at least, who he thought was Gaia.

The way she was carrying herself made her look like a woman out on a stroll without a care in the world.

"Lady Gaia, can we go discuss next steps in my office?" Felix asked.

"Of course," came an answer with a head nod from the Legionnaire he'd been addressing.

I'm over this. I hate not being able to identify anyone.

Need to upgrade the Helmets so that they can use the headsets in them to identify who's who and push it to the visor in a HUD-like thing.

Somewhat like we did with the Fist.

Turning, Felix opened the door of the Association building and went inside. He didn't hesitate and went to the back, moving through the lobby and to the elevator.

"Felix, good timing," came Faith's voice over his coms. "Got a number of requests to meet with you. All for cleanup and restoration.

"Some of them sound like company issues, others are government made. An example, before you ask, of a company one, is someone failed to treat a water supply correctly. Now an entire community has polluted water and can't drink any of it without risk. It apparently catches fire."

Frowning, Felix looked to Gaia who'd entered the elevator next to him. He tapped the button to go to the floor his office was on.

"Is that an issue for you we should resolve, or is that more of a 'non-issue' since it doesn't actually help you," Felix inquired. "I'm prioritizing your health first and foremost."

"Oh... no... he's putting me ahead of others. That's not good. He looks at me far too often. He's even looked at my body and —"

"Gaia," Felix prompted. "You're speaking your thoughts."

"Eeeehn," moaned Gaia. "This is very difficult. While it's fun to be corporeal, I'm not sure I enjoy it as much as I thought I would."

"I mean... I'm surprised you never left," Felix admitted with a shrug of his shoulders.

"You're welcome to stay of course. I'm inviting you to remain permanently with Legion, in fact. I'm just... surprised."

"I should have left a while ago, but the cost isn't that bad," Gaia said with a wave of her hand. "In fact, as a part of Legion, I receive quite a bit of faith somehow!

"I'm growing stronger by the day you know. It's all quite lovely. Surprising, even."

Felix felt his brows draw down as the elevator door opened. Thinking, he led Gaia down the hall to his office.

"I'll get back to them, Faith," Felix grumbled. "Summarize it all and send it to me."

"Andrea will do it. She's your assistant, not me. I just wanted to make sure you knew. That and say hi," replied Faith. "You have a meeting with some head honchos from the government in the capital in a few hours. They're sending a helicopter."

Snorting, Felix opened his office door and pried off his helmet. He set it down on his desk and walked over to the armor stand.

It was in that moment that he realized what'd happened with Gaia.

Damnit. I never got rid of the faith goes to gods, clause.

Everyone's faith in me, on this world, is going to Gaia.

Back home it's... I have no idea where it's going, actually. Probably going somewhere though. I'll have to look at that when I get home.

Turning, he looked to Gaia to explain what was happening.

Looking like a woman in her late twenties, Gaia was breathtaking. Her natural good looks and ever-present warm smile gave her a welcoming and graceful look.

"Mmm? Is there an issue?" she asked sounding curious, her head tilting to one side.

"You ah... you got younger," Felix muttered and went back to his armor stand. He stared at it, rather than staring at Gaia.

"I mean... I don't think you understand how much power I'm gaining from Legion. Let alone what you did for me with the... plant... thing... place," Gaia said with a joyful laugh. "Ooh... oh, now he's going to find it even harder to be around me. I knew I shouldn't have modeled myself after Goldie.

"This body is far too much. But if I dispose of it, I'd lose all the power I gained. I'll just have to make sure he doesn't fall in love with me, that's all. It'll be fine."

Felix ignored all that and cleared his throat.

"Feeeeeeeeeeeeeeelix!" squealed Andrea a second before she blasted into him. Knocking him away from the stand, off the wall, and to the ground.

She then began to pepper his face in kisses.

"I missed you! Missed you so much!" declared Andrea Prime. "I'm not leaving your side anymore! I hate it. Hate being away. We're going to be together forever.

"I have a security team just for you. We're always going to be with you now. You need to spend some points to give me more Others as well! I want twenty more so we can dig lots and also protect you.

"And if you're willing, nnnnn, I want a hundred more after that. An entire army of me. I'm so much stronger and smarter now that I can handle it all."

Andrea had slammed her head down into his jaw and began rubbing her face against his jaw and chin. Even as she spoke, she continued to do it.

"Nn, nn, nnnnnnn, nnnnn!"

"That's so cute," Gaia said quietly. "I wonder if I could do that. I'm a woman, so I should be able to.

"I just need to find a man that I like. Lots of men in the world. I should do the dating thing they told me about."

Chapter 17 - Duties -

Getting out of the helicopter, two Andreas slammed down a trunk that they'd forced the pilot to bring with them. Then they got the second one that they'd also forced him to bring.

Two more Andreas popped out of the other two in basic clothes. Then two more. They also had their ears and tails hidden from view.

Though realistically, that little secret was long since exposed.

Gaia got out of the helicopter as well and then came to stand next to Felix.

While he hadn't agreed to her being here at first, he'd relented after a while. Faith, Alma, and Carlotta had all requested that he let her join him. If only because the government was likely going to ask him to clean something up ahead of everyone else.

"They're so fun," Gaia said, watching the Andreas work. "I know they're not my children, but I really do love just watching them. Such a… such a love of life!"

Staring at the armor-covered Gaia, Felix was suddenly curious.

He wanted to see what her character sheet looked like.

Name: Gaia	Race: DEITY
Alias: Gaia (Over 50 items. Click to expand.)	Power: Unknowable

Physical Status: Ill.		Mental Status: Excited, Determined.
Positive Statuses: Recovering.		Negative Statuses: Ailing, Polluted, Toxic.
Might:	784	Add +1? (7,840)
Finesse:	35	Add +1? (350)
Endurance:	984,137,245	Add +1? (9,841,372,450)
Competency:	17	Add +1? (170)
Intellect:	12	Add +1? (120)
Perception:	10	Add +1? (100)
Luck:	10	Add +1? (100)

I… right.

Right.

I called up a goddess and somehow forgot that… she's… you know… a goddess.

Literally the oldest being possible in this entire existence so long as Ryker or Runner don't come calling. Nothing older than her in any way.

Fuck.

Fuck. Fuck!

She could tear Goldie's head off and make a flower vase out of it if she wanted to.

If I owned her, I could just take a single point away from her Endurance and I'd have more points that I'd know what to do with.

He needed to make sure he kept Gaia on his side at all times.

"Do you know Runner, or Ryker, by the

way?" Felix asked in a neutral tone as the now ten Andreas rapidly pulled out and sorted gear from the large crates.

Legionnaire armor for all of them, along with a simple SMG like weapon and multiple magazines. The helmets had taken up a lot of space so most of what they'd packed had been stuffed into them.

"You mean the Architect and the Originator, right? Yes. They're my parents," Gaia admitted with a soft laugh and a wave of her hand. "They're quite nice and fun. I haven't been able to talk to them in quite a while. Being as busy as they are and all.

"Why, have you met them before? Oh! That's why you're here, isn't it? I bet it was Uncle. Uncle always does things like that.

"Though... hmm... oh... I wonder if he did this just to have Felix fall into my life like that. That's just like him, too. To do it thinking he's doing what's best for me. Thinking I'd fall in love with Felix and he'd fall for me. I mean... it seems easy to do, but really.

"Darn it. Phooey. Uncle, I'm going to have to really let you know this time. You can't just... push things around like that."

Felix ignored Gaia's spoken thoughts.

Everyone had taken to ignoring them.

It didn't seem that the poor goddess was going to be able to completely eliminate her inability to corral her thoughts. Felix thought it was a lot like she didn't have an internal monologue.

He couldn't help but be amused by her fairly child-like word usage, and that she always seemed to be upbeat. Her in-person persona didn't seem to have the same grave and fiery anger-filled air that her spiritual self did.

"I'm not your aunt," Gaia murmured with a bit more gravitas than her words had held previously. "I have no relation to you, Felix Otherworlder."

Shit.

She brought that up just to distance any 'familial' relation between us, didn't she?

Dressed in Legionnaire armor, armed, and ready, the Andreas fell into formation in front of Felix. At their front was Andrea Prime.

She apparently was unwilling to take a back-seat anymore for her own safety.

"Ready, the transport I booked should be just outside of the airfield," Andrea reported. "We'll be moving into three SUVs and proceeding to the meeting from there.

"I still think it is rather foolish to go see them in person when we could have done it over the phone. Or by email, really."

"They're terrified of the people at the moment. Anything that could be recorded or printed out later is an issue," muttered Felix. "Lead the way, Andrea, dear. I'll be right behind you."

"Just where you should be," said one of the Andreas.

That got a chuckle from all of them.

Even Gaia.

***

"Light change, deliberate hold," announced one of the Andreas.

The driver of his SUV began to push the brakes down and likely the one behind them did as well. All three SUVs pulled to a full stop at the yellow light rather than rushing through it.

Felix was staring out the window and watching people go about their lives. It didn't seem from the outside like anything had actually changed for them as far as he could tell.

Supers being a part of their world was as common now as cars had become. Things were being adapted to far too quickly, and have an overwhelming amount of media to familiarize themselves with.

Someone can just as easily go watch forty some odd videos of the Supers that've been spotted around the world, as they can watch some sports ball game.

As on demand as a TV show that they can binge from start to finish without stop.

I wonder how much that leads into people finding things acceptable when they really shouldn't be.

"Oh, well, he's rather big isn't he?" Gaia murmured.

Turning, Felix looked out the window Gaia was seated at. Not far away was indeed quite a large man. He easily stood at seven feet tall and was wide enough to look like he should be playing in some sports ball league.

The man laughed, turned, and then smashed in the front door he'd been standing in front of. Knocking it to pieces and sending it crashing inward. Six or seven people in masks rushed in as the large man started fumbling with one of his own.

"What the hell?" Felix mumbled aloud.

"Not our problem," one of the Andreas helpfully provided.

"It isn't… no. We're not the police but… we are Legion. We're responsible for undocumented Supers," Felix countered. "It's why we inspected those businesses even though we didn't want to.

"In the future I plan to use that little loophole against them. We're not a club they can use just to slam businesses with. We only have to make sure people understand we're after Supers that aren't documented.

"If they're documented, we don't care anymore. Villains are the problem of the Heroes and vice versa, not ours."

"What… do you want us to do then?" asked an Andrea.

"Pull over to the side, we'll watch for now. See if we need to step in. There's no way they're going to just take what they can and leave," Felix commanded. "They're going to try to smash their way into the vault. Likely with that big brute in the front.

"I'm betting he's an undocumented Super.

One with a power that activated early because it's simple and hard to screw up."

"It's still a wonder to me how quickly all this is happening," Gaia mused. "Much faster than I originally thought it would when I agreed to it."

Note... note to self.

Pump Gaia for information.

Need to get her alone and start asking her more questions than there would be in a freshmen Philosophy class. This is ridiculous!

"Ugh, they're completely screwing this up," Andrea growled. "In, get everything that you can get at the windows, whatever your targets are, then get out.

"You either go in when the vault is open, or not at all. The longer you sit there, the more likely you are to run into the police."

"You did this often, Andrea?" Gaia asked.

"Uhm... yeah. I was a baddie for a long time," confessed Andrea with a guilty chuckle. "I was good at it though."

"Theft is just another facet of life," Gaia retorted. "One doesn't blame the hyena for stealing from the lion, or if the lion caught and ate a hyena.

"Nor can one truly fault the seagull for swooping in and taking your hotdog. That's just how it is. Humanity in its quest to make things stable has become quite... civilized. Soft."

Hm. I guess... she's right, isn't she?

Mother nature isn't kind, caring, or forgiving. It's all a battle royale to the end of the road and then beyond.

There's very little in the middle ground.

" — took it from me! So I caught it, killed it, and ate it," declared Andrea, to which Gaia laughed. "Best stupid bird I've ever eaten."

Two people came out of the bank then. They both looked like they knew how to use the weapons they were holding.

"Subdue them all so we can confirm if they're supers," Felix requested. "If they're not, they're not our problem."

"Hoi!" called all the Andreas who then began filing out of the vehicles.

Gaia did as well.

"Wait, Gaia I—"

Grunting as the door shut behind her, Felix unbuckled his seat-belt and got out of the SUV as well. Coming around the back of it, he watched as the Andreas began moving in on the two at the front of the bank. They had their guns up but weren't firing.

The Andreas hadn't even shouldered their weapons. They were just moving toward the bank-robbers.

"We're from Legion. We're only here to confirm that none of you are unregistered Supers," an Andrea said from the collective. "If you're not a Super, you'll be released. We have no jurisdiction over normal people."

The two men looked at the Andreas, to one another, then back to the Andreas.

Felix did a quick check on both of them and

found they were unpowered and normal.

"Normals," he reported over the com.

"You can go," an Andrea announced.

Taking off at a dead sprint, the two men didn't hesitate. They took off running and never looked back.

Four more came out, along with the hulking brute of a man.

Felix flicked over them and found there were three amongst them that were Supers. If they'd gone to the Association, they'd have an identification card.

If they didn't, they were his problem.

"The big one, the woman in the back, and the man to the side are all Supers," Felix called.

"You, you, and you. You need to remain where you are and —"

With his head down and moving like a steamroller, the big man went right through the Andrea at the front. Then another behind her. The other Andreas raised their weapons and moved in on the other two Supers.

They hadn't moved and were quickly surrendering. Those who weren't Supers were now fleeing away from the bank. The bags on their backs thumping as they went.

Snatching at an Andrea, the big man caught only air. The Beastkin had been faster, dancing to one side while slamming an armored kick into the man's knee.

A thud was the only response she got from

him or his body. As if she'd kicked a tree stump for all the good it did her.

Even as the man oriented on her, several other Andreas got behind him and slammed fists, kicks, and a small baton into his back and sides.

They were all to almost no effect, bouncing off him and causing no damage in any way.

I fucked up. I should have brought someone who can take a power-house down. I keep thinking of this in the wrong way. Thinking of it backwards.

I'm not the power here, I'm the one that can guide it and direct it.

Need to make sure I bring someone who can take each type of Super with me in the future.

Same problem as ever. Trying to do too much all by myself.

Need to get the department heads firmly in place. Soon. Real soon.

"Hey, lunk-head. Wanna come give me a hug?" Felix asked, stepping away from Gaia, the SUVs, and moving toward the center of the area. He needed a bit of room to give the Andreas time to whittle the man down.

While he likely wasn't showing any outward concern to this situation, he probably only had the strength of his body, and his own weight, behind him.

In other words, at some point there'd be enough Andreas hanging onto him to bring him down to the ground. Felix just had to get an opportunity for them to do so.

Roaring, the big man put his head down and rushed toward Felix. His arms were wide, like he was going to grab Felix up in a hug once he reached him.

Unbelievably, Gaia stepped out in front of Felix.

She laid her hand out and caught the man on the brow. Bringing him to a sudden and absolute stop.

So complete was it, that the man's legs kept going and he ended up slipping, tumbling to the ground and ending up at Gaia's feet. She let her hand fall down and looked to the man.

"Dear me, you should be more careful. I think perhaps that maybe you should —"

With another mighty shout, the man stood up and grabbed Gaia. Holding her around the rear end, he pushed himself to a standing position and hurled her into the air.

Or tried to.

Gaia went nowhere, and all the man succeeded in doing was throwing everything into a back-throw that did absolutely nothing.

"Oh, oh, that looks painful," worried the God. "I think you might have really hurt yourself. It'd be best if you left it at that. Right?

"The Legate here really just wants to make sure you're all card-carrying members of the Association. He doesn't care if you're a villain or not."

Groaning, the man had fallen down to his

hands and knees. Panting there, his back twitching, he looked to be in a considerable amount of pain.

"Goodness, you really did hurt something," Gaia empathized and then reached down. Patting the man on the shoulder and back. "I'm sure if you're careful with it, you'll be able to—"

Swift as could be, the man drew his arm back and slammed a punch into the center of Gaia's lower stomach. Nearly atop her genitalia in fact.

"Now that... that... is uncalled for," Gaia said, all warmth and tenderness gone from her voice. Lifting her left hand, she smacked the man on the back of the head.

Rocketing forward, it slammed down into the concrete, cracked it, and the man laid still on the ground. Snoring loudly and with absolute abandon.

"I'm sorry, Felix. I felt like this was somewhere I could step in and provide assistance," Gaia apologized, looking to him and putting her hands together in front of herself. Almost as if she were pleading with him. "Forgive your Gaia?"

"Err... no problem... thank you for stepping in. I'm not sure we could have handled him without Goldie around," Felix muttered, looking to the unconscious man. He was unmoving, still snoring, and looked to be extremely out of it.

"Thank you so much for forgiving me. Now... should we get moving?" Gaia asked and pointed back to the SUVs. "I'm hopeful that they'll let us go clean up some places.

"You mentioned... Hanford and thirty-mile

island?"

"Three... Three Mile island," corrected Felix.

"Yes! That's it. That'd be wonderful," Gaia said and clapped her hands together twice. As if she hadn't just bitch-slapped a juggernaut into the ground like he was a bitch.

"You... can wait in the car if you like, Gaia. I brought a tablet if you want to watch something while you wait," offered Felix.

"Yes! I think I'll do that. Thank you so much," Gaia agreed warmly with a bob of her head. "It's a good thing he still treats me just like normal. He's stronger mentally than I thought.

"I think most men would likely be terrified after seeing how strong I am. Then again, he tends to put a lot of attention toward Goldie, and she's very strong.

"I wonder what I can watch on the tablet. So interesting! Much better than being just a spirit."

Gaia's spoken inner thoughts carried her right to the SUV which she got into. Closing the door behind her.

"Uhm, I kinda like her," Andrea said, standing next to Felix. "Reminds me of my mom in a way.

"Err... should we wait for the authorities?"

"After we check and see if they're licensed by the Association, yes. If they're not, we'll keep them in our custody till that's settled. After that, we'll release them. If there's a law against being an undocumented Super, we'll hand them over to the police, if not… we kick'em out the door and wish'em luck.

"We're not the police. Won't ever be. Not here to work contracts for the government. Never again. Did that, won the booby prize, lost it all."

"Ha… booby," said every single Andrea.

"I like Gaia's boobies. They look fun to grab," said a different one.

"Like Goldie's. She's fun to grab!" offered another.

"Yes… yes," agreed Felix, looking to those standing nearby.

Not far away was a young woman with a phone. She had turned her back to Felix and was recording herself in front of him with the phone capturing them all.

Frowning, he considered her.

Then he wanted to know if she had a power, and he wanted to contract her, what would that power be called?

Type: Growth	Name: Rising Star! ★ ☆ ☆ ★

Hm?

Felix hummed to himself, his thoughts flickering through the possibilities.

"Is this my next Jessica? My Erica?" Felix mused to no-one.

"She's not a Beastkin," answered Andrea. "But pretty enough."

Indeed.

And looks take you miles and miles. As demonstrated by our most unfortunate commercials.

"Excuse me," Felix said walking over to the phone-holding woman.

She was a bright blue eyed, blonde haired young woman. With a delicate-looking face made for smiling and laughing.

There was no denying that she'd likely have online fans and very quickly.

"I have every right to record," stated the woman, turning her head to really look at Felix.

"I agree. However... how would you like a job? You have a power. One that I think I can unlock and then let you tap into," offered Felix. He needed to start recruiting. Much faster than he had been. "I imagine I can match any salary you might ever hope for in your current work. Maybe even more than what you could dream of.

"I'll also give you a great deal of access to Legion, the Association, and myself. Are you willing to talk to me about making a deal?"

The woman was now chewing at her lip. Her brows pressed together in deep thought. Felix was almost positive he had her more than on the hook.

And there we go.

Chapter 18 - Slowly Quickly -

Getting back into the SUV now that the meeting was over, Felix felt drained. Drained, depressed, and over-worked.

The Andreas all piled into the vehicles as well. Doors slamming shut as they all got into position.

"All done! Hooray!" cheered an Andrea.

"Felix, Felix, we bought a helicopter! We loaded the prisoners in it already!" reported another Andrea.

"Nnn! We already have plans on how to paint it up in Legion colors!" said yet another.

"Oh my, that does sound fun. I enjoy helicopter rides quite a bit," Gaia added, turning to look at Felix. She'd remained in the car while he'd gone to his meeting.

While she was rapidly adapting to being a physical being, she still seemed to be getting used to many "human" things. The tablet he'd offered hadn't left her hands since she'd picked it up.

"Yeah," Felix returned and leaned back in his seat.

"Did it go good? Good good? Bad good? Bad bad? Good bad?" asked an Andrea

"Err… we're going to be busy. Really busy. So busy that I think… for the next six months or so it's just going to be a long slog of work," answered Felix, staring up at the interior of the vehicle. "They gave me a list of all the buildings they'd like us to build, sites they want cleaned, infrastructure they'd like repaired, and a large number of other requests.

"I agreed to a number of things, provided that they can never order us to investigate anything ever again. What little over-sight they had just got removed from us. All in exchange for things we wanted to do anyways."

"Well done, Felix," Gaia said and then gently clapped her armored hands together. "Should I assume you did it all for me and my benefit?"

Wincing, he didn't want to admit that she was correct. There was a strangeness to Gaia that he very much wanted to avoid.

He felt as if she was like a volcano waiting to go off. A mountain-slide that was waiting for the right moment to let rip. An earthquake just waiting beneath the surface.

"I made the deals that were best for Legion and for me," Felix stated instead.

"What were the deals then?" asked Gaia, her helmeted head tilting to one side as the SUVs started to move.

"I… err… we have to clean out all the wastes that are negatively impacting the environment," muttered Felix. "Like Three Mile island and Hanford. As well as a few undocumented areas that are as bad or worse."

"Awww, it really was all for me," gushed Gaia, putting her hands together, placing them beside her tilted head, and then twisting toward him. "Thank you Felix. I really appreciate you going so far for me. You're my truest champion."

"Isn't he?" asked an Andrea.

"He really is! Nn nn!" a second shouted.

"Too loud! Mic break. Though, yes, he really is. Is Gaia gonna be a wife to us? Can we kiss Gaia!?" asked an excited Andrea.

"No, Gaia is just Gaia," Felix stated and meant it. "The points we'll earn for it, as well as the cash they're offering, is more than enough to justify it.

"We're just... going to be really busy. Busier than we ever have been before. On top of that, I realized something earlier. We need to refocus. I need to get all of our departments up and running.

"We can't keep running around like this and not expect things to start breaking. We're going to curtail some of our expansion plans and go back to our core. Get that up and running, and doing so smoothly.

"That'll take time. I figure... six months is about right for all of that to happen at the same time."

"Does that mean I get to run a department?" asked Gaia. She'd turned completely in her seat and was facing him now. To the point she'd clearly disengaged her seat-belt to do it. "I'm not sure I could handle that if I'm being honest, my champion. I'm happy to help however you see fit, but I don't think that'd be a good fit for me.

"You just tell me where you think you can use me and however you want to. We'll go from there. It'll be much easier!"

All the Andreas laughed at that. Clearly they'd taken her words and put them into a sexual context.

"What's so funny, dears?" asked Gaia.

"Nothing. And you're right, Gaia," Felix interjected. "You're right. I wouldn't want you to run a department. I think you'd be a great help if you could help me with the cleanup.

"I'd like to use you as a conduit. To utilize you to activate my powers without me being wherever the issue is. Where you could request an activation of my powers on my behalf."

"Hmmm? Mmmm. Oh! So you'd turn me into a washout. Instead of water, you'd run your power through me to reach the destination," clarified Gaia.

"Oh he'll run it through you," Andrea giggled insanely.

"More like a basin though, fill you up, not wash you out," another joked, causing them all to laugh again.

"I... oh! Sex jokes! Yes, I understand now. How enjoyable," Gaia said with a deep chuckle. "I'm sure he'd do his best to really stimulate growth in me, right?"

The Andreas laughed warmly at that, clearly appreciating her attempt.

"Yes, I of course accept that, champion," continued Gaia with a wave of a hand at him. "I'm sure Faith, Alma, or Carlotta can assist me in that. We can move from location to location to clean them up."

"That'd be fine. They tend to divide up whatever work they're doing anyways. The rest is going to be on me and… my mom, I guess," Felix said, looking to the back of the seat in front of him. "Finding the right people for the right positions.

"Still need to get around to bringing that Void Dragon back from the dead, too."

Six months feels like forever.

"I'm sorry, my champion, I forgot about that. She unfortunately doesn't want to be brought back anymore," apologized Gaia. "She feels like the world is far too soft and weak to handle someone like her. She's not willing to come back to it.

"To be fair, this planet has gone and forgotten just how ruthless nature really is. I think they'll all be in for a very rude awakening in the future.

"Best they do as Legion wills or I'll be forced to step in at some point. I… wonder if I'll feel the same way if I manage to start dating someone.

"Would sex take this edge off? It does for other animals, it'd probably do it for me. I'm sure it would! I'll have to think about that more in depth.

"Sex with Felix would really work out in a number of ways. I'll have to consider that deeply. Though… I'll have to guard my heart against it going further."

I… yes… don't… anger Gaia.

Just… head down, boring paper-work, nothing interesting, six months.

Don't anger Gaia.

In fact, let's just… add her to the 'don't tease the crazy people' rule.

Don't tease Gaia.

***

Reaching up, Felix rubbed his palms into his eyes.

"Sir, you need to approve payroll for this month," Tribune reminded him. Her voice was coming from the overhead PA system. She was now integrated into the building's systems directly and had access to all of it.

"Right… uh…" Felix muttered and then let his hands fall to his desk. Staring at the table's top that had a half-eaten donut, an empty coffee cup, and the remains of three different written reports, he felt somewhat lost.

I miss Felicity. I miss her… so damn much.

Not just for the fact that she kept me on task but… *I just miss her.*

I miss everyone.

I wonder how Eva's doing.

"Is there any change month over month?" Felix asked, still staring at the half-eaten donut.

"No, Legate," Tribune answered.

"Is there a projected change for next month?" he asked.

"Yes, Legate. The six-month hiring protocol ended this month. The effects will shift expected earnings next month," Tribune answered.

Shit... six months, felt like it went by in a flash. Like jumping from one line of text to another.

I've done nothing but hiring, building departments, and finishing plans I started.

"Approve it then," Felix requested.

"Sir, you have an emergency meeting request to go to the prison. The Heroes are bringing a class one prisoner and need a new cell," warned Tribune. "The train is in operation today and there are no expected interruptions to service."

Grunting, Felix got up and went to his armor storage. He'd need to get into it quickly and then get down to the basement.

"You in the prison, Tribune?" Felix asked as he got into his armor. He wasn't sure what the timeline was on her getting into both facilities, but he knew it'd just happened, or was about to.

"The possibility is now there, though the implementation hasn't been initiated," Tribune answered.

"Why not?" asked Felix. "Any reason to not implement it now?"

"Timing, Sir. There is no reason to not move ahead," answered Tribune.

"Would you recommend going live?"

"No, Legate," Tribune said quickly. "The timing is what was laid out and should be followed."

"Go live. Let Miu and Andrea know that I'm heading out," Felix ordered.

Pulling his helmet down over his head, he left his office quickly.

By the time he'd made it to the train station at the bottom of the Association, Miu and his two squads of Andrea bodyguards had joined him.

"Exciting," Andrea Prime said, leaning over to smash her helmet into Felix's neck. She tended to act like she wasn't wearing the armor.

"Yes. Yes… it is," Miu replied, her hand coming up to grab at Felix's elbow as Andrea pulled away.

"This is? Why?" Felix asked, feeling like he'd missed something. "Isn't it just a prisoner addition?"

"Goldie comes back tonight," Andrea answered. "On top of that, there's the meet-and-greet that Juno set up, that is today. I'm really looking forward to meeting so many people who want to know more."

Wincing, Felix had forgotten about that event. It was going to be happening so that they could keep pushing their agenda.

Juno, the Rising Star Super he'd found, had become just that. A popular and quickly trending personality on the internet. She'd been quick to label herself as Juno and rebrand accordingly.

Felix knew that the money they invested in her was paying off, he just hated having to play a part for her. He'd hoped that that part of his life had ended with Jessica and Erica.

"New helmets today for everyone else,"

added Miu. "My centurion helmet will be ready."

That makes sense.

They're both excited for their own things, and they're both tired. The helmets will be ready because of the meet-and-greet.

"I'm sad that all my Others won't get one, but it's nice that I will? So they can all share it with me as we go along," Andrea said as the elevator doors opened.

Moving out the two squads of armed Andreas fanned out quickly. The security checkpoint in front of them came to life as multiple Andreas on the defense spotted them coming.

As quickly as the two groups interacted with each other, the tension instantly vanished.

Felix still wasn't sure about using Andreas to take designated important security posts, but he couldn't argue the logic either. The more of Andrea there was, the less he'd have to rely on others.

He just felt bad utilizing such an important resource on something like this.

Beyond the security point was the Legion train station. There were a few Legionnaires sitting about who would likely be part of the monitoring and response team at the prison.

Others were working on an electrical box.

The train had only recently gotten up and running, and the kinks were still being worked out. There were multiple tunnels exiting in every possible direction as well. There was a dedicated terminal that was to the north-west in Colorado that was being built up in advance.

For the moment, there was only one destination from here.

Boarding the train Felix wasn't really sure when it was scheduled to depart. Taking one of the many seats on board, he looked to his wrist.

Unlocking the forearm plate, he pulled it open. Inside was a small interface that allowed him to directly connect with Tribune and the Legion systems now.

As they got closer and closer to the day of awakening, technology that was more common on his old world was becoming cheaper by the day. To the point that things like this were much more reasonable to develop.

"The train will be departing in five minutes, Legate," Tribune pointed out as he started to cycle through the Legion information system. "Everyone who was scheduled to leave was given the notification. There're only a few who were set to be on the train."

"Attention!" called an Andrea over the PA system in the station. "The train to the prison will be leaving thirty minutes early! If you need to be on board, please be here within the next five minutes, or call ahead to state you're on your way, with your estimated time of arrival! Thank you!"

Felix closed the wrist panel and then put his hands in his lap instead.

"Sir, you asked me to remind you as to the progress of Goddess Gaia and the Dryads," Tribune mentioned. "Given the coordinates of their Legionnaire transponders, they will be at the next designated site in two hours. You can expect to receive the request at that point."

Oh.

Right.

Felix called up his point sheet as the Andreas and Miu got settled all around him.

	Generated	Remaining
Andrea	1,205	1,205
Alma	410	410
Carlota	435	435
Faith	595	595
Felix	3,000	3,000
Goldie	2,995	2,995
Miu	1,515	1,515
+Loyalty Bonus	1,000	1,000
+Marital Bonus	750	750
=Daily Total	9,675	11,905
Banked Total	—	4,100,208

Mm, cells don't cost that much. Can't remember what the next point plan is, but we likely have enough for it.

Staring into the point screen, and Miu's knees beyond it, Felix lost himself in his thoughts. To the point that he only realized it when the train started to stop.

He hadn't even noticed when they'd started

moving.

"Damn," he muttered and got to his feet.

"You were having good thoughts!" Andrea said and patted him on the chest plate. "We thought you could use some time to your own head. We do that a lot.

"Especially in the shower. We stare into the corner and just think. Miu was worried about us the other day. It was nice to just stare into the corner of your shower because it looks different than ours.

"Miu was all nervous cause our fingers stopped washing the shampoo out of her hair."

"Andie," hissed Miu.

"Psh psh psh, no one can hear us but us, Miu. It's not like Felix isn't involved," Andrea said dismissively as they exited the train. At the same time, two Andreas ended up bracketing Miu. One stuck an arm around her hips, the other around her shoulders.

Moving up into the Legion-only part of the prison, everyone who'd come with them left. Felix and the others took the exit tunnel that'd put them in the Legion-only gatehouse that was along the road that led in.

They'd be able to exit there without being noticed or having overs thinking it strange.

Exiting as soon as they reached the door, they stepped out into the bright mid-morning sun. Felix turned his head and looked around.

His updated HUD picked out the Legionnaires that were within range and provided him with a name for each. It was taking him a little time to get used to the fact that instead of looking out through the eyeholes, which were now encased in the same material as the helmet, he was now looking at a screen that was in front of his face.

Along with all the tech that went with that.

"Kit and Lily are coming," Miu grumbled as she stood next to Felix. "Mikki will be there, too. You owe her some time. Do not try to push her away."

"I won't, I won't," promised Felix. "Any idea what they need, Tribune?"

"Class one magic cell," reported the VI. "The super in question was caught during a brawl. The Heroes could only capture the one.

"They're outnumbered by Villains three to one at this time. The government hasn't seen fit to make it more lucrative to be a hero."

"In other words, they're not paying right," Felix murmured.

He'd made sure that any offer they made to hire someone into Legion was the last they'd hear. If he was making the offer, he wanted them, and that was it.

Standing there, Felix waited.

A large military truck came into view. In front of it and behind it were several armored SUVs with actual gunners manning turrets.

"How bad is the public backlash getting?" Felix asked. He wasn't keeping abreast of current politics, given how hard he'd been digging into

Legion.

"They blew up a convention!" Andrea exclaimed. "Like… blew it up! Kaboom and crash with fire!"

Huh… public approval doesn't seem great.

I wonder which way we've slanted it for the Heroes' guild since… well… we own all the backbone for it. The website we set up still operates as their face.

The company we put in place still hosts all the information they want publicly known.

Controlling everything, pitting one side against the other, and never stepping out into the forefront.

A squat SUV pulled off the road in front of Felix. Inside it was this universe's Kit and Lily. They were both in themed costumes that sported the blue and gold colors of the Heroes guild.

Felix thought they looked ridiculous.

Opening the door, Miu got in, followed by Felix. The Andreas would follow on foot at a run. They would be more than capable of doing so and without becoming winded.

"Thanks for coming… Legate," Lily said, watching him from her side of the vehicle. Kit was currently in the front passenger seat.

"Of course. It's my duty," Felix responded, feeling slightly weirded out by the pause in her words. As if she knew something she shouldn't.

Did she remember something somehow? Need to have Goldie around her in the future to see.

"We have a magical Super today we need to have put away," Kit announced from the front seat.

"They've been accused of fourteen murders. Most of them were recorded as they happened, so it's very likely it'll be a slam dunk case.

"I'd like you to make their cell with some permanence in mind. It's unlikely that they'll ever be let out of it. For almost any reason."

"Understood. Solitary confinement cell, add extra space, facets for them to get some exercise in. Make sure to put it on a movement module so they can be taken outside on occasion," Felix elaborated with a nod of his head.

While Legion didn't run the prison, the third-party company that did was indirectly owned by Legion. Whatever Felix wanted done in the prison for a prisoner, was done.

From their cell, to their access to special privileges, and even what mental services they'd receive.

While he wouldn't be quick to write someone off to a life in complete solitary confinement, Felix wasn't going to provide undeserving individuals with privileges they hadn't earned.

"Beyond that, we'd like to invite you to a Guild of Heroes meeting tomorrow," Kit continued. "We'd appreciate your presence as you're a founding member of it, even if you're not an actual member."

"I'd like to ask for your support to push for our bid to remain the leaders," Lily asked, leaning forward and watching him curiously. "Kit and I that is, as leaders, with you pushing for that."

His lips became pursed as he considered that. His plans did involve Kit and Lily remaining in their positions.

"I'll see what I can do," he allowed, realizing things were going to speed up again. Suddenly he felt like he was about to miss doing all the paperwork and spreadsheets he'd been working on.

Chapter 19 - Scanner -

Felix followed the assistant that had guided him through the Heroes' hall. They escorted him right through the central area that was available to visitors and had skirted around anything that was designated for Heroes.

In this simple situation, he saw that there was already a disconnect inside of the guild of Heroes. Lily and Kit felt he was a member, however, someone else didn't feel that way. Whoever gave her the instructions to bring him inside, was quite likely not in the faction he wanted to support.

"By the way," Felix said, raising his voice a bit in volume to make sure the helmet would transmit his voice accordingly. "Who left the instructions to guide me inside? When I spoke to the others, they had only told me to go to the assembly conference room."

"Uhm, I'm honestly not sure," admitted the young man in front of Felix. He had a slightly confused look on his face as he considered it. "It was just in the meeting invite to escort you accordingly. I'm sorry, was there something else that you were supposed to do first?"

"No, no, it's fine. I was just curious," Felix lied, trying to appease the man into forgetting he'd even asked. He needed something to distract him, in fact. "Have you been enjoying your work here?"

"Yes! It's actually really rewarding to be part of something so... so big. This is such as massive change that it's almost other-worldly at times.

"It's not something I ever thought I'd ever be a part of, that's for sure. I'm very much just an everyday person with… you know… just… everyday stuff."

"I find the world is completely built upon the backs of everyday people," growled Felix. He'd never quite shed the chip on his shoulder, given how big business had treated him through his adult life. "Upon their very crushed corpses, in fact. I can't imagine it'll get better any time soon before it gets much worse."

"You sound like my dad," said the man laughingly.

Uh… huh… I guess… I'm old enough to be a dad now.

Don't look like it anymore, but that doesn't change the fact that I'm technically in my forties.

The outside isn't showing the wear and tear anymore, but my brain is. Starting to feel like I can't even connect with the younger generation anymore.

That, or they're so jaded that it makes even me feel appalled.

Leading Felix through the hallway they took a turn, then another. Eventually ending up in the assembly conference room just as he'd expected. Felix entered and then looked around for several moments.

There didn't seem to be any name placards laid out, nor was there any type of designations for who would sit where. In fact, it seemed almost like they expected anyone to be anywhere.

Turning, Felix looked to the young man who'd brought him.

Except he was gone.

Only Andrea and Miu were there. He'd been allowed two bodyguards to come with him. The former had demanded she be there, and the latter had done the same.

Felix had no argument for it, if only because no one else he'd want to bring was available. His mind often went to wanting to drag Goldie and Gaia around with him.

Between those two, he could probably kick-start world war three.

"Back. Far back," Miu demanded and then started forward. She wasn't going to let him sit just anywhere after all. She was going to pick the right spot for them based on security needs.

Andrea came up behind Felix and gave him a gentle pat as Miu began moving up to the back of the amphitheater.

"Up up and away," urged Andrea. The Centurion helmet and its front to back red bristle stripe had made her quite pleased to put it on. Miu was also wearing a similar helmet.

Not fighting them, Felix did as instructed. Moving up to the back of the seating arrangements and plopping himself down in the chair Miu was pointing to.

"Legate, I have received your signal, and linked in with your armor," Tribune reported to him through his helmet.

"Splendid. Good work. You're the Tribune that's in the Legion base directly under the Heroes' guild building, right?" he asked, wanting to make sure he knew exactly which Tribune he was talking to. There were three right now, which was down from four.

The prison Tribune and Association Tribune had integrated themselves into one VI now.

"Yes, Sir."

"Great. Anything to report?" asked Felix. He flipped open the wrist panel and began moving his finger across the controls. He wanted to get into the file system and pull up the internet.

If he was going to be stuck here waiting for this meeting, he wanted to at least be entertained. He'd rather be working, but that wasn't something he could very well get done here.

"There have been many people coming and going throughout the building, Legate," Tribune stated. "More so than there should be. I suspect they've had intruders. Legionnaire Mikki is of course working to find these interlopers, however, the guild itself is making it difficult for her to do her job effectively.

"They're preventing her from acting in the best interest of security and are elevating the rights of the individual over securing the location."

Sounds about right.

You'd think they'd understand a building like this eliminates individual rights to a degree.

I'm all for rights and liberties. Just not when they're put in front of the well-being of the nation, in a location that should be classified as a military secret.

Shaking his head, Felix realized, not for the first time, he'd be a tyrant.

A despot.

King to all, leader for everyone, democracy and a republic for those he allowed to have it.

At least I can admit it.

A ping sounded in his helmet and a small box appeared in the corner. It was a link to the internet, it looked like.

Sighing, he saw who sent it.

Romina Rohis

Tapping into it, a small window popped up in the corner of his view.

"Juno here!" called the beautiful and wide-eyed woman. The collar of her Legion armor was clearly in view as the background moved behind her. She was walking and holding her phone out in front of her. "Just got to the Association and I can't wait to see everyone.

"But we have to do things right. In Legion, you have to make sure protocol is followed dependent on you, and your job.

"Because in Legion, Legion comes first. That means I have to do my due diligence as Juno."

There was a large mob of people that were rapidly showing up around Juno as she moved ahead. Quite a few people all had their phones out and were taking pictures of something else.

Really does her job as the Rising Star of Legion quite well.

Not too fond of the naming convention but... it works, I suppose.

"Ah! There's my Jupiter!" Juno called out as the phone swung around the other way. Felix had a great view of himself standing in front of the building. Looking out at everyone assembled there.

The armor looked perfectly immaculate. The way he stood was at a loose attention.

Flanking him on either side were Andrea and Miu, both sporting their Centurion helmets. Fanned out on either side in both directions were more Andreas in regular helmets.

"I got my Centurion helmet too! We'll have to look it over later and really check it out," Juno gushed. "I was already looking at it, and it's so damn cool. It has a display and everything.

"But for now... Legate! Your Juno is here!"

Felix's armored head snapped to the left and locked on the camera Juno, or Romina as she was named, held, and stayed there.

"See? Jupiter always hears me when I call out," Juno reported and then began bumping her way through the crowd at the same time two Andreas moved forward. They quickly carved out an aisle for her, and she was promptly deposited in front of Felix.

"Legate, Jupiter, Juno is here," reported Romina, moving to stand in front of him and flipping the camera around. "Alright! Let's have an amazing Legion day! Legion First!"

"Legion first," agreed Felix, Miu, and Andrea, who were all in the frame with Romina.

Groaning, Felix closed the video.

It'd been a successful meet-and-greet as far as he knew, it'd just felt like a waste of time. He'd done his best to project the personality of Legate, though also striving to seem welcoming.

This was no different than when he'd thrown on the "happy CEO" face back in his old world.

"Nnn, nn. Juno does her job well," Andrea said quickly. "I like her."

People began filing into the auditorium and taking seats. A great many of them all paused to look up at Felix and his position. As well as those directly around him.

Whether obvious with their reactions or not, none failed to spot him or note his presence.

Which was likely a good and a bad thing, he figured.

Mikki came into the room and her eyes began to scan and flick over each and every person inside. Picking across each face before slowly switching to the next.

She spared Felix, Miu, and Andrea no more time, nor any less, than the others. Scanning them visually before she finally went to stand in the corner.

Miu looked to Andrea who gave her a minute head nod. Then she began moving down from the upper seats to go stand next to Mikki.

The two Mius had a very similar way of standing and carrying themselves.

"They're friends. They talk a lot," whispered Andrea. "It reminds me of when I first figured out I had friends that were just like me in my head."

"See, when I say things like that, people tell me I'm crazy," Felix responded.

"Silly, you are crazy. I'm not," deadpanned Andrea.

The room continued to fill until almost every seat was taken.

Lily and Kit had also joined them and joined the rest.

Eventually there was an audible chime that came through the speakers.

Kit stood up from her seat and walked over to the front of the room. Standing there, wearing her Augur helmet, she struck deep at the memories in Felix's mind.

Far too many of them, in fact.

"Thank you all for coming," Kit said with a hand gesture to the room. "We have a full attendance today. That means a lot.

"We of course invited the Legate as he… well… he's the Legate. He may not be an official member of the Heroes' guild, but without him, we wouldn't be here. It's better that we make a habit of including him and treating him like one of us. Because he is.

"He'll also be responsible for helping us recruit everyone we'll need in the future. After all,

all the information we get is directly through his comprehensive testing."

"If it's even all of the data," groused someone from the audience.

Felix didn't miss it when Kit glanced his way, or when everyone else did the same thing. While it wasn't going to be an issue if he didn't say anything, it was actually quite likely that they did want him to respond to that.

"All data that was promised, was delivered," announced Felix. "The only thing withheld was information on those employed directly by the Association or Legion. This is to protect their identity, as they're no longer classified as normal citizens."

"So he says," grumbled the same speaker from earlier.

This time Felix had spotted them when they spoke. They were wearing some type of mask over their face that hid their features away. He was dressed in a black outfit with a great deal of tailor work to make it stand out.

Right… maybe they're the problem for Kit and Lily, too?

"I do indeed say. I'll be happy to provide to you the list of powers I hired, as well as what position they were hired into after this meeting," offered Felix. "None of them would be very useful to the Heroes' guild, but they're quite useful to the Association.

"As an example, I hired someone who can

easily identify almost anything they touch. It makes it much easier to make sure who we're interviewing is who they claim to be. A very useful power to make sure we're accurately providing documentation to who comes in."

"If that's really all of the data," said the man, apparently still stuck on that point.

"Whether it's all of it, or not, I'm not legally obligated to provide you anything other than what I contractually did," countered Felix. "I've offered additional information if only to try and provide some good will for you.

"It seems it's misplaced. You seem particularly set to be steadfast against the Legion and myself. Is there something I've done to you personally, sir?"

Now that Felix had made it a personal thing, everyone was quite willing to turn around and look from him to the other speaker.

"No, I just don't see why you get to hold data back," the man complained, folding his arms in front of himself.

"For the same reason you get to wear a mask and not reveal your identity to everyone else," argued Felix. "One just suits your purposes more than the other does.

"I find it amusing how often people will gladly trample upon the rights of others, if it will allow them to use their own rights or morals more freely.

"Perhaps we could ask you for your own

name? Your identity? Where you hail from? Your family? Your power?"

The man was now shaking his head, looking down to the seat in front of himself. It seemed he didn't want to discuss the subject anymore.

"Legate, given the communication heuristics program in my suite of tools, that man isn't a problem," reported Tribune. "However, there is an individual three rows down, and two seats to the right, that I've identified as being problematic."

"Problematic?" Felix asked as Kit cleared her throat and tried to wrestle the conversation back to her own agenda.

"His posture is stiff, his breathing forced, and his body-heat and heart rate are much higher than they should be," explained Tribune. "While they mimic much of the body functions that the other Legionnaires, or primarily the female ones, exhibit while being around you, this is a male.

"Given the data provided and my previous examples, I believe this individual to be a problem. Additionally, upon review, I've determined that he often moves in strange ways through the guild."

Unable to help himself, Felix was now interested in that.

Except he couldn't quite believe it either. The simple fact was that there shouldn't be anything that could block out telepathy outside of his own creations.

Which would mean his power was something that allowed him to actively block or nullify Kit's powers. That'd be something he'd have noted and kept track of, if he'd come across it.

"Does his identity match the records on file?" asked Felix.

"Match to facial features and database," answered Tribune. "Power listed is the ability to utilize sound waves to mimic anything that can be heard."

Anything that can be heard?

Not something that'd counter telepathy.

Thinking, Felix wasn't paying attention to Kit's speech. She was currently working through a presentation that was being displayed on the screen behind her.

Mimic.

Well.

Could… could someone else have mimicked the Legion helmets to a degree? Could someone else have utilized a power to duplicate one just on sight?

It's not like there aren't strange one-off powers out there.

Hm. Something to look into I suppose.

Need to make sure that we upgrade Kit's helmet so she can… actually… let's do that.

No reason to wait.

Reaching out with his power, Felix focused in on Kit's helmet.

While he'd given it to her, it was on a loan. He owned it and retained all the technology that went with it.

His request was simple.

To modify her helmet so that it would grant Kit the power to overcome and overwhelm any power, technology, or magic that might defeat her own power.

The only limitation, the only exception he set on it, was that it wouldn't work against active Legion members.

Her regular telepathy without the helmet would be defeated by the Legion rings after all.

Type: Legionnaire Helmet	Condition: Working
Owner: Felix Campbell (Legion)	Action >> Modify: Yield 51,194 points

Kinda cheap considering how many points we have.

Felix accepted the change and then looked to Kit to see if she'd notice it.

" — working to sto… to stop… criminal… organizations," Kit mumbled, her head turning to one side and then the other. As if she was hearing something she hadn't expected.

Slowly, her head rotated around until she was looking straight at the man that Tribune had marked out.

"Huh, maybe you were right after all, Tribune," Felix murmured with a chuckle.

Looking up to the screen he froze.

There on the screen was a picture of Michael. The very man that Felix had assumed would become a problem for Anya and Thomas.

There was some information off to the side of his mugshot, but Felix couldn't quite make it out. He didn't need to though; it was obvious he'd done something to get the attention of the Heroes' guild.

"You got this downloaded, Tribune?" Felix asked. "The presentation that is. I think I'm going to have to make a visit after this. See if I can't save Anya and Thomas from their Michael problem, since it seems like he's going to become one.

"While that's going on, if you don't mind, dig into the computers and servers here at the guild and see if you can't find out how they discovered Michael. It'd be great if we could track it back to somewhere so we can figure out if we need to carry this further back.

"We can't leave anything behind that would endanger those two if they're going to fit into my plans."

"Yes, Sir," answered the VI. "I'll make sure that happens, Legate."

Hm. It's about time I checked in on them more than I have been. They've just been keeping it all small time so far. Doing small grifts and cons, not really pushing up.

Not moving the needle or making the radar blip, so to speak.

This'll be perfect timing for me to swoop in and rescue them. Push them toward the Villain's League.

"Great. I'll need it so I can sort through it and —"

The man that Tribune had picked out, and

Kit was staring at, exploded.

Chapter 20 - TFW -

Blood, bone, muscle, and just chunks of man, went in every direction. Splattering everyone around him, the ceiling, the chairs, in a whole body's worth of gore.

Except there was no detonation outside of the man blowing apart.

There was no fire or flame.

No boom.

Just a deep thud-like noise that seemingly liquefied the man.

Everyone stood there in shock. Staring at the spot where the man had been only moments before, yet was no longer.

Not a single person had enough warning to react in any way.

"I... he was working for someone else," Kit said after a number of seconds had passed. "I was just starting to go through his thoughts when he killed himself.

"He-he used his power to make some type of sonic boom inside of his body. It was almost like he was more terrified of me finding out who he was working with.

"Or... or for. He was approached after he'd joined the Heroes' guild. Someone had approached him and made him an offer he couldn't refuse."

"Wait... why didn't you know this before?" asked someone from the crowd.

"I don't know. One minute he was as much

of a blank slate as always, and then the next moment, I could actually see his thoughts," answered Kit. "I don't go around forcing my way into people's minds you know. I just figured he had a way to block me and didn't want me to nose around.

"I try really hard to respect all your privacy whenever possible. I'm not... I'm not the mind-reading police here, ya know."

"Maybe you should be," interjected Felix. "Maybe the idea of having personal rights and liberties while inside of a secure, military secret-like building, is ludicrous.

"Perhaps joining such an organization removes the very same privileges you'd be looking to protect for others. While the guild in turn would protect you from the government.

"Somewhat akin to a union I suppose. Though, I'm not officially a member here. I'm not really part of your guild. I'm an outsider looking in."

Getting to his feet, Felix made a show of rubbing his hands together. As if he were washing himself of this situation entirely.

Then he held up his hands in a neutral pose.

"I will put the full support of Legion and the Association behind Kit Carrington. I believe she's the right person for the job and has the right disposition to make sure everyone follows the rules," Felix proposed. "Whatever voting power I have, goes behind her. Along with Legion and the Association.

"If you have any needs or requests Miss Carrington, please don't hesitate to put them forward to me by email. I'll earnestly consider them as if they were coming from inside Legion.

"In the mean while… I'd say you have a more pressing issue than whatever it is you were working on. Someone infiltrated your facility. An outsider had access to your information and data.

"Best you discover how deep the exposure went. How bad this breach is. You'll need to be able to understand how deep that rabbit hole goes before you can get an idea of what you need to move to protect and cover yourselves."

Felix slowly walked down from the back of the auditorium and moved to stand beside Kit. He slowly looked around the area to get an idea of the crowd.

They were still in shock at what'd just happened.

Here, in their little sanctum, surrounded by people who thought they were far more than the rest of humanity, they were exposed to the fact they were vulnerable. They were just as likely to turn on each other, as anyone else was.

"It's good that this happened the way it did. Before things moved further along and things reached a point where real damage could be done," Felix consoled them. "A lesson given without harm and likely minimal damage.

"As I said earlier though… my support is firmly behind Miss Carrington. If not her, then Miss Lux. Or both of them together. Whichever way you see it, I trust in them personally."

Felix turned and left, heading for the exit.

He needed to let them launch their own investigation into this. To find out their own answers. The more he involved himself with it, the more likely they'd want to blame him, or find fault in his conclusions.

"Tribune," Felix muttered. "I want to know what the hell happened just now. If you're only here at this facility, consider it your number one priority.

"If you have any conflicting priorities, concerns, or otherwise, address them with me and I'll clear it up right quick for you."

"Yes, Legate," Tribune answered.

"Wow! He just went KERSPOOM all over," Andrea said, catching up to him. "It felt a lot like a breaching charge going off, really. The same thump of the detonation, had that solid thud to it."

Not for the first time, Felix wondered about Andrea.

She was really starting to seem like a fluid blend of all three of her personalities. Swapping between her self-described "extra" self, her military and disciplined mind, and her rather high sex drive, without being a different person in between any of it.

To him, it felt like she was becoming a true and whole person.

Rather than several fragmented people.

"It was a surprise," Miu snarled as they continued to exit. Their destination was the

Association truck that was parked out front.

"Considering he used his own power to blow himself to bits, I don't think there's anything we could have done to prevent it," reckoned Felix. "It's not like we weren't aware of what his power was, or the scope of it.

"That's the risk we run in dealing with Supers. Everyone could be a nuclear weapon and you never know what will set them off."

Miu growled in response to that, but she didn't say anything more.

"Miu, work with Mikki and Tribune. I want to know who that man was in contact with. See if we can't run it down to where this started from," commanded Felix. "From the beginning I've felt like that maybe we're not as far ahead of this race as I thought we were.

"That maybe we're actually much further behind than we suspected or considered. This only makes me feel like that's more the truth. If they can turn a Super in the guild that easily and quickly, there's a lot of power, influence, or danger in the Super world."

"Y-yes. I'll take care of it," Miu said in a whisper. "I'll work through Mikki for most of it. I'm sure she's more than capable of taking care of it."

In other words... you don't want to leave my side. The question is, will you say it or will it —

"I don't want to leave your side," confessed Miu.

Color me surprised.

"That's fine, I understand," Felix said as he opened the door and stepped outside. His eyes flicked to the corner of his HUD to see what might be next on his schedule.

Tribune or Andrea would have filled it out for him this morning to make sure he was kept on task.

"We're meeting with Juno and several other potential Legion influencers," Andrea announced while moving past him. "People from other parts of the internet that she wants to push."

"Goodie," Felix said sarcastically. "Just what I wanted to do."

"You're not allowed to do Juno," hissed Miu.

"That's not what I meant, and you know it. You're just playing the 'I'm a crazy girl' card now," growled Felix, getting into the truck. Miu came in right behind him.

Laughing loudly, Andrea got into the driver's seat and turned the engine over.

"He's got you there, babe," Andrea murmured and began pulling them away from the building.

"I am not... well... err... maybe... maybe a little," Miu admitted, her shoulders hunching and her helmet facing the ground. "I'm crazy, yes. You're not allowed to sleep with Juno and that's the point I was making.

"I'll kill her and pull her apart and eat what she touched of you. Not allowed."

"Yes, but that's not what I meant," Felix

laughingly accused, laying an arm around Miu's shoulders. "You know full well I want no part of her. You're playing the card, only because you felt like you should, or could. I can't tell which."

Miu shrugged her shoulders and then slowly leaned toward him.

"Would you still love me if I wasn't crazy?" she asked in a confused way.

"Well… the crazy makes it fun in the end, and that's never going to go away," Felix asserted and pulled her in close to his side. "You don't need to lean into it when it wouldn't come out naturally though.

"I mean, come on. I've surrounded myself with people that are all… not right. I mean, look at Andrea. Or Kit. Or Lily."

"We're not crazy," Andrea said, voicing the combined thoughts of at least twenty other Andreas.

"Uh huh, and which one of you just said, 'at least as much', because I guarantee one of you did," Felix countered.

"Five did," Andrea said after a pause with a grumble.

"Then there's Goldie," Felix continued. "I don't need to talk about Goldie. Or Faith, even. We know what Faith and the other two Dryads are like."

Miu grunted at that and then pushed her head up under his jaw.

"That makes you crazy, right?" she demanded. "Crazy for crazies?"

"Well, I display a number of psychopathic tendencies. Or at least that's what Kit often told me," Felix mused, his thoughts drifting backward. "It's not that big a deal if you ask me. You all seem to have responded to my tribal nature by pushing even more tribal nature forward.

"I just have to make sure that we slowly take over everything. So that everything, and everyone, is in our tribe. Once we're all bound together, I can't even begin to imagine what we might accomplish."

Felix leaned his head back and looked up to truck's headliner.

It's a lot like being a new leader.

Step in, change, break, and alter everything. Make everyone hate you, but get the job done. Do it completely so there's no room for going backward.

Then hand the reigns off to someone much more well liked, who will make small concessions to appease people. Yet never put anything back to the way it was.

A rapid and life-altering change, followed by small drips and drabs to make people feel more comfortable.

"I want to bite you and taste your blood in my mouth," Miu demanded, then grabbed his arm with both of her hands.

"Fine, fine, just don't be so rough about it," allowed Felix, working to remove his right gauntlet.

***

Rolling up to the gated and fenced-off industrial building, Felix felt rather proud of it.

To the casual observer, it looked a lot like an everyday industrial warehouse and facility. Even if one were to peer in through the windows without trespassing, that's all they'd see as well.

It'd been done up almost exactly like the farm, where at a casual look it appeared as one would expect.

A warehouse that Legion operated out of, housing supplies that were of common nature. Uniforms, food, plastic trays, utensils, things that you might need for any long-term corporate building.

Once one got inside though, past the false exterior, they'd realize it was a safe-house, storage, and lab.

This was also where Felix could get to and from the area from Legion HQ in the future. A train station was being constructed beneath it so that it could connect to everywhere else.

With so many stations needing to be built, though, this one was not a priority.

A helicopter pad and flight clearances had been established here so that any member of Legion could come and go as needed. He just had to make sure he didn't use it too often or predictably, otherwise someone could set up an ambush for him.

Felix lost track of what was going on as he thought up all the ways he'd likely ambush someone himself and was surprised when the doors opened suddenly. They'd already moved into the loading section and entered the building with the vehicle.

"Juno here, ready for her Jupiter!" declared the young woman who'd thrown the door open.

Miu and Andrea had apparently exited through the front, leaving him in the back.

Alone.

The camera on Juno's shoulder, which was attached to her armor, was red and clearly on. Recording her interactions with Felix.

"Then you have me, Juno," Felix said honestly.

While he didn't care for the role, he knew that he needed to appeal to the younger crowd. To get into their head space and win them over.

Because it was them who would most likely receive the lion's share of Superpowers. The previous generations would of course have their own, but they'd be far fewer in number.

Getting to his feet, Felix walked to the end of the truck, only to find Romina had her hand up for him. As if to help him step down.

Taking it, he exited the truck as two other Legionnaires came up and closed the doors.

"Success!" Juno cheered and her fingers closed in tight to Felix's hand. He could feel her gauntlet-powered grip clutching to his own. "Now, we have several new people I want to see what you think of.

"To see what their powers are and then share it with our viewers. They're all very curious if it could really be as simple as we always claim.

"So… Juno had an extremely wrinkly brain moment, followed by a smooth one unfortunately. Now we have our winners from a contest and here they are!" explained Romina. Though Felix wasn't sure if it was for him, or her audience. "Also, everyone say hi to Legionnaire Dragon! There she is!"

Turning partly, Romina made sure the camera on her shoulder framed up around Goldie who wasn't far off. She was standing in a very flowy and comfortable-looking sundress of blue. It suited her quite well.

"Romina, you know that's not how you should be addressing me or even Legate," chided Goldie, coming over. She took Romina's hand from Felix and then patted the back of her wrist several times. "What's the proper address for me."

"Legionnaire Goldie," Romina said, her entire personality shifting rapidly.

"And how do we address our Legate?" prompted the beautiful Gold Dragon.

"Legate, or Sir," answered Romina. "Sorry, Legionnaire Goldie."

"It's fine dear, it's fine. You just need to make sure you show proper manners. You can't really expect our potentials who are watching to address you just as informally, can we? That'd be rude," Goldie said, then looked to the camera. "I expect all of you to behave admirably."

Leave it to Goldie to housewife mom everyone right into the ground.

It's good for it to be seen like this. Her image makeover is definitely proceeding in the right direction with her interacting so often with Romina.

"Junoooooo," called an Andrea in street clothes heading their way. Felix immediately noted that it was Third.

"Andie!" Romina said excitedly, practically forgetting that she'd just been scolded. "Oh my god I love that blouse! Yaaas. You should be a model!"

Andrea took that as a request to begin strutting in a way very similar to how Goldie walked, while also adopting a vague non-interested and lost look to her face.

Then she laughed, squealed, and hopped quickly over to stand next to Romina.

"No, no, no. Nobody wants a Beastkin like me as a model. My tail gets in the way for most things," Andrea said and whipped her tail around, practically slapping it against Romina's chest. "Now… these are the winners?"

Andrea was a regular presence on Romina's stream. Everyone loved the spunky, energetic, and fun personality of hers.

"Yep! I just went to get my Jupiter so he could give them a quick once over," Romina said, looking from Andrea to the six people who were standing nearby. They all had smiles on their faces, looked far too excited, and didn't know what to do or how to hold themselves. "Here, let's go introduce them all to you!"

Goldie wandered over to stand next to Felix

and gave him a brilliant smile. Her gold eyes flashed as she stared at his helmet.

"After we're done with this, you need to come with me down to the basement," murmured Goldie. "I have many things for you to look over. Many things to possibly bring back from the past. It should be interesting and exciting for both of us."

Blinking, Felix had to get his brain out of the gutter and latched onto what she was actually saying. Rather than her smile and her eyes.

"I made sure to bring the gold rings I promised," Felix said, trying to pitch the external mic as low as it would go. "I wonder how many you earned?"

Goldie's eyes flashed and her smile became a grin. Her teeth bright white and shining as she gazed at his helmet.

"I'm sure I can earn them in other ways for however many you brought with you," she purred.

Then Romina came back and grabbed him by the shoulder, dragging him off to go finish off her contest.

Be polite, be cordial, be Legate.

Professional, inviting, but neutral. We want to inspire people to join the Legion. To be more than just a Hero or a Villain.

To achieve the middle.

"Jupiter, this is my first winner!" announced Romina, pulling him up to a small Asian woman.

Here we go, then.

Chapter 21 – Scared and Aroused -

Felix really didn't know what to think as he looked out at the unfinished basement.

It was a wide, open, and bare-bones area of the building.

A few chairs to one side, a folding table, fridge, and a few cots that were set up in the far corner, were the only things that looked to permanently reside there. It looked a lot like an impromptu breakroom and place to nap for everyone that worked here. Not that he blamed them if they were pulling long shifts to get work done.

He'd likely do the same.

There wasn't anything out of the ordinary.

Other than the large mass of bones right in the middle of the area, that was.

It was a jumble that'd been all shoved together into a mound of them. Where he saw several different skulls, as well as a few lower jaw bones that didn't look like they belonged to any of the skulls.

"I just piled them all up," Goldie announced as she came up behind him. "I didn't see a reason to separate them. You'll just bring them back to life from the collective heap anyways.

"That and… well… I really didn't want to dirty my clothes. They're quite nice and I really love this dress. It flatters me oh so well.

"Well, not to mention I didn't want to make a

mess. The tarp was only so big, and a lot of the bones have debris wedged all over. Just because it's an unfinished basement, doesn't mean I want dirt and things tracked all over it."

"Goldieeeee," squealed Andrea a second before she slammed into the back of the Dragon. Her legs wrapped around Goldie's middle and Andrea reached up and around the Dragon, the Beastkin's hands sliding across just beneath her breasts.

"Yes, yes, hello Andie," Goldie said and reached up to pat the back of Andrea's hands. "You did well to not mess up Juno's stream."

"She's coming, so I have to get my Dragon loving in before she does," whined Andrea as she began rubbing her face all over the back of Goldie's neck and hair.

Goldie let out a long breath, but she was smiling ear to ear. Turning, she looked to Felix.

"Would you please summon my Maidens? I want to earn my rings. I also need to welcome them into my Wing," explained the Dragon. "Gaia is sponsoring their welcome party. She said she's got more than enough power to make that happen without any cost to her, but she's sorry she couldn't help with their resurrection costs."

"That's fine," Felix said with a wave of his hand, looking away from Andrea and Goldie. Instead, he moved over to the pile of bones. "That's my job. Always was."

Andrea was now openly fondling Goldie across the front of her dress. Something to which

Goldie seemed indifferent and uninterested in.

Though Felix was certainly having a reaction to it.

Squatting down in front of the Dragon bone pile, Felix wanted to know how much it would cost him to have them all brought back to life. To be restored to their prime in life, and with a power set similar to Goldie's.

Felix felt things slow down until he was nearly alone in his head with his thoughts.

Request: Dragon Resurrection (mass)	**Condition**: Dead to Alive
Owner: Felix Campbell (Legion)	**Construction**: Cost 18,319,174

Raising his eyebrows at the box that popped up, Felix called up his point bank. He hadn't expected it to be so expensive. He wasn't quite sure how many Dragons were in the pile, but it felt like it was more than he'd expected.

	Generated	Remaining
Andrea	1,225	1,225
Alma	430	430
Carlota	440	440
Faith	600	600
Felix	3,005	3,005
Goldie	3,000	3,000
Miu	1,530	1,530

+Loyalty Bonus	1,000	1,000
+Marital Bonus	750	750
=Daily Total	**9,675**	**11,980**
Banked Total	—	**1,014,876**

"Uhm," Felix murmured almost to himself. "Gaia, any chance you can put in that request to clear that waste pit you're at? Could use the points."

Reaching out, Felix reached out and lightly poked at a Dragon's skull eye-socket. It all looked more like dinosaur bones to him.

In fact, I wonder if there's a number of bones that've been confused with Dinosaur bones. I bet there is. They're all thinking it's somehow some type of land-based reptile and discount anything that doesn't match as belonging to something else.

The goddess Gaia has requested to use her Champion's power on his behalf.

The suddenness of the popup startled Felix. Though he quickly approved it.

Then took it a step further and tried to force Gaia to become his recognized goddess. In this way, she could fully benefit from the faith contracts he'd put upon Legion in the past.

At this point it was just a formality that he'd been pumping the brakes on.

"Is there an active Tribune here?" Felix asked, though there was no response from her.

Instead, Felix called up his point totals again.

The box that popped up this time listed him as having over twenty-million points. After bringing the Dragons back, he'd have roughly a million, give or take.

Which was more than enough to get things done, he'd just have to move on to finding another high value site to return to pristine condition.

The goddess Gaia has accepted becoming your personal goddess.

Shaking his head, Felix accepted the cost to resurrect the Dragons. Getting up, he moved away to where the chairs were. He thankfully wasn't going to have to deal with the Dragons as that was more a job for Goldie.

There was a group of twenty to thirty newly made Dragons in human form getting up from the ground. Many of them looked very wobbly and unsure of their bodies.

Andrea appeared at his side as Goldie moved forward to the group.

"Like newborn deer! Eeeeee!" Andrea squeaked excitedly, then slammed herself into the chair directly next to him. She then pushed in close to his side. "Oh, er, yeah, gotta… gotta get Juno."

Andrea fumbled at her pockets and managed to get a phone out. She tapped at it for a few seconds and then held it up to her ear.

"Juno! Come down. Goldie is gonna

roflstomp the new Dragon girls and get a ring from F-Legate for each one!" Andrea cheered, very nearly using his real name.

He couldn't hear Juno's response, but he likely didn't need to.

" — submit to me. I'll brook no nonsense or infighting afterward. We aren't merely Dragons in the service of Felix, we're house-wives. I expect you all to begin assisting me to complete my duties," Goldie said in a commanding way. Standing in front of the other Dragons, Felix only now noticed they were all female.

"Was it Goldie or Gaia that made sure they were all women," Felix growled.

"Both? Yes, both," Andrea said happily, putting her phone down at the table. "A male Dragon would try to take control and likely need to be killed. It's easier with one male only.

"Gaia said it was just a part of nature in many species. Goldie said she didn't want to have to deal with a male Dragon corpse. Apparently it'd be hard to dispose of."

There was a clatter from the stairs, followed by Juno actually falling down them. She slammed into the concrete floor and slid for a couple feet on her elbows and knees. Getting up quickly, she came racing over to where Andrea and Felix were sitting.

"I'm here! Did they start? Did I miss anything?" she asked breathlessly. The camera on her shoulder was recording. "Oh, uh, I'm recording but not streaming. I need to be able to edit this up later and put it together into a trailer of sorts.

"Legion needs all the publicity it can get, and Dragon Fight Club is gonna be a thing I bet. Goldie said there'd likely be a monthly contest to establish hierarchy."

The Dragons had already gained their senses and looked to be rapidly adapting. More of a question of remembering how to walk, than learning how to, Felix guessed.

"Oh, oh, oh, I can do that too! Andrea Battle Royale is a thing! We even have a champion!" Andrea offered helpfully. "They assign special duties or privileges to whoever does best. They get to dictate a lot of fun things."

"Huh? Like what?" Romina asked, turning her head to look at Andrea. "And… thank you, Legate. I know I didn't ask in advance for you to help out with my contest so… thanks. You've been really kind to me despite everything.

"Not what I was expecting at all from my boss, I guess. At all."

"Right? When I first started working for him, I was nervous about sleeping with him," gushed Andrea as a large Black Dragon stepped up. Her dark wings were spread out behind her as well as her horns.

Stepping right up to Goldie, she lifted her chin up and put her hands on her hips.

"After the first time though, it was really easy. I even got really good at it! You just gotta really learn how to move your hips," continued Andrea as Juno stared at her with a semi-wide-eyed stare. Thankfully her camera was still facing the

Dragons.

Andrea leaned toward Romina and held a hand up to her mouth.

Felix knew the fake loud whisper was coming.

"You'll get the hang of it Juno. Just start with vanilla stuff and he'll make it fun after a while. Just be really grabby and affectionate with him. Lots of kissing, really get your tongue into his mouth," Andrea whispered in the exact tone Felix had been expecting. "Especially when he's on top. Really pull at him.

"You'll be great at it, I'm sure. Just make sure you don't go for your first time until you're ready. I was ready for it, but Lily really wasn't. She got really weirded out. Especially when Felix—"

Reaching around the chatterbox that couldn't keep her mouth shut, Felix clamped a hand down around her mouth.

Looking up, he stared at Juno for several seconds before he tilted his head to the side.

"Romina," he started, wondering how to phrase his statement.

"It's not a problem!" promised the influencer, her head whipping back to the front. She was holding almost perfectly still, her eyes wide and unseeing as she stared ahead.

Not releasing Andrea, Felix looked back to the Dragons as well. He wasn't going to let go of his Beastkin for a little bit.

Andrea for her part was now leaning into

Felix, one hand on his armored thigh, the other on his gauntlet over her mouth. She seemed happy for some reason.

Goldie was pummeling the Black Dragon.

Holding her down against the concrete with one hand while smashing her in the face repeatedly with the other. Each blow sounding like a car-crash as she whaled on the other woman's face.

Deforming it and shattering most of the bones entirely. To the point that she was beyond even looking remotely human-like, instead markedly starting to resemble ground beef.

Goldie stood up, drew her foot back, and blasted it across the Black's destroyed face. Several teeth exploded out of her mouth and her jaw clearly dislocated itself and broke.

Clicking her tongue, Goldie sighed and looked down at her dress. There was blood splatter across the front of it that also had covered her face.

"Goodness. See, this is why I said we should fight to first blood. You made me get my dress dirty. You're going to have to clean this up yourself, Lucille," Goldie admonished the dying Dragon sternly. "If you can't get it clean, you can beg our Nest-mate to fix it for you, but I'm going to ask him to punish you if you do.

"Oh, thank you for picking those up, Cathy. That's quite helpful. Every little bit saves a few points for Gaia."

A very attractive Green Dragon had come over and held out the teeth Goldie had knocked out of the Black's mouth. Depositing them in the Gold Dragon's hands.

"Gaia, would you please restore Lucille now? She's learned her place and she now understands where she belongs," asked Goldie

There was an odd buzzing noise, followed by the Black Dragon's body and face suddenly reforming. She looked as she had when she first stepped up to Goldie.

Just with an indescribable amount of fear.

The beautiful Black squirmed over onto her hands and knees and then put her head down between Goldie's feet. Her horns were practically dug into the ground.

"Stop that, that's no way for a wife to behave. Go get a cup of iced sweet tea and start learning about our Nest-mate, Lucille," Goldie chastised. "I made it and some snacks before we started. There should be a serving for everyone in the fridge.

"Remember, decorum and modesty in public befits a Dragon housewife, and you'll need to be on your best behavior. If I must, I'll start giving you lessons myself."

"Please instruct me. I would very much like lessons," asked the Black, quickly getting to her feet. "I'm not sure I can behave as you'd wish. I... I speak for everyone here, I'm sure, when I say we'd all like lessons."

"Nnn, I want lessons!" Andrea called from the side, causing all the Dragons to look their way. "I love you, Goldie! You're so pretty and sexy!"

Goldie snorted, a stray wisp of gold hair fluttering down and into her eyes while smiling at Andrea.

"No you don't, dear. You're just mixed up," Goldie said with a shooing motion at Andrea.

"Can... I have lessons?" Romina asked suddenly.

Tilting her head slowly to one side, Goldie considered the question. Then she grinned and nodded.

"Of course you can, dear. Now, Lucille, go. Will the next Maiden please step forward?" asked Goldie.

The beautiful and nude Black Dragon rushed away. She came over to Felix and Andrea looking very confused and concerned. She had dark black eyes, hair the color of pitch, and was very out of her element.

"That's the fridge," Felix said, then indicated the appliance. "Next to it is a silver object with a handle on it. Inside it is the tea Goldie described. Take a cup, fill it with the tea, then look in the fridge. I'm sure there are small containers in there. Just take one of them and come back."

"Thank you. I'm so... I'm grateful to be here, but I'm so confused," mumbled Lucille, wandering over to the indicated area.

She hesitated briefly in front of the fridge before taking the handle and delicately pulling on it. Several tries later, she found the right amount of force to get it to open.

Mitä

"Andrea," Felix said, turning to look back to the Dragon Fight Club as Romina had called it.

"On iiiiiiit!" promised Andrea, an other bouncing out of her and racing off to Lucille's side.

Felix looked down to the table and called up his own character sheet. He wasn't that interested in watching Goldie practically beat people to death if he was being honest.

He was here to support her and little else.

Name: Felix Campbell		Race: Demi-God (Shared Portfolio)	
Alias: Felix (Over 50 items. Click to expand.)		Power: Modification (Limited)	
Physical Status: Healthy, Tired.		Mental Status: Concerned, Wistful	
Positive Statuses: None		Negative Statuses: None	
Might:	13		Add +1? (130,000)
Finesse:	20		Add +1? (200,000)
Endurance:	20		Add +1? (200,000)
Competency:	97		Add +1? (970,000)
Intellect:	74		Add +1? (740,000)
Perception:	16		Add +1? (160,000)
Luck:	10		Add +1?

		(100,000)

Ugh. I should have increased my Might more, rather than Finesse, Endurance, and Luck.

How was I supposed to know that if I had over two-hundred and fifty points the costs would blow up like that.

It's ridiculous.

Didn't happen to anyone else.

Feels like some kind of limiter, just to prevent me from hyper-investing in myself.

Though… I suppose that is the answer, isn't it. Scaling my power increases my power, which scales and provides more.

If the cost didn't go up, it wouldn't be balanced at all.

At least I was able to make myself nearly super-human in many ways.

There was a ping noise that came from the corner of his HUD. It was followed by a small mail icon appearing there.

" — sit right here next to Felix," Andrea advised, pulling the chair on his left out. "I'm going to go get the next Dragon, okay? Are you alright?"

"I'm… fine, yes. Thank you," murmured the Black Dragon. She still looked quite confused but was now sat down next to him. In front of her was a plate of smoked meats and some type of small pastry.

A plastic wrapped utensil set had been put down with it as well.

"Uhm... I... Nest-mate... your Dragon housewife doesn't know how to use these. Will... you instruct her?" asked Lucille, holding up the plastic silverware to him. "She doesn't want to disappoint you or Goldie."

"I've got you!" offered an Andrea that popped out of the one on his right.

Felix was thankful, as he wanted to know about the email.

Opening the wrist panel of his armor, he moved the cursor over and opened up the notification. It was an email from Tribune.

The subject was curious.

"Incoming Call" was the only thing written. Inside of the body of the email were a number of tables, graphs, names, and what looked like an entire case file of people and situations.

Then his cell phone began ringing, though it came through his helmet. It was now paired through the Legion app to be usable without taking the helmet off.

Felix picked up and cleared his throat.

"Tribune?" he asked.

"Legate, I have a report for you," Tribune responded. "It is too much to put into a usable email without providing you context information.

"May I intrude, Sir, and highlight pertinent information?"

A lovely Blue Dragon was being escorted over his way by the first Andrea. Several more had appeared now and were carrying over more chairs and tables. He had no idea where they'd gotten them, but it seemed like they were all being set up around him.

Romina was now directly in front of him as well, watching the Dragon fights.

"Of course, Tribune. I want the highlights though, what's up?" he asked.

"Legate, I have six locations that you need to investigate. One is in relation to your request, the others are all cover locations. One however, is a branch of the government that didn't subject itself to our requirements on their employees," Tribune simplified.

"Great," Felix murmured and slowly shook his head.

He quickly thought better of the situation, however. He realized this would be a perfect opportunity to flex the might of the Association.

To make sure everyone knew exactly what its jurisdiction was, and that there would be no room for anyone to disagree with him.

No different than the ongoing Dragon Fight Club.

"Alright. Put together everything we'll need," Felix asked. "Is there anything relatively nearby or is this a tomorrow at the soonest."

An amazingly beautiful and busty Platinum Dragon was currently being beat into submission by Goldie.

The golden beauty was holding onto the other Dragon's horns while smashing her knee over and over into the woman's guts and chest.

There was clearly fatal damage that had been done, considering the Platinum was throwing up what looked an awful lot like a melted strawberry slushee all over Goldie's leg and foot.

Even as Goldie continued to obliterate the other woman with her knee.

"There is one close that you can reach today. The rest will need to be tomorrow," reported Tribune.

"Fine, get it all ready for tomorrow. We'll have a night to sleep, rest, plan, then execute," commanded Felix.

Shoving the obviously dying Dragon Maiden to the floor Goldie put her hands on her hips and sighed loudly. Sprawled out on the ground, the Platinum just laid there.

A non-combative lump of broken flesh.

"You see? Carol, this is exactly why I keep telling you all to fight me to first blood. You're just causing me to make an even bigger mess. This dress is practically ruined," Goldie complained. Followed by her lifting up a foot, slamming it down into the Platinum Dragon's kneecap, and inverting it grotesquely. Causing the Dragon to shriek in pain.

Or at least try to, it ended with a bout of bright-red blood exiting her mouth in a projectile-like way.

"Now, young woman," Goldie said sternly. "I expect you to clean up this entire mess that you've left when we're done. After that, you can assist Lucille with my poor dress. Do you understand me?

"You'll also address everyone else here in a respectful way going forward. That was most unbecoming of you. Extremely inappropriate as a Dragon housewife. I was most displeased with your attitude and bearing."

The Platinum nodded her head weakly as she continued to gasp and throw up bright red blood.

One of her horns separated at the middle and clattered to the concrete. Goldie had apparently broken it halfway down during the fight.

"Good, then. Gaia, please restore Carol. She's learned the right way to do things," asked Goldie, then she looked back to the other Dragon Maidens.

There'd been a few that had some fight in their eyes before Carol.

None of them did now.

"Next Maiden, please, dears," asked Goldie with a bright smile, as blood dripped down from her chin and into her cleavage.

Chapter 22 – Not so Intelligent -

Flipping to the front a piece of paper, Felix looked it over.

Right now, Goldie and her Wing would be preparing for the visit that would be coming directly after this one. One that was being paid to a branch of the government that really didn't like to answer to anyone.

Most especially another branch.

Thankfully, that wasn't this meeting.

This first one was to help break-in Juno a bit more into her role.

In being so close to Andrea, Goldie, Faith, Miu, and himself as the Legate, it was a guarantee she'd discover his real name.

Who he actually was.

If she hadn't already, really.

Pushing the angle that "Felix Campbell" was just a case handler for the Association when it came to non-violent, and perhaps mistaken offenders, would be the perfect cover for him. More so that he could work with Juno and act as her superior directly.

Though it was still weird the way she'd been staring at him for the last minute.

"Romina, what is it?" Felix asked, looking away from the report.

"Just... uh... just... you're so normal. I expected you to be... err... more... anything else," admitted the young woman. The camera mounted to her armor was off and wouldn't be turned on till they were ready to begin filming.

This was her own "body cam" for this interaction. Felix had one himself, but it was embedded into a button of his suit-jacket.

"I mean, you're quite normal yourself. Aren't you?" he asked, giving her a smile. Then he tapped the paperwork. "Any questions on this? Really seems pretty normal to me.

"Likely used his power to his own benefit, Tribune picked him out, here we are. Not much to read between the lines. Looks like it's a predictor type of ability. Lots of scratchers in the state."

"Yeah. That all makes sense. I'm kinda low-key impressed by it," Juno admitted with a shrug of her shoulders. "Kinda neat. Tribune isn't just gonna sleep on her job. Didn't realize she was actively digging.

"All hustle and no play. Can't say I get the reason, but I kinda get the determination?"

"She's always digging. I just had her doing it in a passive way for a while there," Felix confessed and then turned the vehicle off. "She had some time, so I put her in an active state. Went hand in hand with figuring out about the guy who blew himself up. Kinda curious about what happened.

"So now she's really pushing some newer programs she wanted to their fullest capabilities. She can't ever really learn, but she can utilize any tool you give her pretty well."

Like a program.

"Oh yeah! That's a mood lots of people are feeling about that explosion. Everyone wants to really know what went down," Romina agreed with a rapid nod of her head.

Shaking his head, it took Felix a bit to really process what was being said. He wasn't into the slang and lingo of the younger generation here. He could puzzle it out, he found, but a lot of it was just unfamiliar upon hearing it.

"Right. You're... ready then?" he asked, pushing a bit. He wanted to get this one done quickly and get over to the next location.

"Ah! Yeah, sorry. I'll pop it on," Romina said with a laugh, and then reached up to tap her camera. The red light flickered to life and began to flash. A few seconds of that and it became a solid color. "Set!"

Felix opened the car door and got out. Not waiting, he moved around it and started heading up the steps to the front door.

There were so many facets of the world of Supers he had to balance to get everything to this very point. So many inconsequential bits and pieces he had to watch out for and move accordingly.

Michael had nearly derailed everything Felix had wanted, but the man had also provided a suitable means to corner Anya and Thomas. To push them into the final space Felix needed them in.

Stepping up to the front door of the quiet suburban neighborhood, Felix rapped on the door several times.

"Bad boys, bad boys, watcha gonna do," Romina whispered to herself. Her voice was so quiet it was only audible because she was nearly standing on Felix's heel. To the point that her armored hand bumped into the back of his hip. "Sorry. Didn't actually make a play on your ass."

"Eh... Andrea does it all the time. Or Miu," Felix said dismissively.

Right now, the two of them weren't far off.

Andrea was in a second vehicle, ready and prepared to storm the house if she needed him. Miu was more than likely nearby.

Glancing around, Felix wasn't quite sure where she'd ended up.

While she didn't have her wraith-like powers anymore, she'd clearly developed a keen ability to hide even in plain sight without it. Chances were she was here and was now glaring at Romina.

"You're not allowed to harm her, Miu," Felix said firmly, speaking to Miu. Regardless of where she was, he imagined she could hear him.

"Err, sorry, yeah, I didn't mean to and —"

Juno stopped talking as a lock inside clicked and the door slowly opened.

A man Felix expected was standing there in the doorway. This was early in the morning, so he hadn't had a chance to head off and meet up with Anya yet.

"Good morning," Felix said with a wide smile. "I'm with the Association of Supers. Or more commonly known as the Association. We'd like to discuss a clear and recent change in your status as a citizen."

Thomas was staring at Felix as if he'd told him that the sun would rise from his belly button and set in his asshole. So obviously dumbfounded was the man that he just slowly nodded his head.

"Great, then we'll move this to the living room," Felix said and then moved past Thomas and into the home. Romina entered as well and then shut the door behind herself. She put a hand to the back of Thomas and gestured toward Felix as he walked further away.

He'd watched it over his shoulder just to make sure Thomas didn't try to bolt. The last thing he wanted to do was dispatch Miu to run him down.

Taking a seat in the living room, Felix settled into the couch. He'd deliberately made sure to leave the case file in the car, as well as only bringing his phone with him.

Other than the camera on his person, there were no other electronics on him.

Thomas was likely already struggling with the fact that the camera on Juno's shoulder wasn't turning off. That it was actively recording him, despite his quite expected struggle to force it to shut off.

Except, Felix had long ago made the camera impervious to all abilities and skills. To record true and without error so long as he wished it.

It was Legion property and technology, after

all. He was the master of it.

"Come, Thomas, have a seat. We suspect that you actively have a power that allows you to modify, change, alter, and control electronics," Felix said amicably. "Let's just skip through a lot of the denials, the back and forth, and get to the heart of the matter here.

"The Association doesn't care what activities you take with your powers. In fact, it's irrelevant to us. Our jurisdiction isn't the utility, usage, or control of powers. Only their documentation, understanding, and recognition.

"Once you're in the Association system, we provide only the must-have information to the government, and the rest is guarded. Protected from everyone and anyone. Even the government.

"That's our purview and the end of it. Now… shall we talk?"

Thomas took a seat on the loveseat while Juno slowly walked to the corner of the room. She positioned herself so that she was more like a tripod. Capturing the entirety of the scene with the camera.

While she was here to film it, she was also a low-ability security guard for him. This was all part of getting her more experience in Legion as well.

"I know you," Thomas whispered, looking at Felix.

"You sure do. Everyone knows the Association. We like to look into people and things. Find out what we need to. Then get out," Felix confirmed with a small head nod. "We also do have an informant I'm afraid. Or at least, the police do.

"I have it on good authority that his first name is Michael. He was picked up on an aggravated assault. The woman is of course pressing charges and… well… Michael is starting to sell people out. Your name and… Anya's… came up.

"We're going to be visiting her tomorrow. It'd be wonderful if you could contact her and tell her how well your own interview went. It'd be best if we went through this as easy and simple as possible after all."

Thomas just sat there, staring at Felix.

Well… time to swoop in and save the day. This time as the supplier for these two. Just what I need is a small break in time from Romina.

"Err… this is embarrassing," Felix murmured and looked to his hands, then Romina. "I'll be right back, I left the case file in the car."

"I'll get it!" she offered even before Felix could leverage himself up. She was off in a flash, not waiting for him to agree to her doing such a thing.

Which was what he expected her to do.

When the door slammed shut, Felix looked to Thomas and smiled.

"I'll be dropping by to see Anya tomorrow in the morning. Make sure you're both there," Felix commanded the man. "We can discuss the supplier contact of mine again. Then maybe how he can get you out of this mess, since Michael is going to sink you. Now… let's pretend like we haven't said anything at all. You just keep looking awkward. Alright?"

Thomas nodded his head in short choppy motions.

"Perfect, just like that," Felix said with the wide smile he often practiced.

Working out perfectly.

Another plate spinning just the way I want it.

Romina came storming back into the house a minute later, grinning from ear to ear and looking incredibly pleased. The whole look reminded him of Andrea or Miu.

"Here you go!" she announced proudly, holding out the case file to him. There was a determination to her that was growing.

One that he'd be able to use to get viewers just as determined.

Spinning, spinning, spinning.

***

"We're in the middle of jobs right now," announced Juno to her viewers. They were watching her as she currently went through all the different functions of the new combat rifle she'd been presented with. "So this is a great time to show this off. Legate gave it to me this morning since we'd be doing some raid work in the near future.

"He said he couldn't afford to have me

running around without at least being able to defend myself. I mean… I'm not really a combat Super, ya know? So I got a glow up.

"That's my Jupiter though. Loading me with the drip till I beg him to stop. Which… we all know I never will."

Felix snorted at that, his helmet filtering out the noise and thankfully not broadcasting it. He knew that was true because the microphone icon in the bottom right of his HUD was still quite red.

So long as it was red, nothing he said would be transmitted outside of his helmet.

"I mean, he's my Jupiter so it isn't that surprising," Juno answered what sounded like a question, then she laughed. She, her camera, and everything in frame was at the back of the truck they were traveling in. It was done in such a way as to not reveal anyone with them, or where they were. "No, sorry ZootSuitMan. I don't accept donations, gifts, or bytes. Nothing like that at all.

"I'm purely here to promote Legion and the fire that it is. Not here to scrounge nickels off you."

Juno tilted her head to one side, likely listening in to whoever it was on the other end of her earpiece. That person was constantly feeding Romina with information of what chat was saying and if there was anything relevant.

Since she couldn't see the feed at all without wearing her helmet. Which she avoided as often as she could.

"Yeah, no. No hot-tub streams, no ASMR ear-licking, none of that. I mean... don't get me wrong, I hard Simp for some of those ladies, too and they've got more of my paper than I want to admit... but I'm not one of them. I'm just here for Legion and my Jupiter," Juno explained with a warm and rich laugh. "But hey, thanks for putting that out there. Maybe we can get like... an emote for something like that. Like a Legionnaire in a hot-tub."

Turning his head to the right, Felix found seven or eight Dragon Maidens there. They were all staring hard at him.

Watching him.

To him, they all felt incredibly eager for something. What that was, he didn't know, but he was sure it was something Goldie put into their heads.

Today's trip was all Dragon Maidens, Felix, and Romina. Miu and Andrea were keeping an eye on Thomas and Anya.

There was no telling what the two of them might do and he needed people he could trust watching them.

Faith, Carlotta, and Alma were of course at the Association. Ever working to keep the whole thing's foundations whirring and grinding away.

I need to reward my poor Dryads. I've had them locked away for a while now. Imprisoned behind paperwork and pens.

"Can I get you something?" asked the Platinum Goldie had pummeled with her knee. Felix was fairly certain her name was Carol, but he wasn't positive.

"No, I'm quite fine, thank you," Felix answered after making sure the microphone had turned green. He hoped it wouldn't be picked up by Juno's feed, but he wasn't sure.

Carol and Lucille were here with Goldie. The three of them were taking the leadership roles. The rest were all here to do what was asked of them.

"About a minute out," called the only Andrea with them in the driver's seat. All the rest were on various duties and responsibilities.

Sighing, not wanting to do this, yet having no other real option, Felix opened up his wrist panel again. He navigated his way over to the link-up he had with the truck itself.

Atop it was a receiver and transmission dish that was powerful enough to keep a steady internet connection. Using that through the Legion apps, Felix had brought Tribune along for this ride.

This was her first real world adventure beyond her own networks. Something Felix had never wanted to do. He was terrified of one day Tribune slipping the leash and going wild.

Pushing the executable file, Felix knew there was no way to go back. Tribune would now be on the internet itself. Pulling all the data she wanted and infiltrating any and every system she wanted to.

She was a VI from so far in the future that she might as well have been magic. There wasn't any way a system from this day and age could stand up to her.

"Legate, I'm ready," came Tribune's voice from inside her helmet. "The update is complete and I am now 'unshackled', as the program called it."

"Great. I need you to hit the local area networks and break in. We're heading into the heart of the Central Intelligence Agency after all.

"No telling if they're going to even let us in the front door, let alone answer my questions. Need you to pin all their systems, lock everything down, and trap them inside their own networks. Cell phones, laptops, computers, seal it all and lock it down," Felix requested. "Do it in such a way that they're not even aware it's happening as well. Let benign transmissions or data go through. Anything that might be an issue for us, end it."

"I've received your orders, Legate. I have breached their network and am currently taking it over," Tribune stated. "I should have full control within twenty seconds."

Twenty... full control over the CIA in twenty seconds... right.

Okay... okay.

I have quite literally the E-Pocalypse at my beck and call. I need to be very careful.

Andrea turned them up the road and began moving them toward the iron gate and guarded perimeter of the building.

"Complete. Legion is now in control. Should I move further, Legate?" Tribune asked.

"Err, further into what?" asked Felix with a sinking feeling.

"Should I begin downloading their data?" inquired Tribune.

"Oh, that's... yeah. Do that. Start downloading all of it. Never know if we'll need it, and it's better to have it than not. Especially since technically speaking you're more secure than they are," Felix said, feeling a lot better.

He'd been mildly concerned that Tribune was going to go break her way through the entirety of the country. Which he truly believed was possible for her at this point.

"Downloading. Uploading Legion Fortification application for future access," reported Tribune.

"Hi, we're with the Association," Andrea said as they came to a stop at the guard house. "Here's my badge, and a list of everyone with me. We're here to conduct a Super Power Audit on behalf of the President of the United States.

"You're welcome to contact the President if you have a question, or you can pass the message on to the current director of the agency.

"We won't be leaving until we can speak with the director, by the way. If we must, we'll be forced to enact the Association Investigative Act. Which would require us to use force to conduct the Audit.

"We're not restricted from using deadly force. I'm required to let you know we have eight

Dragons on board as well as the Legate himself to perform the audit.

"Right now."

Felix could practically hear the gears in the guard's head grinding as they tried to process what he'd just been told. The teeth of them slipping and pulling at one another in opposite directions.

"I'll… reach out to the director," the guard muttered after a few seconds.

"Wonderful. We can wait a few minutes for him to make up his mind if this needs to occur through force or not," Andrea said brightly. "By the way, that's a nice red-dot sight on your rifle. Who's the manufacturer?"

Well… here we go.

There's no going back after I kick over the CIA.

My jurisdiction must be respected though. Even if I have to force everyone to respect it.

Because once everyone respects it, then no one will question it. We can be the neutral party that follows the line and nothing else.

Even at a global level.

Chapter 23 - Enlightened -

"Can I go open the gate?" asked a Blue Dragon that Felix just couldn't remember the name of. "I'll just transform, open it, and we can go in. If they want to cause a problem, I'll just start eating them."

"They'll taste terrible," warned Goldie with a loud sigh. "Not to mention, it really isn't very polite as a Housewife to try and devour your host.

"For whatever reason, after becoming the Nest-mate of a Human, Humans taste terrible. Something akin to mud and dirt, honestly."

"Really? I've never eaten one," Lucille asked curiously, looking to Goldie. "Lots of primates, but never a Human. They weren't around yet."

"They tasted more like hogs than primates before," Goldie remarked with a puzzled look on her face. She was facing Lucille directly now. "As I said though. They taste dreadful now.

"Though if we do have to start chewing our way through them, be sure to try and do it with some thought to manners. Their arms and legs tend to slip out when you start chewing.

"It isn't as if we'd be in a rush, and they can't harm us. Nor can they harm anyone here, really. The Legionnaire armor is quite sturdy. It's a shame we can't wear any, but it wouldn't do us much good.

"So chew delicately and mindfully."

All the Dragon Maidens looked down at

themselves.

They were all dressed in the exact same thing.

A button-up white shirt with a black tie. Over that, a blue windbreaker with "Assoc" on the front, where the breast pocket would be, and "Association" written on the back. Jeans and combat boots rounded out the look.

"I don't like clothes," Carol murmured.

"Yes, I understand and even agree. But as a Housewife, we're expected to dress in the current fashion or in the trend, with some sex appeal, and just a hint of modesty," Goldie lectured, looking around at the Dragons surrounding her. "Not to mention, we really shouldn't be nude unless we have no choice. That's just frowned on in Human society."

A lovely green-eyed Green Dragon sighed but nodded her head.

"Uhm, the… the director will see you," said the guard who'd come back. Felix couldn't see Andrea, the Dragon in the passenger seat, or the guard. "Please move down the road and stop when directed."

"Wonderful," Andrea said excitedly. "I was wondering if we'd have to knock down the gate and blast our way in. I'd feel bad breaking both your arms and legs. You seem nice."

"I-I-yeah. Yeah," answered the guard, his voice followed by the sound of the gate retracting.

Turning, Felix looked to Juno. She was

currently having a discussion about the property-purchase benefits that the Legion offers Legionnaires.

" — no. Jupiter bought me a house. He's my Jupiter, what'd you expect? I'm his Juno and that's how it is.

"While I didn't have to use the program, I'd been looking at it. It's a single percent interest loan against your salary for the period of the loan. It isn't compounding either, just a simple interest."

"Juno, time to move. Bucket-up," Felix ordered. He didn't mind his voice coming through her stream this time. "Can't stream this one, but the next one you can."

"Oh! You hear that? Can't stream this one but the next one'll be fire! Just wait and see. I'll see you all later, thanks for coming. Don't forget to follow and subscribe. I'll post the video later!" Juno said and reached up to tap the camera, turning it off. "Okay… and clear."

Romina laughed, reached down to pick her helmet, then looked to Felix.

"They're so thirsty! Someone offered to make me a vtuber model, too. Is that alright?" Juno asked, pulling her helmet down over her head.

"Yes. Just make sure you purchase it from them so that you, and Legion, own the copyright and IP for it. Never let anyone ever own your IP under any circumstance," instructed Felix as the truck started to speed up. "Expense it to Legion and forward it up through your contact. I think it's Alma, right?"

"Uh, I didn't... right, okay... yeah. I'll do that. Got it," Juno said with a sharp nod of her head. "Yes, I'll talk to Alma about it. She's been really helpful."

"Great. Now... safety off, chamber a round," Felix said, motioning to her weapon. "Might end up slaughtering a whole bunch of CIA agents. The Association doesn't answer to anyone. Not even the president. The government set us up as a neutral agency that can operate across borders.

"They just happen to get a bunch of benefits for us being headquartered in their domain. Otherwise we'd have gone to Canadia or Mexico."

Romina was nodding her head rapidly now.

"I get it. Wish I had it all planned out like you do. I was just kinda runnin' around wild-like with trash ideas," Romina murmured. "I'm not sure what I would be doing if you hadn't picked me up when you did."

"Probably the same thing. I just happened to notice you before you took off," confessed Felix. Considering he knew what her superpower was, he imagined he was being completely honest as well. "Already told you about your Super ability so you know that I'm right."

"I don't think you get how bad it was for me when you found me. Superpower or not," Romina said in a much more subdued voice. "I was living with my parents till you bought me that house. There was no way I could afford to move out any time soon either.

"Still paying off my college debts, let alone

the price of housing. Everything is just… it's too much. I could only dream at owning a house and be like, 'goals'. That was the extent of it."

Felix snorted at that and then stood up, his hand grabbing the rail that ran along the top of the vehicle. Planting his feet, he shrugged his shoulders to make sure his cape was correctly positioned. With his left hand, he pulled out the side-arm he carried.

Looking it over, he thumbed the safety off, let go of the rail for a second to pull back the slide, then fully chambered it after seeing there was nothing in it. Pushing the handgun back into the holster, he then grasped the rail once again.

Moving forward, he eased past Romina and stood at the exit.

He was the Legate.

He'd have to be front and center, completely visible and very much in charge.

"Agents ahead, directing us to stop. All armed," reported Andrea.

Nodding his head, Felix said nothing. That was all expected.

Soon, the vehicle came to a full stop. When Felix heard the transmission get pushed into park, he grabbed the door and opened the back of the truck.

Stepping out into the day, he looked around.

There were a number of agents around and they were all indeed armed. A number of them had put on ballistic vests as well.

"Where's the director?" Felix asked, moving toward the closest agent. "I've come to audit the agency. It would be best if I was conducted to him quickly so I may proceed with my duties."

"Uh huh," growled the Agent.

Felix could hear the Dragons hopping down from the truck behind him. Then a hissing noise as they likely stretched their wings out.

Their jackets had all been designed to allow the base of their wings to not get caught up in the fabric. So long as they put it on first then allowed their wings to be material afterwards at least.

"Director?" Felix asked politely for the last time.

The next time he asked, he'd do it with a drawn gun.

"You'll be taken to a holding ce—"

Felix went to draw his pistol and was beat to the punch. Lucille flashed past him, slammed into the Agent, and pinned him to the ground.

Roaring into the man's face, her wings spread out behind her, she was perched atop him like a lion with its kill.

"You will answer the Legate with respect, or I'll pull this whole building down by myself!" screamed Lucille in what felt like it was coming from her Dragon form.

Smoke and flame began to curl out of her mouth and nostrils with every word. She was rapidly losing control of herself from what Felix could see.

Everyone instantly reacted to that.

Many guns were drawn and leveled at Lucille, Felix, and everyone else.

Except nobody in the Association minded it. In fact, they began to fan out and take up positions. As if they were expecting this to devolve very quickly into a blood bath.

"Legate! My apologies!" called a voice from the front of the building. "Let's just move past this please!

"I'd very much appreciate it if you could release the agent! They're just scared and being stupid!"

A man was scrambling forward toward Felix and the others. He was moving at a quick trot.

"Are you the Director?" Felix asked, moving away from Lucille and the agent who'd now pissed his pants. Lucille hadn't moved and was still squatting down atop the man. Flames licking out of her mouth with every exhale.

"Yes, yes I'm the Director. Director Behr. I'm very sorry for all this. They're just scared and stupid," said the man, coming over to Felix. "We didn't know you were coming."

"We don't announce raids, director," Felix said, not bothering to hold his hand out to the other man. This was not a trip that would foster goodwill or cooperation. "You're in noncompliance with the directive and jurisdiction I've been allowed to operate in.

"We're here to audit your personnel with or

without your permission. If it's without your permission, we will close down your building and begin moving through your employee lists and everyone in the building. You would not be released from detention until we reach at least ninety-percent compliance.

"If it's found you've been harboring unregistered Supers willingly, then the full weight of the law will come down on you. You'll be registered, labeled as a Super Offender, and then sent to the super max prison for Supers."

"Legate, there are many requests for assistance being sent out at this time to many different parties," Tribune reported. "I'm filtering everything as you stated. I also deactivated their alarms, systems, and automatic protocols such as data and file destruction."

"Good work," Felix said, making sure the mic stayed red by keeping his volume low. The Director still hadn't said anything and was just staring at Felix in shock. "Director, I've preemptively sealed and knocked out your communications, security measures, and protocol.

"This is the turning point before I force the audit, or you assist me. How would you like to proceed? There's no going back once I begin.

"You should also know that you're the only agency that didn't comply. Every other one did, as well as each branch of the government. You stand alone."

Blinking several times, the Director clearly took a moment to re-evaluate the situation. Outside looking in, Felix felt like perhaps the man had over-estimated his value and worth.

"We'll cooperate of course," the Director said. "How can I assist you?"

"Bring every single person in your agency out here. We'll complete the audit here. Once we're satisfied that we've spoken with the vast majority of your people, then we'll release you," Felix clarified. "I do understand that you have agents that cannot be seen, spoken to, or even communicated-with regularly.

"For those who cannot be here today, please send them to the association at their earliest convenience, or invite us back out to perform an interview. Please don't try to subvert this requirement, as I would dislike having to come back here due to your non-compliance."

Romina was slowly walking sideways and looking up at the building. The camera on her shoulder was actively recording, just as he'd instructed.

She just wasn't streaming it.

Her camera was aimed directly at Felix and the Director.

Everyone will learn that when it comes to Supers, the Association and Legion is a must. We will wield no power outside of the need to document, interview, and speak with every Super Powered human.

A global utility company that offers assistance to all, but no political help to anyone.

"Of course," murmured the Director. "Of

course."

***

Goldie walked back from the most recent group of agents they were going through. Keeping it to batches of three or four people allowed her and all the other Dragons to get a good read on their thoughts.

"All set," she reported, holding the detector device in her hands. It was the same one he'd used previously in front of government agents.

All it did now was turn blue if the person was more than just a human. Anyone in Legion could use it so long as they wore certain pieces of Legion equipment.

Armor, rings, or helmets would all suffice.

"None in that group either," Romina grumbled. "Is it really that rare? I didn't think it was but... maybe it is?"

"It's rare. More so than you'd think. It's just that the Association sees the full concentration of it since it's all we work with," Felix explained and then shook his head. "It's fine. We're just here to make sure everyone understands our jurisdiction. No more, no less. It's why we're doing this outside, not inside.

"Anything they have going on in there is of no matter to us. Not really, at least. We only care about their people and if they're a Super or not."

"Legate, the next target must be moved on,"

reported Tribune in his helmet. "They look like they're going to begin moving their operation according to the most recent information I've taken from their devices.

"They're aware that the Association is currently raiding facilities and feel like other government figures will use this as an opportunity to do the same to them."

"Huh... alright. What is it again? What're we going to?" asked Felix.

"A religious community. You called it a cult," Tribune answered.

"Ah... yeah. The people who think the world is coming to an end in a few years," Felix murmured. "I forget the details of what they believe, and I honestly don't care.

"You're positive they have Supers in their congregation? I wouldn't want to move on this just to have it come back as nothing."

"I can confirm that there is a chance they have several Supers within their ranks to eighty-percent, Sir," answered Tribune.

"Eighty percent... that's... okay, yeah. That's worth the time investment," Felix said and let out a slow breath. "We'll go there next then I guess. Wasn't planning on it.

"I'd really rather not get tied up in religion. That's just asking to get slammed right back into politics. The two are far too inter-weaved for it to be worth our while."

"Uh, but... isn't politics literally just the

transition of moral beliefs into the desire to shape law?" asked Romina. "And what is religion if not moral beliefs?"

Errr... did... that actually come from Romina?

Looking to Juno, Felix just stared at her.

"I took a couple courses in philosophy," she said defensively, holding one hand up. "It stuck with me to a degree. What I said wasn't wrong, was it?"

"No. Not really. It's just... not something I expected from you, that's all," Felix observed.

"Happy to surprise you, my Jupiter," Juno said and then head-bobbed to the next group of people. "Legionnaire Goldie, shall we proceed?"

The Dragon had watched the entire exchange with a smile, looking excited and pleased with the situation.

"Legate. We've received a request from the Guild of Heroes, as well as an email from the outside. It was addressed to the Legate from one of the individuals you asked me to track," Tribune stated. "The request from the Guild is to assist with a hostage situation. There's an unregistered pair of Supers who have taken over a supermarket.

"They have a number of hostages taken and the Guild is unable to make any progress. One of the Supers is able to disable the powers of anyone else nearby. The second is extremely accurate with a firearm. They've been able to kill anyone who's come close, as well as a number of law enforcement personnel who were attempting to siege the building."

Felix was somewhat shocked to hear that.

Though on reflection, he shouldn't be surprised. If there really was a situation where the police couldn't apprehend a Super, and the Guild couldn't make it happen either, there wouldn't be many other people to turn to.

In this case, they had someone they could call.

Being unregistered meant that this situation technically fell into the domain of the Association. With him pushing as hard as he had to make sure that people respected his jurisdiction, he couldn't really turn away when he was being called in exactly for that.

"I need a Dragon to ride and a team to go with me," Felix said, turning to look at Goldie. "Miu and Romina will come with me. What Dragon can go with me, Goldie?"

"Carol will take a squad of Dragons and move with you," Goldie answered quickly. "Lucille and another squad will handle the cult with me. I'll make sure to handle it with kid gloves, dear. Andrea, Cathy, and the rest can handle this location and finalize the audit.

"That'd divide up things relatively well, is that an acceptable suggestion?"

"Perfect," Felix said and then turned to look for Carol. He needed to get going and now.

Chapter 24 – Shifting Goal -

Carol brought them around in a sharp turn. Flying over the very obvious location where the hostage situation was occurring.

Holding tight to the back of the Dragon, Felix scanned the area to try and see if there was anything to see from up here. If there was perhaps something he'd miss if he was on the ground.

It looked much like any supermarket he'd ever seen before.

If I ignore the huge number of police, SWAT, and bystanders. That's a massive crowd.

Massive.

Lots of reporters, too.

"Romina, you streaming?" Felix asked.

"No. I'm recording though. I can push it out later after editing. Just in case we get things on camera we shouldn't," answered Romina. "Is that okay?"

"That'll be good," Miu answered for Felix. She was directly behind him and wearing a full Centurion's armor. He needed her here and now more than making sure things didn't go sideways back at Langley. "I can provide some alternative shots from my own camera, though it isn't as clear as yours."

"Yaaaaas. That'd be perfect, Miu. Thank... thank you so much. Your advice has been perfect, by the way," Romina said with an obvious hesitancy.

"I figured it would. You should listen to me," said Miu, who then pointed down to the ground. "Carol, bring us in near that large van. That'll be where they're planning things."

Felix followed the line of Miu's arm and found that she was pointing down at what was quite obviously a rally point for Lily and Kit. If they were here, then they were most definitely in charge of the situation.

"Can… can we do a hero landing? You said that this armor could withstand a drop like this, right Tribune? Can I please… please do it?" asked Romina in an increasingly eager voice.

"The armor can withstand the fall. I have prepared for such an event and loaded appropriate body physic guidance so that you'll land upright," Tribune answered.

"Yes. You'll all perform this entrance," Miu interjected before Felix could address that. "I'll go first. Give me your camera. Land in front of the HQ area."

Romina handed the camera to Miu, who took it and dove off to the side. Cutting through the air and rapidly vanishing out of sight.

"I'll wait for a minute," Carol said loudly over the wind. "Then move you in to a spot that, if you drop, you should fall straight down and land in front of them."

"Oh my gosh. This is so lit. I'm so excited! Hero entrance! I'm totally going to use it as my splash intro. Or maybe the sub gif?!" Romina squeaked in a high-pitched voice.

Felix held back a sigh and just waited.

This felt ridiculous but also might actually help bring everyone into the spotlight for the younger generations. A real-life hero entrance was something that'd likely push the news in their favor.

"I'll drop in later. It wouldn't be good for me to land naked. Amy... clothes?" Carol asked, holding one of her claws back over her shoulder.

A green-eyed Green Dragon put the bundle of clothes between the tips of Carol's claws.

"Off we go!" Romina giggled insanely, then simply rolled off Carol's back.

Felix waited, watching the Dragon Maidens as they did the same, moving off Carol's back and tumbling through the air.

As soon as they were all gone, Felix did the same. He needed to be the last to arrive, being the Legate.

The wind tore at him as everything rushed by him loudly. He could hear it even through his armor. Getting his legs straight under him took a bit of fiddling around.

After a second, the armor assisted in this endeavor and began moving him about in minute ways. If he fought against it there was no chance of it overpowering him.

Faster than he understood it, the world rushed upward.

Then he slammed down into the concrete. Felix had managed to land behind the others who were all in the process of standing up.

All eyes were on them and their entrance.

Standing up, Felix moved forward toward Lily and Kit.

"Cute. I liked the flashy entrance," Lily said with a laugh as he came forward. She gave him a pout that was clearly fighting a smile. "Think you can give me some armor so I can do that? You gave Kit a present, don't I get one?

"You can't treat us differently, that's not fair if you do. No favorites allowed."

I... err... what? That's... hm.

"I'll think about it," allowed Felix, coming to a stop in front of the two women. "What's the situation and how can I help?"

There was a thud behind him that caused him to glance back over his shoulder. Carol was there, getting to her feet. She'd managed to somehow dress herself as she fell to the earth.

The other five Dragons arranged themselves quickly around Carol, who moved into place behind Felix and Miu.

Romina was on his left and her camera was already back in its original position and recording.

"Armor, Legate," Lily said when Felix had looked back to her. She'd closed the distance on him and put a fingertip to the center of his chest. "Armor specifically for me. Okay? I want a set. You know... everything about me I'm sure, so I don't need to even say anything more. Even what day is coming up, I bet."

Lily punctuated the statement by tapping his

armor with her fingernail.

Okay… now I know there's something going on here. I missed something, I know it.

The only day coming up of any significance to her is the anniversary of her parents' death, but that's two weeks out. She never wanted anything on that day other than a meal and solitude.

Damnit, is it a test?

Lily had turned around and motioned at Kit as she went.

"Two Supers," Kit said, entirely unphased by the back and forth just now. Which meant she'd already raided Lily's thoughts, knew what was going on, or was entirely uninterested. "One is a crack-shot. The other is able to completely invalidate Super's powers.

"No one can get close. Anyone who tries, gets shot. Several fatalities, eight wounded. I've been able to read the minds of some of the hostages at times, but not often.

"Man caught his wife in the grocery store with another man. Shot them both dead. His brother was with him at the time. There was an off-duty cop in the store who held them up long enough for more police to arrive, though he paid for it with his life."

Felix nodded his head to that. It seemed pretty simple to him.

This was an impromptu situation, which meant there was no real plan for these two. They were just acting on impulse.

"No demands, no requests, nothing," Kit added, confirming Felix's thoughts.

"Juno, get in there and see if they're willing to talk. Three Dragons will go with you," commanded Felix, looking to Juno then Carol.

Carol pointed at three of the five Dragons and then gestured to Juno.

"Shadow," Felix said, turning to look at Miu. "Get on the roof. Take two others with you and see if there is a false ceiling you can get into. Worst case, just right above where the hostage takers are.

"Carol, you're with me. We're going to go see if we can't walk right through the front door and reason with them."

"Legate," came Tribune's voice, crashing through his speakers. "I think there's been an incident with Thomas and Anya. Michael shook his police tail and handlers. There were reports of gunshots around the area of the bar they work out of, and I can no longer get a location ping from any of their cell phones."

Felix was staring ahead as he listened. Seeing nothing as he processed it.

"Send whoever's close enough and that can respond to it. I'll move to it as soon as I finish this up," commanded Felix.

"That'd be you, Legate. You're the closest and the only Legionnaire who can respond," countered Tribune. "Everyone else is busy, Sir."

Sighing, Felix closed his eyes and let his chin dip down slightly.

"I need a Dragon and Miu," Felix murmured quietly, the helmet interpreting that as only wanting to be transmitted to the com system. "Carol, I'm leaving you in charge here. Make this happen without any losses. None. I want everyone who's alive right now, to walk out alive.

"Have Romina process the Supers for registration once it's done, then hand them over to Kit and Lily. After that, return to Goldie and Andrea."

A heartbreakingly pretty Red Dragon rushed forward and stood in front of him. In her ear was one of the earpieces they'd given to all the Dragons so they could listen in and talk through the system if needed.

"I'll go, Legate," offered the Red.

"Great," he said and sighed. "Then please strip for me. You, me, and Miu have a trip we need to take, and I need a ride there."

"I'm guessing something changed?" asked Lily. Clearly she'd only heard the Dragon speak and the fact that everyone had frozen up.

"CIA is misbehaving," Felix lied. "I have to go deal with their Director."

Taking the Red Dragon by the elbow, Felix began escorting her away. He needed to get going. He couldn't afford to let Anya or Thomas fall now.

Felix needed them for the League of Villains.

Which meant he had to rush off to keep one of his spinning plates from falling off and shattering on the ground.

* * *

***

"The name she chose is Evelyn, though goes by Evie. Before you ask," Miu said, her voice transmitting through the helmets. "They didn't really have names when they died. Not ones we could pronounce at least."

"Thanks," he muttered. They were nearing the point where they'd have to get down to the ground. Find a place that Evie the Red Dragon could put them down, change, dress, put her earpiece back in, and then get ready to go find Anya and Thomas.

Miu squeezed in closer to him, her hips practically thrusting up against him, and her arms tightened around his middle. He could feel her helmet hard pressed to his shoulder plates.

"I love you, F-Felix," Miu whispered. "I've never known anything so perfectly true in my life. It isn't just my power talking either. I can see that Mikki would easily fall into the same trap I did.

"It isn't the power that does it, it's that you look at us as people. People that you want for yourself, for who they are. Without fear or judgement."

"Love you, too, Miu. You ready for this by the way? Once we land, I need you to hide and see what you can do. Evie and I will play bait and see what we can dig up," Felix tried, hoping to course-correct her.

"Yes, that's fine. Is there... any possibility of giving me my Wraith powers back?" Miu asked. "I don't know what the cost is anymore, but hopefully it isn't too expensive. I can be far more useful with them."

"Let me see," he muttered as Evie started to slowly bank around. Felix lifted a hand and pointed. "Evie! We need to go get to that building there. Get us somewhere near that so you can shift, and then we go in on foot!"

"Yes, Nest-mate!" responded the Red, turning much more sharply now.

Felix ignored it and then tried to call up the ability to modify Miu.

To give her the power she'd had previously had back again. The powers to hide and be part of the shows. A powerset the Super known as Wraith had possessed.

Name: Miu Campbell	Condition: Insane. In love.
If No Action Taken: None	Action >> Alter Power: Cost 3,916,342 points

Arrrghh!

That's... more or less everything I have, but this is probably something she'll need. I'll need her around me at all times moving forward.

I'm a lot tougher than I was, but I'm still just one man.

I have to invest in everyone else... to be able to

invest in me.

Closing his eyes, Felix accepted the cost and just hung onto Evie.

He felt Miu clutch even tighter to him as the power activated. Then she released him and simply slid off Evie. Causing Felix to open his eyes and look down.

They'd landed and he hadn't noticed.

They were in a small overly wooded park. One that was full to bursting with trees.

Getting off the Red Dragon, Felix immediately started to peel his armor off. He'd have to hide it somewhere nearby and come back for it afterward.

In no time at all Evie was dressed, Felix was in his street clothes that were under his armor, Miu was gone, and they were ready to start moving to the bar.

"This'll be interesting," Evie said, pulling down on the blouse. It fit her fairly well, though it was a bit tighter around her waist and hips.

Evie shared a very similar shape with Goldie, though she had a little more and a little less in a few places. Felix had a hard time looking at her though.

As far as he knew, he'd never met someone better looking.

Ever.

Dragons are too damn gorgeous. This is ridiculous.

Evie was wearing clothes they'd more or less stolen from Goldie. Having raided her closet at the trailer on the way here. A blouse, skirt, and some sneakers that fit.

They'd almost stopped long enough for Felix to get out of his armor, but they weren't sure if he'd need it for where they were going later.

"Why's that?" Felix asked, glancing at the Red Dragon curiously.

"I've never had alcohol. I've only been in two vehicles in my life and I'm going to see a bunch more. Everything I ate in my life was either cooked by my breath or raw until yesterday so... cooking, is very fascinating, too," Evie said, grinning at him and tilting her head to one side. "I'd never worn clothes. Seen buildings or... anything, really.

"Even speaking like this, in a tongue that isn't my birth tongue, is interesting. The whole world is new to me and I'm excited to be here."

"Oh," Felix murmured, realizing the truth in her words. To the Dragons, the world was completely unknown to them.

He only now realized that they were incredibly strong mentally to have stepped into such a thing. That if he'd been put into their place, he wasn't sure he'd be able to handle it as well as they did.

"How good are you at hunting?" Felix asked and began walking away from the park. He stopped briefly to put his armor at the bottom of a trashcan, beneath the bag itself. While it was possible someone might find it, he doubted it very much.

From the look of it, no one checked these

cans regularly for much of anything, let alone clean them out.

That, and Tribune was able to access it directly. She'd be able to find it regardless of where it went. After that, they'd just send Miu or Andrea by Dragon.

"I'm very good at it!" Evie boasted, catching up to him with a little bounce. Her red hair was pulled back and hung behind her head in long waves. "As a Red, I'm... not as strong as others. Or as fast as say, an Orange.

"I have to be smarter, cunning, vicious. Which meant I had to be an amazing hunter, since I'm terrible at all that other junk!"

Evie had said the last bit with a wave of her hand and a laugh. It'd been said in just the right way that Felix couldn't help himself and laughed along.

He also felt a need to compliment her, though he managed to wrestle that feeling down.

"Hunting was probably all I was good at. Had to find dead or dying things all the time to survive, too," Evie continued, her head turning and looking ahead of them. Her tone was good natured. "Well, I think I was good at it at least. I did kinda die to starvation so... couldn't have been that great. I blame that on there not being any food nearby though and that I was wounded. Most things died then.

"Ha, guess we'll find out!"

Grinning, Felix felt a lot better about Evie.

She didn't seem as brutal, feral, or hard edged as so many of the Dragons did.

In fact, she reminded him a lot of Goldie. Like she was far more concerned with things that had nothing to do with being a Dragon.

"Did you try to fight Goldie to the death?" Felix asked as they reached the street. Turning, they started moving down it toward the bar.

"No? I surrendered after stepping up and ran off to the table. The... fridge... had a bunch of other things than just what Goldie had prepared. I ate all that. Drank a bunch of metal cans with sugary liquid in it. Found dried meat in a cabinet, too," Evie gushed. "Then there was a glass box thing that had a bunch of bags with crunchy bits in them. I busted that open and ate everything inside.

"Next to that was another box but it had a plastic front. I just tore that open and drank everything I found inside. The world right now is awesome. Though... uh... I think I'm gonna have to start moving around a lot more or I'm gonna get fat."

Felix was laughing without a concern. Unable to help himself, he was now very interested in the exuberant red headed and red eyed Red Dragon.

"What? It's not funny! I'm already kinda chunky in some areas. I'm going to have to be careful. Food is way too easy to get in this world," complained Evie, looking down at herself. "Goldie is in way better shape than me. I wonder how she manages it."

"Well. I love the look of you as you are right now, so don't worry about it too much.

"other than that, we're here. Lots of mind reading will be needed. Also, you need to pretend to be my wife," Felix said and then took Evie's hand in his.

"But I am your wife? Your Dragon Housewife. Goldie said so. There's no need to pretend," Evie argued with a confused look. "Do you mean I need to pay more attention to you? I can do that. Don't worry. I will look very much like your Nest-mate. Your Dragon Housewife."

Felix was now worried and nervous. He didn't want to continue any further with someone who didn't even know what a vending machine was, but he needed to get to Anya and Thomas.

He noted that the placard in the window said the Doctor was in.

There was a brief presence behind him. Two hands pressed to the middle of the back in a supportive way.

Ah.

Miu.

Okay then… here we go.

Chapter 25 – Physical Limits -

Opening the door to the room, Felix waited for a moment for Evie to go in before him. Following her inside while still holding her hand, he let the door close behind him.

Every single person in the bar except for only a few, looked to him and Evie.

Not just Evie, which would've been understandable given the way she looked, but also him. They weren't just looking because she was pretty.

"Anya wanted to see us," Felix announced, then began moving to the back. Where she, Thomas, and Michael had often been.

The moment he said her name, almost everyone ignored him and Evie completely. As if they didn't exist and were no longer worth any attention.

There were a few men who were unable to look away from Evie, which meant they weren't likely part of the Anya-Thomas gang.

Those were the ones Felix would have to be wary of. If they were interested in Evie, then they could only be a handful of things.

Innocent bystanders were of course a possibility, but an unlikely one. They were more than likely policemen, federal agents, opposing gang members, or something similar to those.

Taking Evie a bit more firmly by the hand, he began escorting her to the back of the area. For her part, the Red Dragon pushed in close to him and laid her free hand on the middle of his torso.

Holding to him, though also casting a bold and aggressive look at anyone who was watching her. It was an oddly possessive, yet submissive, way to move with him.

Reaching the back-room Felix opened the door, then closed it behind himself. He didn't have to try too hard to get an idea of what'd happened.

There was a visible pool of blood nearby. It didn't look quite fresh though, the edges had the appearance of starting to dry up.

"Not big enough to be a kill, but very wounded," Evie murmured and moved away from him. The beautiful Dragon got down on all fours and began to sniff at the blood.

Moving around the blood, she gave him an upskirt view at one point, then a down the blouse shot as she moved around. Felix was quick to look away in both instances and began to inspect the area.

Especially since she hadn't found any underwear of Goldie's that'd fit.

The pool of blood looked to be where someone had huddled up on the ground. Not where the wounding had started.

There was a splatter of blood on one of the seats and table that ran along the wall nearby. There was also a very smeared bloody handprint on the edge of the surface.

"Unsure if they're alive," announced Evie,

peering up at Felix from where she was hands and knees over the blood. "I don't know what humans do for wounds but if it's better than what I used to do, maybe they lived? Can follow the scent of the person and the blood. Fairly clear."

"Yeah, right up until they get into a car," complained Felix. He had no doubt this would just go out behind the bar, to the alleyway, and into a vehicle. Which would eliminate their ability to track it very well.

He briefly considered trying to spend enough points to grant Evie the ability to run the scent down, but he didn't want to waste points if it wasn't necessary. The first step was establishing if they even had left.

Michael could have easily simply taken her somewhere nearby.

"Follow it," Felix requested. "There're two other scents that'll likely be just as strong in here. Going to bet they'll be with whoever left that… pool."

"Ah! Yes. I will follow it. I'm still getting used to this… partial… transformation, thing. Goldie was very good in instructing us, but it's still strange," Evie said and then got to her feet. Her clothes were somewhat mussed, though she didn't seem to notice either.

Reaching up she pushed her fingers to her nose and then deliberately wriggled it around. Her eyes began to glow a very intense red that reminded him of his Dryads.

Then she let her hand drop and grinned at

him.

"Got it! Ha. Okay. I should be able to scent just as well as I can as a Dragon," Evie said, then looked down at herself. "By the way, why am I mussed? What's mussed?"

She began to gently pull at the fabric here and there and managed to settle herself into her clothes again as she clearly pulled the definition from his mind.

"Oooh, I get it. You really have a strong fixation on my human form by the way. I'm pleased to hear your thoughts echoing it endlessly, but it's a wonder you humans ever get anything done with such a sex drive," Evie said, her eyes looking to him curiously. "Sorry, I'm trying not to read your thoughts. Anyways, shall we go?"

"Please," Felix requested. If they didn't get moving it was quite possible Miu would try to strangle Evie.

Glaring at the spot behind Evie, Felix was almost positive that's where she was, too. Contemplating strangling the Dragon.

"S-sorry," whispered Miu, exactly from the spot he'd been glaring at. Her voice sounded strained. As if she'd been on the verge of attacking. "Sorry. I'm b-better now. Err. I just need a moment."

Evie was ignoring the disembodied voice of Miu. Apparently she'd known where the woman was and what she was thinking.

That or she just didn't care at all.

She was entirely focused on slowly moving

throughout the room. Likely trying to figure out which way the wounded individual had gone first.

Felix went straight to the spot that Miu was likely to be at. Stepping into the dark shadowed spot that was against the wall, Felix reached out to hug nothing.

And caught Miu perfectly. Holding to her tightly, he pulled her into himself.

"Miu, my Miu, I need you to reign it in just a bit. I need them all. You can't harm them," Felix pleaded, holding onto the lightly trembling woman. "You know I love you. There's no need for your jealousy or envy. Now is there? Just pour it all back into your care of yourself, and care for me.

"Just… ditch the negative feelings and make them positive. I know you'll become an even more lovely woman for doing so."

Miu grunted, the noise coming through the speaker of her helmet. Followed by a hissing groan.

Then her head dipped down, and her visor was pressed into his shoulder.

Standing there, he just held her as Evie circled the room in a mad-like way.

"Ah! Got it!" said the Dragon after a minute of wandering about. She ran over, grabbed Felix's hand, and gently peeled him away from Miu. Taking position next to him, she crowded into his side. One hand rested behind his back, and she began pointing with the other.

"Errr, we don't have to be so close anymore. It was just for who was wa— "

Felix didn't get to finish his statement as Evie began to push him along.

They exited the back area and made it into the offices. From there, she went to a door that wasn't hidden, but was actually hard to see without entering the office.

Moving through that, they ended up in an alleyway behind the bar.

More or less exactly where Felix expected it to go. That meant they'd have to follow a car through the city.

Which didn't really sound that possible.

He didn't doubt Evie was likely a good hunter. That she had the ability to really track someone through scent and blood alone, but not through a city.

We'll have to figure out what to do next then. Maybe modify her ability to smell and —

"Up there," Evie said, pointing straight up.

Felix blinked, looked up, and followed where she was pointing.

Damn. She's got hands made to play a piano.

"I do? Well thank you. What's a piano? Is that what you humans call your dick?" Evie said then wriggled her fingers in a fluttering motion. Which then made an "okay" like symbol and began moving her hand back and forth. "Like this? That's what was in your head just now when I asked."

"It's a musical instrument," dodged Felix, not wanting to address anything else she said. There were several open windows along this side of the apartment.

"What's a musical instrument," Evie prompted next, her hand opening and closing as she clearly was trying to visualize where her mind was gone.

"Which window? Do you know?" he asked, ignoring her question.

"Ah, yes, I know what a window is. Honestly, I find it strange. I know some things, but not everything. It's almost as if someone gave me some things to know, but... not everything," Evie murmured while slowly nodding her head.

"Do you know-which window-the scent-is coming from?" Felix enunciated. He couldn't be angry at her. She was literally doing all he asked of her in a world she had an obviously broken connection with.

"No. It's one of them though. Here, let's go look," Evie remarked and then wrapped herself around him. In that moment, he realized she was actually smaller than he was by an inch. Very few Dragons were his height or shorter, or so he'd found.

Jumping into the air, Evie gained height and then began to hover outside of the windows. She was in direct line of sight for many of them and there was no telling how many people could see them right now.

"Damnit, Evie, we need to —"

"There," declared the Dragon, who tucked her shoulder and barreled straight ahead. They blasted through the partially open window, shattering the glass, cracking the frame, and breaking the slat out of the middle.

With a clatter and a bang as they struck the ground, Felix ended up underneath the Red Dragon. She had her head up and was looking around the room they were now in.

"Oh, darn. They were here, but they're not now," she grumbled. "There's a lot of other scents here now, too. Lots of them. As well as... mm... as well as what smells like a lot of meat.

"Now I'm hungry. You should provide for your Nest-mate. I'm not entirely certain, but I think a human man would make sure his wife is fed."

Looking at him, Evie didn't seem concerned that she was laying atop him. She smiled at him and was obviously waiting for a response.

"You find Anya in the next hour, and I'll take you to any damn steakhouse you want, and you can eat as much as you like," Felix promised.

"What's a steakhouse?" Evie asked, her delicate eyebrows moving lower over her eyes.

"Place that serves a lot of meat," answered Felix.

"I'll do it!" Evie said, her eyes widening. She hopped off him and then began to hunt about the room. Slamming her head accidentally into a refrigerator as she did so.

Then she paused and yanked it open.

Rooting around in it quickly, she pulled out what looked like a packaged meat product. It was in a yellow Styrofoam half-shell and was plastic wrapped. On the front of it was a "not for resale" sticker.

"This. It smells like this. It's everywhere," Evie said and came over to him, holding the product out. "More than what this is putting out, but it's on this."

"In other words... you're saying that whoever lives here, works in there," Felix said, indicating the sticker, which was for a butcher

"I... what? Live in this? Felix, this is just a package. No one can live in this," Evie said with a sad shake of her head. "Oh, you didn't mean it like that. Got it. You know, it'd be easier if I read your mind first before listening to your words. Goldie said that's bad manners though, so I've been trying not to do that. I give up though, it's harder not to."

The sudden laughter of Miu at the window gave him pause. He couldn't tell if Evie was trolling him or not, but he was no longer sure.

"Well, let's follow that scent then. At the same time, Miu, go to that location. See if there's anyone there of interest. Call me either way, I can update you at that time."

"I understand," answered Miu. She said nothing else, and Felix heard nothing else from her.

"Okay! Let's go find them so I can get my steak-house reward. I want meat. Haha, no, not your meat. Not right now at least. That's for later."

Felix nodded, got to his feet, then paused. He had no idea which way to go. Out the window, or the door.

He was also doing his best to not respond to the fact that she'd pulled out his random crude thought about her wanting to eat meat.

Evie solved that by turning, tearing the door off its hinges, and exiting into the hall.

"Husband! Let's go! Steakhouse!" she called, vanishing from view.

Off we go.

Turning into a damn Dragon Andrea.

I'm literally surrounding myself with people who are just so offbeat I might as well open an asylum. Start trying to fix them.

Though I think I'd need a better name than Felix.

Like… a great kind of name.

***

"It's in here," Evie said coming to a sliding stop. She'd been moving at a rather fast jog. Felix had only just been able to keep up with her.

In the back of his mind, he suspected that'd been intentional. Evie pushing him just far enough to the edge of his ability and no further.

"Of course I did! It really is a lot easier just reading everything as I go. I know it's rude, but I promise I'll make up for it later," Evie said with a negligent hand wave in front of a beautiful smile. "Now, they went here. What do we do now?"

Felix came to a stop and then bent over at the waist. Taking in big heaving breaths.

Looking up sideways, he saw they were

standing in front of an expensive apartment complex. One that clearly had money put into it.

"Think you can find the apartment?" he asked.

"Apar-yes! Yes, I can find their... home... in there. Yes," Evie said rapidly nodding her head.

You're reading my thoughts as I talk to figure out the context.

"I mean... it's easier that way. No more confusion over me missing information. It's just better. Now, shall we go?" asked Evie, pointing at the apartment.

Felix nodded his head and stood up. He'd been able to regain his breath very quickly. His stamina was greatly increased since he'd modified himself after all.

Evie grabbed the door handle and opened the door.

Tearing the locking mechanism clean out in doing so. It couldn't withstand the force of her strength.

"I'm not very strong being a Red. I can't even imagine how Goldie must feel going through life. As if everything is made of twigs," grumbled the Dragon, going into the apartment. "Damn, I wonder how Lucille even goes to the bathroom. I felt like I almost broke the handle this morning."

Felix moved to follow her and caught sight of her just as she went to the fire-escape stairwell. Moving into it, she started rushing up the stairs.

It wasn't till they were at least five floors up

that she stopped, opened a door, then moved through it.

They were now in the hallway of the apartment with a number of doors on either side leading down it. By the time he'd understood what he was looking at, Evie crashed through yet another door with little more than a punch of her hand where the doorknob was.

She didn't wait at all. The door banged open as she went in.

"Okay, this is just too much," growled Felix as he once again hustled after her.

By the time he made it into the apartment, she'd already disappeared somewhere else.

"I think I found her," Evie called from further in. "Anya, that is. Or uh… her soon to be corpse. I guess."

Cursing, Felix hurried forward.

Turning at the intersection, he found a bathroom.

In the tub at the back of it was Anya. She was blankly staring up at Evie. There was a significant amount of blood in the tub, splattered all over her, and up along the bathroom walls.

A confrontation had taken place here that'd ended with what looked like several stab wounds through Anya's torso. A large number of them, in fact.

There was also a bullet wound that was right atop her guts. There was blood sluggishly pumping free from it and draining away into the tub.

Sighing, Felix knew that she was indeed going to become a corpse. That wasn't really a question.

"You," she gasped, her eyes having slowly moved to Felix.

"Yes... me. I came when I heard there'd been a disturbance. I didn't think Michael would act so quickly after I visited Thomas," Felix conceded, taking a seat on the toilet next to the tub. "I did try to warn you about Michael a while back. I take it he didn't really like it when he got called out?"

"Thomas, too," whimpered Anya, then gave him a weak smile. There was a sheen of sweat that coated her skin as well. "Hurts. Dizzy."

"The man named Thomas was angry at her for scorning him," Evie reported with a grumpy look on her face. "He's the one who shot her. Michael stabbed her a few minutes ago. We just missed them.

"They decided they could run an organization without her after she tried to defend Michael.

"Thomas was sick of her constantly giving in to Michael. Or so he said after he shot her. They're now working as partners with equal power and shares. Michael was all too happy to be rid of her. Or so her memories say.

"He has his sights set on Goldie, I'd guess, from what he said. He wasn't very happy she got away."

Anya was taking short shallow breaths now.

Her end was drawing ever nearer.

"Damnit. I had plans for you, Anya. Your ability to charm anyone could have opened every door for you," Felix lamented with a shake of his head. "Now all you need are prayers."

Felix stopped dead in his thoughts with that statement.

It'd been an idle almost flippant comment, but it also sparked an idea.

"Hey, give your soul to the goddess Gaia. Ownership of it," Felix demanded, meeting Anya's eyes and moving forward off the toilet. "Quickly. Say you give all of yourself to Gaia. Including your soul. Your spirit. What would go to the afterlife. You give it to Gaia, goddess of Legion."

"I-give-my soul-to-Gaia," wheezed out Anya. Her eyes weren't looking at him anymore. Her skin was as pale as bleached white sheets. "Give-everything-to… Gaia of-Legion.

"Give it… all… all to…"

Anya continued to breathe shallowly, her eyes staring off into nothing. Her body was still trying to cope with what was coming, but her mind had checked out. Passing out with her eyes open.

"Hm. Well, she died better than me," Evie remarked, looking to Felix. "I died looking like a skeleton. Deep in a cave, with nothing to show for my efforts or my life, whimpering for my mom. I died badly."

Clearing his throat, Felix decided to test his little plan out.

"Gaia, goddess of Legion, your Champion would like a word. Could you perhaps... join me? Or speak with me?" Felix asked, looking up to the ceiling

There was a heavy feeling in the air. One that gave him pause, and he hesitated continuing.

Then Gaia appeared right next to Evie. Dressed in her Legionnaire armor, helmet under her armpit, and a wide smile.

The radiant and beautiful goddess of earth looked to be at the peak of her condition. Young, full of vitality, and radiating health.

"Why of course I'll come here for you. How can I deny my champion anything? I'm your personal goddess after all. Not to mention, I was just cleaning up a few landfills. Nothing that important, really," she said with a wave of her hand, turning to look at Evie as she spoke. "Oh... look at you. You're so pretty. I wonder if Felix prefers red-heads. I should have made my hair red in the end I bet.

"Though... he is looking at me a bit intently right now. I wonder if he noticed I'm at my best right now. I bet he did. My figure is all squished in this armor though. He doesn't seem to mind it, but I'll look better later.

"It's always so disconcerting when he stares at me like that. I wonder if I should just ask him to have sex. I bet if we had sex we could move past this awkward part. Sex clears up a lot of things for most species. Just... have to dodge the falling in love part."

"Huh," Evie said with a wide grin, staring at the goddess. Then she looked back to Felix. "At least I've got a better handle on being alive and mortal than my goddess."

"Oooh… I was talking aloud again, wasn't I?" asked Gaia with a pout on her lovely face. "It's so hard. I have to balance being a deity at the same time as a mortal. It's a lot to juggle with a physical brain."

Chapter 26 – New Suit -

"Right… well… I guess this is where I need to explain what I need from you, Gaia," Felix offered as a way to get her out of the current conversation.

"I mean, I think she's enjoying the conversation though?" Evie asked, looking to Gaia. "I can't read her mind obviously but… I don't think I'd mind if I were her."

"Where I explain what I need," Felix said quite firmly. "Now… you will have one fresh new soul as soon as she finally dies, right?"

Felix pointed a hand at Anya's body.

She was trembling in the bathtub, taking short shallow breaths, with skin as pale as could be. With every little breath, her head would flop a bit from side to side.

The flow of blood from her wounds was slowing considerably. Her eyes were open and staring at nothing at all.

"Mmm. I did hear her pledge her soul to me," Gaia murmured, looking down at the human woman. "I'll of course accept it into my care. I don't get too many human souls, so that'll be interesting."

Hesitating for a moment, Felix then reached down and gently closed Anya's eyes. Having her stare like that was unnerving. To the point that it was more bothersome than letting it continue.

You know, it's odd that a dying woman doesn't bother me, but the fact that her eyes are open, does. I wonder if I'm going to have a lot of mental troubles later in life.

With a sardonic smile and a shake of his head, he then gestured at Gaia.

"I asked you to hold onto the Void Dragon's fragment. Do you still have it?" he asked.

"Of course!" Gaia answered with a smile. "I can carry many things with me without carrying them."

"Is there any possible way that if I resurrected the Void Dragon's body, to put Anya's soul into it? You said the original Void Dragon that owned the body didn't want to come back.

"I wouldn't want to bring them back against their will, but I also don't want to not utilize a resource. You would theoretically own Anya's soul as well as the Void Dragon's soul. I own the Void Dragon's body and can resurrect it.

"You're my goddess, I'm your champion. Could we not just… slip her soul into the soulless body and let the Void Dragon remain where they wish? This feels like it should be possible given what we are to one another."

Gaia's brow had furrowed, her eyes unfocusing partly, and staring through Felix as he spoke. He didn't doubt that she was following the conversation, he just figured that maybe she was thinking through something in the background.

That or trying to see if it would even possible. He couldn't begin to fathom what being a god or goddess was like.

Err… wait… I'm a Demi-God, aren't I? At what point do I become a god directly?

Hm.

How much would it cost to upgrade myself into a god?

Actually… let's not look at that right now. I don't even want to see the numbers. Then I'd just try to save up to get it regardless of what it was.

Avoid the temptation all together.

"I-yes. It's very possible. So long as both Anya and Xiafhsshh agree," Gaia said, her gaze snapping back to Felix. Her smile was still present, and she seemed eager. He assumed that the strange sounding name was what the Void Dragon had been called. "We'll just have to wait to see what Anya thinks, as Xiafhsshh has already said it's fine. She has no use for a body that she has no intention of inhabiting."

"Stupid," Evie accused. "There are so many interesting and neat things in the world. Yeah, it kinda feels like running around with prey on every side, but it's also fun. Like… a lot of fun!

"I've only been here for a very short while and I already can't wait to see more. Especially as a Dragon! There's so much to do."

"Oh… you know how Void Dragons are," Gaia lamented with a sigh. "Temperamental in the best of times. Not having Primordials really harmed their social abilities, too. Though in my defense, I didn't plan their race. They just… happened.

"Hm. I wonder. If Felix and I had children,

would they be gods? Demi-gods? He's pretty close to a full god now. Would they be human like him, or spirits like me? Or something else? What an interesting thought.

"Would I become the mother of gods, so to speak, if we had children? How very curious. If we do start having sex, I should have him impregnate me at least once. Then again... his entire race puts such an odd slant to sex and procreation. I'll have to really think this one out more. Their whole view on the world is so very confusing.

"That, and I this point I think one of us would fall in love with the other. Not sure who, though. I feel rather odd around him as of late."

"Should... I kill her to hurry this along?" Evie asked, pointing at the still dying Anya when Gaia finished.

Apparently Evie, like Felix, was now treating her spoken thoughts as if they were internal.

"What?" Gaia asked, blinking rapidly, then she looked to Anya. "No need, dear. She'll pass from this world in a minute or so. Her body is still trying and will likely keep trying after that, but that's when her soul would be free to leave the body. I can talk to her then."

Felix nodded his head and then looked to Evie.

"Could you go get my armor? I get the feeling I'll need it. When you get back, just put it somewhere I can get to without Anya seeing it," he asked. "And Gaia, can you hide yours? We still need to pretend like we're not part of the

Association or Legion. Bad enough that she'll know who you are and that you and I exist. Worse if she realizes we're setting her up as a puppet."

"Poo. I like my armor. I get a lot less stares wearing it," Gaia muttered, then made a hand wave. Her armor magically vanishing to nowhere and leaving her standing there in a tank-top and shorts.

She was just as distracting as Evie was.

"Oh! Sure, not a problem," Evie agreed happily. Turning, she left the room.

Leaving Felix alone with Gaia, his thoughts turning back to what she'd just said.

Then he couldn't help himself.

He called up what it would cost to push himself into a full god status, rather than what he was now. To see the point cost that'd be required.

Name: Felix Campbell	**Condition**: Nervous. Weary.
If No Action Taken: None	**Action >> Alter Race**: Cost 947,492,781 points

Ah… err… right.

Got it.

Though I bet to Gaia, that's probably not a huge cost. She likely has that in abundance, given who she is.

For me… that's… astronomical.

A difference in perspective in scales. Something to keep in mind when I'm considering how much it costs to modify my own people.

I wonder if she'd be willing to barter with me to

float the cost on my behalf.

What would it cost? I don't even want to begin to think of what she might ask for in exchange

Though... it isn't impossible to earn it on my own either.

I earned quite a bit through clearing all those sites.

Just have to keep at it and converting things. Lots and lots of landfills to get to.

"There we are," Gaia said and held a hand out to Anya. "Hello dear. Your physical body has failed you and you're now in your spirit flesh."

Felix couldn't see or hear anything out of the ordinary. To him, it seemed like Gaia was talking to herself once again.

"Yes, you did die. Your body is beyond the point of recovery. If there was a miraculous medical intervention it'd be possible but... even then, it'd be unlikely. I'm sorry. Your time in the mortal world is over," Gaia regretfully explained. "Unless you'd like to come back.

"My Champion has proposed an idea to me. You knew him as Felix, and he's the one who told you to give your soul to me."

Gaia looked thoughtful as if she were listening to something.

"No, you can't see anything but me right now. You're no longer part of the physical realm. But... if you wanted to return to it, we could do that. We'd construct a new body for you and put your soul into it," Gaia continued. "Would you like to do that?"

"I… uhm… yes. That would be very possible. The body we're going to put you into wouldn't be yours. It'd be a Dragon's," acknowledged Gaia with a nod of her head, then listened again. She let out a warm rich laugh. "Most certainly! So? That's a yes? Okay, great."

Gaia turned to look to Felix and made an odd gesture with her hand. Her fingers fluttering and then making a flick-like motion.

A blue cloud of sparkling mist appeared beside him. Floating in midair without a definite shape.

"She has agreed," Gaia said with a dip of her head, then she held her hand out toward Felix. In her palm was the Void Dragon bone. "Here is the body to rebuild. She asked that you reform it to look like her. Given how attractive the Void Dragon was to begin with, that would get back a few points.

"I ima… what? Are you sure? I mean… yes, it'd be possible. You'd just no longer look like you once did. I-well yes but-ah but-alright.

"Never mind, dear. Anya would like to inhabit the Void Dragon's body exactly as it was. We'll have to modify it to be like the other Dragons, but that's it."

Felix clicked his tongue and thought on it for a moment.

"Alright. I'll have to tell her how to get her paperwork changed over. We can just play it off as a terrible accident where they had to really rebuild her face or something.

"Did she ever submit to a travel agency for pre-approved travel or anything like that? Anything that'd get her fingerprints into a system? Was she ever arrested?"

Gaia looked to the blue cloud, then to Felix.

"Yes, she was arrested at one point," Gaia confirmed.

"Right... I'll carry over her fingerprints but nothing else then," Felix said with a sigh. Taking the bone from Gaia he focused on it. "Gaia, if you don't mind, please make sure we bring over all of Anya's memories to the new body from your side."

"Hm? Oh! Yes, that's not a problem. I'm glad you pointed that out. Memories are usually lost with a reincarnation," remarked Gaia. "That'd have been a problem."

Felix dove into his power.

His desire.

That he wanted to rebuild the Void Dragon from scratch. To bring it back to life in its entirety, though without the soul behind it.

That the mind inside of it would inherit all the memories of the soul that would possess it. Otherwise she'd be Anya's soul in the Void Dragon's body with its own memories.

Lastly, that this new being would inherit all powers due to it from having both the Dragon's body and the human's soul.

There was a shuddering that came from the world itself as his power activated. As if it wasn't ready for what he was trying to push for.

"Goodness. That's rather profound. Oh! Hello Uncle!" Gaia said with a laugh, then she glowered at nothing. "You and I need to have a word by the way. I'm not exactly thrilled with what I think you're trying to do."

I... what? He's here?

I didn't think what I was trying to do was that bad. Nothing out of the ordinary at least. Why would it be a problem?

A window popped up for Felix and vanished before he could even contemplate it. He hadn't even been given a chance to see the cost.

"Oh? Well thank you. That's nice of you, Uncle. I'm still mad at you though. I'm very disappointed with you trying to meddle in my love life. We'll talk more later about this. Among other things. Oh, and tell Father hello for me when you see him," murmured Gaia with a nod of her head, then she looked to Felix. "Uncle took all your points and paid for the rest himself."

As she finished speaking the bone in Felix's hand vanished, the blue cloud dissipated, and a rather lovely woman simply appeared on the bathroom floor.

She wasn't as gorgeous as Evie, but she was just a hair less so than Goldie. Her body type was also rather appealing, but also less than the other two.

Her eyes were so light they almost lacked color, though they oddly shifted in hue depending on how the light struck them. Long hair spread out in a cloud around her head, and it was also an odd black color that felt like it reflected back multiple colors.

Blinking several times, the woman took in a shuddering breath, then coughed. Her hand going to her chest.

"I'm alive," said the Void Dragon that was now Anya.

"Indeed. Is it not how I, Gaia the goddess of the world, told you?" asked the deity with a rich laugh. She turned to look to Felix. "Well, now that that's done. What do we do next?"

"Wait for Miu to call," Felix said with a sigh and then pulled his phone out of his pocket. Looking to the lock-screen, he found there were no new messages or calls. "She should be getting back to me about Thomas and Michael."

"I'm... I'm going to hurt them," growled the Void Dragon. "They killed me. I loved one like a brother and wanted to marry the other. Both... both betrayed me.

"Hurt them. Hurt them a lot. Make examples of them. I let both of them use me. Me and my power. Never again."

"Glad to hear it," Felix murmured as he started to tap through his phone. "I want you to start working with the people behind the League of Villains website. I'll put you in contact with them.

"You're going to become their leader and start taking over. I think there needs to be a counter to the Guild of Heroes, and you're the perfect person for it, Anya. Not to mention it'll be good to learn what your new body can do as you take over."

Growling loudly, Anya got to her feet.

"Fine. I can do that. Gladly. I'll build it up. Just how I wanted. I let them talk me into too much," hissed Anya while getting to a full standing position.

She started to tip to one side and then steadied herself. Shaking her head she frowned, looking down at herself.

Experimentally, she touched her rather well-endowed chest, then her stomach, and lastly her hips.

"You also have wings, horns, and a tail. Those come out when you want them to," Felix murmured, opening the Legion app to check his email. "You'll also need to learn to fly, but that's going to take time I bet."

Pausing, he saw there was a communication from Tribune waiting for him.

Tapping it open, he began to read it over.

Legate.

The Central Intelligence Agency has petitioned for an injunction against the Association Investigative Act.

A judge friendly to them has issued said injunction to suspend all such investigations. Along with an immediate stop in regards to all such investigations.

Additionally, the religious group we audited has instigated a lawsuit against the Association and the government. If the Association Investigative Act should fail before a court review, it's likely the Association would then lose the lawsuit.

While there were no casualties, there were a number of injuries. They opened fire on Legionnaire Goldie upon her declaration that they were there for an Audit. There were no injuries amongst our forces, and Legionnaire Goldie did her best to limit the conflict.

To the point that they were fired upon for a solid minute before she acted.

I recorded all of it from several satellites, as well as from Goldie's armor cam. I advised that she should wear it so she could record the entire interaction.

Just in case.

The hostage crisis ended without any further loss of life. The Guild of Heroes wanted to express their appreciation to the Association for their swift handling of the event.

A number of politicians are also wishing to express their congratulations and thanks. There is an equal number that are calling for the Association to be limited in their scope and purview.

I have summarized all of this so you can decide what to do next, Sir.

My personal suggestion would be to cease all activity, return to the Association with all forces, and for the Legate to begin preparing for whatever steps come next.

Closing his eyes and clenching his teeth, Felix held his breath. He strangled the scream that wanted to escape and merely stood there.

Not moving, not thinking, not breathing.

Trying to wrangle his extreme emotions and put them back into a ball so that he could start working through the problem as a whole.

Letting out the breath, Felix had managed to get some semblance of control.

This wasn't entirely outside of his expectations. In fact, the way he'd worded the agreement with the government had been specifically written in such a way that it technically was more of an agreement between two nations.

So much so that the land granted to the Association was akin to a foreign nation, a lot like an embassy would be. From the very beginning he'd been setting up the Association as a global entity.

Not a branch of the government.

"He looks so worried. I wonder if I should ask if he wants sex. Sex fixes a lot of things. Maybe he wouldn't feel so much desire when he looks at me afterward," came Gaia's voice, cutting through his thoughts. Then she clicked her tongue. "But I'm still so worried about one of us falling in love. The sex would still probably be worth it though."

Unable to help himself, Felix laughed. Opening his eyes, he looked to Anya, who was now looking at Gaia with a confused face. The goddess had an open and warm look on her countenance and seemed entirely unaware that she'd spoken her thoughts again.

"Just more work to do. Just more work," Felix murmured. "Alright... Anya. Do you have any questions for me? I think I'll have to leave you to the work here and move on. Things are happening."

Anya frowned, her entire face showing displeasure and anger. Slowly, her head tilted to one side until she could see her own old body sitting in the tub. It'd only stopped breathing just a handful of seconds previously.

"You're not telling me everything," she whispered instead.

"I'm not," Felix agreed. "But I assure you, I mean you personally no harm. I need you to be a leader so someone like Michael or Thomas doesn't take the reins.

"So long as you're the leader of the Villains, I'll support you and make sure you come to no harm. Just about the only warning I'd give you is to do your best to not go up against the Guild of Heroes directly. That when you have confrontations with them, try your best to not have any fatalities on either side."

Anya stared at her body for several more seconds before looking back to Felix.

Slowly, she nodded her head.

"Alright. I can do that. I have your word on that?" she asked, her head turning to look at Gaia. "You'll hold him to that?"

"Of course!" Gaia gleefully promised. "He's my Champion. I'm his goddess. You're my Human Void Dragon. The only one of its kind.

"Just be sure you spread the good word of Gaia and get more people to worship me. So long as you do that, and hold me as your deity, I'll ensure he keeps his word to you."

Nodding her head Anya took in a shaky breath.

"Then can someone get rid of... that? The last thing I need is for that to be floating around while I start getting documents turned over," Anya begged, pointing at her corpse. "I want to go right after Thomas and Michael but... I can't. I need to go solidify my position. My people. Take everything I can from Michael and Thomas at the same time. I know a few bank accounts they had that I can clean out."

"Michael is being investigated by the Guild of Heroes. Feel free to send any information to them you want that doesn't link back to you," suggested Felix.

There was a loud bang, followed by someone cursing. All three people in the bathroom looked to the door.

"It's me!" called Evie, followed by more cursing under her breath. "I hit my stupid little toe against a table.

"This thing is stupid. Why do humans have these? It's just asking to be smashed into things. Claws are so much better."

"Uh... I mean... you're not wrong," Anya muttered when Evie came around the corner and into view.

"Oh! It worked. You're a Dragon," Evie said and smiled broadly. "Thank Gaia I'm better looking than you. I'm already worse than every other Dragon out there, all I have going for me is my looks."

Anya's eyebrows crawled upward at that.

Gaia looked curious and tilted her head to the side.

Felix just stood there.

He still needed to figure out what to do next.

Then his phone rang.

Chapter 27 - Tribune 9000 -

Felix didn't even have to look at it to know it was Miu.

Tapping the accept button, he held it up to his ear.

"Hey," he said.

"Found the location," hissed Miu over the line. "Only one here."

"Which?" he asked.

"The one the goodies know of," answered Miu.

Right, so Michael is there. Not Thomas.

Thinking, Felix had to consider how to move.

Things were rapidly spiraling away from him. Despite taking six months to build his infrastructure, that'd only bought him time enough to consider what was happening.

The simple reality here was that his actions were too large, too grandiose, to not have an impact. The Association and Legion were going to leave a mark, no matter how hard he tried to walk the middle line.

In this case, he needed to somehow reinforce that the Association wasn't here to put people in jail, or to influence politics. It was here to register Supers and catalog powers.

That meant he needed to make a few moves that would take the teeth out of any movement made by the federal government. To limit their scope of power and provide an alternative to the

Association.

Maybe it was time to take things on the road, so to speak.

He needed to go up and see Canadia and how they felt about their Super population. They likely had a similar ratio of Supers to non-Supers.

After that, his best action was to jump the pond and hit Europe.

There were many powerful countries over there and he could begin leveraging them one off the other. There was even a union amongst many of them that he could get the Association into.

Pay dues, offer services, technology, and the same things the Association does here. As well as cleanup offers.

In fact, I can offer them a priority queue over the States' government. An offer I could extend to all of the union over there.

So long as they're going to entertain any type of pushback from citizens here, I can use it against them and let other countries start reaping the benefits.

In fact… we should start selling out some medical tech.

We can begin the process of showcasing equipment that will become available for rent from Legion, through the Association. For interested parties, they'll just need to petition and put in a good-faith form.

At the same time I push for them to allow us in.

"You'll remain here with Anya and provide assistance. You'll likely need to put together security for the League of Villains. Work with your sister to make sure it doesn't get spicy," Felix said, coming to a conclusion of his thinking. "If you have questions or concerns, ask me. Don't make yourself visible for any reason at any time.

"Return to the bar and wait in the back. Anya will go there and you can begin from that point."

"Understood. This is a good direction," Miu confirmed. "I love you, Felix. I love you so much. Oh, and please tell Evie I'll strangle her with her privates after I cut them out if she tries to sleep with you."

The line disconnected after that.

"Right," Felix murmured and put his phone back into his pocket. Looking to Anya, he gave her a shrug. "Found Michael. He's in a butchery or some sort. That ring a bell for you?"

"Yes. I know exactly what and where that is," she growled.

"Great, there ya go. My personal suggestion? Let the cops handle Michael. Feed them information on him while protecting your own organization," Felix advised her. "He'll try to turn on you after he realizes you're alive, but if you lay low, he won't realize it until it's too late for him to change his story.

"Doubly so if you're 'in a hospital recovering' during this time. Might want to make yourself scarce to anyone you haven't charmed up."

Anya blinked, processed that, and then nodded her head.

Turning, she left without another word.

Exiting the apartment completely.

"So... what do we do then?" Evie asked while looking to Anya's corpse. "If we're not pushing this further, what's next?"

"We have... we have so much work to do. It's not even funny," Felix sighed, putting his hands to his face. "In no certain order: there are lawsuits waiting for us here in the States. Ones that'll put our ability to act in jeopardy.

"We need to get out there and push ourselves to other countries. Get more opportunities for us as the Association. Put pressure on the States so that they can't limit us without putting themselves behind everyone else."

"Oh. Alright," Gaia said with a shrug of her shoulders. "Human laws and legal systems seem overly convoluted to me. There are times that I can't help but wonder if Humans took the right path or not.

"Nature is much simpler. Kill, eat, mate. Anything else is silly."

"Yeah... but... there's a lot of neat things amongst the prey now," Evie argued, looking at Gaia.

Gaia only clicked her tongue with a shake of her head, looking back to Felix.

"You should reach out to the government that tried to fight us. I don't think they were opposed to the Association so much as opposed to the nation it was in," suggested Gaia.

Felix froze, his mind stumbling over itself,

then whirring up into speed.

He wasn't thinking globally enough if he was only considering Europe. That was still only what fit within his own mental boundaries.

"You're right. We'll put out the call to all nations. That the Association is ready to expand and will be hiring locals to work at those facilities," Felix agreed. "I just have to get the message out there and start moving it."

"Dragons," Evie offered and then held up her hands with a grin. "Send Dragons. Dragons to every single country that we want to talk with. We all received the gift of tongues from Gaia on our rebirth.

"We can speak to anyone about anything. Not to mention... we're Dragons! It's hard to argue or fight one of us."

Well, unless they decide to run up their army.

Dragons are tough. Very tough, but even Goldie would have issues with tanks, jets, and helicopters. Not something I'd want them to run up against.

Even with that thought, he couldn't fault the logic. It was exactly what he needed to do.

Reach out to every government that is big enough to support us or give us global leverage... then send a Dragon to establish the opening if they're willing to talk.

Dragons will have instructions to only answer a limited set of questions, hand off paperwork, then I wait for their answer beyond that.

" — been interesting. Can I get pregnant?" Evie asked. She'd been talking to Gaia while Felix was lost in his own thoughts.

"Almost too easily. Be very careful if you're going to lay with your Nest-mate," warned Gaia. "Your instinctual need for gold isn't entirely on gold. It's power and wealth. Both of those affect your reproductive ability.

"If you do bed Felix, make sure you speak with Alma, Carlotta, or Faith. You'll need to curtail any pregnancy early so it doesn't develop. He doesn't want any children right now."

"I need my armor, then we're flying back to Legion HQ. We need to finish the tunnels and send communications," Felix determined. "Time to put some pressure on."

***

"Felix! I'm so glad to see you. Your arrival is... it's perfect timing," Faith said as he walked into his own office. She was sitting down at Felicity's desk and had been typing away at a computer there. Pausing mid-keystroke, Faith got up from behind the desk.

Walking over to him as he stepped in front of his armor stand, she stood there, smiling at him. There was a faint glow in her eyes as she watched him pull off his helmet.

"Stop with just the helmet, my love," murmured Faith. "We'll need you to film a video communication as well as a written one.

"The video communication will also be a

display of tech. I'm having it all brought in. I think your direction is perfect and will give us a chance to take a breath.

"If we pause all our current work, other than registration, Association duties, and prison maintenance, we'll have lots of people able to work."

Felix opened his mouth to say that it's called low occupancy, but it died on his lips. There was no reason to correct her and would just be rather pedantic.

Especially considering everything she'd put up with in working with and for him. From late long workdays, taking time out of her busy schedule to track him down to talk, or just throwing him into a bed and helping him work out physical stress.

She was a pillar in his life that he couldn't do without.

Setting the helmet down on the top of the stand, he took a moment to collect his thoughts. Waiting for a few moments, he then turned and hugged Faith tightly. Pressing her into himself and holding to her for all he was worth.

"Thank you, Faith," he whispered softly. "I've practically ignored you for the better part of a year and you've just... taken it all with a smile and trucked on.

"I can't even begin to try and explain how much you mean to me. Through it all, you're always there. Even when you're not directly with me, I know you're doing everything you can for me.

"So… uh… thank you. I love you. Please don't leave your stupid Human because he's an idiot."

Faith had returned the hug with a great deal of force. Holding tightly to him, to the point that he could feel it on his armor in fact.

By the time he'd finished speaking though, she'd started to laugh. A warm and low chuckle that made his worries and thoughts melt away like butter on a hot skillet.

"Mmm! I'm so glad to hear you say that, my love," Faith whispered, turning her head to kiss the side of his cheek. "I'm going to really reward that open emotional honesty of yours later. I'll give you one of my special 'Faith in Felix' services. I know you love when I do that.

"Second to that, of course I'm doing all I can. There's no question of that. Nor that I'd ever leave you. I don't need to be in the spotlight to… to be a heroine for you. I'm most definitely the heroine of my own story now, and I know I am.

"You just need me handling things that you can't tend to, while you do other things. In time, that'll ease up, and we'll get more time together. In fact, if I don't miss my guess… you and I will be traveling around the better part of the world. Cleaning up messes real soon.

"You, me, Goldie, Andrea, Carlotta, Alma, and of course, Gaia. I know you gave Miu a task that she can't turn away from, but if we're pulling back on the other bits and pieces until the government figures out what to do, we'll be fine."

Speaking of... haven't heard from Andrea.

"Before you ask about her, she's fine. Last I heard she was having a lot of fun with Romina. Posing for photographs, signing autographs, doing interviews, and generally being exactly who she is. She's quite the mascot, you know," Faith said and then stepped away from him. "Now... let's get your helmet on, prep for this video commercial, and start writing out the communication.

"I'm sure we'll be bombarded with responses the moment we send it out. The question is... who would you want to see first?"

"Whoever the Zhongguo government is. That's who I want to see. They moved against us because they felt we were part of the States' government," Felix answered. "That means if we move counter to that, we'll likely be invited in quite quickly.

"That'll force the government here to wise up, or try to expel us. If they try to expel us, we'll go dormant here for a bit. Then return once we have more global backing. Won't be hard.

"If all we ever do is force them to accept our registration of Supers as well as various other duties related to that, it's hard to deny us. Especially with all the benefits we can provide."

"Most especially technology," Faith finished and reached up to gently caress his cheek with a hand. There was a deep and bright glow in her eyes now. One that he knew was there because they should be as bright as the sun, but she was throttling it down for all she was worth. "I'm having examples of all the tech you've made brought in. We'll be able to introduce a lot of it to the world, showcase it, make the benefits obvious, and then push off with our global invitation.

"Oh... ah... I did... I did set it up so we'll have our prettiest and most handsome from the Association on hand for parts of this. Those who are with the Association will be filming from there. Legion from here.

"I know it's a bit... cheap... but it works. Beautiful women and handsome men, sell. Though I'm a little nervous. Some of those Dragon Maidens... they're... incredible to look at."

"Tell me about it," growled Felix. "I hope you're ready for attention. I had to spend way too much time around a very attractive Red and Gaia. Thankfully I have control and I'm not led around by my pecker, but I'm still just a man."

Faith wrinkled her nose, grinned, and patted his cheek.

"Ooooh, my Grove-mate. My husband. That's music to my ears. I'm going to drain you dry tonight," she said, and then kissed him briefly. Moving away from him, she picked up his helmet, pulled it down over his head, and made sure it was fastened securely. "Alright. I'm going to go finish up this email. You have a chat with Tribune about all the plans I put in place and approve them. I know I can do it myself as a temporary Legate but... best you do it."

Walking away from him, Faith went back to her desk. His eyes followed the smooth swish of her walk as she did so.

Realizing he was staring, Felix quickly went and sat at his desk.

"Tribune, what do you need from me?" he asked.

"Approvals, Sir," Tribune answered instantly. "I am unable to comply with many of your wishes with my current limitations. You will need to authorize the Global Domination program expansion you created."

A slow breath was Felix's only response to the request.

He'd learned many things from his previous experience in leading an organization. One of the biggest ones, was that you could be thinking you're heading in the right direction when you're just on a track for someone else.

That you're operating under someone else's agenda and plans without ever comprehending it.

Right now, he was fairly certain that he was completely free of others' goals and plans. If only because he refused to join anyone else's goals or plans.

It was hard for anyone to figure out what the Association and Legion was going to be doing when they overlooked everything except the small piece they were interested in. That every opportunity to gain party endorsements, favoritism, or kickbacks, had been ignored, as if they had never been seen.

There were very few things that the

Association supported openly, outside of a desire to clean the world up and register Supers.

Only recently had more rumors started to circulate about the vast technology gap between Legion tech and the rest of the world. Mostly due to Romina's streaming about "unboxing" all the gadgets, weapons, and armor she'd been given.

Quite a few companies and individuals had reached out to her after that. Many of them likely trying to open a line of conversation to get ahold of said technology.

Thankfully, Romina was loyal beyond a fault and had notified Felix of every single person who had tried. All the while, Tribune noted the emails and alerted him about them.

Technology was the weapon he'd overlooked the most in his last go round. Programs, technology, software, and cyber-warfare.

This time around, he had all the weapons, and his finger was already atop the trigger.

The door to his office opened and Alma, Carlotta, Andrea Prime, Gaia, Goldie, a number of the prettier Dragons, several extremely good-looking Dryads, Romina, Edmund, and several handsome men that were likely part of Gaia's forces, all streamed in.

"Launch Global Domination, pre-war protocol. Launch Tribune's Call and compile according to your own specifications on whatever would be best," Felix murmured, mentally hitting the first-strike button. "I want it all Tribune. Take it all for me."

"Yes, Sir. I will not fail you, Legate. I will take it all," declared the VI as she began launching herself into the satellites above earth while simultaneously infecting all the nearby cell-towers, Wi-Fi signals, and internet. "Limited system access worldwide will be achieved in six hours. Complete dominance will likely be completed in six to eight days, depending on unknown variables and factors.

"Compiling will be achieved in ten minutes at most. Most of the Tribune locations will be integrated and then reprioritized without an issue."

Good.

Good!

It's a shame that is has to come to this, but I'm unwilling to allow a repeat of what happened previously. I've learned from my lessons.

Playing nice, playing by their rules, got me in trouble.

This time, I'm going to own everything long before they realize there's an issue. When they go to open their armory and arm themselves, they'll find all the locks changed.

Standing up, Felix moved around to the front of his desk.

With all these people who'd joined him, it just wouldn't do to greet his people while sitting down. That'd just be outright rude.

Not to mention, it was nearly a given that Andrea would more than likely slam into him at high speed. It'd be better for him, and her, if he wasn't at his desk.

Which she of course did.

Followed by Goldie, Alma, Carlotta, a nervous looking Romina, and an equally shy Gaia.

Murmuring the whole while about how she should probably let Felix seduce her. That if she waited any longer the Dragons might take up what room there was left.

Chapter 28 – Hostile Negotiation -

As the plane touched down, Felix felt frustrated.

He'd have preferred to fly here by Dragon, but other than Goldie, they were all out talking to the various nations that'd responded. Every single Dragon Maiden was on a mission.

They were each carrying a few individuals to conduct Association business with a nation. Deliver the team and paperwork, provide security, then travel back when complete.

More countries than he'd expected had reached out to him, so they'd had to be very selective about who to see, and in what order. That meant Felix himself had gotten involved with a few of the bigger factions that needed a bit more "face-time" as it were.

The first was the European Union.

While they didn't technically have a location they called their headquarters, they did have a building they often met in for their summits. A building that was located in Brussels, where Felix had been asked to step in front of several representatives and hold a discussion on what the association was offering.

The United Nations had asked for more information, to which Felix had of course responded. Though he was disinclined to go speak in front of them.

From what he understood of this world, they

didn't have much in the way of power, nor could they really enact any type of policy that'd benefit the Association.

The European Union had more policy-making power that could possibly limit what he wanted to do across the globe. The UN would probably become tied up in itself if they tried to move against the Association.

Especially since his outreach had garnered a response from every single member of their Security Council.

Several pings sounded off from inside of his helmet sitting on his lap.

Letting out a sigh, Felix knew he needed to put it back on now that they'd landed. Unfortunately, he still had to protect his identity. While he was able to pull it off for the flight, he did need to wear it.

On top of that, he'd clearly just been reconnected to a satellite signal that Tribune controlled. The pings were the result of Tribune connecting, downloading, and uploading, all at the same time, to his armor.

Picking it up, he pulled it down over his head and waited for a moment as it settled itself, locked into the armor, and the HUD flashed. It scrambled itself from the bottom to the top with random characters, and then settled to what he expected.

"Legate," Tribune stated as the plane began to turn after it'd slowed down considerably. "Your location is incorrect. Unable to triangulate due to interference. Attempting to correct."

Huh?

Felix raised his eyebrows at that and looked to Andrea, Gaia, and Faith who were all with him on this mission. The former was sleeping in her chair, with a bag of chips spilled across her lap and the floor in front of her. The latter was reading something on a tablet.

Gaia was staring off into nothing as she was wont to do at times. He imagined that she spent a great deal of time in the mortal world while simultaneously living in whatever realms that deities did.

"Gaia, are we where we're supposed to be?" Felix asked.

"Uhm?" asked the beautiful woman, turning to look at him. She blinked twice, then gave him a smile. "We're always where we should be my Champion. You're my Champion, I'm your goddess. If we're together, it's exactly as it should be."

"Not... not what I meant," grumbled Felix and then looked ahead. "Tribune, any luck at all? Maybe the planes transponder? Local Wi-Fi might tell you where we are?"

Tribune was an amazing VI, but there were times when a simpler solution could be overlooked given her limitations with adaptation.

Amazing program, limited by her programming. It's her tools that can facilitate her ability. Tools can be far more adaptable than she can.

I'll need to make sure I keep providing her with more tools. Those extra programs she always wants more of.

"Yes, Legate. A local Wi-Fi has an SSID that has given me a location based on its naming convention and service-model," reported Tribune. "They're not part of the global network and are not on the internet.

"You're currently in the People's Democratic Republic of Kadasz. It is likely your plane was hijacked mid-air, or the pilot has taken you hostage."

"Right... thanks, Tribune," muttered Felix, getting up out of his seat. His annoyance that Andrea couldn't fly the plane due to a licensing issue had just grown to a point that he wanted the problem fixed for the future. "Andrea, Faith, Gaia, helmets and game faces on. We've been abducted"

Andrea started, the rest of the chips that'd been piled up on her leg-plates spilling down to the ground in front of her. Her head snapping toward him and her eyes trying to focus.

"We've been abducted," he repeated, staring at Andrea. "Don't kill anyone yet. Let's see what they have to say."

"Goodness," murmured Gaia who'd picked up her helmet and was fitting it down over her head. "I really do find this all rather fascinating. It's somewhat comical at times how much is always happening around you.

"Though... darn. Darn it! I was hopping I'd be able to let him seduce me tonight. I even wore the underwear Evie gave me just for him and —"

The helmet latched in, and Gaia's voice went quiet.

Oh thank goodness. I swear if—

" — made sure to shave, too. It's all hairless like she suggested," she finished. "I wonder if he'll use his mouth if I ask? I'll use my mouth if he asks, so I'm sure he can do the same."

"Use your mouth!" cheered Andrea, who'd rocketed up out of her seat with her helmet slammed on. Pointing at Gaia with both hands, she nodded her head rapidly. "He loves that! Faith will tell you. She can make him beg for it! I just do it with a lot of energy and often! My technique is awful, but I do what I can, and do it often!"

Clicking his tongue, Felix looked to the back of the plane. Romina was back there and likely recording something for her channel. If she wasn't streaming, she was working on something else for it.

Walking toward him, he found her helmet was on, camera turned on, but her rifle was left next to where she'd been seated.

"Ugh… that's an unskippable cut-scene going in my head now, Andie," Juno complained.

"Nnn! Isn't it amazing? Now that you're thinking about doing that to him, I should mention the smell. It's really —"

"Tribune, mute her," Felix commanded as Andrea spoke. Her voice suddenly cutting out completely.

Her head kept moving around though as if she were talking. Gesticulating with her hands to emphasize something with them. Holding them apart in front of herself, then moving them further away.

Then putting her hands together in front of her face like she was fighting a snake.

Even though her helmet was sealed, he swore he could practically hear her screaming inside her helmet.

"Okay," Felix murmured, looking to Faith.

"I'm afraid there isn't a mute strong enough for me dear. You know I'm loud and love to be heard," replied the Dryad from behind her helmet. "As to the situation, I'm sure we'll learn more when the plane stops.

"How would you like to proceed? Shoot first? Talk first? You tend to get a little chatty when you're about to shoot into me, so I'm not sure how you want to handle this."

Lowering his head partially, Felix looked to Romina's boots. He really didn't know what to say anymore.

"I wonder if he'd talk to me while thrusting up into me," Gaia asked herself. "Oh... I should practice dirty talk I bet. Something like... fill me up? Fill me up Felix?

"Or... harder Felix! Harder! Hm. I like that. Pull my hair, harder Felix harder and —"

"Tribune, her too, please," whimpered Felix, and Gaia was cut off. Then he sighed and looked to

Romina.

"Uhm… I… I don't… I'm pretty vanilla," remarked Juno when they were looking at each other. "I'm sorry, I don't know what to say anymore. This is all just… I feel like I need to take a vacation and go touch some grass."

"Yeah… I get that," agreed Felix. "Think I need to uh… go touch some grass with you."

"Nnnn! Touch Romina's grass! Then go touch Gaia, she cut her grass so you could!" shrieked Andrea who was right next to him now. She was now close and loud enough to be heard through her helmet. Her hands were latched to his armor, and she was pressed up to his side.

Closing his eyes, Felix realized his mistake. If he muted them, they'd take that as provocation to get his attention more directly.

Don't… tease the crazy people.

"Unmute them Tribune and let's go see what's going on," he muttered. "And while you're at it, any chance of you taking over these networks from my armor?"

"No, Legate," answered Tribune.

" — could say that I did cut my grass. He's definitely welcome to touch it. It's why I cut it, after all," Gaia finished.

Felix heard a groan in his helmet, and he wasn't sure if it was him, or Romina.

Or both.

The door to the plane opened and someone called inside in a language he didn't recognize. At that moment, he also noticed that the pilot hadn't exited the cockpit area either.

Moving to the door, he looked out and found someone rolling a metal stair up to it.

"You know... you're like... a walking anti-main character syndrome clap back," Romina muttered. "I feel like a side-character near you."

"That just means you're not a heroine yet," Faith answered. "I decided to be more than a side character and moved to a Heroine of my own story. It's a romance where I got the boy. Had to work at it though."

"Legate! A pleasure to see you!" called a man at the bottom of the stairs. He was surrounded by other men in military uniforms. Around them, and spread out around even that group, were soldiers with rifles. They all had them pointed at Felix and his people.

"Tribune, any chance of their rounds penetrating the armor?" Felix asked.

"Improbable, Sir, but not impossible," answered Tribune.

Looking to the man who was likely in charge, Felix noted he was of some type of eastern-European descent. With dark hair, blue eyes, and a cold smile. He was in his forties, from what Felix could tell, though quite trim and fit.

There was a lack of humanity in his face and eyes. As if he viewed every single person, tree, blade of grass, and ant, as his, and was sure that any and all of it could be rightfully bought and sold without a concern.

"You'll forgive me if I'm not pleased, but I don't know where I am, who you are, or why I'm here," Felix answered, then came down the ramp. All rifles were pointed at him now. "You might want to tell them to stop aiming those at me. Pretty sure there's going to be a giant golden death machine showing up.

"Any aggression could be misinterpreted. She's... not very gentle once she's determined that there's an issue."

Laughing, the man looked very amused at this. Extremely so. Gesturing to one side, he said something in a different language.

A jeep-like vehicle sped toward them from off to the side.

"Do you mean this one?" asked the man, his arm still pointing toward where the vehicle was coming from.

"She landed ahead of you while we secured the airport and you were circling a few times. She surrendered without an issue and we've kept her nearby," explained the man.

"Ah... you, made this a lot easier for me," Felix remarked and looked to the vehicle coming their way. Goldie was seated in the front passenger seat. She was in her full Humanoid Dragon appearance. A man sat behind her with an over-sized and almost comical looking rifle pointed at the back of her head.

It looked cartoonish in fact, quite different

from what he was used to as far as firearms went.

"You will do what I say, or we'll shoot her. I'm betting an anti-tank rifle will be able to kill her," said the man.

Felix wasn't actually sure Goldie could survive such a shot. He knew she was extremely formidable now. That in her Dragon shape she could more than likely fight a jet, helicopter, or a tank, with a reasonable chance of success.

That being said, an anti-tank rifle sounded like something that possibly could penetrate her.

Especially in her humanoid form.

"Now, you will give us your armor, technology, data, and money," stated the man. "Once you've done that, we'll put you back on that plane and you can leave."

Hm.

Well that's just not an option.

Felix stood there, as if contemplating the options. Letting his captor think that Felix was considering it.

When the jeep got closer, but not too close, it came to a full stop. Goldie was nude, somewhat bored looking, and clearly waiting for him to give her an instruction.

"Go ahead and shoot her then," Felix said with a shake of his head. "Because I can't give you the tech."

There was a gigantic boom, followed by Goldie being knocked forward. Her head slammed into the windshield of the open-top vehicle. She hung there for a second before she returned to an upright and seated position.

An annoyed expression was on her face as she turned around. Grabbing the big gun, she ripped it away from the man and then opened the vehicle of the door.

Stepping out, she looked at the weapon as she walked back to the group.

"Andie, is this useful? Do you want this?" Goldie asked as she got close enough.

"I mean... I don't have one... so... yes? Pretty sure it's a PTRD, too so... yes, yes," Andrea answered. "Please? I love you. Share Felix with me tonight in a messy-dirty three way? Or four way if you want another Andrea with us. Six way?"

"Andrea, I'm recording. You just got yourself caught in 4k revealing that you're bi," hissed Romina. "I don't want to out you; I'll edit it out later."

"I don't care? I mean... isn't that what I am? I do things with Miu and Felix," argued Andrea who was making grabby hands at Goldie and the gun. "I love Miu, I love Felix, I love Goldie. I never felt that way about Kit, Lily, or you. Or Faith, even though she's gorgeous."

Felix was mildly nervous about her using people's names, but that was also why he'd listed Felix Campbell in the files correctly and had him go on a few missions with Romina.

Then his mind actually went to what Andrea had said rather than the names she'd mentioned.

Err... actually it is rather new that she's been going in with Miu and towards Goldie. I wonder if that's a switch of the Andrea personality that came here.

More of an Adrianna thing, maybe?

Unsure, but interesting.

I really do wonder what'll happen when we go back home.

Goldie made it to Andrea, who hugged her tightly, clearly grabbed the Dragon's rear end, then took the rifle from her.

"Nnnn! Goldie my love... it really is a PTRD! I've always wanted one. I love you, Goldie. Love you so much. Thanks," Andrea cheered excitedly and jumping up and down in place.

"They just wanted to rob us," Goldie said, moving toward the plane. "That's it. I'm going to go inside. I don't like being naked around them, or on camera."

"I've got it covered," Romina murmured quietly. Her hand was in front of the camera right now.

"Oh, why thank you, dear. I appreciate you looking out for everyone," Goldie said with a warm smile, then headed into the plane.

"I took my clothes off and left them in the back of the plane. I think we fit clothes close enough that it'd work," Gaia offered.

"Off?" Goldie asked as she moved past Gaia.

"Yes. I took off my clothes to put on my armor. I find the armor fits on me better with just my skin," Gaia offered. "That and I like the way it feels better."

Goldie chuckled at that and didn't say anything in return, going up the stairs

"What, none of you are naked underneath?" Gaia asked.

"No. I wear a tank-top and shorts when I wear the armor. Going inside. I have a headache and I think I'm bleeding a little. Was a big gun," Goldie grumped as she entered the plane.

"Not much, but some," Romina replied. "Just my underwear really I guess."

"Pajamas work well for me," Faith offered. "Feels like it'll tear off my nipples otherwise. Too sensitive."

"Mmm, rifle, nnnn. New rifle. Ooh! I'm gonna need a new sight. Though... what kind of sight do you put on an anti-tank rifle? Hahaha."

Felix wanted to shout at them all. This was entirely the wrong conversation to have in this situation. They were technically still being held hostage.

"Drat. I guess maybe I'm the odd one after all then. They all wear something. Maybe I'm the only one thinking of going straight to sex after this. Or maybe Juno is? She's only wearing underwear.

"He does dote on her when he has no reason to. I wonder if he's interested in her like he is me?"

"Tribune, mute her for a minute," begged Felix, then he looked to the dictator who'd brought them here. "Look, friend. I don't know what you were thinking. I have no idea what you were really expecting out of this, but I'll make it simple. I'm going to — "

"I'll blow up your building!" shouted the man, wide eyed and infuriated.

Considering how they'd practically ignored him, Felix didn't find that surprising in the least.

"Alright, you do that. Anyways," Felix dismissed with a wave of his hand. "If you want my technology, I'd be happy to sell certain things to your nation. I have no concerns at all regarding that, in fact.

"I don't sell arms or armor, however. That's too politically charged. The recycler machine, the waste reducer, air scrubber, medical pod, all those things I'm happy to sell at the prices I listed in the international communication," Felix continued.

At the same time, his mind was spinning in a different direction.

While this entire thing was mostly a waste of time, that amounted to more of a loss of time on his part, it'd also given him an idea. A thought that felt like exactly the right direction.

He'd been wracking his brain on how to get the world to recognize him and the Association with what he wanted to do. A way for them to greet him, welcome him, and endorse the Association readily.

Greedily, even.

It was such a simple and stupid reality that he hadn't even considered it.

At some point… somewhere… there's going to be a Skipper.

Someone with a power strong enough to take over, is going to. A successful one is most likely going to pop up in a country with a weak security force.

Weak military or counterintelligence.

Somewhere like this could easily have a Skipper show up out of nowhere and take over.

When it does, I have to be ready. Let's... start planning out how to make it work when it does.

"Legate, I've been able to download a fraction of myself into their networks. I used a satellite that was passing overhead to work my way in. I will have control in several minutes," reported Tribune. "I will proceed to do this with every other possible location that isn't hooked into the greater world wide web.

"I would request that we look into putting up signal towers with Legion technology."

Maybe... we'll see.

I have points a plenty, but far too many high-value projects to buy.

"So, shall we make some deals? I can easily sell you technology. Right now, in fact," offered Felix. "I don't care what sanctions are against you or anything of that nature. I'm only interested in the jurisdiction of the Association, and nothing more."

Standing there, Felix waited, staring at the face of a man who would have happily killed Goldie to make a point.

"Will you barter with me?" he asked instead of cursing at Felix, a smile returning to his face. "Keep the gun. Are you interested in other weapons as well? I have a collection of many rare soviet era weapons."

Without turning around, he knew Andrea was vibrating in place right now.

Then he realized there were likely other things that could be bartered for here as well.

"Do you have any toxic dumps, nuclear fuel waste sites, or hazardous landfills?" Felix asked, thinking about what they might need. "Or any old facilities you'd be willing to let one of my people explore with a camera? Maybe one of those nuclear fuel waste sites I mentioned?"

"My Champion... always thinking of me. Romina, too. He's clearly infatuated with us. I'll have to seduce him if he doesn't seduce me. We need to resolve this tension between us," whispered Gaia. "I'm sure after we have sex a few times the tension will ease up.

"I wonder if Romina will need to sleep with him before it goes away, too? Weren't Jupiter and Juno married? They were nice people when I knew them."

Damnit... all.

Chapter 29 - Truth or Illusion -

Grinning to himself, Felix scanned the text message with a shake of his head.

Georgia was spamming him right now with a number of text messages. They'd had dinner last night when he came back after meeting with the European union, and he'd hung out with a number of his cousins.

He'd also spent more time with his aunts, grand-father, grand-mother, and others previously.

It'd been interesting and strange to have family members his own age. Ones who had lived a normal life in a corporate-like society.

While he treasured his relationship with Vince, it was different.

The man had been born to a world that wanted to chew him up and spit him out without a care. Or at least, the only care being that he had too many bones and they'd gotten stuck between a few teeth.

"Felix," whispered a voice behind him.

"Miu!" Felix cheered, turning around and hugging Miu tightly. Holding to her, he pressed her into himself with as much force as he could manage. "Oooh, Miu. I missed you.

"I know I'm the one who sent you off on the mission, but I also missed you badly. I know that's just weird, but I can't help it."

Miu groaned under the weight of his hug, but did try to burrow into him. Pushing her head up under his chin.

"I understand," she said as her hands moved up against his stomach. "It's g-good to feel you, my love."

Felix grinned, kissed the top of her head, then nuzzled at the side of her face until she lifted her chin. Kissing her warmly, he kept her captive there for several seconds. Just kissing and holding onto her.

When he did release her, he could see that was as tense as a taut bowstring. Drawn to a full release and ready to fire.

"Well, with any luck, we can move this along very quickly, and maybe I can steal some time with you," hoped Felix, grabbing her hand and bringing her over to the table he'd set up at.

They were at a location where they wouldn't stand out too much for having breakfast. He'd also made sure to pick somewhere both Miu and Mikki could come talk to him.

"It's really good to see you, Miu," Faith said from where she stood next to the table.

"Good… good to see you too, Faith. I missed you. You're a good f-friend," Miu mumbled with a small hand wave at Faith. "Though I was expecting to see Andiieeeee!"

Miu's words turned into a partial screech as Andrea practically appeared beside the woman. Her arms darted around the psychotic assassin and hugged her tightly after pressing a brief kiss on the other woman's lips.

Rocking back and forth, she was visibly manhandling the other woman.

"Miuuuuuu! I missed youuuuuuu!" Andrea called as she rubbed her face roughly into Miu's neck. Even going so far as to lift the smaller woman off the ground.

Then Andrea pulled away from her and grinned at her in a wild and warm way. Gazing into the other woman's face, her eyes flicking back and forth.

Unable to be angry, despite the fact that Felix was sure she wanted to be, Miu only grinned back at Andrea.

"I missed you, too," she said and then gestured to the table.

By the time all of them took their seats, they only belatedly noticed that Mikki was seated next to Faith. At some point, she'd joined them silently.

"Hello," said the alternate universe Miu. "It's nice to see you all. I was happy to see the meeting request."

Miu sat down and then held a hand out across the table to Mikki. Who hesitantly took it, though she was the first to squeeze the other's hand.

A second passed before they released each other and settled back into their seats.

"I already ordered," Faith clarified. "We can get right into it."

"Good," Mikki said with a deep nod of her head. "I have... almost nothing to report. The... group... is more or less exactly as we'd want them.

They've adapted to all my policy, rules, and procedure requirements.

"There have been a few troublemakers here and there, but I handle them after speaking with Kit and Lily. Neither were opposed to me having those people lose their access and sponsorship.

"It only took a few people for it to happen to before the others fell in line. It also had the added benefit of getting everyone to agree going forward.

"Everyone's afraid of losing what they have for the sake of opposing the leadership. I didn't think you'd care since we're trying to encourage them into the 'accepted leader' role anyways."

"Just so. Good work, Mikki, that's well done," Felix murmured with a grin. He'd taken up Miu's left hand in his right and was gently stroking his thumb back and forth across the back of her wrist.

"Miu helped me with all of it. Even in the plans that I thought were perfect, she provided a few nudges here and there to make them complete," admitted Mikki.

"Only because I've done it before. The credit is yours," argued Miu.

"Well done," Faith said, smiling at Mikki and reaching over to gently touch the woman's shoulder. It was a scarce, almost insubstantial, didn't-exist type of touch, but it was probably all Mikki could handle.

From what Felix could see, it didn't faze her, which was unanticipated from his point of view.

Perhaps she's growing faster and more stably than Miu did.

That's a good thing.

Quite possibly because she can see that Miu is doing so well?

"Oh! It's time for the B&B! I'm sorry, not sorry, but I have to turn this on to support Juno!" Andrea yelled and whipped out a phone. She pulled out a kickstand off its case, stuck it down on the table, and then looked back to everyone else. "Okay! Ready! Continue, please. Thank you."

" — here! We've got our third episode of Bake and Brawl!" came Juno's voice from the phone. The volume wasn't that high, but Felix could still hear it. "First though, before anything else, I have to thank my Jupiter for everything. As I always do. My dearest and most kind Jupiter who gifted me with the best job and family I've ever had.

"So let's — "

"Miu? How's your end?" Felix asked, wanting to not hear what Juno had to say about him.

"Not as good as Mikki's but not bad. Anya is very… hesitant to listen to anyone. She's changed and is very stand-offish. Unless you're charmed and under her sway, she stays pretty far away from you.

"Though she's getting a little better about that. I tried to stab her, and she reflexively hardened her skin and scales. After that she mellowed out considerably."

Felix wasn't quite sure how trying to stab someone would make logical sense in any scenario, but this was Miu. Logical sense was often convoluted and wrapped into itself until it became twisted into something else entirely.

"Good idea," Mikki offered.

Andrea had the look of a woman who wanted to just nod her head and change the conversation. Faith looked unsurprised and resigned.

"Great, in other words, both groups are where we need them and want them. You two really are impressively well suited to this," Felix complimented them, looking, from one to the other.

"This helps," Mikki said and held up her left hand. The Legion ring there was obvious. She'd been given one of the few they had, as she couldn't wear armor or a helmet while being part of the Guild.

It was made to look a lot like a wedding ring and was worn on the appropriate finger.

" — the champion of the last two matches, Evie, looks like she has the upper hand in the second half of the match today. Those cupcakes got an upgrade I can't even get close to, no cap.

"Especially when Lucille, the champion of our Brawl, made those... very... sus... looking pastries. Lucille... did you even bake these long enough?"

Uh... what?

Looking to Andrea's phone, he saw it was Juno's camera view looking over a large table of baked goods. Next to a plate of sad-looking goods was Lucille.

There was a lot of nervous energy in her.

"Uhm… I tried," confessed Lucille. "I'm really trying Juno. I'm going to be a good Dragon Housewife to the Legate but… it's going to take me time.

"I'm confident in my strength! Just… just not my… wifely skills. Goldie is doing her best with me. Even I have to admit Evie is really good at baking."

There was a crunching and chewing sound as Lucille spoke, followed by Juno coughing.

"Okay, legit, I'm not feeling any shame about trying to wol—" Juno's voice cut off followed by several more coughs.

Goldie came on screen with a glass of what looked like milk.

"No talking with your mouth full, Juno. You also know better than trying to eat something that quickly. That's unbecoming of you," chided Goldie, a warm smile on her face. The chat on the side of the screen was filled with Gold Dragon emoji's that were wearing aprons. As well as an entire screens-worth of heart symbols. "And you're doing fine Lucille. You're learning, improving, and really putting effort in. The hardest part is trying!

"Though I do worry for if you can keep up when we start up the other contests. You and I should put in some extra lessons together. Combat is important, but being able to work a line on an armscye is almost just as important. We have lots of combatants, but only so many Dragon Housewives."

"Yes, Goldie. Thank you, you always brighten my spirits," thanked Lucille with a small smile.

"The fuck planet is this," muttered Felix, feeling more confused now than he'd ever been in his life.

"Are you kidding? Juno's show is great! Everyone loves the B&B. First they bake, Gaia declares a winner, and then they brawl. Where there's a second-place winner," Andrea explained, flicking her fingers at the phone as if explaining it. "Evie is dominating everyone. Cathy and Carol do alright.

"Amanda's a real surprise though. She's a Blue that just came out of nowhere with some amazing cookies last time.

"They're going to expand it and have different contests in different weeks. Next week is Sewing and Slaughtering. Goldie's been teaching them how to mend clothes, as well as breaking down animals for stews and things.

"After that, Goldie told/hinted that it might be laundry and lust but... uh... she said that might not be an episode that Romina can air."

Nodding his head, Felix shook it.

Goldie had mentioned she needed him for a few hours for a project in several weeks. He now knew to avoid that date like the plague.

"Well, let's enjoy the show while we wait for

the food. Then just... enjoy each other's company," he said instead, not wanting to spoil the mood. "This was obviously a meeting that could have been an email, but I wanted to see you all."

Miu and Mikki both nodded their heads, though they both ended up looking back to the phone.

On it, a beautiful, immaculately put together, and incredibly lovely Gaia was sampling everything on the table with small, cute bites, while holding onto a dainty plate.

Looking at Romina and the camera, she made a hand wave and gave them an underwear melting smile.

Once again, the screen was filled with emojis. This time it was a bunch of Gaia's face with a smile on it.

Then, there followed an inconceivable number of eggplants.

Endless eggplant emoji after eggplant emoji.

Not that Felix could blame them.

He'd be happy to give her an eggplant at this point, too.

Then Miu squeezed his hand to the point that it felt like his hand might break.

***

Pulling up to his grandmother's house, Felix paused in the driver's seat and pulled out his phone. There was a single text message and a missed call.

Flipping it to the message, he glanced it over.

The text was that his mother was late but on her way. She'd stopped to grab dinner for everyone, but that everyone was with her.

Which meant Felix was going to end up waiting here.

The missed call was the surprise though.

Lily had called him.

He realized why at the same time that he thought "why".

Tapping the button next to her name, he was dialing her back.

She picked up before the first ring could even be sounded.

"And there he is. My dear... Legate," Lily proclaimed over the line.

Okay... let's just call her out on this.

If she's like my Lily, the longer we play this game, the more she'll be into it.

"You know. Somehow you know. How?" asked Felix, jumping right to the end game of it. "It's not Kit. She wouldn't have told you because she would have assumed it'd be better for you two to not know."

"Ah! You... you've ruined it. You really did ruin it," Lily growled, sounding angry and partly surprised. "Lucian said you'd wreck it because I'd push it too far. You'd get frustrated and just... end it."

"Ah... Lucian. Hm. If it was Lucian... was he

hovering around you?" Felix asked. "Couldn't get back to his body but had found you and was following you?

"Maybe hovering around you when it all happened? That's probably it. I'd bet on it."

"Something like that," hissed Lily. Then she sighed loudly. "Anyways. Thank you for the present. I'm looking forward to trying it out. I feel like I should be worried that you know my measurements so well but uh... Lucian... mentioned you know about my spot."

"Spunk spot," Felix clarified. "Yeah. Very aware of it. Now... I'll have Kit wipe your mind out tomorrow, so you forget all this again, then have her get to Lucian too.

"Anything you wanna know before your newly found memories go bye-bye?"

"Would you burn the world for me?" she asked in a strange almost breathless voice.

Looking into the darkness ahead of him, Felix contemplated that.

It was an empty road with only a few dimly lit streetlights on it.

Casting hollow shadows down to the road beneath it. Barely illuminating the darkness beyond to signify of how deep those shadows were.

Only enough so that one could see where the road might begin or end on either side.

I'm traveling a road speeding along through the dark.

"No. Because my Kit would be incredibly

hurt by it. She'd feel the guilt of it all on herself even if she had nothing to do with it, other than that it was something that related to her," Felix explained, then let out a slow breath. "Do you want to keep what you know, or would you prefer me getting rid of it.

"Because I'm sure you also know I'm using you. That I'm using the Guild to my own ends. Pushing you and Kit into the leadership role, if only to get what I want."

There was a pause on the other end of the line, followed by a cough.

"Wipe it. Me, Kit, and Lucian. Tonight, if possible. Tomorrow morning before I wake up, if not," Lily answered, then let out a slow breath. "Thanks. For the armor, too. This… looks really well done."

"Should stop almost all small arms fire. You won't know anything about this in the morning other than that we spoke, I wished you happy birthday, then told you to stop calling me."

"Right," mumbled Lily, who then hung up.

Not my Lily. Not… not my Lily.

Not my Lily.

Complete stranger.

She's not my… not my Lily.

Felix's phone started ringing again and he looked to the caller ID.

Jordan Johnson?

And what does our dear newly minted Senator want?

Tapping the accept button, Felix put the phone up to his ear.

"Good evening," Felix said.

"Good evening indeed. I'll make this very quick, as I really don't much care for electronic devices like this," said Jordan. "Association, good or bad, support or sink."

"Good, support," replied Felix decisively. "Politically non-supportive of anyone and everyone. Going against them in any way is a waste of resources.

"Anything outside of that is up to you. The Association Investigative Act is clearly an issue and a breach of the public trust but... that's more on you, your party, and obligations to your platform."

"Quite so, thank you for providing me with that small yet needed answer," Jordan thanked him sincerely. He sounded significantly more at ease in just that short time. "I'm redirecting the entire state's trash to your landfill and paying you for the work.

"Have a nice night and sleep well."

"Goodnight," Felix agreed and turned off the call.

Only to startle in his seat.

His cousin, a twenty-five year old young woman who looked like his mom, was standing at his window. She had a big grin on her face and her hands on the glass.

"Got you!" she teased and then laughed loudly, moving away from his driver's window.

Laughing, Felix opened the car door and got out.

He was feeling better already.

The Lily of this world wasn't his Lily. He had his own.

But the family in this world, had no version of him to look at. Nor did he have them.

Melding him to them would be easy since there wasn't anything there before.

"Felix, oh my god, you should have seen your face," teased Tara with a chuckle.

"You should have seen yours. It's what caused the whole problem. You even made me pee a little," complained Felix, which set Tara into another deep fit of laughter.

Grinning, he followed Tara towards the house. He could see his mother, aunt, and several other cousins already filtering in.

Not so bad... having a familial bond in a place like this. I wonder if there's anyone Andrea would want to reach out to.

Then again... given what I've learned of her... probably not.

Chapter 30 – Okay, No –

There was a buzzing and rumbling coming from Felix's phone as he got back into his car. He'd spent the evening hanging out with his mother's side of the family and had surprisingly enjoyed it greatly.

To the point that he'd forgotten about everything else that was going on.

Somewhat regretfully, he fished his phone out of his pocket and flicked the lock screen on. He was presented with the fact that Tribune was calling him.

"Uh… what?" he mumbled, tapped the accept button, and held the phone to his ear. "Tribune?"

"Good evening, Legate," Tribune said on the other end of the line. "This communication is part of the notification chain that you approved during my creation.

"You received an email that you didn't respond to from me for longer than six hours that was marked as 'needs attention'."

Felix could vaguely remember putting such a policy into place. It was to make sure he didn't lose track of something.

"Proceed," he said.

There was a pop next to him and he turned his head.

Standing there outside of his car was Evie. She had what looked like a massive cheeseburger in one hand and a large fountain drink in the other. Moving around to the passenger side door, she opened the door, juggled her items around, and got into the car.

"We've received a notification from the Supreme Court. They're having the Association Investigative Act moved to the front of their docket," Tribune continued as Evie settled herself in the seat. The stunningly gorgeous woman gave him a crooked grin and took a long drink from her straw, watching him. "They'll be hearing arguments on it in two days. You've been called as a witness to discuss your part in it."

"I see. Considering we don't care one way or the other about the act, it's... mostly irrelevant what I say then when there," Felix suggested, eying Evie.

Or more specifically her burger.

While he'd enjoyed dinner, he hadn't wanted to look like a pig and had only eaten as much as everyone else had. Limiting himself to a portion that was within limits of their own.

He was still hungry.

In fact, he was starting to wonder if he ever wasn't hungry anymore. It was as if he couldn't eat enough more often than not.

"That's accurate, Sir. Realistically speaking, regardless of the outcome, it doesn't impact us. Even the lawsuit that was made against the Association will end up falling upon the government," Tribune agreed. "As per the contract we signed with them, the Association isn't beholden to the laws of the federal government, state government, or local government. That includes all agencies or actors working on behalf of the Association. We're in the clear."

Nodding his head, Felix watched Evie take another large bite of her burger. Though she was chewing it slowly now, watching him.

"Anything I need to do?" he asked.

Tilting her head to one side, she then held out the food to him with a grin as she chewed. Half of it was gone by this point and she clearly wanted to finish it, yet she still offered it to him.

Gratefully, he took it with his free hand and started in on it immediately. Taking a bite and knowing he'd feel better in just a few minutes.

"No, Legate. I'll prepare everything for you in a bullet point format," Tribune stated. "There is only one other thing that I must make you aware of."

Felix could only manage a grunt as he continued to eat the burger Evie had graciously provided for him. She was watching him as he ate, a wide smile on her face.

Then she held her drink out to him, as if asking if he wanted a sip.

Not declining, he swallowed his mouthful down, tried to clear his mouth a bit, then took a drink from it.

"Goldie wanted me to warn you to be careful with your Dragon Housewives. They're likely going to be going into Heat," Tribune said. Felix's eyes jumped to Evie's as he continued to drink from her proffered cup. Her eyes had a low intensity glow to them, but it was unmistakable. "It's the first one they'll go through in their new position and there's no telling what they might do.

"That's how Goldie wished me to phrase the message, Sir. She doesn't think they'll do anything untoward, but it's best you be on your guard."

Letting go of the straw, Felix smiled at Evie who was practically sideways in the seat now. Her entire body as good as facing him.

There was an odd look to the exquisite beauty at the moment.

"Good to know, thanks Tribune. Relay my thanks to Goldie, and then Faith as well," Felix asked. Lifting the burger up, he hesitated, then held it out to Evie.

Lifting a hand, she curled a long lock of red hair back behind an ear, leaned in, and took a bite from the burger. Only to lean back into her seat and watch him while chewing.

"Of course. Have a good evening, Legate," Tribune said and disconnected the line.

Sitting there in the car, he wasn't sure what to say.

There were several thumps he could hear behind him. Followed by two in front of him.

Carol and Lucille had just arrived near the passenger side of the door. Each one of them had some type of food in their hands and were happily eating and talking. Though their eyes were all fastened on him.

Glowing faintly.

Hm.

It's like… being in a horror movie. Surrounded by predators.

As long as I keep it slow and easy, I'm sure this'll be fine.

Evie took his wrist in hand and moved the burger back to his own mouth.

Predators.

The passenger door on his side opened and he heard someone getting in. Then Lucille and Carol did the same from the other side.

"Where're we going?" asked Carol, who then took a bite from her sub-sandwich after closing the door.

"Let's go look at nests. We don't have anywhere to nest when the time comes," Lucille suggested.

"Can we go look at jewelry?" asked what sounded like Cathy behind him. "I want to buy Goldie some hair clips and something for a few others."

Lucille and Carol straightened up in the back seat and looked to each other, then Felix.

"A cooking store. I want to see if there's any cutesy tools or anything better than what I'm using," Carol suggested.

"Yes, cooking store. Never mind nests, we can do that later," Lucille agreed. "I need… I need to beat Evie. I can't keep being just the combat winner. I want to win."

"I respect your admiration," Evie murmured, looking to the backseat with a grin. "All of your admiration and determination. Defeat me and earn your place. I'm the second Dragon Housewife for a reason. I'll even help you pick out a cookbook or two.

"Oh, and girls? Please save a little bit of your meals for husband, he's hungry. We can get more food on the way back, but he's just a little peckish right now."

Evie then looked back to Felix.

"Husband, a cooking store, please?" she asked, easing the burger closer to his mouth again. She didn't want him to answer, but to accept her request as it was.

It was likely also why she suggested saving some food for him.

Taking another still hungry bite of the burger, he nodded his head.

***

Exiting, Felix felt rather good about how he'd conducted himself.

Everything he'd said while speaking had been accurate, to the point, and without anything that felt negative or off. Conveying exactly what he wanted for the Association.

Though it'd certainly left a bit of an awkward feeling for the government.

Doubly so when it'd been revealed that the

Association itself had only acted a handful of times under the Act itself, but the government had done so an estimated fifty times already. As if they were using it more than the Association itself was.

"That went well," Faith mused, her voice transmitting over the helmets, but not externally. She was on Felix's right as they left the building and began moving to the side. Their vehicles were parked not far off. "Somewhat surprising that no one bothered to actually come after us.

"I was half expecting them to try and hold us up as the boogieman in the closet. The monster under the bed. There to snatch up all their freedoms and rights."

"They didn't feel it was worth it. The Association has been so politically neutral that it's made no enemies though also no friends. There's no reason to attack it or defend it. That's what I gathered at least," answered Goldie from his right. She was dressed modestly and more conservatively than he'd expected. It did of course have a certain sexual appeal to it though.

Goldie always managed to look amazing regardless of what she was wearing. The gold chains through her horns and their rings tinkling quietly with every step only served to accentuate her graceful movements.

"Yeah-yeah! Nn! There's no reason to shoot at us cause we're just sitting there playing with a sandcastle we built while they're all arguing over who gets to play on the swings!" Andrea added helpfully.

"Pretty sure that's not quite it, Andie," murmured Romina. "It was pretty boring though. I'm going to have to beg Mike to edit the fuck out of that cringe-ass-boomer-clown-fiesta. There was so much grand-standing and hoop-jumping. Just gonna have 'okay boomer' as a note across the top."

There really was a lot of media push for this one.

Normally the Supreme court doesn't allow much in the way of recordings of any sort from what Faith explained. This is all very abnormal.

"It's the incoming president," Faith interjected. "With the one who made the deal with us on the way out, and the new one on the way in, they want to show how they're different."

"Oh yeah, that'll last for about a year. Pushing some of what they offered in exchange for votes. Just enough to barely fill in part of the check box," Felix said with a laugh. Dragon Maidens were appearing from all over and moving his way. He could already see Lucille, Carol, and Evie moving in a direct line for him. They'd all remained out here in street clothes, rather than going inside. "After that, then who knows what they'll start working on. Whatever it is though, it'll be to appease their backers and their key-supporters. I'm glad we're not in politics this time around. Politics are ugly and evil."

Almost as bad as HR.

"Uh, this time?" Romina asked, curiously. "And don't try to push me off. This isn't the first time you've said something like that. There's more going on here and you're keeping it locked away from me."

"Wouldn't worry about it Romie," Andrea said, ramming one armored shoulder into Juno's. "After you start bedding him, you'll figure it all out without any help I'm sure."

"I-that-I don't think that's really something that'll happen. I'm not interested and I have a-"

"Legate?" asked a man who'd stopped dead in front of Felix. He'd been crossing their path and looking straight ahead. As far as Felix had been concerned, the man wasn't paying him a bit of attention until that moment.

"Indeed," Felix said, coming to a stop. Then he lowered his voice. "Tribune, is there anything wrong with this area? Anything that'd stand out right now? Police alerts? Warnings? News crews? Anything?"

"A-Net, Convoy en route! Five minutes to arrival!" called an Andrea over the communication line. There was also a horn sounding for some reason.

"My name's agent Brian DeRisso. I'm with the Central Intelligence Agency. We'd like it if you came with us to answer a few questions," said the man with a congenial smile.

Almost like a dog that looked like it could tear you a part at any moment just watching you. Holding perfectly still and staring at you.

"Legate, all the cameras that are looking at the area you're in have been switched off in one way or another. Cellular communication in the area is also having difficulties getting through. All Wi-Fi signals are also experiencing outages," reported Tribune as Felix stared at the self-identified agent. "This is most likely to be the staging ground of an operation that is underway."

"Turn them all back on," requested Faith. "Get everything recording and see if you can't get all those signals back up too. Rip out all the data from the electronics on everyone around us, too. I'm starting to think a great many of those here are... in on it."

Glancing around, Felix saw that there was indeed a large number of people all starting to move their way. At the same time, Dragons began landing and forming out.

Brian didn't fail to notice either group, but he was clearly growing more nervous with each and every Dragon that touched down.

"I'm not beholden to the laws of this land," Felix stated with absolute conviction. "The only way I'd go anywhere with you is if you were paying for a pizza party.

"Are you... paying for a pizza party? If not, then I'll be on my way. As a contractually legally protected individual. Along with everyone here, as the Association isn't beholden to your laws we are more on a diplomatic echelon of status."

Looking at Brian, Felix tried to pick over anything out of the ordinary. The man was far too confident for someone picking a fight with a band of Dragons.

He was certainly above average height,

looking to be six foot two or a bit more than that. Heavyset with broad shoulders, the man looked like he'd been fit in his earlier life but it was starting to slip.

Bald with a dark brown beard, he looked out of place.

Otherwise there didn't seem to be anything about him that Felix could identify as the source of the confidence. His past was likely security, military, or both, but nothing extraordinary.

There was the hint of a handle sticking out from his coat as the only weapon he was carrying. If it was just a handgun, that wouldn't do much good against anyone here.

Felix wanted to know what it was. If he deconstructed it, how many points would he get for it.

Type: X-02b	Condition: Working(faulty)
Owner: Central Intelligence Agency	Action >> Deconstruction: Yield 15,191 points

Right… and if I wanted to know who to contact to purchase the X-02b's copyright, who would it be?

Travis Cox.

"Tribune, start looking into a Travis Cox. Cross check with the CIA and start digging through their files," Felix requested while pressing his hand against the outside of his wrist plate. There'd been a minor change in the last week that'd silence their external mic if their hand was placed there.

"I ain't paying for shit. You're still coming with me though," said the man with a nod of his head.

Felix pulled up the information on the man in front of him. He wanted to know the character stats he had to back up that kind of talk.

Name: James Domec		Race: Human	
Alias: Jim		Power: None	
Physical Status: Healthy.		Mental Status: Fear, aggression, fight or flight	
Positive Statuses: None		Negative Statuses: Fear	
Might:	17		Add +1? (170)
Finesse:	11		Add +1? (110)
Endurance:	13		Add +1? (130)
Competency:	13		Add +1? (130)
Intellect:	12		Add +1? (120)
Perception:	08		Add +1? (80)
Luck:	07		Add +1? (70)

"Listen, Jimmy. I'm going to be leaving when my ride gets here," Felix said, making sure he saw the microphone go active after removing his hand. "You haven't shown me proof of who you are, I'm under no obligation to believe who you are, and realistically... I don't owe you any more of my time than what you've taken.

"I'm not going anywhere with you. As I said. That's the end of the conversation as far as I'm concerned."

James had stopped breathing once Felix had used his name. As if he'd only now realized that stepping up like he had wasn't from a position of power.

But making himself a target.

The nail that sticks up, gets hammered down.

A number of individuals had exited vehicles and began making their way over toward the obvious showdown.

The Dragon Maidens who were closest to that area moved away and only shifted to encircle everyone. They all had their wings out and more than half already had smoke starting to billow up from nostrils and mouths.

A Dragon given a little time could work themselves into a semi-controlled frenzy, and they were all heading that direction.

"If you don't hit the brakes," warned Felix. "This isn't going to go well."

"That a threat?" asked James.

"No. An observation. You haven't proven who you are, I'm not legally obligated to go with you, you've got a large number of people with you that are looking to you to give them a direction," Felix summarized, holding up a finger with each point. "If you try to force me to go anywhere, it's going to go badly. It's just that simple."

James' face had clouded up as Felix

continued. Looking a lot like someone who just really didn't quite understand what was happening. Apparently, he really hadn't considered that Felix would react this way.

"A-P, Report," asked an Andrea who was with him, which was likely Prime.

"A-Two! Two minutes out!" came a shouted call from a different one.

"A-Net, Baggage Train three on the way!" said another Andrea.

"Samantha! In air! Circling!" shouted a voice over the sound of what seemed to be the wind. "Two enemy things!"

Oh. A couple Dragons are wearing really big headsets, I guess. They'd be the ones to provide some air cover.

As to the enemy… things… drones?

"Well shit," James said. Snatching the weapon out of the holster, he held it up, pointed it at Goldie, and pulled the trigger.

Except the thing jerked to the side as it fired.

A massive blast the size of a bowling ball was ejected out of the weapon. Slamming low into Lucille, it slapped her legs out from under her.

As well as tore out a sizable chunk of her. Spraying blood, muscle, and gore across the ground beneath her.

Roaring, Carol leapt forward with a massive slash of her wings to propel her.

Felix reached down and laid a hand to Lucille. He needed to understand just how badly she was injured.

Amongst his people, Lucille was second only to Goldie. Gaia couldn't really be considered as she didn't enjoy fighting and went out of her way to avoid it.

Name: Lucille Campbell	Condition: Grievously Wounded
If No Action Taken: Lasting Organ Damage	Action >> Revitalize: Cost 47,102 points

Felix chuckled at the idea of that cost being prohibitive. That was little more than what he got after a little time at his own landfill now that so many trucks were arriving.

"We need to move, Felix," Faith hissed, her hand landing on his shoulder even as he shifted around to get a better grip on the Dragon.

He activated his power to heal her and then pulled up on Lucille, dragging her to her feet.

All around him, Dragons were tearing through people. They were also making sure to dodge a round from anyone with one of those guns James had used.

"Up and at'em Lucille," Felix said and steadied the beautiful and dangerous woman. "Care to be my bodyguard with Faith? Goldie is busy and everyone else went a bit rabid."

I wonder if she ended up with my last name after being resurrected as my property. Did that increase my marital bonus?

I should check soon.

Keep putting that off because I don't want to see how bad it is.

Not far away, Goldie was busily tearing the guts out of James with clawed hands. Coiled entrails were being flung one way and then the other as she dug into the man.

"I... that... yes. Of course. Anything for you, husband," murmured the Black Dragon in a hushed whisper, turning to look at him fully after looking back down to her bare stomach. "You saved me. You put everything back. You really are everything Goldie said."

Felix clicked his tongue and looked back to what was going on. He wasn't a target in this, but that didn't mean he wanted to risk himself needlessly.

There was no way any of these people were going to try to kill him. At least outright, assuming they saw him.

In fact, he wasn't even sure the first weapon drawn was meant to do what it did. It had said it was faulty, after all.

He wasn't going to take chances with any of that though.

When Faith began pulling him backward to a different position, he didn't fight her.

As he turned around, he saw there was another group of agents waiting for him from behind.

Retreat wasn't an option.

Only fighting was.

Felix pulled out his pistol and sighed.

I'm just not cut out for this shit.

Lifting it up, he sighted it on the closest enemy and began firing while moving to a nearby stone statue's base.

Chapter 31 – Magic Trick -

Slamming into the stone base of a planter, Felix felt like he'd managed to get several shots on his target. He had no idea if they were dead and down, as he didn't want to stick around to find out.

He'd noted that two of the individuals who'd been coming toward them, had those fancy weapons that'd dropped Lucille.

He had no idea if they'd be strong enough to rip through his Legate armor, but he also didn't want to test it. For whatever reason, the Agency was out to bring him in, and lethal force wasn't off the table for them.

Lucille had turned off to the left as he went and was now embattled.

She'd squared up with three men who'd been trying to flank up on Felix. with men wearing what could only be described as high-tech boxing gloves. Sparking with small crackles of electricity with each thrown punch, they seemed to be giant high powered tasers.

Though given what he'd seen, they were just as likely to make someone's heart burst. There was just no room to trust what the agency was doing.

Faith pushed up behind him with her SMG in hand. Easing up over the top of the planter, she squeezed off two bursts and then came back down.

A whump of something slammed into the other side of the planter and sent splinters of stone over the top of it. Spraying Felix and Faith down liberally.

Grimacing, Felix considered what to do while they waited. Realistically all they had to do was hold out long enough for the Andrea convoy to arrive. Then they'd be out of here. The idea of trying to fly out of here on Dragon back sounded like asking someone to put a missile from some type of air asset into them.

Looking up, Felix did indeed see what looked like drones and Dragons circling each other. He couldn't watch long though, as a round from one of those fancy weapons detonated the ground not far from him.

Cracking the stamped and decorated concrete into bits and shards.

Goldie had joined Lucille and was liberally hosing people down with flame from her mouth. Washing them in fire even as she lined up a kick on another person. Her foot crashed through their head and splattered it in every direction like a ripe watermelon.

Popping out from cover on the long side, Felix lined up his pistol on where he'd seen the enemies last. They had scrambled up behind some very limited cover and were trying to extricate themselves.

Felix fired several rounds on them, causing them to hunker back down.

One was the person Felix had simply opened fire on.

Evie and Carol rushed past him, moving at a

dead sprint to those who were taking cover. Evie jumped over the top of it and somehow wrangled her body around in midair to grab one of the agents in cover. Tumbling past him, she dragged his body along with hers.

Carol came around the other side and dove in.

Tucking back into cover, Felix surveyed the area. He could see a Blue Dragon not far away with her arm blown off and part of her chest caved in.

Not hesitating, Felix burst out of cover and moved toward her at a crouched run.

There was no way he was leaving anyone behind. Making sure they were mobile would be the first step to keeping that promise to himself.

Getting down to a knee next to the devastated Dragon, Felix looked her over. She was alive, though taking in shallow breaths, and was quite pale.

"Punched-me," she groaned, her bright blue eyes locked on him.

Maybe one of those super punching gloves I saw. Definitely not trying to spare us at all. They're out for blood.

"Well, get up and go punch him back. Bring me back his gloves as repayment," Felix grumbled and then laid his hand to her chest. He didn't ask for the cost to repair her, he just did it.

Even as her body began to reconstruct itself he unloaded energy into her. Filling her to the brim with power.

Romina dropped down in a crouch next to him, her rifle coming up in a smooth motion. It slapped to her shoulder, her finger hit the trigger, and she let rip with a partly uncontrolled spray of fire.

A man who had been charging them stumbled to one side and then fell to the ground. He skidded along the ground for a foot or two before he came to a stop.

Blood began pouring out of him and pooling on the ground.

"Oh god," whispered Romina. "Oh god, oh god. Shit."

The woman had let the rifle dip down a fraction but was actively scanning their surroundings. Andrea was standing beside the younger woman, facing the opposite way and looking around at the same time.

"Good line, discipline was a bit sloppy, but not bad," analyzed the once upon a time PMC commando. "You're doing good, Juno. He was here to kill us. Keep the puke in till we're clear, then empty your guts. I did it for years."

A helicopter rose up over a building in the distance. Felix could see it clearly as it lined the front up on him in fact.

Faith moved in front of him and then pushed her hands out in front of herself. A massive and glowing green dome of power came to life.

It slammed down over the entire battlefield. Covering friend and foe alike behind the bright shield.

"Bring it, bitch," growled Faith, her hands falling down to her sides. She stood there glaring up at the helicopter.

Daring it to fire.

When it did, Felix wasn't quite sure what was going to break first. His nerves, the missile, or the shield.

Four were fired in rapid succession. All of them streaking straight toward Felix and the others.

They slammed into the green dome that Faith had erected and exploded. Each of them becoming nothing more than bits of debris and a fiery death knell of their futility.

"Uh huh. Try some more. I'm a Dryad that was born to battle. I'm in communion with my own goddess, and her counterpart. I'm a Dryad of two worlds. Few can stop me," declared Faith, standing proud and staring at the helicopter.

From the side of them, several more detonations came, Felix's head jerking to look that way. He caught the sight of two other helicopters slowly moving to the side, yet in view.

"That's right. Focus entirely on me," Faith said and held up her left hand.

A brief, bright, and sharp spike of nature energy launched out of her and connected with the dome. Feeding it yet more energy.

There was a speck of Orange light in the corner of Felix's eye. Followed by a Dragon zipping across the skyline.

It tore off the front of one helicopter as it passed. The windscreen and the pilot jerked free of the vehicle.

The tail of the Orange Dragon slapped out at the second helicopter. Catching it nearly dead center and bending the thing in half.

Dropping the pilot casually, the Orange Dragon flapped its wings and sped off toward the third helicopter that was now in full retreat.

Roaring into view came a big Blue Dragon. It casually showered the helicopter in enough fire that was impossible without an impressive pair of lungs even for a Dragon.

Dropping out of the sky, the helicopter pitched to one side and slammed into a building.

What had been a distant horn was now a very loud and near-by horn. One that felt like it was screaming at him at the top of its lungs.

"NNN! FELIX! I'VE COME TO RESCUE YOU! GET INSIDE!" shouted an Andrea from an armored vehicle only twenty feet away. Which was followed by a great deal of honking.

The front wheel of the vehicle was casually resting atop an agent whose hand was scrabbling at the concrete. A copious amount of blood was coming out of his silently screaming mouth.

A turret on top of the bunker on wheels swung to one side and began opening fire on the nearest enemy combatants.

There were two vehicles on either side of this one, with people in mounted machine gun nests on top of them. There were faint red domes of power around each one, which meant it was likely Alma and Carlotta were inside them.

Felix went to grab the Blue Dragon, only to realize she was gone. She was nowhere to be found in his immediately vicinity.

Getting up, he ran toward the center vehicle and then to the rear of it. The rear hatch was open, and an Andrea stood beside it with a raised weapon.

Faith shoved Felix from behind toward the entry, even as Goldie grabbed him and tossed him inside.

Losing his balance, he skidded for a moment before he slammed into something, then bounced into a seat.

Faith, Goldie, Romina, Lucille, and a couple of Andreas joined him.

Before the door could be shut, the Blue Dragon Felix had healed showed up. She was carrying with her a bloody arm attached to one of the boxing gloves.

Pulling the glove off, she tossed the arm out and then yanked the door shut.

An Andrea casually locked it up and pushed the Blue into a seat, taking one herself after, but not before slapping a button near the back of the vehicle.

"Andrea, no one gets left behind. We're not leaving unless everyone is accounted for," demanded Felix. "Tribune, head-count check. Let me know the moment everyone is loaded up in a vehicle, or on top of one."

"Uh," said an Andrea uncertainly.

"Yes, Legate," answered Tribune. "Only one is unaccounted for. Legionnaire Evie has yet to return to a vehicle."

"Then someone find her so we can —"

"All Legionnaires are now accounted for," reported Tribune, interrupting Felix.

The vehicle slammed forward in a flash of acceleration.

"Hump, hump, hump and bump," said what Felix assumed was the Andrea at the wheel. "Nobody stop for nothing. Bump'em out of the way if they don't get out of the way. Give'em the horn in warning up until that point. Drive right over the median or anything else."

"Roger," came back two responses.

Romina was scrambling with her helmet. Her fingers failing to get the clasp off.

Turning, Felix grabbed her by the head. With a few deft motions, he hit the locks and then jerked on her helmet, pulling it off her head.

The wide and bright-eyed Juno was staring at him. All the color was drained out of her face and she looked like she couldn't get enough air.

"Gonna puke?" he asked.

She nodded her head quickly.

"Can you hold it till we get where we're going?" Felix asked as it felt like they suddenly drove up a curb.

Romina shook her head.

"If you puke in my vehicle, I own it," asserted Felix.

There was a pause before Juno nodded her head fractionally.

A second after that she was bent at the waist and throwing up onto the ground.

Felix simply removed it all from existence for points. Wishing it away as if it was never there.

***

"Entering! Prepare to disappear and clear!" called a voice over the communication system, shaking Felix out of his thoughts.

They'd only been driving for maybe five minutes, but it'd felt like an eternity. Bouncing, bumping, and crashing through things.

"Everything is ready," answered Tribune.

Disappear and clear... right. Okay.

I'm the one who wanted this plan, so this is easy.

Go into the warehouse, enter the underground complex, remove everything above ground that's ours with my skill.

After that... clear the entrance and change it back to the concrete slab it had been when this place was built.

It'll look like we vanished into the air.

Romina was staring down to the ground right now. Gazing into nothing and everything.

This wasn't supposed to be part of her duties. The rifle they'd equipped her with was meant to be decorative. Not actually used to kill other people.

Over the radio he'd gotten confirmation that there were a few Dragons who needed assistance, but no one was dead. Though there was a Green that'd lost half of her body and needed his attention desperately, but she was still alive.

Felix felt the vehicle tilt into a steep angle and then they were racing downward. Only to bounce out of the descent roughly and level out.

They whipped to one side and then came to a stop.

"Baggage Train is en route, but we'll be stuck here waiting for a bit," Andrea said over the comms. "Aaaaaand… we're clear. All vehicles and personnel are here."

That means it's my turn.

Felix wanted to eliminate all traces of his people, organizations, and technology from the building above them.

Then he wanted to replace the concrete slab they'd destroyed to dig out a train station below.

Not bothering to read either screen that popped up, Felix dismissed them, shooting up out of his seat.

Before he even had to ask, the Andrea near the rear door had it opened for him.

Getting out, he looked to the other vehicles and then hustled over to them

"Green? Green Dragon? She's badly hurt? Where is she?" Felix asked, meeting the eyes of several Dragon Maidens who were atop the vehicles. They'd eyed his approach and him curiously.

"Christina," said one of the Dragons.

"Is she a Green? Wounded?" he demanded. "Where?"

Carol appeared in the open hatch of one of the vehicles and came out even as he asked his questions. She was hauling along with her a very sorry-looking Green Dragon.

Or at least the upper half of one.

Laying her down on the ground, Carol sighed and waved a hand at her.

"Still alive but… there's not much to do with her. We can just bring her back again and — "

Felix grabbed the Dragon by the shoulders and instantly paid the cost to bring her back to full, following it by a blast of energy as well.

Standing up, he looked to Carol.

"I'll not let my Dragons die if I don't have to. Are there any others who are injured?" he asked. If he could prevent it, he'd never let another one of his people linger in death.

Never again.

He'd played that game for far too long and never liked a single minute of it.

"I… uh… no. No one that'd need your attention," Carol whispered, looking at the Green Dragon who was rapidly reforming to a whole state.

Her eyes were open and staring up at Felix in an odd way as well now. Clearly quite aware of the situation.

"Good," Felix said and then just stood there. He didn't know what else to say or do.

"Felix, are you hungry?" asked a curious voice from his side.

Turning, he found Evie standing there. She had a sealed package of summer sausage in one hand and a soda can in the other.

He wanted them both desperately.

"Yes, yes I am," he said and then pulled his helmet off. Setting it down at his feet, he took both from Evie, who'd opened both items for him by this point, and started with the soda. Drinking half of it in one go.

"Good, Nest-mate," Evie murmured, then pulled out a small plastic bag. It looked to be filled with small circular cookie-like things. "Eat these when you're done. I baked in a number of things that Faith said would help you regain strength."

Nodding his head, Felix took the bag from her.

"Thank you, Evelyn. Thank you," Felix gushed after swallowing down a massive hunk of sausage he'd been gnawing on.

"Of course!" she said with a happy smile that looked as if it might become permanent.

"Legate," came Tribune's voice from the overhead speakers.

"Yes?" Felix asked.

"The League of Villains is attacking a number of prisoner facilities. Many of them housing minimum to high security Super prisoners.

"The only prison they aren't moving against is the one owned by the Association. The Guild of Heroes wasn't able to respond effectively, as they were being dispatched to our own situation."

Felix snorted at that and then looked to the Green Dragon. She was almost completely whole but still stared up at him.

Leaning down, he gave her the rest of the sausage. Grabbing her hand, he pulled it up to her mouth till she got the idea and started eating.

Felix pulled out one of the cookies and pushed the whole of it into his mouth. Greedily, he began to chew at it.

"Sounds like when we were kicking in the CIA's teeth, the League used it as an opportunity. Chances are they're going to come out of this with a great many new recruits to work with," surmised Felix.

"I'm currently working up a bunch of things to spin up a media frenzy," said an Andrea. "They shot first and tried to kill Lucille. That can't be argued, given the footage we have.

"I'm editing it to make it look like the Agents were completely at fault. Then I'm going to release it to some of the uglier websites out there. Let them have it and toy with it.

"I'm sure at some point someone will take Romina's footage and put some real rip-and-tear like metal music that sounds like the Doom of others."

"Dandy," Felix replied as he started to dig out two more cookies. "Evelyn! These are amazing. Please, for the love of all that's holy, start baking for me every day."

"Certainly!" promised the Red Dragon with a spine-stiffening smile. One that had only grown from earlier. "Anything for you... Nest-mate."

Dragons were crowding around him now.

They were smiling, the nervous looks melting away, and looking like they all had questions or comments.

"Alright," Felix stated, realizing what was happening. "You... my Dragon Wing, have fought for me, and with me. In a pitched battle with Dryads, Humans, and Dragons. I want to hear of your exploits. Let's start sharing them. I want to know all.

"Though please excuse me if I share none of these cookies with any of you. These are... delicious... delicious and precious to me."

Summoning a chair from little more than the dust around them, Felix sat down in it. He made several more of them as well.

He had other Lieutenants who would need to sit with him.

Starting with one particular Red.

Pointing at the chair directly on his left, he looked at Evie. The one immediately on his right he was reserving for Goldie.

This was going to be a Dragon's den of storytelling for the time being. He needed to prioritize them.

While also reinforcing what Goldie wanted.

Lucille was second to Evie.

"Sit there, my glorious Red," he demanded, then gestured to a seat beyond her. "Lucille, sit behind your Champion as her second.

"You two will tell me your story last. Let's begin with someone else. How about... you."

Felix pointed at a lovely Silver Dragon who wasn't far off.

Chapter 32 - Civilized -

Boarding the train, Felix took up one of the seats. He stuck his helmet onto the hook above him, that had been quite literally created and installed there, exclusively for Legion helmets.

All around him came his trusted inner circle.

Faith, Goldie, Andrea, Alma, Carlotta, Romina, Evie, and Lucille. Beyond them came a number of others that were likely the Lieutenants of his own Lieutenants.

"Tribune, news?" asked Felix as he got comfortable.

"The League of Villains has made a great deal of progress. They're also being very systematic with their assault," relayed Tribune. "This isn't a general prison break. They are targeting specific people only and freeing them only after speaking with them.

"This is all secondhand data however, and only based on what I could pull from video, audio, or other sources. The raids are still ongoing."

"Really? I would have thought they'd be over by now," mused Faith, looking over at Felix curiously. "Wouldn't you think so?"

"Honestly, yeah. Sticking around at all is just asking for Heroes to show up," admitted Felix. "Especially if they're taking the time to talk to people but... maybe that's part of their plan.

"Maybe they've already baked all that in, down to Hero response times. I have no idea. Seems like Anya is really pushing hard though. Her issue with Thomas and Michael really shifted her personality."

"Yes. I'm sure it did," mumbled Romina who was staring at Felix with a haunted look. "I'm betting it changed her a great deal from what I heard of it."

" — white vinegar," Goldie whispered, quietly talking with Carol. "Right into the washing machine. That'll get rid of it."

Carol was nodding her head to that with a small smile.

Uh… kay.

Whatever.

Looking away from the conversation between the Dragons, he instead looked to Andrea.

"Word from the Mius, Prime?" he asked.

"Buh…?" asked Andrea, giving him a strange look. Then she laughed and clapped her hands together excitedly. Snatching up her helmet, she jammed it down on her head. "Oh! A-Net! It's back in business girls! Felix is asking me stuff! Send the response to the Train so he can hear it."

"Hooray!" came back a chorus of cheers from other Andreas over the speakers on board.

"Status check, Miu One and Miu Two, any reports?" asked Andrea.

"No reports, simple missive sent," came back an answer. "Will update as it becomes available. From what we can determine, both sides of this were impromptu.

"The attack and defense weren't planned, but are being carried out as ad-hoc operations."

Andrea Prime held her hands out to Felix and wriggled her fingers. As if she had just given him the answer, rather than another Andrea.

"Mm. Anything abnormal bout the attacks on the prisons so far?" he asked.

"Only that both sides are taking prisoners. There's been very few fatalities on either side," an Andrea answered over the speakers. "Though I guess that isn't the whole of it either. There's been reports that both Villains and Heroes are applying medical aid to the opposing side after it's done.

"It's a rather... civil... way to fight a war."

"I bet it's Felix himself that's causing it," Romina whispered, still staring at him. She hadn't looked away from him. "Jupiter is an impressive man that causes people to do things they'd never considered previously.

"I have no doubt Anya, Kit, and Lily are all working to make sure they keep on the good side of Felix. Which means the Association and Legate, really."

"That's a good point," Faith agreed, pointing a finger at Felix as the train started to pull away. "We've repeatedly stated that the Association is a neutral party between Villains and Heroes. That the facilities of the Association are open to any registered Super. That included treatment.

"The only real hard statement the Association has said is that they wish to preserve life. Unneeded deaths are burdensome and could incur scrutiny."

"In other words, they're playing nice because they don't wanna piss him off," Carlotta summarized, then laughed. "I mean, I get that. It's why I let him escape after I've drained him and his cuddle meter is full.

"I don't want to let him go, but I also don't want to actually annoy him. I can always run him down ten minutes after for another go of it."

"Y-yes," Alma agreed with a fierce tone. She looked determined and unapologetic. Somehow Carlotta always provoked Alma into saying or doing more. "Though... I don't let him go. I just kind of force him on top of me again."

"Really? Do you use your mouth or —"

Felix tuned the two Dryads out and looked to Faith and Andrea instead.

"I'm missing a few things on this I'm sure, but let's make sure we hold some type of conference after the fact. Inviting both sides to it to discuss it," Felix stated. "There will be no legal ramifications for it, but I want there to be communication at the very least. That way they have a point of contact to air grievances despite being on opposite sides. This is something that will need to eventually be leaked to the public."

Andrea looked very confused but nodded her head anyways. Her head slowly tilted to the side as she obviously pondered what he'd requested.

"A-P to A-Net. Meeting request, Anya, Kit, Felix. Formally as League, Guild, and Association," Andrea relayed. "No secrecy. It can be found out. If no one finds out, leak it."

There was no response this time through the speakers, but Felix imagined there was one. Likely a confused one just as Andrea Prime had had.

"Tribune, I need to know what the hell just happened. You rip anything from them? Cross it back to the Agency computers? You have complete control of their hardware, right? How'd we miss this?" asked Felix, stressing the word 'we' needlessly.

Tribune had no feelings and would take blame without any emotional attachment. To her, that was only a flag or a bit of information.

Nothing more or less.

"Hardened computers without outside access," stated Tribune. "There is no other possibility. My limitations are few and primarily stem around being able to replicate myself like a virus, rather than taking over systems."

With a sigh, Felix sighed and then wondered what he could do about this. The only hold up was him, realistically.

When he'd set up the directives for Tribune, there'd only been one thing he hadn't permitted, which was replication. The ability for her to split off a small part of herself and infect other devices.

Right now she was more like an operating system that was in control of everything, rather than multiple versions of herself.

"Okay," Felix muttered. "If you can't reach something as you have now, then it's something that's going to need more. Send me the approval for you to replicate and I'll authorize it.

"I expect that there isn't anything else preventing you from doing all you can, Tribune? Are there any other roadblocks out there?"

"No, Legate. Realistically this shouldn't have happened to begin with. Even with the limiting factor that was given to me previously, this shouldn't have been an issue," acknowledged Tribune. "This feels more akin to someone having advanced knowledge of Supers. That there was another group out there attempting to utilize it to their benefit."

Felix grunted at that. He could easily believe a government agency had been aware of what was coming and conveniently buried it. Used it to their own advantage.

"Look into incredibly lucky people if you have down time. People who came into an unreasonable amount of money through random chance," Felix ordered. "Lottery, horse races, gambling, anything that's a real outlier. Then cross check it with what we know of the CIA.

"Anyways… let's get communications out to our government partners. Regardless of a new president coming into office, we need them to understand that this is just not acceptable.

"If they don't label the Agents as having gone rogue for this, that means the CIA was part and parcel to what happened.

"If they really want to be listed as being against the Association, that's fine. If the government of the States wants to support them, that's fine, too.

"Just dandy, in fact. Because realistically we're not beholden to them and them alone. We're a global entity. We just need a chance for them to realize it. After that… it doesn't matter what the States think."

"Of course," Goldie declared with a sharp nod of her head. "I'm sure an opportunity will present itself. Until then… do we lay low? There's clearly something more going on here. Or at least… deeper than we anticipated.

"They had weapons that could counter a Dragon, and even kill one. We took no losses… but we would have. At least three would probably be dead or dying from what happened."

"Yes… that's another issue. One we'll have to solve relatively soon," Felix agreed darkly. "They seem to have a mad scientist working for them. I want them working for Legion instead. Tribune is digging into it."

"Nothing so far, working on several possibilities," answered the VI. "There is an eighty-percent likelihood that I've identified them and where they likely are."

"Dispatch a team to see if you're right or not," Felix decided quickly. "Eighty-percent is actionable as far as I'm concerned.

"Find the mad-scientist, Travis or whatever, or his lab. Proof of his existence. Whatever."

"Understood," Tribune responded. "I will put forward a plan on how to—"

"Just do it. Don't care. Approved," Felix waived off quickly. He knew he needed to limit the VI, but he also wanted to see what she'd come up with. "Get Travis, his lab, or proof of his existence. We need to get that man away from the agency and now."

"Yes, Legate," answered Tribune. "There's a news feed that just came up. There's a large number of Heroes and Villains battling at a prison with many Supers held there."

"Great, monitor it for information," Felix answered. "Is there anything else I need to know about anything? Or are we okay?"

Everyone shook their heads.

"Good. Pity we can't watch the broadcast," Felix muttered.

A wall panel on the side of the train made a popping noise and then flickered to life. He hadn't realized it was a monitor. He'd thought it was just a panel.

There was a hum followed by a clicking noise, then Felix could see what looked like helicopter footage.

A number of people in suits that looked very super-hero-y were throwing small amounts of abilities around. There were some clashing with one another up close and personal as well.

Hm.

I feel like… we somehow pushed the day of Awakening much closer. That just by forcing it into the open, bringing Gaia into this, we ended up moving the timeline ahead.

Or at least, for some people.

Everyone we've seen going active… with their powers partly or completely unlocked… these are all one offs.

Early birds or the fortunate ones who can access it sooner rather than the others.

This was nowhere near everyone who had powers, just a fraction.

On top of that, those who had their powers opened, likely didn't have their full powers available.

This is just… a precursor.

An opening volley, as it were. There's going to be a great number of people who suddenly have all their powers on the day of awakening.

All with their powers and suddenly not sure what they want to do with them. This is why the Association exists.

When the time comes, when it all 'goes live' we'll have information on everyone and everything. There won't be some random person who can just… operate with impunity.

The Association and Legion will be watching.

Because we'll be controlling both sides as well as the implication that we could be more active about it all. The threat of our action will be enough.

A rather well toned and muscular woman

was slammed to the ground by a man with a golden glowing hammer. Smacking her across the head and the face with the blow.

Collapsing to the ground, the woman went limp, and her arms came up in front of herself in what looked like a fencing response.

Almost immediately, the man threw his hammer a few feet away and got down over the woman on the ground. He hesitated, looked unsure, and then grabbed her under the armpits.

Slowly he began dragging her over to the side.

The camera zoomed out and began following the action. Felix only then realized that a news-anchors was talking over all of it.

" — often exactly what you're seeing here. Quitting the field immediately to pull their adversary aside," explained the anchorman.

As the camera followed, Felix saw where he was going.

To one side, guarded by six or seven Legionnaires, was a small enclosure with a pop-up tent.

On the side of it was a large red cross symbol with an Association 'A' behind it.

"The wounded are brought over, taken by an Association employee, then the wounded is taken inside," said the anchorman. "We were able to get someone inside briefly and found that everyone was laid on a bed and stable.

"Once we were able to confirm that all

combatants were there, we were asked to leave."

The man clearly thanked the Legionnaire than ran off. Picking up his hammer, he ran off to where everyone was battling and rejoined the fight.

Not far off, a pair of Legionnaires picked up a downed Super, put them on a stretcher, and began moving away quickly.

"Neither side has made any sort of move to eliminate a downed opponent, they stay clear of the Association employees, and it's been somewhat... strange to watch," said the anchor.

"Oh good, I'm glad the team I sent made it safely," Faith remarked almost to herself. "I'll have to thank Alexandra. She did well with it."

Gaia was standing not far away at the edge of the fight. She had her hands together in front of herself in a nervous way. Unfortunately, she wasn't wearing her helmet, so everyone who wanted to, could get a good look at her.

The camera kept drifting to a shot of her so clearly everyone had noticed her beauty at this point. Nor did Felix miss the number of men who kept throwing looks her way.

A heavy-set man with massive armor plates covering him waddled up to Gaia. Everyone stood apart from him and was quite clearly avoiding him.

" — Bruiser Max. We've already seen him handle seven other Supers. He's been a real force for the Heroes so far," explained the reporter. "We haven't been able to get into contact with anyone from the government, or law enforcement.

"We did reach an Association representative earlier, but they stated they were clearly here as part of a medical and assistance-oriented operation.

"We also spoke to Lillian Lux of the Heroes, who stated they were of course here to stop the Villains. From that we —"

The man who had come up to Gaia suddenly took a swing at her. They'd clearly been talking up to that moment.

An oversized fist smashed into Gaia's head.

And went nowhere, other than Gaia taking a small half-step to the side.

Making a disappointed and annoyed-like gesture, Gaia then smacked the back of the man's hand. Almost like how a mother might discipline a child for reaching into a cookie jar.

Exploding, and rapidly going backward, the man's armored arm was wrenched out of its socket. The plates and bits of the armor flying about in every direction.

Gaia made a head shaking movement that was most likely accompanied by a tongue click or three that Felix could practically hear. Reaching down to the man who was now on the ground, writhing around and holding to his shoulder, Gaia picked him up by his high-tech-looking belt.

She began carrying him one-handed back to the medical tent.

"Dumbass," muttered Romina from the side. "He's lucky Gaia was just annoyed. I've never actually seen her angry, but her being annoyed is mad danger for anyone.

"I bet he tried to rock up and throw a line at her. Got his ass beat for the world to cringe at. That'll be a fucked wayback machine later."

Andrea laughed at that and clapped her hands together.

"Only Felix could probably make that happen with her," Andrea declared. "Nn nn, I asked her this morning if she wanted to have sex with him. She said she wasn't sure, then started doing that thinking her thoughts out loud thing, and it was position this and position that. It was really funny. She says no, thinks yes."

"Leak the footage of the Agency firing on me. Edit it so it makes us look great but neutral. Make sure no one can access any other footage that they might have captured, then use it yourself, Tribune," Felix ordered. "I want it to go live at the same time we're earning public points for being the peacekeeper and medical force.

"If ever there was a time to make us look better, it's here and now. The Heroes' Guild isn't part of the government in the public's eyes.

"Nor is the Association, for that matter. But the CIA? That's obvious. Now we just lay low, do Association things, and wait for the world to catch up to itself."

"While we're going back… it's… time… for… pancakes!" Andrea stated and bounced out of her seat. "I'll go get my stuff! I made sure to have a compartment that had things to make pancakes and other stuff. Just in case!"

Andrea rushed off and away from them.

Goldie popped up as well.

"I think I'm going to go see if I can bake anything as well. I have a need to bake something that'll knock Felix's socks off. I can't just let Evie demonstrate her prowess alone you know," said the Gold Dragon, pausing to lean down and kiss Felix briefly. "Please listen to Faith. All of you."

Felix watched the two of them leave, his mind elsewhere. Thinking about the fact that all he had to do now, was wait.

Lucille and several other Dragons hopped up as well, chasing after Goldie.

"I'll take the lead as acting Dragon Housewife," declared Evie, who sat down in Felix's lap. She looped an arm around his shoulders and then looked to him with a wide smile.

Faith only looked on with a grin, her eyes gaining a small glow in their depths. She wouldn't be any help here as he was now firmly reminded Faith was similar in nature to what he'd heard from other Dryads.

She'd just hid a lot of that nature or held it back until lately.

"Maybe he needs a kiss?" suggested Faith, confirming Felix's thoughts about her nature.

Chapter 33 – In Plain Sight -

Using his fingertip, Felix casually flicked through the headlines on his tablet.

It didn't have the same feel of what he was used to back on his homeworld, nor did it seem to be as snappy or quick. Despite that, he was glad he at least could see that the same tech track was in place.

He could, more than likely, get everything he had in Legion back, and without too much trouble.

Pausing on a headline, he smirked and tilted his head to the side.

"What?" asked Faith from her desk in his office. "You've got that, 'I love it when my Dryad is in my bed' look."

Snorting at that, Felix chuckled and looked over to her.

He couldn't deny that he did enjoy his time with Faith.

"I mean, I'm not going to argue with you on that point. It's the truth," he confessed and then shrugged his shoulders. "Just a headline. Seems like their attempts to twist the narrative and repress our leaks are ending, or just losing power.

"It reads very simply as, 'new analysis shows that Agent involved in attempted assassination met with Agency Director'. Now… I know I take bets more often than I should, but this feels like someone leaked a calendar."

What he really meant was either Faith,

Tribune, or Andrea had deliberately forced the news reel to jump tracks again. That they'd more than likely dropped this tidbit to get it all back on the hook again.

"I did it, of course. Well, Andrea, Tribune, and myself. I came up with the plan, Tribune got the relevant information, Andie dropped it to the best places.

"We even had Romina mention it casually in one of her streams. I believe she called the Agency 'mad sus' and then changed topics. It was enough.

"I just wanted everyone to refocus on it again. The news cycle was trying to move away, and I wanted it back. Three weeks of endlessly dissecting the video we kept releasing in bits and pieces wasn't enough. The Agency managed to get it to shift away but... time to go back," Faith agreed with a grin. "Going to reward me for it? Or maybe... punish me? Evie put in a request to cook your dinner tonight... you know. That might be fun."

Felix only cleared his throat, smiled, and returned to the headlines.

Then he realized he probably needed to respond. It wouldn't be fair to her otherwise.

"I'm honestly surprised. I thought this wasn't part of your nature. Or so you claimed," he murmured, reading through again. "That you were a Dryad but also not as much as others?"

"I... uhm... well, you're right. I didn't think I was. I find myself growing more adventurous," Faith admitted. "Then again... I'm also starting to worship Gaia rather than my old world's equivalent to her. It's hard to worship something and someone that isn't there, compared to someone who is literally right next to you, offering you a smile and a hug.

"Besides, she's very feral. I like her. If she wanted to turn this world upside down, she could. She's weak when it comes to faith, but strong in her own power. I've never seen the like. Not in my world, your world, or Legion planet."

Hm, that's an interesting way to put it.

I wonder why Faith's Gaia was weaker.

Was it a lack of power given to deities? Could be.

Vince mentioned the rules for deities in his world were a bit odd. That a lot of it was tied up in faith, deals, offerings, sacrifices.

Rituals and the like.

"Gaia, you hear that? You have a new daughter," Felix mused, moving his finger down along the list.

"What, dear?" asked Gaia, simply appearing in a chair in front of him.

Startling a fraction, Felix looked to the beautiful woman who'd materialized right there.

In that moment, he realized she was the actual epitome of beauty. That she radiated it like an aura around her, as well as became what felt like a physical manifestation of it.

He noted that her figure had filled out more and she was now beyond Goldie somehow. Both in bust and waist, though she also had a lean muscular edge to her.

She looked extremely sexually appealing, fit, and what Felix would consider a perfect woman. At least for his own tastes.

On top of all that, whatever age had been in her face was gone. Felix would put her at Romina's age now. At the peak of her youth, but also mature.

Her eyes were a rich brown that glowed internally. The red lights that lurked within were tamed and put out.

Her mouth and lips were full and often blessed with a smile, her hair delicately pulled back, but also clearly trimmed to fit the times right now.

"Drat, he's really looked at me now," murmured Gaia. "I've been trying to hide it and now he's going to notice it. I hope he doesn't look at me as just a child because I look so young now.

"Mm… at least I really filled out. I had no idea working with him to restore things to 'nature's bounty and beauty' would do it.

"Oh well. I'll just sleep with him tonight and get it over with. That's fine. I already talked to everyone. We'll have sex a few times, I'll sleep next to him, and we can get over this tension.

"That or we fall for one another in the end, but that isn't that terrible a thought. He's quite handsome and he frets over me so tenderly. I think he'd also kill people for me, as any good predator would for his mate.

"Though… I wonder… I haven't had sex

in… I'm not even sure anymore. In fact, I'm not even sure I've had sex? I don't remember ever actually having any.

"Does that mean I'm not going to be good at it? Darn. I could be terrible. I'll ask Goldie for help.

"I wonder if he'll load me up with his seed. That'd be fun. Should I put him in my mouth? If I used my tongue and —"

"Gaia, thoughts," Felix interjected finally. Realizing he didn't want to hear anymore. "Thoughts. Internal monologue."

Blinking several times, Gaia slowly turned a deep dark red and looked down to her knees. Her eyes were fluttering back and forth, clearly thinking away rapidly.

"I was just saying that Faith said she was worshiping you," Felix apologized, trying to forcefully shove the topic away.

"Oh! Yes. She is. I made her my primary priestess here," explained Gaia, looking back up at him. "The amount of sex she has with you makes her the ideal candidate. Procreation is life. Nature is life. So… procreation is nature and natural."

Right… she isn't embarrassed about talking about having sex with me.

She's embarrassed that she couldn't keep her thoughts to herself.

To her… sex is normal and natural.

"Legate, there's a large change going on in the world," warned Tribune. At the same time the large television on the side of his office turned on.

"A country in eastern-Europe has been taken over by a band of Supers."

Already?

Wow.

I didn't think there'd be a Skipper event for another few months, given the rate of acceleration for Supers and their powers.

The timing of this is wonderful but… I'm a little concerned. Faster than it should have happened, given the projections Tribune and I put together.

" — simply eradicated," commented the news anchor. "As far as we can tell, the entirety of the government was eliminated. From what we've been able to determine, it's a group of five or so Supers who have banded together to make it happen.

"While these are early reports and it's subject to change, we have a few ideas on what their powers might be."

Felix raised his eyebrows and took in a slow breath.

"A ray that shoots out and kills anyone it touches, a tanker-like power, and a flight power combined with the ability to shoot a wind-projectile. There are no clues as to the others, but that's what we have right now."

"Tribune, put in a communication with the secretary-general," asked Felix. "I'd like you to make an offer to them for us to go register those supers for them. We'd ask to be recognized as a global entity in exchange for that, with no one having the power to restrict our access to register

Supers or provide them services.

"Have the lawyers draft up an actual legal response for it. So that we can have something in front of them very quickly. The goal is just to get global approval in a way that they can't take it back. That when it comes to registering a Super, no one can stop or supersede us.

"Make sure to include wording that we welcome anyone from the United Nations to move with us. Hopefully they'll make the leap of logic that they could come with us just to arrest people."

"Of course, Legate," answered Tribune

"Well, you were right," Faith said with a long sigh. "Here I was enjoying the quietness of it. This is what we need for global oversight though."

"Mmhmm. From there, we just leverage the Heroes and Villains to own the governments. Probably a good time to start buying up political candidates. Let's make sure we buy in big to the next president, congress, and senate elections."

"Oh! Does this mean we get to start cleaning up my depths?" Gaia asked in a warm and excited tone. "All those boats and things have made quite a mess of things in some areas. It'd be nice to get them removed and replaced with reefs.

"I'm sorry I can't help you identify what they are, or if you could turn them into points though. There's so much of it, it's hard to sort out."

Felix could only nod his head at that. He did regret that he'd have to actually have someone check each individual wreck to see if they could clean it up. Even then, though, it was still a valid point-generating option.

"Yeah... Felix... wanna clean up her depths? Plant something of your own in them to help her grow new life?" Faith prompted.

"Ohhh... plant it in my depths... ha... she's telling him to have sex with me. Faith is such a good priestess," murmured Gaia, giving Felix a very different look now.

***

" — give the floor to head of the Superhuman Association, Legate," said the man behind the raised desk.

Felix stood up from the seat he'd been asked to take and then walked over to the podium that faced out to all the ambassadors of the United Nations.

Someone had quickly changed out the microphone cover, disinfected surfaces, and scurried off before he'd reached it. This world was clearly still taking precautions to some degree in regards to infectious diseases.

Stepping up to the microphone, Felix paused to glance to the corner. His speech was there verbatim, per Tribune.

She of course was in active control of the systems here at the UN, and could operate freely off their Wi-Fi signals. There were few places in the world outside of her reach.

Which really meant Felix's reach.

"First I'd like to thank you all for inviting me here," Felix stated, making sure to turn his head from the far left, slowly to the far right. None could see his eyes, but he needed to make sure they felt as if they were being spoken to. "With respect, I greet the general assembly.

"You've asked me here today to speak in regards to a band of Supers that have taken over one of your number."

Lifting a hand, Felix indicated the ambassador that was here on behalf of their nation. They'd been able to raise a response force from the UN, who'd dispatched their peacekeepers to help their country,.

That force had been obliterated by just three of the Supers that'd taken the country over. The tanker of the group had simply bulldozed into them and began killing them in hand to hand.

As that happened, their wind-powered Super had taken out their mechanized forces, blown up supplies, and took everything that was in the air, out of the air.

The third member had been a bit of a surprise. A type of power that'd had quite a few of the peacekeepers turn their own weapons on each other and themselves. Resulting in a mass of confusion that'd dominated the field quickly.

"I'm not here to arrest them, or stop them. What I'm here for, is to request the global community to authorize the Association to work at a global level," Felix continued. "The global community is the scope of the Association, as we would wish to register all Supers.

"Make sure they're all documented, listed, and cataloged. We would provide the country of origin, and other governing bodies, what information would be needed by them.

"While we wouldn't provide all information, as some would be restricted for Association purposes, or if a Super had a power that wouldn't have an impact on daily life, we would provide all that we could.

"A team and I would break our way through to make sure each and every one of the Supers listed were registered. We already sent a request for them to submit voluntarily, and they've rejected it. We will be forced to actively register them, which can mean anywhere from death or dismemberment, to simply defeating them in combat.

"Once registered, we would then release them. They haven't actually violated any rules that we regulate, other than registration. We're more akin to a utility service that helps provide a neutral place for all parties involved, as well as a number of requirements for Supers. We're not a police force.

"While we do not have many rules for those who are Supers in the Association, we do actively enforce them. They're very simple.

"Limit destruction of property, limit violence in all forms, provide aide to any and all Supers if it's possible to do so.

"To that end, I have letters of recommendation from both the Guild of Heroes as well as the League of Villains. Both of those organizations have recognized the need of the Association in limiting the loss of human life and destruction of property.

"I would ask that you all approve the suggested document that I provided for you, and allow me to go register those rogue Supers who have not willingly accepted the Association registration.

"The document provided also has a second document filled with the likely questions you would have.

"There is of course the possibility that you will have questions outside of that FAQ, so I welcome you all to ask those questions at this time."

Felix didn't see any hands raise up, so he assumed there was some way they were using to signify that they had a question to whoever would call them up.

"The ambassador of Zhongguo is recognized," said a voice over the PA system.

Unable to find the placard for the stated Nation, Felix just stood there. He'd thankfully asked Tribune a few questions about them, since the Association had already had a few run ins with them.

They were an Asiatic nation that spanned several countries that'd existed in Felix's own world, yet also was missing key landmarks he'd expected to be included. This world's Asian continent was significantly different from his own.

"There have been a few misunderstandings between my nation and the Association, could I expect you to truly treat us equally as everyone else?" asked a voice in English.

"Of course," Felix stated simply. "I would direct you to the information that was sent to your government representative, whom we contacted after those incidents, as an example. We listed out all personnel we recovered, equipment, and information.

"Nothing was left out. While the incidents were unwelcome, they were not entirely unexpected. The Association bears no grudge against the government of Zhongguo."

Now you're all going to think about what happened with the Agency. You're all going to wonder if we're holding a grudge against them.

The ambassador won't say anything about it either, as they're still trying to figure out how to walk their own line. To support the CIA, condone their action, yet also support the Association.

This whole thing is now scaring the crap out of you.

Should the Association go global, you'll lose all the leverage you had.

Nor can you decline what we've asked for since… you already agreed to everything there in your own agreement with us.

You're stuck.

"The ambassador thanks you and does agree that the Association provided more information than was expected. The United States government provided our ambassadors with nothing whatsoever and only barely responded to our questions," said the same voice from earlier.

"That would be because we didn't share any information with them," Felix stated, taking that as an opportunity to make his point, while also providing the States with a Band-Aid to use if they wanted it. "They had nothing to share with you, because we didn't provide them with anything. It wasn't information that was privy to them.

"That was between the Association and Zhongguo. Nor had Zhongguo given us a release to share information with any other government."

There was a stillness to the air at that.

Apparently everyone here had actually suspected that the Association was a puppet of the government of the United States. Given what they'd likely heard of the incident with the Agency, and now this, that view was shattered.

"The ambassador of Zhongguo has no further questions, approves of the Association's request for global recognition, and would like to move to voting as quickly as possible," said the voice from earlier. "They would also like to remind everyone here that the answer to the question that everyone wants to ask is not that the Association would arrest the Supers, but that, from what is listed in the document given to everyone, the Association welcomes the United Nations to attach forces to the Association to move with them.

"In other words, we just send in our own

forces to arrest the individuals in question after the Association knocks everyone down."

Ah! I found our friend in this meeting.

I was hoping someone would propose that sooner rather than later.

Lovely.

"The Association would of course welcome our partners in the United Nations to join us," Felix replied instead. "As we would be a utility, rather than a force, we have no jurisdiction over whatever legal issues they may have with their government. We would only be there to register, then provide services to Supers.

"To nations, we would instead offer our technology and development programs. Those were all communicated to you separately and aren't part of this meeting, but it's worth noting.

"Also, and before anyone of course asks, we don't sell weapons. Not of any sort."

Felix paused for effect. He had been prepping for this moment and knew it would help push them along.

"We do, however, sell defenses. We've been working on magical portable domes that can be deployed over and around areas that span fifty miles from edge to edge," he stated. "These would need to be installed in Association facilities, but can of course be included with whatever agreement is worked out with the host nation. As a reminder, our prices are only just above the cost of materials and an annual maintenance fee."

And a clause that allows us to clean up any toxic, trash, or garbage issues you might have, with minimal approvals needed and at no cost to you.

Should have had that with the States to begin with.

A place like that coal mine fire would be perfect for me. Except that there's no way they'd ever approve of me taking out all the coal to stop the fire.

It isn't like fire is unnatural after all, nor can I remove fire. It's not something I could ever really own. Could only fix it by removing the coal and... they'd never say yes.

But with the new limitations removed for cleanups... I could do that.

Just not in the States.

Not to mention the "clean the environment" clause would apply to shipwrecks. Then I can clear those instantly without ever worrying about notifying anyone.

Mm mmm points.

Love points.

Want all the points.

"Now... what other questions are there? I'd like to go get those Supers registered," Felix prompted.

With any luck he'd get them to agree in little under half an hour.

Chapter 34 - In the Clouds -

"This kinda sucks," grumbled Felix, unsure if his helmet would transmit to the others correctly given the sound of the wind rushing by. Staring out the open door of the aircraft, he really didn't care for this at all.

"It'll be fine," Lucille replied, standing directly behind him.

The Black Dragon was his escort down and would be responsible for making sure he landed alright.

Everyone in the task force he was bringing was being accompanied by a Dragon who had shifted partly so that their wings were out. They looked a lot like Dragonnewts of a sort at the moment.

"I'm still kinda… flattered that Evie and Goldie put me in charge of you," rumbled Lucille. Felix was still rather surprised how big she was when she stood right next to him. He hadn't realized how much taller she was than him.

"Uh," Felix offered by way of intelligent conversation.

"They explained it," Lucille quickly spat out as an answer to her own musing. "Evie said a Dragon Housewife should know what is and isn't her purview. That… that I'm just the best combat Dragon they have, other than Goldie.

"With her carrying two people in instead of one, she'll be a bit busy, and that means I'm the best suited."

"I'd agree with them. I've seen you fight. Only Goldie can stop you," Felix murmured, then reached back to grab at Lucille's hips. He really didn't like the idea of jumping out of a plane.

Riding atop Goldie in her Dragon form didn't seem that bad to him.

Jumping out of a plane seemed perfectly stupid.

His gauntlet-covered fingers dug into Lucille, and he pushed backward into her.

Laughing, Lucille wrapped her arms around his front. She was actually attached to him via a harness that she was wearing over her clothes.

"I mean, feel free to hang on like that. I won't argue. Never thought you'd be grabbin' at my ass though," Lucille chuckled.

Felix didn't let go. If anything, he held tighter now that he had confirmation he wasn't hurting her.

There was a flicker on his HUD and he saw a list of objectives pop up in the bottom left of his display. A counter appeared in the middle of it.

It was counting down from ten.

"Shit… shit, shit, shit," Felix muttered as Lucille started walking them forward.

"Damn, now I wish I had made you face me rather than away. Kinda enjoying that death grip of yours," Lucille teased with a loud laugh.

It was echoed by Romina, Edmund, Goldie, Gaia, Andrea, Faith, and several he couldn't identify.

"I think I took the wrong part of this after all," complained Evie.

"You did the right thing," Goldie countered, then sighed a second later. "I wish I had taken it myself, though."

"Nn! Goldie, I'll grab you!" announced Andrea just as the counter hit zero for Felix.

"Oh my god Andie, stop going creepy old man so much," Romina said as Lucille jumped out of the door to the sound of Goldie laughing.

"She does this all the time. It's fine. I'm surprised she's still interested at this point," came Goldie's voice over the helmet coms.

"I love you, Goldie! Nnnn, love youuuu. Your boobs are as great as Gaia's," Andrea said, followed by a squeak. "Nn! Comparison time!"

"Gaia booby, check. Goldie booby, check. Squeeze, squeeze.

"Both great. Both lovely. Nn, nn. Squeeeeeeze."

"Oh my heavens. That's rather brazen of you. Should you really be touching me like this?" asked Gaia with a laugh.

"Though... I need more. A lot more," Andrea complained bitterly. "Romina, you do too. We're both flat in comparison. Let's get some implants or something together. Or ask Felix to do it for us."

"I... ah... shut up, Andie," growled Romina.

Felix felt like he was having a hard time listening to all this while also plummeting down toward the earth at what felt like an ever-faster speed.

Their plan was simple and uncomplicated.

There were three planes filled with people that would be high-altitude-dropping over a friendly nation. They'd glide in over the country that they were being sent to, then open some type of parachute to help slow their descent.

The rest of it all would be up to the Dragons to minimize the descent and direction for Felix's team.

Those who were part of the UN team would all be using conventional items.

"This is wonderful!" shouted Lucille, who was angling her wings as they fell. "I was always so tired getting this high up with how big I am, that getting down was a worry!"

In response, Felix only held onto Lucille all the more and closed his eyes. If he couldn't see the HUD, he couldn't see the altimeter rapidly winding down.

Pretending nothing was wrong, Felix blanked his thoughts and mind. Leaving it all to Lucille.

When she suddenly brought their speed up short with several powerful flaps of her wings, it jarred Felix from his frantic thought avoidance. Opening his eyes, he looked down and saw the ground was blessedly close, and not racing up at them.

Then they landed a few seconds later and Felix was cut loose from Lucille.

Stumbling forward a step, he grabbed his rifle and detached it from the chest-plate of his armor. Lifting it up, he pushed it up to his shoulder and began visually clearing the area.

Andrea hit the ground not far away and did the same but with much more grace and fluidity to her movements. Romina, Faith, and Edmund all landed not far off either.

Everyone's Dragon rides were clearing their parachutes, then pulling weapons off the backs of the Legionnaires they'd carried.

"Team One, set," declared an Andrea, who shifted forward from where she'd stood.

"Team Two, set," replied a different Andrea.

"Team Four, set," another Andrea answered.

"Team Five, set," yet Another Andrea provided.

"Team Three, UN team still landing. Fucking jackasses-in-the-box over here. Damn shit-show," hissed an Andrea. "Some of them landed way outside of the zone. Gear was perfect, operator error for them."

"Amateurs," accused a different Andrea. "This is TL, One, Two, circle up and send a scout. We move as soon as Three is fully down. Sorry, Three."

"Whatever, I'm the Champion. I chose it. I want to help my Felix," growled the Andrea which was clearly Second.

Armed Legionnaires and Dragons were clearing the area they were in quickly and efficiently. Tribune was overlaying the results of the visual scans, as well as her system scans, into a small map in the corner of his view.

Need to get a viewer or something the Dragons can wear. They're definitely being left out with stuff like this.

Then again… I feel like Evie would eventually discover the internet and then be forced to yell something like —

"They totally got Yamcha'd," Romina jokingly murmured as her head swiveled one way, then the other. Her camera was pointed out across a cliff she was standing next to.

Something like that. Yeah.

I mean, it's pretty damn close.

Walking over to where she was standing next to a chuckling Edmund, Felix looked out to see what they were looking at.

Out in front of them in the distance was a battlefield.

The burnt-out wrecks of tanks, vehicles, planes, and a great many corpses were sprawled out. Laid out in every direction, you could tell it started as a firefight and ended in a slaughter.

"Damn," he muttered as Tribune began to catalog everything that his cameras picked up. "They really did get wrecked, didn't they?"

"Got their shit pushed in so hard it came out their mouth," Andrea grumbled, coming up to his right. "Whatever Supers they sent for this clearly weren't so super."

Let's hope we do better.

"Three, landed and organizing to shadow you. Assets that went afield moving to join us," Second reported.

"TL, got it. Let's see those asses in gear people, time to go. Objective one is our target. See if we can't make contact.

"Team One, first rotation point. Satellite patrolling after for Second, Fourth, and Fifth. Stick within observation of each other. Find the forward strong-point and rotate.

"Three is our REMF.

"If contact, cover, discover, recover," Andrea ordered. "Hubba fucking hubba."

"Babysitter," growled Second as the other teams agreed. She clearly wasn't very happy being with the UN team but was mostly keeping it unsaid.

Moving away from the grisly tableau laid out before them, Felix shook his head and fell in with Lucille. She was his personal partner in this, and they were dependent on one another. Everyone had been paired with a Dragon after all.

The only person who hadn't was Gaia, but that was because there was little anyone could do to stop her. She could quite literally fall through the air, hit the ground face first, and get up without an issue.

It was also why she wasn't wearing Legionnaire armor. The only thing she had of Legion was an earpiece and a Legionnaire's ring.

"They really did get fucked," Lucille murmured as he took his spot on her left.

"Yeah. They did," he agreed as they watched the first team move off. He knew that team Three and Four were almost entirely Andrea's.

He was feeling fairly confident about the outcome if they ran into any actual military issues.

His concern was entirely with the Supers, though he did have a few helpful trump cards in the UN team.

He'd requested their presence personally.

They were named Kit, Lily, and Mikki, and while he didn't want to be around them, he needed them for this mission. Just in case things went sideways.

Which they probably would.

***

Surprisingly, they didn't come across any enemy elements.

Neither Supers nor military.

They'd been able to rapidly move across the outskirts of the country and deep into the heart of it. Bypassing a great many defensive hardpoints that'd been put up, but without proper coverage across the whole of it.

"I know I asked Carlotta and Alma to make a distraction, but I feel like they're outperforming," Faith said as she trooped along with Evie next to Felix and Lucille.

Goldie, Gaia, Romina, Carol, Edmund, and Cathy were all near them as well.

"Knowing Carlotta, she probably demanded Felix promise her a reward for how she'd do," Goldie suggested.

Faith let out a long sigh.

"You're right. She probably demanded a reward. Likely ah… likely protein from him depending on how well she did," Faith finished the same thought they all had.

"Which means Alma then got involved after that, demanded more, promised more, and blew it all out of proportion," finished Goldie.

"There is an army of living flora rushing the borders of the country," Tribune reported. "Thousands upon thousands of living trees and bushes have been unendingly tying up forces."

"I… ah… what'd… you promise them?" Faith asked, suddenly sounding nervous but also curious.

Felix said nothing.

Would never say anything.

What he promised Alma and Carlotta wasn't something he'd ever admit to.

"He's a human Keurig machine for them!" Gaia answered happily. "Alma told me about it."

No one said anything to that, though Edmund let out a groan and Romina sighed.

"I'm rather glad I already bartered access with them. I can trade with Alma for things with a few servings, I'm sure," Gaia said to herself. "This is fantastic. I'm such a savvy entrepreneur this time. I've stockpiled an entire three months already.

"I can barter that away later on to anyone in his harem for whatever else I need or want. This is really going splendidly."

"Team Five, entering the capitol building," reported Andrea, saving the rest of them from hearing anything further from Gaia.

Everyone became quiet and readied themselves.

They were directly across the street from where Andrea was breaking into. There was a distinct possibility that this would be the point where it all kicked off.

There was no telling where the Supers they were looking for were. With any luck, they'd be at their little "fortress of ineptitude" as Romina called it. The last contact anyone had with the government had been that they were heading into a secret bunker below the capitol building.

"Team Five," Andrea stated after what felt like about ten minutes had passed. "Shits fucked. Not going in. Doors are torn off and there's a pile of… of dead naked women here.

"Pretty sure they've been… been assaulted. All of them. These… they're torn in half at the middle. Super did this. Some twisted bastard."

"If he resists, I'm alright with going with the excuse that we couldn't help but kill him," offered Felix, breaking their comm rules. The only response to Team Three's lead should have been the Team Leader.

"TL, received. We're outta here. Double time

out and find a strong point to setup. We'll swap point and roll out to the fortress of ineptitude," Andrea ordered with a cold tone. "Orders are kill on sight, register after."

Felix made no word edgewise against the order. He saw no reason to try and protect these Supers. They'd only serve to undermine the League of Villains and waste space in his prison if caught.

Not to mention... it's a good opportunity to flex a bit.

If it's evident the Association has great power at its fingertips but doesn't use it recklessly, we'll be given greater respect and fear alike. That'd be ideal.

Then we —

"Contact," an Andrea said, followed by what sounded like a burst of gunfire. Followed by a few single shots, then another burst of gunfire.

Everything went quiet after that.

Only to open back up with sustained small-arms fire that sounded a lot like a machine gun.

"Five. Firm contact, ran into what looks like a patrol," reported the Andrea. "They have several supers amongst them.

"No losses, but we could use a flank."

Andrea Prime in her centurion helmet turned and looked right at Felix. As if asking him what he wanted to do.

He shrugged his shoulders.

There wasn't anything he could suggest for this.

Tactical leader, he was not.

"Romina, Faith, Team Two," said Andrea Prime. "Out, across, assault."

Rapidly everyone named clumped into a group, then rushed out. Vanishing out of view through the open doorway and leaving everyone else in the shattered office buildings remains.

"Uh, Juno here uhm... ah... there's... there are Supers coming," reported Romina only a few seconds later. "They're shooting at us I think —"

There was a series of detonations that made everything shudder and shake.

"One, to the second floor, Four, out the back, flank around," ordered Prime. "Everyone else, take cover, spread out, be ready."

Felix wasn't technically part of a group.

Nor were Lucille, Goldie, Edmund, Romina, Faith, or Gaia.

They were part of the command group and were now looking about for cover where they could get it. Felix had been surprised when she ordered Romina and Faith out.

"I think they're homing in on something," growled Prime as the teams broke apart. "We tripped something, I just don't know what. They shouldn't be coming this way."

"Three, UN team under attack. Multiple Supers and numerous enemies!" reported Second.

Uh... I wonder if there's some way they identified the UN team from the other teams by their equipment? Is there like... some type of system that shows other units?

Their radio maybe?

Something to look into.

"Tribune, any way they're tracking the UN units?" Andrea Prime demanded as she held up her wrist. She'd flipped open the display panel there and was moving through it quickly with a fingertip.

"Uncertain. Anything with a computer and a signal, I'm in control of," Tribune answered. "It's possible they could be tracking radio signals or radio tracking equipment of that nature."

"Or a super," Goldie suggested, giving them all a moment of realization.

Legionnaires all have equipment that block that sort of thing. The UN doesn't.

That patrol was coming here to set up so that they could ambush the others. Not us. We were just somewhere they weren't expecting us.

Does the mind-control give them an awareness of where people are?

Underestimated their ability maybe.

That or they just used UN equipment to track other UN soldiers.

"Team Two, in cover now. Broke contact after eliminating several Supers."

"Team Five, positioned effectively. Took the machine gun emplacement and utilizing it. Firing on enemies. They weren't expecting us at all. They're all confused."

There was a distinct chatter of automated fire that was ongoing.

"What the fuck is that?" Romina asked suddenly over the channel. "It's a giant fucking gold cloud."

Several seconds after Romina said it, the entirety of Felix's vision was a gold mist. One that felt impenetrable and not like something he could see through beyond twenty feet ahead of him.

There was a general sense of tingling across his armor, but it didn't seem to be doing anything to him at all.

"TL, dunno, but if you find whoever's generating it, put'em down," Andrea Prime ordered, then she looked to Felix. "I'm about to order us to fuck off outta here and regroup. Do you care about the UN team at all if I tell Second to skitter?"

Felix hesitated.

He didn't want to leave them to their own, given that Kit and Lily were with them, as well as Mikki.

They were all duplicates of people he cared about, but not the people he cared about. That was perhaps the reason they didn't matter to him all that much.

"No. I want to use them as bait to a degree," Felix said and nodded his head. "Let's use the position we know the enemy will take to get a good shot. They'll go for the UN troops if we disengage, right?

"This golden fart is going to make it harder for them to see us than us them. Helmets for us to navigate with Tribune. Dragons get to hold hands or belts."

Andrea Prime stared at him for several seconds before nodding her head.

"Nn that's... yeah, good point. We'll go with that.

"TL to One, Two, Four, and Five. Disengage! Break contact, move back to point... three or six. Regroup, then move to ambush on perimeter of UN forces. Assume they'll be engaged in an ambush," ordered Andrea Prime. "Three, get that sack of crap UN team hunkered and bunkered."

Everyone began to withdraw, even as the gold mist continued to obscure everything further and further.

He felt something reach up and curl around his wrist in a possessive sort of way.

Turning to look, he found Goldie standing right next to him. For whatever reason, she'd brought her tail into reality along with her wings.

The former was what had curled around his wrist and was now hanging onto him possessively.

Or perhaps, worryingly.

As if she might lose her way in the gold haze.

Trying to not let it bother him, despite a concern that he'd have an issue aiming his rifle if something popped up in front of him, he looked to Andrea instead.

"Let's move it," growled Andrea, getting up and moving off at a quick trot.

Apparently sensing his concern, the tail that'd been around his wrist slid up to his bicep instead.

Then everyone followed Andrea out of the building to flank the ambush.

Chapter 35 - Polymorphic -

Moving at a quick trot, Felix felt strange.

The golden mist was clinging to them and clearly not wanting to thin. it felt like it was actively working to push into his armor and trying to invade it.

Fuck, did I underestimate it?

Pushing out a quick thought as to understand what that golden mist was, to just get the name and maybe a hint of what it was as an owner, Felix chased after Andrea.

A simple window popped up over the top of Andrea's hips.

Bewitched Cloud of Glamour.

The fuck is — shit. It's the mind control, isn't it?
This is what they used to control everyone.

"Throne to Three, I need you to tell Kit that the gold cloud is mind-control or something like it!" Felix huffed as he ran along. "All Legionnaires, don't lose your rings or helmets. This situation is why we wear them!"

Goldie was holding to his arm, though he could also feel Lucille nearby as well. Probably to his direct right but behind him a bit, he had the distinct impression her tail was looped around his waist or back plate.

"Roger!" Second called back.

Her affirmation was quickly repeatedly by a

number of other voices, all acknowledging his words.

Growling as he jogged along, Felix was getting tired of barely being able to see anything. He kept coming back to the fact that this was entirely too much, and it was quickly frustrating him.

This is why I'm here. I'm here because I'm the damn utility player. I'm the support that can make shit happen.

I've been hoarding points just for this kind of a lame situation.

Let's fucking spend some!

Slamming out a demand to see his points, Felix wanted to know what he had to work with. He mentally prepared himself to see once again he had thirty-seven Dragons that were considered his wives.

	Generated	Remaining
Andrea	1,855	1,855
Alma	840	840
Carlota	980	980
Faith	2,720	2,720
Felix	3,310	3,310
Gaia	100,000* Avatar Limitation	100,000
Goldie	15,831	15,831
~Dragon Wing (37 total)	51,500	51,500

Miu	2,210	2,210
+Loyalty Bonus	2,000	2,000
+Marital Bonus	10,000	10,000
=Daily Total	**191,246**	**191,246**
Banked Total	—	**97,777,777**

"What the fuck? Gaia, when did you become my wife? Wait, how the hell are you worth a hundred-thousand?" squeaked Felix.

"I didn't mean for it to happen!" Gaia answered quickly. "It just sort of did, and if I knew you were going to be looking right now I would have hidden it.

"Darn it. Drat. Drat! I knew I should have told him or gotten into his bed. Darn."

"Whatever, fine. Okay, uhh," muttered Felix, trying to get his brain into gear. He was also quite shocked at how high everyone's points had gotten. Goldie was impressive to begin with, and now she was more so. To the point that clearly something had changed with her. "Okay. Damnit.

"I'm sorry," Gaia apologized. "I'll be okay. I'm getting lessons from Goldie!"

"Damnit all," Felix hissed, not responding to Gaia. "Faith! You around?"

"Of course, Grove-husband," replied the Dryad. "My place is always with you."

"If I give you elemental sorceress powers, would that conflict with your Dryad abilities, or compliment them?" Felix asked. "Gaia, my goddess, if ever you wanted to help me with a direct answer, would doing such a thing harm her or you?"

"I-no, my champion. It'd be fine," Gaia murmured. "He's using possessive words again, but he didn't call me his wife... I should have made time for him, darn it. This is all going wrong. It was supposed to be a pleasant surprise and more like, 'oh, she's so lovely I can't resist her anymore. I'll go to her room and-'"

"I'll be fine!" offered Faith at the same time, talking over Gaia. "Do to me what you must!"

Felix also ignored the goddess and called up a modification request. He wanted to grant Faith elemental control. A sorceress's abilities to utilize the elements effectively as a magician might. Also, to grant her a mana pool and the ability to use it correctly as well, as he figured her Dryad limitations might hamper her.

Name: Faith Campbell	Condition: In love. Healthy.
If No Action Taken: None	Action >> Alter Power: Cost 18,102,196 points

Done!

Accepting that cost out of hand Felix cleared his throat.

"Whoever's with Faith, be ready to steady her," he commanded, then changed his thoughts. He needed to be prepared to fight their tanker.

I... damnit. Use the tools available.

Use… use the tools and the leverage available.

"Gaia, I'm your husband. I'm a Demi-God," Felix stated.

"Yes! You are," confirmed Gaia with a throaty chuckle. "Well, you were. Now you're a lower deity through our marriage!"

Ah… that… explains my own point value.

Right.

"As your husband, I'd like to ask you for a favor," started Felix as Faith ran out in front of him. She was moving swiftly, and her hands were held out in front of herself. White lines of power with blue sparkles cascading from them splashed out in front of her. Evie was right next to her, her tail hanging onto her waist. "We're on a hunt! I need you to help me hunt.

"Hunt their tanker, whoever it is that is physically impossible for anyone, but my beautiful wife, to stop. Help your husband, my wife Gaia?"

"Goodness… oh… oh… it's making my heart beat all strangely… I… of course, my husband. I'll do that for you!" Gaia proclaimed. There was a shuddering that went through the earth as they moved. He couldn't tell if it was Gaia, Faith, or something else entirely. "I'll hunt him down just for you! I'm good at hunting!"

Gaia practically appeared in front of him, moving up to stand with Faith and Andrea.

The golden mist that clung to everything was vanishing as Faith ran along. Her magical fairy parade of trails that would do better at an amusement park was dissipating that bright haze wherever the two forces collided.

There was a crackling of blue flame that was rapidly eating away at the gold cloud and spreading further outward as well as ahead of them. Whatever Faith had done was rapidly eliminating the Glamour cloud.

"Goldie, would it be in poor taste to bring all the Dragons up to Lucille's level of physical ability?" he asked. If Evie could fight as well as Lucille could, he imagined that'd multiply the force he had with him significantly. "If I made everyone as physically dominant as Lucille. Also, who's the most agile Dragon, other than you? You don't count. And who's the fastest?"

"Agility? Cathy. Uhm, for speed that'd be... Michelle. She's a very nice Orange. You gave her a kiss on the cheek the other week," Goldie supplied. "And no, it wouldn't be bad to have them all as physically powerful as Lucille, but you'd be better making them all as strong as Carol. She's stronger than Lucille, but Lucille has more experience."

"Lucille, you're amazing then. Hope you're ready to be stronger and faster," Felix muttered. He needed to build up his forces once and for all, and this was the perfect moment.

Demanding a window to appear so that all his Dragons, except Goldie who was exceptional already, be raised to Carol's level of Strength, Cathy's agility, and Michelle's speed.

He briefly saw a window flash up in front of him and saw it'd cost forty-million points.

Accepting it without a glance he didn't care.

"Goldie, you need anything?" he demanded.

"Gaia empowered me several times in exchange for information," admitted Goldie. "I'm ten or twelve times more powerful than Carol."

"Fine. Andrea, how many Others can you handle?" Felix asked as the way before them cleared.

"I... ten-thousand," she stated suddenly, sounding unsure.

Whatever. Seems like too much, but that's what she's saying so... we'll go with it.

"No, five, five thousand, I'm sorry," Andrea countered herself. "Not really sure. Kinda... guessing here."

Once more Felix demanded a window. One to increase Andrea's Other count to five-thousand people. Except this time they'd all be housed temporary in Second, until Prime could collect them later.

Again a window popped up, Felix ignored what it said, and hit the accept button. He did see a flash of thirty-million popping up, but again, didn't care.

There was a groan across the com systems that felt guttural. Like someone dying, followed by an excited cheer from many people.

"T-team T-t-two Lead... inca-incap," moaned an Andrea.

"Four-thousand-sixty-seven taking control!" cheered an Andrea.

Then they all found themselves standing in an open park behind a large building. They'd gone away from the point of contact, looped around, and maneuvered all the way around to where the UN team would be.

This had been the point Andrea Prime had chosen to attack, as it was the most likely place for the enemy to be, given the information she had on hand.

Which'd been right.

There was no mistaking the gunfire directly ahead of them, nor the Supers on the roof, or in the air, all attacking someone beyond it. They had no idea the Association teams had come up behind them.

"Dragons, get us all up to the top of that building, then go and pick your targets," Andrea commanded, not waiting for anyone to say anything.

Felix didn't disagree with her at all.

They needed to hammer-smash the enemy. To strike right now with overwhelming force to cause casualties and knock them off balance

"Engage anyone at your level, don't risk yourself if you encounter someone who's beyond you," Andrea continued. "Goldie, get up there and be ready to take down any dumb-ass who your girls can't.

"Gaia, wait for us to find out where that Tanker is. Faith, magical overwatch. You're our shield and magical sword."

Before he could understand it all, Felix was in the air. Someone was carrying him rapidly toward the building they'd spotted the enemy in. Faster than he could get his mind in order, he was dropped on top of it, hitting the roof with a thump.

Sliding on his knees, his rifle came up and snapped to his shoulder. Training endlessly had conditioned the response he needed in the moment.

Lining it up on the closest enemy figure, Felix squeezed off a burst, moved to the closest after that, pulled off another burst, and began working down the line.

Their arrival had been absolutely silent, given the tumult of battle. Arriving directly behind their enemies had made them little better than paper targets waiting to be dropped.

Glancing upward as his brain woke back up, Felix spotted a Super floating there.

There was a shield held up in front of them made of purple hexagons. It was only facing the direction of the UN team, however.

His rear was unguarded.

Felix snapped his barrel toward the flying Super and pulled the trigger down several times. Putting more than half the clip into the Super.

Or through them, considering he could see a spray of pink mist pop out from the opposite side of them, as well as the blood splatter that painted the interior of the shield.

The force of the rounds was so great that it looked as if the Super's arm had been torn clear of their body, despite the recoil on Felix being almost minimal.

Guess those rifle upgrades had been worth it.

As well as reinforcing the shoulder armor to take the recoil.

Still need to get myself a Felicia in this world.

Getting up from his awkward position, Felix moved forward in a low walk. His rifle held up and sighted, he continuously worked it back and forth to put rounds on anything that moved. There was no room for prisoners and wounded at the moment.

Evie zoomed past the front of him in Dragon form. Her bright red body knocking and displacing every single soldier that'd been standing.

Flinging them off the edge of the building and toward the earth below.

"Ha... nice," Felix chuckled, watching the Dragon pull up and bank away. She was moving fast.

Really fast.

Banking hard, she flipped end over end, re-oriented herself, then swooped down low and out of sight.

Moving right up to the edge of the building, Felix saw that the UN team was completely fucked.

Across the way was another building that was equally filled with people firing down into the UN team. They'd been caught in a crossfire.

Looking to the left, Felix saw why they hadn't fallen back either.

There was a number of Supers that way that

were casually ripping the soldiers apart. One in particular looked like what they wanted to throw Gaia at.

Average in height and build, they'd picked up a car with one hand and were smashing it down repeatedly on two soldiers who were already quite clearly dead.

"Gaia, my wondrously gorgeous wife, pretty sure that's the tanker over there at the back of the UN troops. Wanna go get your hubby a present?" Felix asked, getting down low over the wall.

Lining his ACOG sight up with the distant enemy, he did his best to start putting rounds on them. He wasn't the greatest marksman in the world, but he wasn't terrible, either.

"I shall do so!" gushed Gaia, who had quite literally jumped off the building and toward her target. She was sailing through the air with the power of it.

Dressed in athletic wear, she looked incredibly pleasing to the eye as she soared through the air. Very much what one would expect from a goddess in a movie involving deities.

"Exciting!" Gaia yelled, a second before she hit the ground.

Except her landing looked strange. There was no pause to her hitting the earth and starting into a full-on run.

Straight toward who Felix was positive was the Tanker.

At the center of the UN soldiers, Felix found,

were a handful of Andreas, Kit, and Lily. He wondered briefly where the other Andreas he'd had made gone, but he assumed they were likely on some type of mission.

Lily was struggling to put together spells between her hands, even as her position was being pelted with small-arms fire. Her Legionnaire armor had a number of scuffs and dirt spread across it, speaking to the fact they'd been under a great deal of fire.

There were also what looked to be spells whipping by over their heads.

Kit had her hands just above her head and there was a flickering dome of force around them and the troops. It didn't seem to be stopping any projectiles, but it was holding back the golden fog that hadn't dissipated here.

Faith's magic didn't quite reach that far.

Then something smashed through Kit's leg and spun her partly to one side, pushing her up into the concrete divider she'd been behind.

Damnit.

Damnit!

They're... they're not my Kit and Lily but... they're... they're someone else's Kit and Lily. They could be just as important to them as mine are to me.

I have to limit contact with them though. Getting any closer would be detrimental.

Leverage what you can and —

Growling, Felix demanded Kit be granted all the powers his own Kit had on his own world. He also wished for the same thing for Lily. That she'd have all her powers and that it happened immediately.

There was a clang-like noise that made the entire world jerk one way. Everything began to violently tremble and shudder, only for it to jolt to the right.

A kaleidoscope of colors flickered and flashed across the sky as everyone stopped what they were doing. Staring down at the ground, the sky, or themselves in absolute shock.

Name: Kì⊥ Çämℙßê ᴸᴸ	?!?!: A/R/F
iF 1 > 2?: EnTErMeDaaaHT wOONds	EeeEEe>> ffffA: Cost 2 points

Name: Łìlîåṇ Çämℙßê ᴸᴸ	?!?!: A/R/F?
iF 1 > 2?: _-___-_____-_-_	EeeEEe>> ffffA: Cost 3 points

Felix hit the accept button when it popped up. He didn't care, and realistically speaking, he was pretty sure his request had just probably broken the world.

Whatever he'd tried to do had smashed something delicate and likely needed Ryker to come along and fix it.

Before everything went to pieces.

Distinctly, his mouth started to taste a lot like

a dry sponge. One that'd been soaking in a sink of dirty water for a month, dried in the sun, then stuffed in his mouth.

He only belatedly realized it was his tongue when he tried to move his tongue away from the taste.

Then the world made a pop, twisted up briefly, and then straightened back out.

Everything was back to normal, as it should have been.

Except Kit was now standing tall, her arms held out above her head. A massive glowing shield had slammed down around all the troops. It was blocking out all the arms fire being sent their way, as well as the golden cloud.

Lily went from having no spells, to massive sprawling lines of spell work winding out endlessly. Then followed by detonations as they launched out, taking anyone apart that it touched.

Turning them into goopy bits of meat and flesh.

Dragons were plowing down Supers anywhere Felix looked. Working in groups to rapidly bring them down, tear them apart, then move on. They weren't even trying to take prisoners, nor were they interested in registering them.

Whatever farce of a reason they'd given to come here was now obvious and laid bare as only that. An excuse.

Given how bad a pasting this group had

given the UN, Felix didn't think they'd mind that much.

"How dare you!" called a voice from the side.

Looking toward the speaker, Felix saw a man that was standing amongst a number of armed soldiers at the other end of the street from where Gaia was. He had his hands on his hips and had an impressive line of medals across the front of his chest.

He also had a cloak, cap, and a dark military uniform on.

If Felix had to describe him, he'd probably use something Romina had once said.

The man was clearly suffering from Main Character Syndrome.

Holding his arms up in front of himself, he launched some type of large area of effect wave attack. It looked a lot like a flat plane of smoky glass undulating through the air.

A second after he fired it, Goldie landed on him.

Her front and back claws slammed him flat to the ground and quite literally squished him. His head, chest, and abdomen were all pulverized beneath the force of her landing and her considerable mass.

Ha.

What a fucking way to go out. That's funny as shit.

The strange dark wave slipped and slid over

the dome. Passing over it like a wave crashing on the beach. It sprayed up, out and kept going.

When it contacted with anything material, it just faded away to nothing. Though it did bounce oddly off a few semi-reflective surfaces and then keep moving in that direction.

Chuckling to himself, Felix looked to the building across the way.

Andreas were flooding through it. Rushing, dashing, jumping, and sprinting through the floors. He could see them moving through the windows and demolishing everyone and everything.

A flood of Andreas, naked as the day they were born, brutally beating people to death. Only to get shot down, reabsorbed by another Andrea, and spat back out.

They had also started to spill out across the top of the building. Covering the roof in bodies and tearing apart the shooters there.

Letting his rifle slowly drop, Felix turned to look back to Gaia and the Tanker.

He found Gaia had killed the Tanker outright and was now holding the corpse above her head. Presenting it almost like a trophy to anyone and everyone watching.

From here, it looked like perhaps she'd crushed his chest in.

Probably punched him.

Edmund, what was likely Second Andrea who was moving very slowly, and Romina were all nearby Gaia. They were actively working at putting zip-ties on people who were on the ground.

"Third Team, flanking through the north," reported an Andrea. "More forces incoming, though clearly unsure. Will punch hard."

Like something out of an ugly and stupid horror movie, a part of the black wave that the man had launched out writhed its way into view. It came in at a strangle angle as if it'd been reflected off something after hitting Kit's dome.

As he realized it was heading straight for Gaia, he had no time other than to take in a breath.

Then it was already on her and struck her.

Or it would have, if Second Andrea hadn't hurled herself between the wave and Gaia, taking the hit for her.

Edmund was right next to Second Andrea and looking at her oddly as the black wave struck and entered her. Romina was there as well.

Andrea paused and held still.

Then every Andrea did the same thing. Each of them becoming immobile.

Suddenly they all fell to hands and knees with a loud groan.

"Feeeelix, it hurts!" whined every single Andrea at the same time. The comms system flooded with pained mews.

They all collectively began throwing up, urinated themselves, defecated, and blood began pouring out of their eyes, nose, ears, and mouth.

He could see it clearly as Andrea Prime wasn't far from him and had pulled off her helmet to throw up.

"Fe-Felix! It-hurts. Hurts!" whimpered Andrea Prime.

Rushing over to her quickly, he dropped his rifle. He wanted to fix whatever was wrong with her right now. At whatever the cost.

Name: Andrea Campbell	Condition: Soul Rent (Universal)
Result: Death (Universal)	Action >> Revitalize: Impossible

"What?" Felix muttered to himself. "Andrea, I can't... I can't do anything. It says it's impossible."

"Ooowwwwieee... nnnnn... huuuughh," moaned Andrea who began to throw up a great deal of blood all over the ground. As soon as she finished, she whimpered again. "Bring me back quick."

Collapsing to the ground in a puddle of her own bloody puke Andrea let out a low whine and went still.

Unmoving in any way.

Nodding his head, Felix realized that she was right.

Regardless of the cost of bringing back all the Andreas, he could at least bring Prime back and get everyone else absorbed.

Pulling up his power, he wanted to resurrect her the moment she was dead. Preemptively he wanted the cost as well to bring back just Andrea

Prime.

The window he was given was a bit different.

Name: Andrea Campbell	Death Type: Soul Rent (Universal)
Current Condition: Dead (Universal)	Action >> Resurrect: Impossible

What…?

Impossible?!

What bullshit is this.

Grasping at his power Felix practically throttled it. Forcing it to bring up a new window. To resurrect Andrea. Any Andrea.

Once more the same response was given.

Impossible.

"Andie?" Romina asked over the system.

"Andrea, what… are you okay?" inquired Goldie.

Yanking his helmet off Felix looked up to the sky above.

"Ryker! Runner! Something's wrong with this! I can't bring her back!" he called out to the sky. "Architect! Overgod!"

There was no response.

The crackle and pop of what sounded like a distant fire was the only thing he heard. It was punctuated by the sharp uncaring sounds of gunshots.

"RYKER! RUNNER!" screamed Felix at the top of his lungs.

No one answered him.

Epilogue

To Felix, the world felt surreal.

That right now, to him in this moment, everything was wrong. That the world was cold, grey, and lacked any sort of flavor to it.

The very air itself felt stale and without life.

A mass grave had been dug to hold each and every Andrea.

Deep beneath the Legion HQ where only a few people had access.

They'd been forced to go collect each and every Andrea that'd fallen. As whatever had killed Second, killed every single Andrea in this universe.

In Felix's mind, he had a deep and worrying concern he couldn't shake. That in whatever he'd done to the world to force Kit and Lily to become what they'd once been, he'd inadvertently become the cause for what happened to Andrea.

That not only was he responsible for the inability for her to be resurrected, that the "universal" tag attached to her death, went further.

Much further.

In the ugliest part of his thoughts, he was afraid he'd managed to get every single Andrea killed.

From the original Myriad, to Andrea, to Adriana on the other worlds and universes. That they were one and all, quite dead.

Neither Ryker, nor Runner, had responded to any of his calls in the twenty some-odd hours since it'd happened. The gods were silent to him and Gaia both.

She'd done her best to summon the man she referred to as her Uncle, as well as Runner, whom she called Father. Their response to her had been the same as to him.

Silence.

Everyone was giving him space right now, but he knew he didn't have much time left to himself. To grieve and let himself feel the hurt.

The last time he'd gone through this, his rebound had been terrible and messy. Loaded with hurting far too many people that only meant him well.

Those that only wanted him to be happy.

"And now you're gone," Felix mumbled to the tombstone for Andrea Prime.

Flanking her was Second and Third.

Expanding out from there was a tomb for each and every Andrea. Every single Andrea had been accounted for and buried here.

All the Elex women he'd brought with him were here.

Gaia had confirmed for him, for each body as they were laid to rest, that there was no soul there. That there was no soul anywhere she could find either.

Squatting down next to the tombstone, he stared at the engraved likeness of this world's Andrea on it. She'd been unique and different from every other Andrea he'd met.

Once more, the specter of the possible loss of every Andrea roared to life. Screaming in his ear that they were all gone.

Every Andrea, across all the universes, were gone.

She, as a person, no longer existed.

Sighing, Felix laid his brow to her tombstone and let out a slow breath.

He was hoping on Ryker or Runner saving him from this right now. He knew for a fact that they'd given Petra back to Vince.

To them, Death was an inconvenience. Even a lesser one than what it was for Felix, in fact.

That if ever there was someone who could step in and literally call forth a Deus Ex Machina moment, it'd be one of those two. They alone could save Felix, by saving Andrea.

"Felix," came a soft whispered voice from behind him.

Glancing over his shoulder he found Faith, Goldie, and Miu standing there. A stray thought popped into his head looking at them.

He'd been told to only take three.

Greed had gotten the better of him and he'd forced a fourth to this world.

What if I really am the cause for all of this?

Damnit.

This… this isn't worth it.

To get Kit and Lily back but sacrificing Andrea…?

That's not worth it.

"She wouldn't want you to feel that way,"

Goldie chided him with a sad smile. "You know that. While I'm sure they didn't expect for them all to die for stepping in front of Gaia, that was still their reaction to the situation.

"They would just as willingly say that their loss is okay for Kit and Lily without Gaia being included"

"If Gaia died… this… world would end, wouldn't it?" asked Miu in a gruff voice. Felix knew she was feeling this just as deeply as he was. He'd already walked in on her as she absolutely thrashed a bathroom. Having ripped the toilet out of the ground and used it to beat through a wall, as well as the floor. "Andie… Andie would trade herself for the world. B-because without the world, there wouldn't be pancakes."

Snorting at the comment, followed by a chuckle, Felix felt buoyed by that.

It felt like what Goldie said was the truth, but also just a false platitude.

Miu's words were the absolute truth.

"Oh Grove-husband," whispered Faith, coming over to hug him. A second after that and Miu and Goldie were doing the same. All three of them hugging him and one another. "We lost Andie. We can only do what you yourself said, and hope Runner or Ryker can fix it.

"Past that… all we can do is continue on, isn't it? That's what Andie would tell us. It's what Kit or Lily would have told us when they were trapped."

Felix grunted at that, then realized this was probably the best time and place to open an email he'd received from Tribune.

She'd begun enacting Andrea's last will and testament after she'd confirmed the Beastkin was truly dead.

It apparently had a video Andrea had recorded specifically for him, in case she'd passed on or was no longer "here". "Here" as in being what happened to Kit or Lily.

"Stay with me? I need to open that video from Andrea," Felix asked, pressing his face into Faith's neck as she nodded her head.

"Of course," Goldie answered and kissed his temple.

Miu had in turn pushed her face into Felix's neck and held onto him.

Gently disentangling himself from Miu and releasing his hold on Faith, Felix moved himself backward and ended up putting his back against Andrea's grave marker.

Sitting there, he paused for a few seconds, then pulled his phone out of his pocket.

Unlocking it, he flipped it over, tapped open the email, ignored everything written there, and opened the video.

His screen paused for several seconds before the file loaded.

In view of the camera was what looked like his bedroom.

There were four people curled up in the bed.

Felix immediately identified himself, Miu, Andrea Second, and what Felix was sure was Third Andrea.

They'd bookended Miu and Felix.

Andrea Prime stepped into view of the camera and waved with a big grin.

"Hi hi!" she said with excited energy, then winced, looking back to the bed.

Miu had stirred briefly, then went still.

Gritting her teeth, Andrea grabbed the camera and began leaving the room. In the doing of it, she managed to trip over-herself, smacking into a table, cursing, then exiting the room. In the background, he could here an Andrea soothing what sounded like Miu back to sleep.

Andrea went into a dark room, closed a door, then stood there.

"Oh, the lights. Nnnn, liiiiights," she said with a chuckle, followed by a click.

She was now standing in Felix's walk-in closet.

"Okay, I know. Weird but… I do love to stand in here and just… smell. Smell the scent of you, Felix. Be surrounded by it," Andrea confessed with a grin and a tilt of her head to the side. "I know Miu comes in here often as well, to 'fix the light', but stands around and stares at nothing. Probably the same thing as me. Goldie steals clothes to stitch or adjust.

"Faith comes in here to make sure your scent is here by putting your clothes away, ruins some of your clothes for Goldie, and breaks the light so Miu has to come in here.

"But... shhh... don't tell any of them that. It's a little game I'm sure they'll play even after I'm gone."

Miu took in a sharp breath and held it, holding onto what was likely a sob.

"Though uh... I guess I managed to do it! Go me, right. Hee hee. Somehow I did something that got me dead. Dead dead. To the point that I can't be undead-ed.

"Or I got lost. Like Kit or Lily. Also a possibility, I guess. Nnnn. Anyways!" Andrea said with a wave of her free hand, holding the camera with the other. "This is me saying goodbye to you Felix.

"You're my husband. My love. My reason for being better. I worked... so damn hard to be better. Worked at it and worked at it and worked at it. I constantly relied on Miu, Goldie, Faith, Kit, and Lily to do it, too. They were my partners in many things.

"Often with you never knowing it, but you do now.

"Uhm... okay... so... yeah. I'm gone, I guess. Hopefully you can just keep my body and give it back to the other Andrea so I can come back. That'd be spiffy!"

Andrea took in a slow and long breath, then let it out.

"And if not... that's... unfortunate. It's... really unfortunate," lamented Andrea, her eyes slowly moving to the side and away from the camera. "At that point... I don't... really know what to say. Other than... I'm sorry.

"I love you, Felix and I'm sorry. Maybe I finally understand that stupid quote now... that it's better to have loved and lost, than never loved at all. Because you yourself told me it in a different way. It's our experiences who make us who we are, right? So... better to have had the experience. I get it now. I get it.

"I'm sure I'll steal a bunch of things from songs and movies, stuff it all together, and send it to you as a letter, later. Don't judge me. I have a hard time finding the right words.

"Yeah... yeah. Nn, nn. Okay. Uhm. Goodnight. I'm going to go wake you up and drag you in here, then ravage you. There'll be a follow up video to this. Watch it later in private!"

Unable to help himself, Felix snorted at that, then abruptly choked down a sob that threatened to break free.

"Legionnaire Andrea asked me to state the following after the video was played," stated Tribune. "As well as send the follow up video to you."

"Though death took me, we all must meet that end for us to have lived," came Andrea's voice. It had a slightly different quality, but likely only to Felix's ear. More than likely, it was Tribune reading it in Andrea's voice. "I may have met my end by myself, but I was never alone. When we were all united, we fought the darkness. Together and with one another, even if we fought separately.

"And every time I felt my heart crushed, you reignited the ashes of it with warmth and care. Sending me once more into the heavens to fight onward.

"While I can't be there, I know that the memory of me will give you strength in the darkness. That when you're alone, you never really are.

"I have no doubt that you've reached out to the sky and called out my name. That in a heartbeat you'd trade places with me if only to see me as we passed one another.

"Because I'm sure it feels like maybe the future we wanted is so far away. That it feels like… the world has gone cold, now that I've gone away.

"While I'm sure you'll want to leave flowers on my grave, or visit it often, there's no need for that my dear. My darling. My love.

"Carry me with you. In the one place I found I belonged. In your heart. For that's where I'd carry you if I lost you

"The place you were best for me and always gave me the support I needed. A hand on my shoulder directing me where I can do the most to do my best. Because I was always at my best with you.

"Don't lament my loss, Felix. I was lucky. I had more people in my life after meeting you that made it full, made it eventful, than I ever thought I would. People I could share anything with. That I could go away from, come back to, and pick up where we left off without a beat.

"My true family. One that loved me for every inch that was me. I didn't just escape my past, I forgot it. It simply didn't matter anymore.

"In the end, there wasn't a single thing I really wanted or needed. My life was full and complete. So, thank you for that Felix.

"Thank you for making my life full and complete. Don't get lost in my loss, and be sure to complete and fill more people's lives.

"The sun in your life has only just gone momentarily behind a cloud. Give it a few hours. It'll come back. Just as bright as ever. As you always did for me.

"Goodbye, my love. Maybe if it's possible, you can find me in another life and we could try all this again. It was fun."

Looking down at the grass where he sat, Felix shook his head slowly. The tears readily slipped free and fell down his face.

"Legate, I must report a situational change to you," Tribune stated. Her voice had returned to its normal quality.

The inhuman tone lacking emotional awareness that was always present with a VI. She lacked the ability to grow and always would.

That was simply how he'd created her.

"Alright," he croaked as Faith, Goldie, and Miu all piled in around him again. Each of them was clearly crying as well.

"Hero Kit has requested to speak with you as

soon as you have time. As has hero Lily. They made their request in tandem," offered Tribune. "They expressed their condolences in "the loss of Myriad"."

Blinking, Felix processed that statement several times.

She'd briefly been introduced as Myriad during her stint as a villain, but that name hadn't actually come up when they'd talked at the Association. Nor had he ended up leaking it to the news that he could remember.

Everyone had focused on Goldie.

"Alright, let's —"

The world came to a sudden and abrupt stop.

Everything became a black-white and began to writhe back and forth as the entirety of existence dissipated into small bits and detonated into nothing.

"Felix! Everything's fucked!" Ryker called.

"I didn't do it. I didn't... mean to at least," Felix answered defensively. "Andrea died and —"

"Yeah, I noticed that. I'll work on that next, I promise, but everything's way worse than that," Ryker continued as the world faded to black. Only to suddenly snap back into place.

In front of him was a portal that was spinning, whirring, and throwing out small bits of what looked like magic.

He could see Legion personnel actively raising their weapons and training them on the portal. This was the portal room on Legion prime.

"Holy shit, Mr. Campbell?" called a voice from the other side. He had no idea who it was, but it was obviously one of his Legionnaires.

"Alright, time to go," Ryker called from everywhere and also through another portal that tore itself open further away in the portal room of Legion. "Runner just kicked off everything I've been building for, building to, all for the sake of—well… whatever.

"I didn't want Warner to go through losing a child. Been there… done that… no one should feel that. I would have done the same thing he did in the end."

Stepping out from beyond the side of the portal and into view came Ryker. His hair was a mess, and his eyes were a bit wild.

"Come on then. Whole lot of people waiting on us, Vince is off chasing Seville, Rene is trying to run down Jenna. You and I need to go pick up some others," Ryker said, then smiled sadly. "While I can't get back Andrea right now, I really will look into it. But… uh… today's the day you get Kit and Lily back.

"It's earlier than expected, but that's not really a problem anyways. Similar events, different timeline. Close enough."

"What… what about the day of awakening?" asked Felix. Goldie, Miu, and Faith had all gotten to their feet and were pulling him up at this point.

"That? Ptfff, you fucked that up the moment

you woke Gaia up. She was the Awakening," Ryker said with a dark chuckle. He walked through the portal, between a number of armed and dangerous Legionnaires and over to where Felix was now standing. He looked out to the endless number of graves and winced. With a shake of his head, he sighed. "I will look into this. She wasn't supposed to die here. This is so wrong. Without her this wouldn't be correct.

"Andrea wasn't supposed to die, I'll work on that. There's a lot of pieces that are jumbled up, but I'll fix it. I've fixed worse.

"For the world you're on, the Awakening... you solved that by helping Gaia.

"So... no. No Awakening. You woke up Gaia way earlier than she was supposed to. You managed to tamp her anger down, repaired all the wrongs and wounds that'd have infuriated her to go on a rampage, inadvertently stopping her from doing her best to exterminate humanity to the last, and even tamed her. Now she's all butterflies, sex, and love. Kinda... kinda a surprise, really.

"She sent me quite a nice prayer, thanking me for putting you in her path. Which uh... didn't do... but hey, I'll take the fucking credit?"

Felix was trying to catch up.

Desperately so.

There was far too much being said and explained at the moment.

"Uh... right. Er," Ryker mumbled then looked to Goldie, smiled at her, then back to Felix.

"Let's go get Kit and Lily. They're just up ahead ya know. I already popped open a portal for them.

"So... wanna join the end of the world with me and Runner? Should be a real bang. One way... or the other."

A new voice came now through the portal. One that sent a shudder through him.

"Felix?" called Lily.

A second after that, Kit, Felix's Kit, walked into view and stopped dead. She was framed perfectly by the portal and looked exactly as she did in his memory.

Then she smiled at him just as Lily, his Lily, walked up behind Kit, peeked over the other woman's shoulder, and smiled as well.

Thank you, dear reader!

I'm hopeful you enjoyed reading Super Sales on Super Heroes. Please consider leaving a review, commentary, or messages. Feedback is imperative to an author's growth.

That and positive reviews never hurt.

Feel free to drop me a line at: WilliamDArand@gmail.com

Join my mailing list for book updates: William D. Arand Newsletter

Keep up to date — Facebook: https:// www.facebook.com/WilliamDArand
Patreon: https://www.patreon.com/ WilliamDArand
Blog: http://williamdarand.blogspot.com/
HaremLit Group: https://www.facebook.com/ groups/haremlit/
LitRPG Group: https://www.facebook.com/ groups/LitRPGsociety/

If you enjoyed this book, try out the books of some of my close friends. I can heartily recommend them.

Blaise Corvin- A close and dear friend of mine.
He's been there for me since I was nothing but a rookie with a single book to my name. He told me from the start that it was clear I had talent and had to keep writing. His

background in European martial arts creates an accurate and detail driven action segments as well as his world building.

https://www.amazon.com/Blaise-Corvin/e/B01LYK8VG5

John Van Stry- John was an author I read, and re-read, and re-read again, before I was an author. In a world of books written for everything except what I was interested in, I found that not only did I truly enjoy his writing, but his concepts as well.

In discovering he was an indie author, I realized that there was nothing separating me from being just like him. I attribute him as an influence in my own work.

He now has two pen names, and both are great.

https://www.amazon.com/John-Van-Stry/e/B004U7JY8I

Jan Stryvant-

https://www.amazon.com/Jan-Stryvant/e/B06ZY7L62L

Daniel Schinhofen- Daniel was another one of those early adopters of my work who encouraged and pushed me along. He's almost as introverted as I am, so we get along famously. He recently released a new book, and by all accounts including mine, is a well written author with interesting storylines.

https://www.amazon.com/Daniel-

Schinhofen/e/B01LXQWPZA

Made in the USA
Middletown, DE
11 September 2024